Minimally Effective

(or The Teacher's Catch)

By J. Arthur Weber

SRCLB Press

ISBN: 978-1-7331730-0-1

This is a work of fiction and satire. Names, characters, businesses, places, events, locales, and incidents are either the products of the author's imagination or used in a fictitious and satirical manner. Any resemblance to actual persons, living or dead, or actual events, past, present, or future is purely coincidental and quite possibly a figment of the imagination of a massive ego.

Acknowledgements

Thank you to my wife for giving me the freedom to take time away from one dream to pursue another.

Thank you to my "school mom" Sherry Ransford-Ramsdell for emotional support and editing advice and general proofreading. (Even English teachers need help sometimes).

Thank you to my favorite writer, performer, musician, and comedian Spencer Henning for reading my rough draft and providing feedback.

Thank you to Abby Thomason (www.abbydey.com) for her beautiful cover work.

Without these people, this book would still be rough notes in a spiral-bound pad.

Dedicated to Eric Bock,

my friend

Praise ignorance, for what man

has not encountered he has not destroyed.

Ask the questions that have no answers.

Invest in the millennium. Plant sequoias.

Say that your main crop is the forest

that you did not plant,

that you will not live to harvest.

-Wendell Berry, "Manifesto: The Mad Farmer Liberation Front

"I ate civilization. It poisoned me; I was defiled.

And then," he added in a lower tone, "I ate my own wickedness."

— Aldous Huxley, *Brave New World*

Prologue

Niles was a newly minted high school English teacher. He had just joined the ranks of the last gatekeepers between the teeming, unwashed masses of belligerently ignorant and egocentric adolescents and the rights and responsibilities that awaited them as belligerently ignorant and egocentric adults. His search was underway for a full-time job doing what he trained for in college. The only way to begin a career in professional education was to take a job on a short-term basis in the district for poverty wages and a much lower level of cultural respect than even the low level that he aspired for. He first had to be a substitute teacher: a placeholder, or as most of the public labeled him, "an overpaid babysitter."

He was slotted in to substitute at one of the local elementary schools in the Pianosa Springs school district where he lived. Working with high school students was tough enough with all of the distractions that they were already culturally programmed to respond to but working with elementary students was a whole other beast. To say that it wasn't a good fit for him would be an underwhelming statement, like saying that the American flag was not universally loved while watching a foreign demonstrator soak it in gasoline and burn it. He hadn't had any experience with any large number of elementary age children since he was one. And that had been a while.

Niles got the call at 6AM on a Tuesday.

It was always on Tuesday, which everyone knew was the worst day of the week. As soon as they said "elementary" over the phone, he groaned inaudibly. He said "yes" but meant "please no" because if he had said what he meant, then he would be taken off the list of potential substitutes. That was counterproductive because he needed money to survive. A sacrifice had to be made; he would be his own Isaac and Abraham both.

He arrived at the elementary school just before the first bell and checked in with the main office secretary before gaining entrance to the classroom. When he got to the classroom the students were already inside the room. That was odd. He learned during his internship that students were never to be left alone inside the classroom. Someone else had unlocked the door and let them in. They were without adult supervision.

Mere minutes had passed and the classroom had morphed into a fast-food restaurant playland. The only things missing were mysterious brown stains on the plastic in the ball pit and slide. Seven students were standing on the desks dancing to a beat in their heads that was paired with one created by an aspiring musician pounding a beat on his desk with his fists. Two others had the window open and were petting a stray dog who found the playground to be a very amenable ground to play indeed. Pencils and papers were flying across the room in a mock re-enactment of World War I era trench warfare. Niles stepped inside the door with his school map and door key in hand and closed it loudly, hoping to get their attention.

It didn't work. The barbarians had found the gate open and they weren't going to go back from whence they'd come easily. There would be a struggle.

"Good morning class." He announced forcefully.

They ignored him.

He loudly cleared his throat, accentuating the cough and playing it up so hard that it made his throat hurt.

Not one single student looked his way.

He strode over to the teacher's desk, picked up a large binder and slammed it to the table with authority.

They stopped and looked at him at once.

"Good morning class. I am Mr. Niles, and I will be your substitute today."

They looked at him blankly.

"What kind of name is that?"

"It's my name."

"It sounds stupid."

"Be that as it may, I need you all to settle down and take your assigned seats."

"We don't have assigned seats."

"I find that hard to believe. Please take your assigned seats so that I can take attendance and we can get started today." He looked around the desk. There were no lesson plans. Usually a teacher would leave a binder, a folder, or a clipboard that was clearly marked "Substitute Plans." There was nothing to be found besides the giant binder that was full of copy masters from a dozen workbooks. There was not a seating chart, a class list, or anything at all that would indicate an orderly plan of education. He scanned the walls. The children watched him anxiously while climbing off the desks and moving slowly away from the window where the wet dog waited. Sometimes elementary teachers posted seating charts on the walls along with assignments and folders. There was nothing but reward and punishment charts and markers and motivational posters mixed in with posters that displayed basic tasks and skills for the grade level.

"Okay then, just take a seat. Everyone take a seat." They began to mill about, obviously sitting next to their best friends. Some of them even pulled chairs away from other tables to create groups of six or eight at one table. Niles nipped that in the bud. "It looks like there are enough tables, so let's just sit four to a table, okay? Four chairs and four people to a table please," he asked.

Several students shot him looks of death. Who did he think he was, their teacher? But they did as he asked, slowly and begrudgingly. His height and physical size was enough to make them do at least that much.

He looked again for lesson plans for seating charts, rifled through the papers and the binders first on the teacher's desk, then on and in the tops and shelves of every bookcase and cabinet in the room. There was nothing. He'd suspected as soon as he saw the door open when he approached the room that the lesson plans would have been seized and "lost" by the students, but the fact that everything including the seating chart was gone surprised him. These kids were thorough. They had done this before.

"Okay. Where does your teacher usually leave her lesson plans?" He didn't want to accuse them yet or at all if he could help it. He needed them on his side.

"She don't."

"She doesn't have lesson plans? I kind of doubt that."

He moved around the room, peering under chairs and desks, scanning and looking deeply into the garbage cans while the students watched him with anticipation.

"Why would she leave them in the garbage can?" One of them piped up.

"I don't know. Is that a trick question?"

They had him. He had nothing. The lesson plans were missing. There was no way to take attendance. He opened the door to the hallway, peeked out and looked up and down the hallway for help. There was no one of course.

"You guys stay right here in your seats. I'm going to check with another teacher."

4

He jogged across the hallway to the closed door and knocked. No answer. Urgently he knocked again. This time a small boy opened the door and peered up at him.

"Yes?"

He looked into the room and saw the teacher sitting in a neat semi-circle of students with a picture book. She looked at Niles as if he were an annoying fly or a moron. He decided that her look meant both. He was clearly interrupting the most important story time ever in the storied history of story times.

"Hi, I'm substituting across the hall and the teacher doesn't seem to have left any lesson plans."

She frowned and sighed. The children stared at Niles.

"I'll find you some worksheets." She didn't move to get up. "In a minute."

"Thanks. Sorry." He felt sheepish about having interrupted and backed out of the room sheepishly. Meanwhile across the hallway where he had come from, things had gone to the dogs. Niles returned to find that the students had finally pulled the stray dog in through the window and resumed their desktop dance party in the thirty seconds that he'd been out of the room. He closed the door tightly behind him hoping the barrier would keep the dog's excited yips from flowing into the hallway and allowing the rest of the building to hear how well he was doing at being a substitute.

"Who brought the dog through the window?" Niles's voice was getting tense.

"But—"

"No but. The dog needs to be outside. Off the desks. Now." The "Now" was strongly emphasized just in case the students thought that they had more time to plan or tap off the tables stage left like a cartoon Bugs/Daffy vaudeville combo.

Niles tried to wrangle the dog by the collar while he tried to collar the dog wranglers in the room. The dog panted and padded around happily sniffing interesting things. "I need everyone to sit down in a chair right now. Any chair. Take a chair at a table and sit there please." He was speaking loudly, as if the matter were that the children couldn't hear him.

He cornered the dog and caught him while the students whispered and giggled. A voice came from behind him as the dog licked one hand while he grabbed the collar with the other: "You ain't our teacher."

Niles turned and addressed the room, looking at all of the faces in turn. "Right now, I am. I need you to cooperate, lest things become unpleasant for all of us."

The students were unsure. He seemed serious. He had the dog tightly by the collar and even the formerly excited canine looked frightened about what was coming next. The big substitute looked kind of scary. Collectively, and without even speaking to each other, they decided that their rebellion would move a bit more slowly. They had to feel this guy out for a few minutes before their fun could resume.

Niles had just restored the room to some sort of order and ushered the dog back out the window just as the teacher across the hallway came in with a hand full of grammar and math worksheets. The scent of dog was still strong in the air. He brushed the wet fur from his hands and she passed the pages to him wordlessly. She knew what was happening. She rolled her eyes as she turned away. She didn't think he'd catch her judging him, but he did. As he passed the papers around the room he noticed that the students had rearranged themselves again and were no longer in the same groups as just minutes ago. Their plan shifted as well.

"All right. We have some things to do now. I don't know who any of you are, but we have things to do. Can I please have the lesson plans back? Or maybe the seating chart? Please?"

"We don't know what you're talking about. She didn't leave nothing. We don't have seats."

"Okay then. We're just going to sit where we're at and do these fun worksheets quietly. Maybe if we had a seating chart and lesson plans we'd make time to bring the dog in for a desktop dance party." Niles was angry and things were starting to slip.

"Really?"

"No. I'm a substitute, not a retard."

There was a sharp intake of breath around the room. "You're not supposed to say that word. You're not a very good substitute teacher."

"You're not a very good class. You hid the lesson plans and seating chart."

"We told you old man, she didn't leave none. You're dumb."

"Well, I did sign up for this, so you're more right than wrong." Niles cursed himself silently.

They did worksheets or rather refused to do worksheets quietly with Niles stalking around the room heavily, until the principal came to the door and announced that it was almost time for them to load up on a bus for a field trip. Niles hadn't been told that was on the agenda. She sniffed heavily with a narrow nose and gave Niles an evil look before leaving to direct traffic in the halls.

The students sulked and plotted revenge until an announcement over the PA gave permission for their hall to march down to the buses which were loading to take them to a play with puppets about positive citizenship. The ignored Nile's glower and excused themselves from the room, clearly still fuming about being denied the dog.

He felt defeated and his posture showed it. He slumped, his eyes downcast as he stood in the hallway uselessly. The other teachers seemed to feel sorry for the average Joe turned pathetic substitute in Niles's clothes. His students spread out despite his protests and commands that they stay in an orderly line, and the other teachers accidentally corralled his students onto the bus for him and left him to mindlessly mind the rest of the hordes on the buses with little interaction. The ride was short and painful. He kept his mouth shut, lest he show the other chaperones exactly how ineffective he was. The teacher that he was substituting for was already present at the puppet show (for reasons unknown to Niles) and once they arrived she took over doing the things that he didn't know that he was not doing since no one had told him to do them. He felt as useless as he was.

Overall, it was a very educational and effective substitute teaching experience. Niles learned many things that he would apply in his own classroom in due time. This time he learned that the students hated him for being there and that no one would help him, no one liked him, and no one would be his friend.

Niles and people like him who became teachers were products of their own worlds -- distanced though they were from the one he had just become a part of. Once upon a time in America, teachers were made from the children of working class parents. They were taught that education provided a way up and out of the working class life. They were told that the difference between the people who controlled the machines and the people who controlled them was a matter of education. The lines were easy to see. Even without a high school diploma, a worker could see for himself that education made the difference in levels of control. Most of those machine operators understood from the bottom how little control they had in their lives because they didn't have the knowledge that would give it to them.

They dreamed of more than they had for the lives of their own children, so they pushed them toward more schooling. Even with encouraging parents, every child had to decide for themselves how much effort to put into school. Sometimes they chose poorly because they couldn't imagine the difficulties the rest of their life could hold due to choices they made as adolescents.

Niles had made his own choices. Somewhere out there, through a series of complex mathematical equations was another Niles existing in something that wasn't quite theoretical construct, but not quite flesh and blood. That Niles might wake early in the morning and walk through a cornfield that he himself had planted before heading into a barn to feed dairy cattle. He might walk through that cornfield inspecting the life that he planted, that he had put into that ground and fostered, the life that he was cultivating. He might, in that pre-dawn starlight, hold those leaves in his hands, touch the stems and stalks, looking for weaknesses or imperfections that he would work to compensate for, in those plants that he cared for and generated his livelihood.

That Niles would wake up early every day, and walk down from his saltbox style farmhouse to the barn in the dark to check on his animals. Those domesticated creatures were his responsibility too, since they could no longer care for themselves after having had their wild bred out through a few hundred or thousand generations before he might ever pull them, breech and gasping for breath from their mothers' wombs. He would cuddle and feed his dogs, each of them a king or queen of the barn, running through the herd in pasture with their tongues lolling gleefully and knowing their place by heart and soul in the pack. He would watch the cats arch their backs and stretch on the windowsills as he flicked the lights on, and then watch them begin their daily routine with that same self-certainty that all cats wield like a weapon on the hunt.

He would walk through the pastures and pens before starting the day's chores, inspecting the fences and gates, looking over the cows that were laying heavy and pregnant in wait, consulting his records and notes, figuring which ones were due and when, carefully eyeing their feeding and their movements to make sure that they would bear well and healthy. As he leaned on the gate watching them, he might even be nuzzled by the breeding bull that he had hand fed as a calf, the bull that would still gently butt when he wanted his neck scratched and who would follow him back behind the security of the fence like a puppy if ever his curiosity combined with an open gate or a broken wire to venture outside his pasture.

That Niles would milk, and feed, and clean. He would care for all of his animals and his fields -- all the life that existed in part due to his work, and that Niles would wash his dirty calloused hands, the same ones that healed, guided, and dug; those hands that would dance across a page and write, record and figure, ruminate, weave, and create, because that's what a Niles's hands would do.

This Niles was not that same Niles. This Niles had done the mathematics differently somewhere back in time, traded his plants, dairy cows, and dogs for lesson plans, dry erase markers and other people's' children. That other Niles would never stalk around an elementary classroom, hoping to calm humans who were thrown off kilter by coming to school to see someone other than their teacher that they were accustomed to standing in front of them asking for the same things their teacher asked for but who lacked the relationships necessary for those things to happen.

This Niles thought he could be a teacher.

1. Mathematics

It wasn't love at first sight, but it might as well have been. The first time Niles saw the math teacher he was too upset to be infatuated.

He was at the bar hovering over a warm beer that he didn't want to drink. Looking at it distracted him from being anxious or depressed about the overwhelming things which he had no control over. There were many things beyond his control waiting for him when he went back to school.

Niles wasn't at the bar to have a good time - he was there to escape. He didn't know where else to go. Sitting alone at home did him no good. He had to go back to work at the school next week, and although he wanted to see his students again he hated going to work. He didn't go to the bar to drink, he just wanted to lose himself somewhere there was other people around. He wanted to get out of reach of the ennui and despair that was waiting for him in the school building and that haunted him at home. He loved working with teenagers, but the thought of returning there and the misery of the paperwork looming before him made his stomach ball into a knot.

Late afternoon August light streamed in from the windows. People trickled through the doors, more in than out, filling like a small pool in a slow-coming high tide as banker's hours drew to a close. She came in with her friends, chattering and tweeting like birds, high-pitched and excited in the politely unique way of being "rebellious" with her church women's group who'd all gotten out of work early on a Friday to celebrate her new job. She made eye contact incidentally with Niles while scanning the room. He was drinking the scene in.

"How are you?" she asked with a friendly smile, not caring for the answer in the normal way of pretending to be more invested than she truly was. It was politely dismissive. So was his response.

"I am here," was his reply.

"Yes, you are," she said as she moved her eyes back to her friends, smile fading, seeking to disengage the man who didn't give the scripted polite answer that he was supposed to.

"How are you?" he asked her, emphasizing the "you," then took a shallow drink.

"Good, thank you for asking." She looked away.

She was trying to blow Niles off, but he didn't see it. She continued to look above his head at the drink selection board on the wall but was too polite to completely ignore him.

"That's very good. It's good that you're good, because there are too many people out there who are evil. We need more people to do good."

She turned back to him confusedly, "What do you mean?"

"I mean that the world is full of people who have no consideration for anyone else. We need more people who do good."

Her upturned lips went straight. "You're a bit odd, aren't you?"

"I had hoped that you wouldn't see that so quickly. I'm trying to make new friends."

"How is that going?" She rummaged in her purse for her ID.

"I don't know. I'm not optimistic though. You've done quite well in that regard." He motioned toward her flock of women that had wandered away, laughing together at part of God's plan across the room.

She turned back to Niles. "I was trying to be polite to you."

"I often assume that politeness means more than it does. I'm sorry. So why are you still talking to me?"

"You're not the worst man I've ever met in a bar. I don't want to be rude. I also want to order a drink."

"I have an offbeat way of making friends."

"Is that what this is?"

"It's what I was trying to do. I get the sense that it's not coming out that way, is it?"

She sighed deeply and dropped her shoulders in a slump. "My friends are kind of high maintenance. It puts me on edge. I'm sorry if I misjudged you." As a woman, she believed that she was at fault if Niles was offended. Her mother had taught her well.

"No worries. I apologize for being rude. It's how I justify in my own mind the fact that I am sitting in a bar alone." Niles was hit by a sudden inclination to be honest because now he felt guilty for provoking this woman. His mother had taught him well.

His admission tripped a circuit of sympathy within her Christian heart.

"I'm sure that you have friends."

"And that they surround me, as yours do?" He swept his arm in a short circle at the empty space around him. She looked around, then met his eyes again.

"You can come sit with us. We'll be your friends." Niles chuckled softly at her kind naiveté. She wasn't serious and even though Niles suspected that, he didn't indicate it.

"You I might take. Your friends seem... a bit much for me." Their voices rang through the din from across the pub, penetrating it like the cries of gulls descending on a field of garbage. Niles leaned toward her to hear her better over the noise.

14

"Well, they're a bit much for me sometimes as well. My name is Amber Duckett, I'm a teacher here in town." She reached out a hand to shake his.

"Ember? Like ashes? That's unique." Niles couldn't quite hear her over the din.

Her hand was limp, like her name.

"No, Amber, like the patriotic waves of grain." She pulled her hand back, repelled by Niles's touch.

"Ah, I see." Said Niles who did not see. "I'm a teacher too. Also in this town. My students call me Mr. Niles.'"

She was not impressed. The flock was calling. The circuit switched off. "Perhaps I'll see you around?" She absent-mindedly rubbed her hand as if to brush Niles's touch away.

"Perhaps." Niles said, thinking that perhaps not was much more likely. She rejoined her noisy friends. Niles returned to his quiet cell in the open block.

Niles went home that day, shortly after parting from his first experience with Duckett. He went to his garden, sat with his back to civilization and gazed into the branches of the maple tree that danced in the wind there, wondering why anyone would put up with something that consistently made them feel awful and contemplating what else he could do with a degree in English beyond being mocked for his short-sighted choices at the university.

Duckett walked away not knowing that Niles was sitting in front of a warm beer because he was dreading another year of working with an insane staff and insane administrators, another poor yearly review because he was not "using technology effectively" or didn't follow the mandated curriculum perfectly, and that she'd be treated the same as him no matter how "effective" or "ineffective" she was. She also didn't know that they'd be working in the same building in the same hallway. She couldn't imagine having anything in common with him in those moments except being caught in the same three-dimensional space.

There would be commonalities though, beyond those of being closed into the same time and space, philosophical paths crossing common to both the heathen and the blessed alike.

She would find Niles across the hall from her on the third floor that next week, and like Niles had already found, she too would see that nothing she could do in the classroom would be good enough. In their district, they could not teach "highly effectively." Everything would fall short of even their most mediocre goals. Semester after semester. Even though Duckett was just about to start and hadn't been through the same ringer that Niles had been wrung through, she would learn.

It was all just a matter of time.

In three dimensional space, this bar was just around the corner and down the street from the school that Niles had worked at for two years and where Duckett would start working in just a few days, so that made it a likely place for teachers to go when their workday was done. Niles would sometimes go there alone even during the summer, but most teachers visited the place in pairs or small groups similar to Duckett's. When Duckett rejoined her friends that day she brushed off their questions about that man who had detained her and talked instead about plans for that week's Bible Study, but Niles had been a topic of conversation for others who had sat and drank in some of the same spaces.

Just short of two years before, Niles had been a topic of conversation for other teachers, even though they didn't know his name.

Halvermeyer, Trudeau, Geit, Johnson, and Smith had convened on the first Friday after returning to school in the fall to evaluate the new strangers including Niles who had entered the building as teachers.

"What's up with that new guy in the room next to yours, Halvermeyer? He just stands there with his arms crossed staring at students during passing time. Have you talked to him yet?"

"He said 'Hi' and introduced himself." Halvermeyer paused, trying to remember something important. The others waited, as if what he would say next might matter. "I can't even remember his name."

Geit was unimpressed. "It sounds like subtraction by addition. Wasn't there a math teacher in that room last year? I wonder what happened to her. What was her name - Talley or something like that?'

Johnson nodded knowingly. "You remember her because she looked like a member of Destiny's Child."

Smith chimed in, having drained his glass and feeling left out. "That new guy in there looks like a psycho. He's probably like a secret serial killer or something. Geit, you and Halvermeyer keep an eye on him. If people start disappearing, I want a full report."

Geit laughed. "I'll probably be one of the first to go. People like me always get picked off first in horror movies.'

Trudeau snorted incredulously. "You're not black. As a fellow white man, I think we're pretty safe." He paused dramatically. "Unless he's gay. Then a pretty guy like you will probably be first to go." Everyone at the table laughed at the irony. Geit wasn't the prettiest one there. Trudeau was.

Trudeau was the All-American beauty of the group. Just three years out of college, his dishwater blonde hair had barely started receding and his blue eyes were considered the dreamiest by every teenage girl who had him for their English teacher. He was the teacher every woman thought of when they heard The Police play "Don't stand so close to me." He was the star of the high school play every year, and even the local college girls would take the evening to swoon at his performances. He was the guy who was great at everything and could have pursued any career after school, so when he walked down the stage steps with his college degree in Education in hand it flew in the face of the common knowledge that teachers were only people who couldn't do anything else. He was a "somebody."

The conversation drifted and they no longer had anything to say about Niles. Smith shared that he had a good job with a local insurance company lined up but couldn't start until November when the manager he was going to replace would retire. They all drank to his future success, even Johnson, the short, swarthy Science teacher who left to work for the local pharmaceutical company in early October before Smith made his exit and told no one that he was leaving until he was gone. Both had lasted less than three years in the building and Niles would never meet either.

Smith and Johnson were good teachers. Competent, skilled in their areas, but they'd left before they were allowed to have an impact.

The year before that, Niles was in a different district trying to be a teacher.

At Niles's first full-time teaching job as an interim substitute in Leinster Hills, his room was cleaned daily by an hourly janitor hired by and working for the district on a yearly contract. This was an odd thing already, not just that the room was actually cleaned daily, but also that the janitor was a district employee instead of being an employee of an outside company coming in to do the job for minimum wage without benefits.

He would sweep the hardwood floors and dust and even clean the chalkboard when Niles asked him to. He was always in a hurry, but never rushed; even though he knew that he had a full floor of classrooms and offices to clean, he also cared enough to do a good job. When Niles was there late in the afternoon and into the night grading papers (as he so often was that semester) the janitor would talk to him while he cleaned - alleviating some of that after-school loneliness that would have else wise echoed around those hallways usually filled with youth.

He often told Niles that he admired and respected all teachers for the hard work they did. He told Niles that he had been one of those hard-headed and sometimes belligerent kids when he had attended that high school as a student some thirty plus years ago. He knew now, through a lifetime of struggles and hardships of his own, that most of his teachers were right, and that they were honestly just trying to look out for him. He said it was too late for him to find those teachers to apologize for his teenage behavior, too late for him to track them and down and tell them that they had been right after all, but that now he would not miss a chance to tell any teacher that he met how much he honored and respected the diligent and hard work that they did. He wasn't an exceptionally bright man, but age and experience had taught him a good deal about kindness.

Niles responded to him and told him that his work in creating a safe, clean, and comfortable environment for the students to live in for hours each day was also very important, and that if the building and restrooms were not kept so clean and tidy then teaching would be more difficult.

In the years after, Niles would often think of that man, divorced three times, supporting children through the court, on the recovery side of drug addictions and convictions, and of the integrity and dignity with which he carried himself around the school building after the students had left. He thought of that man and then tried to peer into his current students' futures. He wondered how many of them would be like the janitor, would put things together years later after stumbling in life and realizing that the people who'd most consistently had their hands out to help him their whole life had been teachers.

There was a junior ROTC program in place in Leinster Hills. Problem students who showed potential were steered toward it, as were many children of single parent households. Administrators believed that the place of the missing parent could be filled by someone who shouted in a uniform and made them stand rigidly in one spot for an hour four days a week after school. As Niles stayed for hours grading papers and planning after school that semester, he could hear them out his windows practicing standing, shouting, and moving in different directions when someone told them to. Sometimes he would move over to the window when taking a break from grading to lean on the sill like a forlorn poet and watch the students he knew who could barely behave civilly in class get shouted at in a parking lot.

Niles suspected that there was supposed to be a straight line for them to follow in other places beyond that parking lot. Since Leinster Hills was one of the cities in Michigan most destroyed by the retreat from manufacturing (at least outside of "ground zero" in Detroit) there weren't a lot of options for the students who hated school. Military recruiters circled the high school like buzzards on a whale carcass in a Death Valley salt pan. Some teens were easy pickings. Lacking a mother or a father, or both, using school only as an escape from an abusive or violent home, and with no foreseeable future in entrepreneurship beyond selling weed or meth in an alley left them with few options. To them, the military looked like fun. They would shoot guns and travel to places they would otherwise only see in photos. Once the prospect of regular food, sleep, and health care beyond expired pills from grandma's medicine cabinet was added in, it looked like a good plan.

Those comforts weren't the real draws. The real draw was the power that military service seemed to offer them. These were young adults who'd been dominated for years, left behind by family and society, told again and again that they held little value because they were not pretty, not smart, not "talented," or not "white." The military offered them a way to use their anger over rejection and broken promises.

The military would take their anger and give them a gun. A gun was a substitute for money when it came to power, making the two interchangeable in some regards. They simplest way available to get money was through violence. What did the military promise if not the opportunity for sanctioned violence used on other people to enforce control or power? The military might woo young people with promises they don't have to legally keep about money for college, but once someone had a gun what need was there for more? Learning in school took perseverance and work. It was not surprising that college felt out of reach when violence was offered.

Niles wasn't there long enough to see how many of those students followed through on their dreams of guns and violence. He was pushed out by the same thing that gave him a way back to Pianosa Springs: student enrollment numbers. He became just an unnecessary body in the building despite his own large class sizes when the Count Day numbers were tolled and budget money was figured. He was let go after a semester. His dream was that a percentage of those students whose gun fantasies were made good was less than one hundred, or one one hundredth of that, but he had no honest hope of that being the case. There were few opportunities for them beyond violence. He knew that some students would end up in prison or a cheap casket because of the weapons they'd find in their hands.

He was sad when he had to leave Leinster Hills. There was a need for good teachers there and he wanted to be one of them. There was no money to pay them. Pianosa Springs was going to be different though. He believed that the mathematics of enrollment and money would be better there. So many things that he was led to believe would turn out wrong.

2. Kringe

The Assistant Superintendent for Student Services in Pianosa Springs Public Schools, Donna Dinkley, was addressing the new hires that muggy August morning. She was short, but not small. The measuring tape might have stretched equally taut both in length and circumference, and from a distance through smudged lenses she might have been mistaken for a large fire hydrant if she were not so prone to speaking with her hands, but these things would not stand in the way of her making a difference to these young teachers.

There was more than forty of them assembled in this cramped room this morning with another thirty-seven lining up for the same session the very next day. The District had to hire and train so many new teachers every year because they simply had the worst luck in hiring people who could handle the job. Dinkley believed strongly that if only they could ever find good, competent people, people who were prepared and able, people who were smart enough to adapt to change, flexible enough to change when given direction, and dedicated enough to stay with the district and not closeted bigots of the worst kind that then finally, she would be recognized for being as wonderful at her job as she was unquestionably was. She walked into the room smartly, then slammed a large binder of secondary education curriculum nearly as large as her bosom on the table to interrupt the low chatter in the room and gather everyone's attention. They all stopped talking immediately and looked at her. Satisfied that she was the center of attention, she began to speak.

"Ladies and gentlemen, I have the privilege of being the first to officially welcome you as a group to Pianosa Springs Public Schools, home of "The Privilege." You are now teachers in the most promising community in America where wealthy benefactors have decided that normal charity just won't cut it in today's America, especially when it comes to effective tax shelters, and that no one can depend on the government."

She stood bolt-rigid, barely visible behind the podium mounted on the low table as she continued, "You are now teachers in a district where every single child can now attend the college of their choice in this state for four years without paying a dime in tuition. Working as a teacher in this district means that you too are a part of that privilege. Your job is to teach our students the knowledge and skills necessary to succeed in college and beyond. You are important cogs in the machine that is building the future of this city and this state, but more importantly in the futures of each and every one of these children. Without you as partners, our students might fail. Without you as leaders, these students might not know where to go or how to get there. Their success is now your responsibility."

She looked around the room and stood straighter even though no one in the audience could tell. She was a prophet delivering a message to the unwashed masses. She held power over them, the power of the authority that she had mastered as a chosen handmaid of the superintendent. She went on in her version of the sermon of the mount.

"We know that this is a heavy burden to put on your shoulders. If you feel that this weight is too heavy - if you feel that you are not up to the task that we are putting in your hands, then you are free to leave now."

The assembled audience sat stunned in silence. They looked back and forth at each other, trying to figure out what was going on. What did she mean?

Assistant Superintendent Dinkley smiled. She had made herself clear.

A man in the second row sheepishly raised his hand. She smugly pointed to him. "Yes, you there." He was clearly intimidated both by her presence and the weight of the message that she had delivered to his shaking hands. He stood up clutching a battered and weathered Detroit Tigers ball cap and struggled to find the right words.

"Ma'am? This is the bus drivers' meeting."

She paused only slightly as her ego reset her hard drive and the new program compensated.

"And we have a terrible time finding and keeping good bus drivers. Bus drivers who care about our children enough to give them safe, comfortable transportation to school. Will you be the ones to do it? Will you be the ones who are unselfish enough, caring enough, and loving enough to take these kids to school on time when no one else will?" The Tigers fan gulped and sat back down.

Her recovery was majestic and she knew it. Now, these adults were caught on their heels, moving backwards because they had just been attacked. They had been asked not to be as terrible as they were.

"Because if you don't care about children, if you can't find the love and decency in your own heart, you can leave right now!" Her words stung. Why would they have shown up for this meeting if they weren't willing to drive a bus to take the students to school. Why was she accusing them of being bad people? Faces became stern and chins were set. She was issuing a challenge, and these people, if they had any courage at all, would not be pushed around by this fireplug of a woman flaunting the power of her position in front of them.

She knew exactly what she was doing. She insulted the heart of these working class people to manipulate them, to use their pride against them to grow and preserve her own. Already they had forgotten that she was in the wrong meeting. Her words were powerful. Dinkley narrowed her eyes and looked down her nose at them. She smiled a thin smile. This was going to be another good meeting, even if she didn't deliver her long speech about the importance of the student ID card. She could save that until the new teachers' meeting, whenever that was.

If there was one policy that the school administrators believed in without variation, it was the ID policy. It may not have been the first set of commandments brought down from the educational mountain, but it was the second set that was revised in Exodus 34. It may have even been number seven on the stone tablets, but no one could be sure because they were hidden like Joseph Smith's golden plates. In Pianosa Springs, "Thou shalt take accurate and timely attendance" was carved in granite.

High school in America was different before September 11, 2001. Beginning that very morning terrorists could now be everywhere, not just in presidential speeches performed to drum up support for enhanced domestic security policies and undomesticated wars. When it happened, Niles was in college in the Midwest preparing for his career as a teacher. It changed America forever.

By afternoon, all of them learned that they were a target. Paranoia ran wild as local malls and elementary schools began to question "Are we next?" The mall in nearby Boatstown increased its security staff by fifty percent which gave them a full three-man part-time team to watch teens try to shoplift and prevent the next major terrorist attack from taking place in the American Midwest. Schools everywhere demanded that student IDs be visible constantly, in case they were being infiltrated by Bin Laden's operatives, their terror cells intent on ripping apart the social and cultural fabric by bombing or crashing a small plane filled with bombs into Mrs. Weaver's third grade art class at John Blanchard Elementary on Republic Street three blocks away from the high school where Niles would begin working full-time only five years later.

Of course, the threats were well-known. Non-stop coverage of the wars in Iraq and Afghanistan were broadcast on every news channel without fail and with all due patriotic rigor until they became routine and boring and Americans already submerged in a supremely nationalistic and egocentric culture tuned into more intellectual pursuits, like watching singers be humiliated by an English celebrity and a washed up singer/dancer. The American public's attention might have moved on even as the war continued, but the surveillance state that existed in the school system grew beyond any teacher's fever dreams.

By the time Niles became a teacher in Pianosa Springs he found that making sure each student was constantly wearing his or her ID was the second most important thing that he could do after taking attendance four different ways. The ID would make it possible to ensure that only those who were supposed to be in the building were actually in the building, and any student who was not wearing his or her ID visibly was to be instructed forcefully to do so. If students failed to comply, they were to be sent out of class for a disciplinary action that would inevitably mean that they missed that class and part of the next. Students who had lost their very important ID or otherwise found it to be damaged in some way were sent out to receive another from the main office where they would be charged five dollars for each replacement card. The cost of the card was seventy dollars per every one thousand cards but administrative costs had to be added in, and initially the cost of replacement to each student was ten dollars. Remarkably, someone pointed out that it was too punitive a cost when seventy percent of the student body was on free and reduced lunch and it was lowered accordingly to only five dollars one year later after the initial cost of materials had only been paid back fifty-five times over.

"Those identification procedures must be followed" the teachers were told, or else chaos and perhaps even terrorism would ensue. Without proper ID worn around the neck on a school approved lanyard, anyone could be a terrorist. When Niles was a probationary teacher the policy seemed problematic to him, but he was too uncertain of continued employment to try to buck the system. The policy as laid out seemed antithetical to other school policies that were in place. For example: the attendance policy.

The attendance policy said that students were to be in their assigned courses at all times. They can't learn if they're not present. Attendance was mandatory for receiving state and federal funding. According to the administration's ID policy which said that students couldn't be in class without their IDs visible at all times, students had to be sent out for punishment. But the attendance policy said that they also had to attend class. Students couldn't be in class unless they were wearing their ID. Students who had no ID were sent to the main office to get a new one, but if they did not have the money to purchase a replacement, then they would be housed in the in-school suspension for the remainder of the day and then sent home with a billing notice due immediately upon receipt. That resulted in the student missing class. However, Niles and his fellow teachers were to mark each student present, even if they were only in class for one minute before being asked to leave to get a new ID. The student's other teachers were notified via e-mail by an overworked subordinate secretary at some point during the school day or often the next that said student had been housed In-School Suspension and that they were to be marked present even though they had never made it to class.

It was a system designed with everyone's best interests in mind, and was an echo of the district's motto: "Perseverance, Aptitude, Dedication, Determination, Integrity, Nobility, Goodness." Niles considered the policy paradox of the motto and the policies to be brilliant, especially when he realized that whoever conceived of the slogan had no idea of what a paradox or an acronym was. Most of his fellow teachers didn't know what the district's motto was either. They never stopped to consider whether or not knowing the motto and being able to repeat it when prompted made a difference even though teachers and students both were asked to be able to repeat the mantra upon prompting by an administrator.

Gradually during his first two years Niles decided that his personal closed door policy had to change. At first, he did what he was supposed to do: sent his cardless students into the hallway and out of class to get a new ID. From the start, he felt bad about it. It didn't feel right pushing them out because they didn't come back. They would miss the whole class. He weighed his two directives from administration against each other. Push students out who don't have their ID and make sure that students are in class learning.

Niles included both official declarations from administration in his class syllabus and went over them verbally with the class at the beginning of each semester.

"All students must wear their ID visibly above the waist during the school day. Students will not be admitted to class unless they are wearing their ID." Some students were listening, some were daydreaming about sex or sports, and some were planning on losing their ID so that they'd never have to attend class. "Students must be present in class, whenever possible, barring all academic, sports, or personal excused absences."

As the school year progressed, students would try to push the boundaries of the rules. "Sorry Mr. Niles, I can't come to class. I don't have my ID. I gotta go get one!"

"I'll tell you what. Just come to class. I'll send you out at the end of class to get one before your next class." Niles knew that sending that student out for lack of an ID might mean that he didn't see him for a few days, so he kept him in class.

The student would forget to ask to go get a new ID at the end of class, Niles would also forget, and then if the next instructor didn't forget (which they usually did,) Niles would look like a bad teacher who wasn't doing his job. Like most rules and laws in the US, it was selectively enforced, usually only if the teacher had a bone to pick with someone. Wein, for example, became well known for throwing other teachers under the bus to make herself look better and she had decided that she had a few bones to pick with Niles. She was a real team player in the most American sense of the word.

She sent out passive-aggressive e-mails to the whole building on many topics, but student IDs were one of her favorite issues to highlight. There was one of those students who would often try to use the "I don't have my ID" line on Niles to get out of class until he figured out that Niles would make him stay in class no matter what. Wein happened to have the same student the next period. She quickly grew exasperated with Niles not following the rules.

Her email said:

Good morning staff!

I'm sure that all of my fellow teachers are so busy with everything going on in their classrooms, but I just want to touch base about the ID issue!

I know that the school has a policy, and that we as teachers in our rooms all kind of do "our own thing" but it would be so helpful if some of you that have some of the same students that I do would be as consistent as I am in enforcing the school's policy on the matter

If you have any questions about how to deal with the ID issue in your own classroom, feel free to ask me or Ms. Linn, as we both have effective policies regarding this difficult classroom issue! Looking forward to having everyone on the same page with this policy! I looped in our administrators on this so that we can have some cohesion as a building!

Thanks in advance for your support and cooperation!

Niles read:

Hey assholes who are not me!

I know that you're all lazy and lesser than me because I do so much, but I want to call you all out about something basic to try to make myself look better than you!

I follow the school policy because I'm the best teacher here, and you probably don't because you think you're better than the rules, especially those of you like Niles who have the same students that I do.

I'm an expert on everything related to students following the rules, but I'm also going to kiss Ms. Linn's ass because she loves people who kiss her ass and I believe that kissing her ass can get me special treatment! I know that I can embarrass you all into being like me with the passive-aggressive note, since I also sent this to all of our administrators!

Up yours, losers!

Which was clearly what she meant.

Niles was fairly intelligent, so he understood what was said between the lines as well as the size of the margins and the font used. Wein's problem was that she wasn't good at hiding her the size of her ego. She was combatively attempting to make herself look better while simultaneously making others look bad, the age-old practice of the incompetent - usually employed while fawning. Older teachers noticed the dubious relationship that she was pursuing with the with married vice principal who'd grown up one district over and had gone to graduate school in the Deep South for two years before coming back with an overacted Southern drawl and an enhanced hatred of black people, and that poorly hid relationship just made Wein all the more despicable to anyone who paid attention to how awful she actually was.

Niles didn't like Wein. No one else seemed to care. He was the only one. He must have been crazy.

Niles put his feet up on his desk and sighed. He leaned his chair back to the very limit, that place where his students thought he would inevitably crash over backwards upon his bald head but never did. There was an ironic glee for him in such a small detail of existence.

The fact that some students had expressed amazement at the chair's in-built ability to resist the temptation to topple amused him. The chair was designed to tilt, just like it was designed to roll, but the unlikely balance of Niles on the chair's fulcrum dazzled daily. Every time he did it, they gasped, day after day, as if he were performing some new and heretofore unseen miracle. He knew that the key to success lay, like so much else in life, in having long legs. Taller people got paid more money on average, taller people were perceived as more popular and successful in survey after survey as was related in his Introduction to Psychology textbook from college. People with short legs would never understand how a simple act like reaching a grocery item on a top shelf for an old woman would inspire such admiration. In his chair and elsewhere, the long legs gave him a clumsy balance, a counterweight to an oversized head that must have destroyed his mother on his birthday. He spent a good portion of his life in between his birth and his now trying to fill out the space between his head and his legs with something substantial. This ironic glee filled at least part way this cavity in his chest, it swelled him with a substantiality that few other things did. Speaking of legs, this was subtle, silent leg-pulling of the students who paid attention. It was his way of crafting a character to fill the gap that might otherwise have left his oversized head floating off into space away from his legs like a helium balloon lost to its mooring and simultaneously rewarding the students who noticed.

He wasn't the only newer teacher who was given to flights of naive fancy. Reghan Bullox was another fresh-faced new teacher in the high school on the other side of the district who started the same year as Niles. She was bright and full of life and joy, just the kind of young teacher a district should try to hold on to if they value people who do their jobs well and with enthusiasm. She wore her hair in a full afro that would have put a blaxploitation film star of 1970s to shame and which created the illusion that she was much taller than she was. When Niles met her, they stood eye to afro and he fell in love immediately.

The district gave notice that it was looking for some of its new blood to overhaul an aged curriculum that seemed to hold little utility in working with a population of dedicated smartphone users and Bullox and Niles both signed up. This work was paid by the hour like his previous job of working in the factory, which made writing curriculum twenty percent less valuable than building seat adjusters for pickup trucks. It had even less value if measured by the "overtime" standard. Niles already worked fifty plus hours a week in the classroom grading and planning. Writing curriculum was "extra duty." If it had been in the industrial factory, it would have been paid at the overtime standard of "time and a half." By that measure, writing curriculum was roughly fifty-six percent as valuable as building a seat adjuster. Niles marveled at the wonderful complexity of capitalism and wished he'd learned a valuable skill well - something like throwing a football or being a Kardashian.

Also unlike the seat adjusters, the curriculum would be owned forever by the district. Unless they decided to sell it for a profit like General Motors did with the seat adjusters. It was a different sort of capitalistic beast that Niles now served. With the seat adjusters, Niles "owned" each one he built until it made it all the way through the build process up to the end of the final round of product testing, then the seat adjuster belonged to the vehicle company until the expiration of the warranty. If "his" seat adjuster failed during any part of the build or test process, it was removed and sent back to the factory with his marks on it, and he was reprimanded for failing to create a quality piece of equipment.

The curriculum writing for the district however was more akin to creating a living creature through genetic manipulation and sequencing that was owned by a company. If it was good, they could sell it to other districts. If it wasn't, it would go into the dustbin of history with the old curriculum that it was written to replace.

Niles showed up Saturday morning at one of the old school buildings that the district used for meetings instead of classes. The building had been built for the post war population boom in the fifties and was starting to show the effects of neglect on the outside, but the inside had been renovated recently due to a millage vote that allocated money toward upkeep and maintenance of district properties. The school was in a difficult position with the building.

If the district sold it, they were up against a financial wall. Schools weren't built like warehouses and strip malls to be fitted and refitted for multiple different tenants over the lifetime of the building. The only potential tenant to buy the building directly from the district would be a charter school. That would be a detriment to the public district because that meant a competitor in the education sector that wouldn't be beholden to the same laws and regulations. That was unacceptable.

To sell the property to a non-educational user meant that the building would have to be rezoned and demolished to make way for another strip mall or block of chain restaurants, and the monies received would count as income for the district. To tear down the building meant a $500,000 bill because no buyer would pay for the property with a building on it that they couldn't use, so it was on the district to pay the demolition costs. The district was already barely operating in the black, and the costs of demolishing buildings no longer used for classes would push them into the red even with potential profit to be made in the sale due to that increase in taxable income. It was in the best interest of the district to ask the public for money to renovate and then to find another use for each building even though it might be redundant. This building was now used only for training and writing curriculum.

There were ten teachers at the first meeting. Linn and Demarr were there because they had to have their hands on everything to do with English Language Arts. Then four new teachers, including Niles and three female teachers who had also just completed their first year of teaching in the district. Besides Bullox, there was Yung King and Penny Pound, both whom worked with Niles with the freshman in his building. Jong was from the Appalachian region of West Virginia. She was exceptional, being the only Asian descended woman to ever come from the region. She was tall, only a few inches shorter than Niles and she loved teaching YA literature with a passion that Niles admired right from the start. Penny Pound was the copper-haired daughter of a Romanian mail-order bride and a Chicago stockbroker. Despite their differences, the two women had immediately bonded into a highly effective team during Dinkley's practiced speech about the importance of dedicating themselves to the children of Pianosa Springs.

They were joined by Brien Massengill, Linn's lapdog and two more aged English teachers from the high school across town who were on the verge of retirement and looking to bank a bit more money before drifting off into the aether of meaninglessness that awaited every teacher at the end of their use.

Geit, the dark-headed rogue, and Trudeau, the all-American teaching star, had wisely chosen to direct their energies in other directions over the summer. Both men were absent from the curriculum writing in ways extending far beyond the physical.

After the first meeting, Linn dropped out with Demarr, leaving her proxy Massengill there to report what went on back to her. He would suggest a few poems from Langston Hughes be a basic part of the curriculum, which wasn't a bad thing. It was just that like Kaseman the new superintendent, he only invoked Hughes to try to enhance his credibility with black people and "woke" white ones in the same way that a waiter who mentioned that he once served Al Pacino's table made people think he was an actor.

The other teachers dropped out one by one (because they had children of their own or other more important things to do) except for Niles and the three young English teachers who started at the same time. He was the soul male voice in the group, but he hardly counted as male because he was probably a man trapped in a lesbian's body anyway. The curriculum was written by the four of them who promptly had their names removed from the document so it could be published and marketed for the district. It was their lasting work that wouldn't last, but it would last longer than any of the women would work in the district. They were all bright, enthusiastic,

37

compassionate, articulate, and beautiful people. They wouldn't put up with being treated so poorly for as long as Niles would. They went on to teach in other settings. Niles stayed. All of them had become like younger sisters to him during the times that they worked together, enthusiastically sharing books and lessons. Like the colloquial colloquialisms that he shared with other teachers during his career, it made for one of the best periods of his life. For a short while felt like a part of an intentional family.

Within two years of the completion of that curriculum document, the three of them had left for healthier places, places were they were appreciated, had their professional skills cultivated, and were treated with positivity as human beings with value. Within another three years of their departure, no traces of them remained in their buildings where they'd once worked so hard to foster a love of learning. They were gone, and all vestiges of their classrooms were wiped away. No more students walked the halls who would remember them fondly. It broke Niles's heart when they stopped returning his texts and emails, having all moved on with their lives. It made his disconnect all the more wrenching that he'd had something and then had it removed. He heard years or months later that each had gotten married, had even invited many other teachers from the building, including many of his less appetizing department cohorts to their ceremonies. Even though Niles didn't partake of the gossip, he continued overhearing or underhearing about those who'd left in the copy room or at meetings.

In their places other teachers would cycle through, but some of the worst people Niles was to meet in his teaching career were all deeply invested in theirs. They had their worser traits fine-tuned and settled in to keep Niles company on a long-term basis. The district had a very specific type of teacher that they sought to keep and grow, and the others who remained who didn't fit the bill were simply place holders until the district could push them out. Certain policies were a filter to keep sadists and masochists in and anyone who couldn't fit in either broad category would move on.

It was late August and Portia Kringe's first day in the building. She'd moved from Atlantic City where she'd learned to decorate her cleavage with glitter and skip several meals a week to stay trim while working through college as a dealer at a casino. She walked into Niles's room at Linn's heels looked around and exclaimed at him, "Who'd you have to blow to get this classroom?"

Niles was dumbfounded. He couldn't understand why anyone would say something like that before even introducing herself. Niles sat silently sheltering in his desk, his brow noticeably furrowed at Linn and Kringe.

Linn laughed shrilly, clearly amused by her new acolyte. "Mr. Niles is clearly speechless at your fabulousness." They both cackled and exited through the hallway door, giving not another thought to him. Niles's feelings were hurt. He was accustomed to people under the age of eighteen insulting him without knowing him, but to witness the same level of thoughtlessness come from the mouth of a new colleague wounded him. His naiveté was not proving to be an asset in dealing with Linn or the others who subscribed to her code. He stood up, put his hands on his hips and shook his head before walking to the door the cold-hearted pair had exited through to close it off behind them, attempting ineffectually to close the door on the interaction. He looked down at the floor. For some reason there was a faint trail of glitter leading to the door and out into the hallway.

Portia Kringe may have believed (likely from personal experience) that the only way to get a nice classroom was to go above and beyond sound judgment. Perhaps she was a cut above with oral skills and her hands given her experience in the casinos of Atlantic City, but Niles knew from his personal experience that at best it was a matter of luck. It could also happen (and probably did) that some administrators who were in charge of such matters could and would play favorites or least favorites, but Niles never saw either side of that. Niles got his classrooms because the teachers who inhabited them before him retired or moved away. It was simply replacement. Kringe knew that nothing worked that way in her life. She had to be good with her mouth and her hands, better than she was at accusing Niles of using her tactics. Her list of resentments against Niles for things he wasn't would be long, but it started that first day with his classroom.

Niles's first classroom of his own as a teacher was on the third floor of a building downwind from the cereal factory back in Leinster Hills. The scents carried on the breezes were meaningful. On the days when something fruity was baking, the students were fruity. On the days that it was cocoa, they were lazy. On the days that the wind was blowing out instead of in, the students longed for glasses of whole milk.

This first classroom was a "first" classroom and had the original chalkboards from when the building was built in 1908, but not the original desks. They had been sold at auction during the district's decline to some artisanal cutting board maker who had repurposed the seats into cheese boards, believing that decades of student flatulence gave his work a certain "je ne sais quoi." Niles instead inherited a flock of mismatched tables and chairs of all shapes and sizes. Some round, some square, some rectangles, some wooden, some plastic, some metal. They all looked like they'd been rejected - forlorn, broken-hearted and unable to fit in with their surroundings. It was a strange commotion of impressions that the room punched the casual visitor in the face with. The paint, wainscoting, tall windows operated by thin ropes and pulleys, and the elegant trim work evoked a classic post Spanish-American War vibe - like paintings of the USS Maine. The furniture was completely late 80s post-Reagan garage sale.

There was only so much Niles could do with it. Any room that invoked disorder with its design and decoration was going to cause problems when packed full of teenagers dripping hormonal sweat and hate for adults. That first classroom was a riot waiting to happen and the fact that Niles only had to stop one fight where tables and chairs were thrown was a testament to how well he'd learned to work with the animals on the farm.

Milking the cows on the farm was about keeping them calm enough to walk into the stalls where they could be locked in. It was about distracting them from unpleasantness while they were being milking to keep them from kicking the milkers off onto the floor and standing on them. Niles could pet them while speaking calmly and give them a gentle push here and there while he made sure they were getting fed. He couldn't touch the students in the classroom, but some of the same strategies applied. Kindness, calmness, and concentration were aspects of control in both environments. If the stanchions could have been brought over from the farm, it would have made things easier.

The classroom he was placed in when he left the Hills to head to the Springs was as different as different could be in meaningful ways. Niles went back to where he had done his internship, back to Pianosa Springs District. This newer school in the older city was built by the district in the 1970s as a response to bubbling racial tensions in the community which was slow to integrate blacks and whites everywhere but on paper. The district hired a designer whose specialty was prisons. The windows were high and narrow, the hallways thin and enclosed in brick and steel. Natural light was rarely allowed to penetrate its red brick edifice and trees were discouraged from the courtyards for fear that the selected population might climb them to escape. Doors were heavy wood and steel and windows from the hallway into the classrooms were screened with steel netting to dissuade students from making statements with broken glass. Security cameras were everywhere that was legal, forgoing the bathrooms lest administrators be accused of voyeurism.

Niles's first room as a full-time hire in this imposing edifice of administrative discomfort was on the third floor as well, but there were no fragrant cereal factories creating waves of ambient olfactory refreshment to waft through those windows. Nobody there ever wanted milk. Somehow the walls and windows managed to keep smells outside while keeping the ones inside simmering in an at times putrid mixture of dust, spittle, and body odor. That first classroom in Pianosa Springs was unforgettable. It was carpeted in 1974, the same year that the school was built.The carpet had seen more sticky spills than the shower floor in the men's locker room and had not been cleaned well since Carter was President.

Each morning when Niles came in, he was smacked in the face with a stench that was paralleled only by that of the dumpsters behind the building, however the dumpsters were newer and had been cleaned more recently. The carpet was the color of dry vomit, which was surely not coincidental. More than being simply carpet, it was a physical symbol of the care, concern, and finances dedicated to keep the school functional and pleasant. A classroom with carpet was unfortunate for the teacher in a building that wasn't well maintained. The carpeting was unfortunate because in its thirty plus years of existence, it had not been cleaned once. This sad carpet had with it the the deeply embedded odors of every horrid thing that mankind ever created. Students were wont to treat floors of the school as if they were taking courses at a dump, because students were firm believers in passive rebellion. One of the simplest forms of passive rebellion is discarding refuse where one sits or stands - and this floor had been passively rebelled upon heavily for years.

He taught in that room for two years. Upon opening his door each morning, he was violently assaulted by odors that made his days on the farm seem pedestrian by comparison. The first few days each year he had to retch a little and was unable to eat the lunch he'd brought with him. After that, his nose grew accustomed to the smell. Thankfully the students weren't due in class for another week. He tried bringing in plug-in air fresheners, but all they did was change the general scent ambience from "inside a closed dumpster" to "land-fill on a hot day with occasional breeze" so he gave up after the first ones were overcome by exposure to the local miasma.

Unlike Niles, the students were well-trained by the time they arrived in their first week. This was nothing new to them - after all, they'd been going to public schools for years. The only student who ever remarked about the odor of the room was a home-schooler making her first foray into public education for her freshman year. She walked in and announced, "My mom told me it would smell like this."

Niles wondered what other bon mots of homespun wisdom she'd unveil as the days passed, but he was deeply disappointed as they all turned out to be some form of thinly veiled racism that even the least kind of the other students flinched from. She was gone off to the Christian High School across town by the third week. No doubt fully unprepared for this building's "diversity" or the nature of an "urban" district, but very well prepared for an environment where high tuition costs kept the "undesirable" children of non-northern European immigrants out.

Across the hallway from the classroom was the grade level principal's office, and due to that conjunction there were all manner of interesting and entertaining messes taking place just outside Niles's closed door in addition to the ones inside it. The freshmen that came in daily were very similar to feral squirrels. There was a strange, inexplicable transformation that took place whenever they slipped through the doors of the high school: In middle school, they were the "big kids," and they usually could be depended on to behave accordingly, looking to show the younger students trapped there in the same building what a "grown" student could look like. However, during that summer between eighth and ninth grade a switch some-where in the lizard part of their brains flipped and they went clinical-ly insane. Their attention spans, already short in the era of the cellu-lar phone, became measurable in microseconds. A sneeze across the room, a bee flying in the window, a shadow passing over the wired framed window to the hallway, a bare ankle on a girl, the crinkle of a candy wrapper, or even the unsightly wrinkles of a teacher's shirt and a shine off his bald head could set them off and Niles needed twenty minutes to bring them back to a semblance of humanity.

For the feral squirrel-children, freshman year was the year for them to try new things that they hadn't done in a while. They had grown an inch or two in some direction over those months separating middle school and high school and were now even more "grown" and tried to assert themselves in "grown" ways, such as by finding out and then attempting to address their new teachers by their first names. Parents were of little help in curbing that behavior because they believed that what their child did in the classroom was the teacher's problem and not theirs.

This school, as most in the US, was thought of by its citizenry not often, and only when there was some sort of convenient criticism to be voiced for some aspect of it. Niles knew well from where he had grown up how people thought of schools. Just down the road from the farm was a representative American family of six, which was not unheard of in Michigan where the Bible was as strong as the body odor in the finished church basement where the youth group met up to watch Christian Life videos after a sweaty pick-up basketball game.

There was a mother, a father, and six Christian children who were all a part of "God's plan" without birth control or prophylactics or any sinnery of the sort. That family would happily spend 10 percent of its yearly income (after tithes) on basic minimal upkeep and cleaning of its house, repairing broken hinges and burst pipes, new water heaters and furnace filters, even replacing an appliance or two if it seemed like part of "God's Plan." They were open to paying the escalating costs of upkeep year after year on their home that could and had accommodated up to thirty for birthday parties and family reunions on an annual basis. However, that same family balked at paying taxes to maintain and keep up the school. Each of their children would only spend four to six years in the school building at most, so they believed their personal investment graduated when the children did. That family might inhabit the home down the road from Niles's parents for thirty or forty years before changing needs and priorities necessitated a change in residence, but a school was meant to be inhabited for several decades more than a single family dwelling and by several hundred more people at a time.

The average school building was home to several hundred children for several hours a day who worked, played, and studied there, as well as all of the attendant adults, both supervisory and maintenance, who provided for the safety and well-being of those children, and then the teachers. With all of the plumbing in the bathrooms, the appliances in the kitchen for student lunch, all of the wiring for the AV and power hook-ups necessary for each classroom to keep up with the pace of technology and global expansionism, it was very expensive to upgrade and maintain the school.

Those neighbors down the road didn't want to pay the taxes for public schools because they could not see a benefit beyond their offspring. Like most Americans they considered paying for other people to have nice things as being one of the most "un-American" if not downright "anti-American" sentiments that existed. They could pray for it, and maybe even think about it before sharing a post from Fox News about how escalating educational costs are providing diminishing returns, but they would not actually vote to contribute an increase in tax money to it.

Niles knew and accepted all of these things. The middle class apathy was part of the socialization for being American too, and it was taught most successfully to the white students who benefited passively from a system that was inherently unfair to their colored peers.

In the public schools where Niles worked, teachers were expected to pay for materials and goods for their own classrooms. Unless you were Linn or one of her acolytes - then you just sent a student to borrow materials from the Art Department for your dioramas, collages, and multi-genre projects. The art teachers could not turn down the doe-eyed students sent to ask "please?" each week. For some teachers, money seemed to be no object, or at least the money that they spent on themselves.

"Mr. Niles. How come you don't have new clothes to wear every single day? I saw you wear that same shirt and tie last week."

"Is that a trick question?" Niles was confused. "Are you serious?"

"Yeah, Ms. Linn don't ever wear the same outfit twice. She says she has over a hundred outfits in three closets in her house, and she ain't never got to wear the same thing to work twice."

"She told you that? Well, she must make a lot more money than I do. Also, we must have vastly different priorities. Even if I had enough money to wear a different outfit to work everyday, why would I? Who cares what I wear to work? Why do you care?"

"I was just thinking about Ms. Linn. She so cool."

Niles let slip, "What kind of teacher is she to brag about her closet to a bunch of teens?" The student was dumbfounded. "Is her life is so meager that she has to brag about clothes to a captive audience of teenagers? And if she really considers that to be an achievement worth bragging about, what is the rest of her life like?" The question was rhetorical, but Niles would have liked to know the answer.

The student understood what Linn was teaching. "Aw Mister Niles, you just jealous."

Niles saw no point in arguing. There was nothing he could counter with. "You got me. Saw right through me." He moved on. There was too much work to do.

Niles kept walking around the room, asking students questions about what they were doing instead of letting a discussion about clothing take over. He wondered what kind of lesson about selfishness Linn was teaching by devoting class time to bragging about her wardrobe. Was it leading by example? Was it the school administration's favorite game of "do as I say, not as I do," or was it just pure mindless self-aggrandizement? The lesson this student learned seemed to be that Niles was not up to snuff if he couldn't be a clothes horse.

It was the kind of life lesson that Linn was teaching in her classroom. She was truly the best at what she did.

3. Smithson

School should be simpler and more profound at the same time. At least Niles thought so when he first started as an intern teacher.

He was in the same building where he would later find full-time employment and where he was going to spend most of his waking hours for more than a decade, although he had no idea at the time. He was just an intern, interning with other interns who were in the building doing work and observing, but paying for the privilege of doing so because nothing says "desire to work" like paying to do the job you want. The building principal, Dr. Myles Smithson, wanted to meet all of the new faces and say the new names that he would later forget that very day. They all came in, all twelve of them (including Niles) and sat with Smithson at his conference table next to his office.

The conference table was almost as big an oval as the room was a rectangle, so the room was already overstuffed with eight chairs nearly arm to arm at the table and now three extra chairs and five extra people, not counting the extra body that Smithson toppled up and down out of his office chair with constantly. There could have been two of him, but he looked like he'd swallowed his twin in the womb. He led the soon-to-be-teachers into the room, pushing all of the furniture further off kilter before he hefted himself into the furthest chair and sighed with some relief as part of his bulk settled on the table taking a load off his spent frame. The rest of the young almost-teachers shuffled and sidestepped into the room, taking chair by chair and filling the corner spaces until the door could no longer close and if it had, then it would have taken less than five minutes before everyone's breath had condensed into clouds over the center of the faux wood table that they had squeezed over and around.

Smithson exhaled a visible fog of decaffeinated coffee and spoke in his slow Midwestern drawl that made him sound like a carpetbagger mocking Southern farmers, inserting extra syllables in the middle of words that themselves sounded exhausted "Leh-hett's go ah-round the roo-hoom and intro-duhuce hourselves. I am Duh-hoctor Myles Carl-hson, the Huh-ead Prince-hipal of this school. Who are yoo? Sta-harting with this muh-han on my right and muh-hoving that way,' while pointing at Niles and spinning his finger in the air counter-clockwise as if they had lined the wall and ceiling instead of the table. Myles Smithson was out of breath.

It was hard to breathe between the warmth, the stale decaffeinated coffee exhalations surrounding him and the inability to fully expand his chest in the tight quarters, but Niles showed the perseverance and dedication that he would never be known for.

"I'm Joseph Niles, English intern." He said, artificially smiling.

Cutting off the intake of breath of the next speaker on his right just before she spoke, Smithson interrupted: "What kind of a name is Niles? Is that short for something?"

Niles was confused, but responded quickly, "It's the name I inherited from my father, sir." His lip curved upward on one side.

"Are you new in town, 'cause I've never heard that name before and I've been in education one way or another for more than sixty years."

"Sixty years? That's impressive sir, why—"

"Thank you."

"Actually sir, I believe the name is Latin."

Smithson seemed to hear him but clearly wasn't listening. "Is it Viking? Don't all their names end with 'son' or something like that, you know, like mine does?

"You too? I would not have guessed, sir." The grin on Niles's face was spreading.

"But your name doesn't have a 'son' in it. Or does it, and I missed it? Did you say 'Nelson'?

"No sir, it's "Niles." I believe that if there is a 'son' in there that it is silent and invisible." His eyes were finally playful.

Smithson's face went blank as a short-circuit occurred while trying to process that.

"You seem smart. I'll have to keep my eye on you." He narrowed his eyes at Niles.

"Yes you will, sir. Yes, you will." Niles's grinned like a boy at play.

The rest of the interns were quizzed briefly about their names and the meeting ended. The sweating, uncomfortable mass of people exited the room and spread out through the building and returned to their assigned mentor teachers.

But Smithson didn't keep his eye on any of them. And the next day, Dr. Smithson had forgotten there were interns in the building. He had forgotten many things in life, and the names of these soon-to-be-teachers were among the least important. Getting punched thousands of times did that to a person.

Myles Smithson was a former Golden Gloves boxer and had been boxing since he was eight years old. He started competing officially as a lightweight at the age of thirteen when he was listed as being fifteen. Already then, he was slow and ponderous in thought, moving more like a middleweight than a lightweight, not quick at all like most of his weight class, and he learned quickly that he should bulk up to better compete. He never grew taller after hitting his majestic peak of five feet seven inches, but he did continue to put on mass. As he grew into a middleweight, his speed decreased inversely, but also exponentially. His speed was a calculus problem. By the time he was nineteen, he was a super-heavyweight who moved more like a glacier and he began to reconsider his future as a professional boxer. His defense was slow, he couldn't keep his hands up and the punches to the head were adding and multiplying. As the countless punches accumulated his future options dissipated. His ponderous thoughts moved even more slowly after each fight. He had actually started thinking that boxing wasn't going to work out for him when he was sixteen, but hadn't been able to reach the full certainty of a decision about it until he had reached his nineteenth year, so slow was he at reaching distant conclusions. Graduating high school and considering careers felt overwhelming to him. It was a good thing that the program in educational leadership felt like coasting. He settled on that.

At that point, unfortunately for everyone else, Smithson was also a lightweight in terms of intellectual ability. He had lost more than just rounds in the boxing ring. Everyone told him that he'd make a great gym teacher, which made him feel like he was a perfect fit for professional education. He was accepted at the state university in town (almost everyone was!) and he headed straight for the administrative educational track. Local people in positions of authority who recognized his name were pleased to see him rise up. His past in boxing was a perfect precursor to working with combative teachers and the even more combative and unruly children. Being punch-drunk could only be a benefit in PSPS. He was well known around town and from the very start it seemed like he was fast-tracked for greatness. He could be just what they needed. A local boy from the unsuccessful part of town who could rise through athletics to be a leader. It didn't matter if he was qualified or not.

Smithson's years at the head of the school were marked by other people making executive decisions. Leadership depended on who stayed or who left. For some years, it was the Head Secretary who ran the school. For others, it was the Dean of Students. Some years, an assistant superintendent would attempt to control it with sticks and strings from afar. Some years, there was no one but Smithson at the helm of the ship, and those times it drifted aimlessly on whatever current caught it on a given day. That was until Dr. Kaseman came from New York to rescue that small Midwestern school district from its own mediocre self.

The new superintendent of schools, Dr. Kaseman, was not an interesting man. It was largely his own fault, in part because he was so short. Most short men strive to be interesting to overcome their perceived lack of power due to a height disadvantage, but Kaseman simply tried to compensate by standing on other people.

Sometimes he would knock them down first, verbally, with backhanded compliments and passive-aggressive attacks. Other times, he would talk over them until he was standing on their mouths, controlling everything they could say when they were around him. At 4'11", he was less Napoleon than gnome, but most of his energy went into being a tyrant instead of going into hiding under large stones or granting wishes. He wore lifts in his shoes, but the extra inches meant he could only tower over elementary school students. The rest of him was as transparent as his hair transplants, at least to everyone taller than him and anyone who paid attention to him long enough to see his insubstantiality for what it was.

For most personal interactions, he tried to make all of his guests be seated. Then he stood over them and from their chair looked a few inches taller. For his presentations and speeches he had a special podium built, one that could be transported from place to place with him by his building services staff. It had a special double platform that it stood on, and then another smaller platform built behind the podium that he stood on when he spoke. It helped to foster the illusion in his own mind that he was more important than he actually was.

He in some ways was very similar to Brian Massengill. Massengill was only a teacher, but he was ashamed of being born white and tried to make up for it in ways similar to how Kaseman made up for being short. He was the average, unaware white fellow who got placed with Linn for his internship. That ping pong ball lottery pick forever changed his life. He learned quickly that he was a racist (by accident) and that he could make up for a lifetime of accidental racism by doing everything within question to satisfy the whims of Linn, which in reality did not excuse anything at all.

He was a Protestant, and so he didn't know what a penitent was even as he became one for the sins that had been unwittingly perpetrated upon minorities by the affluent and ignorant white middle class of America. By the time he had finished with the allotted time of his internship, he was deeply invested in bettering Linn's state of affairs in the building and was easily brought into the building full-time when a retirement opened up a spot in a classroom down the hall and around the corner from the one teacher he'd had who changed his life forever.

To make up for his life of white privilege, he brought Linn coffee every day. He dragged her cushy chair from her classroom to every meeting, carried bags to and from her car, paid for lunch when she took him out on school days, took her car in for service to the mechanic, brought her flowers on Mother's Day, graded a good portion of the homework that she assigned, spoke for her during staff meetings, shined her shoes, and taught her class during his plan period - just as a start. His internship with Linn meant that he was well trained to be second chair during his whole career in order to elevate hers. And he never did move above second chair, at least as far as Niles knew.

It went on like that for a while, but before Niles even knew, he was gone; Massengill divorced his wife and moved out of state. Niles heard through the teacher grapevine that he'd gone on to marry a black woman three times his age and gave up teaching to be her full-time caregiver. It had probably become the best use of his life, and Niles wished him well. At least Massengill was good at what he left teaching to do. There was some reward in being good at your job, even if there was no summer break in taking care of old women.

Teachers lived for summer break. But in Kaseman's district, summer breaks were always the same. Administration knew that the teaching staff were spending their summers thinking about ways to be more awful at their jobs. The rest of America assumed that teachers across the country were kicking back to smoke smuggled Cuban cigars that supported the island's leftist regime and drinking the finest most expensive whiskeys and bourbons bought with their fat salaries while dipping their feet in pools of the collected tears of students who fought vainly for the Right side against a horrible centrist agenda, but Niles and most others went to work right away each summer again to work on continuing their education. For them, summers were about taking what could have been personal time to work on meeting district requirements.

For Swamp, who had never taught and started as an Attendance Interventionist across town and then came to Niles's school to principal succeeding Fitzgerald, who filled the chair after Smithson, summer meant adding three more classes of Bible study -

two of which were made up of students that she'd recruited from the high school.

Those same two months, Kaseman's underlings were hard at work compiling manufactured school data and spinning it like dollar store tops to achieve what he wanted the data to show. Kaseman needed a new crop of data to use to justify the harsh directives directed toward the teachers at the All-Staff meeting at the end of summer.

The return to school each Autumn meant that the district was compelled to have an equivalent to a brown shirt political rally to "marshal the troops" in a non-campaign year. Kaseman liked the idea of the rally to demonstrate how popular he was. It shined his ego to have all of his subjects applaud him, to see all the sets of eyes riveted to him in the auditorium.

In a healthy school district, it would have been an opportunity for positive encouragement toward the lowly bootlickers at the bottom of the power structure, even if the lens had to be twisted a little bit to make the news look good. Under Kaseman's leadership, the district either didn't believe in positive reinforcement or saw nothing positive to reinforce (which was a matter of choice). Positive reinforcement would make the teachers and support staff feel good about who they were and what they were doing. It might give them a sense of pride and ownership in their jobs. There was no room in Pianosa Springs schools for that style of management.

Each new year, the notice to attend the first major "All-District Meeting" was an invitation for teachers to be told that: A. They weren't doing enough. B. They didn't do anything last year correctly. And C. They had not done enough of what they had not done correctly.

Oddly enough, there was at least one teacher that sort of negativity grated on. Niles sensed a quiet grinding noise from behind him in the audience, as if teeth were being ground into powder, but looked around and saw nothing but faces glued to Kaseman.

Kaseman daydreamed of accolades when he wrote his speech in the week before the meeting. It was mid-August, and the Michigan heat lent itself to fever dreams. The auditorium would be silent with anticipation. The subservient and child-like teachers, quiet and respectful, waited with bated breath for their fearless leader. The lights would go dark save for a spotlight on the stage. Then Kaseman would appear from the back curtains and a spotlight would follow his magnetic presence to the podium to an applause that rose swiftly like a roar. He would raise his arms in triumph to all of the adoring eyes glued to him. The applause would not stop in a practical amount of time, but would be joined by whoops and hollers and he would have to ask the raucously adoring crowd several times to quiet, so overwhelmed would they be with enthusiastic adoration. When he finally calmed the crowd with the skill and aplomb of a master lion tamer, he would speak. Everything he would say would be greeted with interruptions of applause and when it wasn't, he imagined himself imagining that it was. He would lift his hands, grin, and lean back as if waves of adoration were crashing over him nearly causing him to lose his balance.

The actual meeting flowed with a different energy than it had in his head. He would make a statement: "This year, we had gains on standardized test scores in every student category but two. We attribute the reason for the lack of success in those two areas to a great divide between the cultural expectations of our staff toward those two minority groups and the reality of those groups. Every year, we work to re-educate you (teachers) on how to work with students of color, and every year you fail to adjust your behaviors that are making our student population fail." Then he stood at the podium with his smarmy smile and looked around at the audience as if he had told them a great universal truth that would awaken them to a glorious resurrection. Instead, the assembled teachers were entirely silent. They understood on some level or another that they had just been accused of being the cause of their students' failure because they were all racists.

Some of them looked at each other in disbelief with wrinkled and crooked brows. Then Kaseman broke out the slide presentation with cherry-picked data to correlate lack of student achievement with teachers in three different ways while ignoring the correlation between achievement and the economic background of the students because blaming the teacher was the simplest conclusion to find data to support. Every student was expected to achieve the same high scores on standardized tests: whether they were poor or rich; whether they had been sexually, physically, or emotionally abused at home; whether they had a safe place to sleep or not; whether they were fed three healthy meals a day or not; whether they had one parent or four, or even none; if they could come to school in clean clothes that fit or not; if they had to walk three miles or were dropped off in a BMW SUV or not.

The only variable that the district could control through economic strings was the teachers, so that was the only one that mattered to them when it came to measuring student achievement and the only one that was cherry-picked for the yearly presentation.

If there was any positive metric to be reported, it was always attributed to something that the superintendent or another administrator had done at his behest. Niles recalled that just last year, an increase in the number of students enrolled in AP courses had been attributed to the principal taking a hand in "convincing" students that they could handle the course because of Kaseman's directives to increase enrollment. Accolades were showered upon her. He also recalled that several students who had neither the desire nor the aptitude had been steered into his AP course without knowing it until they received their Autumn schedules on the first day of school. They'd gotten no conversation, no prodding, just a late blind notice that they were in the class. Some had even gone directly to their counselors to ask to be taken out of a class that they had no interest in, but they were told that there would be no course changes related to AP.

That was one way a principal could get Kaseman's gold star.

After the first two years of receiving that same speech from Kaseman and feeling unbelievably disheartened and unimaginably dispirited for the first month, Niles stopped going to the meetings. It was not the best way to start the school year. He had no desire to begin in such an overwhelmingly negative fashion.

He didn't miss anything. The annual fixtures were the same. Superintendent Kaseman waddled out on the stage on his short legs, flanked by his assistant superintendent, Thomas Black. Black was known as "Uncle Tom" to the local black community even though he had no siblings. He was the little dog that stayed close to the big dog of the pack for protection, making himself from an epsilon into a beta by being in the right place at the right time. He was a remarkable man, and many people remarked about him for his subservient behavior to Kaseman. Black was black, but he'd always wanted to be white. He was raised by a father, who like himself, hated being black, so he told young Black that all of the problems faced by the Blacks were due to other blacks.

Young Thomas was confused.The blacks' problems were caused by other blacks? Or the Black's problems were caused by other Blacks? Or was it that the Blacks were causing the blacks problems? Was it the blacks hurting the Blacks? Just what exactly was meant by black on black crime? He never did figure that out as a child, but when he got older, he knew that he had to maintain the family tradition.

He'd heard too, that the Blacks and the Hispanics in his community didn't like each other, and he decided as a boy that must have actually meant all of the blacks, since he'd never seen his father have any interactions with Hispanics at all. When he was older and had achieved his position of authority in Kaseman's regime, he decided he'd have to attend to that tradition as well, since he was a black man. As if there weren't enough complications in his life from being a Black, he also had to work on meeting the expectations of being a black! He considered his minority employees of Hispanic origin to be racist to other minorities, because to him, the Hispanics were too favored in the community - what with all of their migrant outreach programs and Spanish as a second language programs that were available. He was uncomfortable with Kaseman's wife too. She was Hispanic. A Cuban immigrant. He hid it well.

To him, "white was right" because he'd been taught well by his teachers, who were all white. If they said that displaying a Confederate battle flag in Michigan was a matter of heritage and freedom of speech, then that's what it was. Whites were benevolent and good, and just like he'd heard on his favorite news channel, slavery had been an institution that had built black communities instead of tearing them down. As a Black man, he worked hard to avoid creating an illusion of favoritism through helping other blacks by not helping other blacks at all, unless they were Blacks, because he knew that he had to take care of his own. No one could ever accuse him of having a bias toward other people who looked like him. He made sure that he was safe from that. He knew who his real masters were and fulfilled his duties to Kaseman with the sort of aplomb that would embarrass even the most obsequious of house slaves. It didn't matter to him if he was a caricature if that caricature was what his master wanted him to be.

His complex knowledge of racial equality was actually very basic. It was white people who had given him his power, white people who had provided him with his education through their Affirmative Action programs. The man who had handed him his diploma was White. Robert White, Dean of the College of Education. He owed a good deal of his success to him and other whites.

"You don't bite the hand that feeds you" was something that his father often said when he sent young Thomas to school without a lunch. He knew his place in the hierarchy, and like Bledsoe from the Invisible Man, he would bulldoze or drive out anyone he had to preserve his precarious position as Kaseman's left hand.

Even if that meant that he had to be black.

4. White

Vice Principals came and went like the principles held dear by political parties. They flexed with racial realities. In politics at least, it depended on who was in power, whereas at Niles's school there was no rhyme or reason to what was and what wasn't. For a few years, there was a Mick Maru.

Vice Principal Mickey Maru was born to a Polish family who'd immigrated to the US just after World War One and had a father who believed in the power of alliteration and loved baseball. Mick believed like other people who were teenagers in the 60's and read Marvel Comics that he had a heroic alter-ego. When he came to work at the school, he became "Captain Suspension" and worked hard to save the school from minority students.

His rules were flexible and infirm, like the stools of his father who was on several medications in the retirement home where Mick never visited him. He had clear favorites, and while they were clear, they weren't transparent, instead being mostly a lily shade of white, but he suspended everyone. His favorites understood it as a gift, a chance to stay home and play video games and do what they wanted.

Maru also had a decided proclivity for suspending minority students. Apparently, they were not his favorites. Every chance he had to make the school a brighter and whiter place, he did.

Talking back to the teacher? Suspended three days. Talking back to the teacher when you came back from being suspended for three days? Suspended seven days. Fighting? Ten day suspension with return dependent on a mandatory parent meeting. The mandatory parent meeting was a tool for stretching out the suspensions to even longer periods because the children that got those often had only one available parent to start with, and that parent often worked at least one, sometimes two or more jobs to support their children,

and those jobs often had hours during school the school day, so taking time off work to come in to see Mick Maru was a much more difficult proposition than simply strolling out of a white collar job for a
two-hour lunch break.

Mick Maru said that he needed a face-to-face with these parents for the good of their child, and who could argue against doing
what was best for the child? Except that sometimes when the parent
missed work, they lost their job, or the parent couldn't get out to the
school on the outskirts of the district where it was built because bus
service was sporadic at best and resolutely American at worst. It was
best for Mick Maru.

Every parent who came to the meetings and tried to argue
with Mick Maru lost, and many of the children whose parents lost
were slipping through the cracks that Maru was widening with long
fingers that were blessed by his principal, the man, the myth, the leg-
end, Miles Smithson. When it came to Mick Maru, Miles Smithson
took his hands off the wheel and let the man who looked like Jesus
drive, even though the only thing that he had in common with the
pictures of Jesus that Smithson saw at his church was that both men
were as white as driven snow. Maru needed only two years in PSPS to
make his retirement happen, so his time in the building was short as
well. Thomas Black loved Mick Maru and was the deciding voice in
his hiring, but he also loved the man he helped hire that came next.

After Maru left for a golden retirement came Jeffrey White.
Jeffrey White was no relation to University Dean Robert White even
though a police artist sketch of one White might have led one to ar-
rest the other White. Many whites looked the same. Jeffrey White did
have one offsetting quality: a case of Bell's Palsy that made Sylvester
Stallone look dignified by comparison. The children that he grew up
with in his coastal town often mocked his abnormality, and it fos-

tered a deep resentment in him that he nursed and turned in other directions later in life.

Jeffrey White had grown up in a school on the state's west coast, but had gone to college down deep in the American south. Before he went to college, he'd doodle Confederate flags in his school notebooks and dream of driving his own version of the General Lee. When he moved back to Michigan, he put a confederate flag on a pole in his front yard, right below his American flag because he believed in "heritage" and "showing it." He kept a picture of white Jesus in a frame in his guest bedroom, mostly for his mom's sake, but when he interviewed for his job with Swamp, he noticed the cross on a chain around her neck, so he played up a new, but heretofore unreal faith in the power of Jesus's love and the possibilities of salvation that existed if only one accepted that love, especially if they would practice forgiveness for the sins of slavery.

Swamp immediately took a liking to this fellow who seemed to understand that showing her obedience would earn him more than just a job. She blessed him with an administrative position underneath her.

White was puffy, like a ripe bud of cotton. He'd put on some extra pounds eating hearty portions of Southern fried food and looked like an allergic, swollen version of the boy who'd left a few years before to make his name at a university that had only recently begun allowing blacks on campus as students instead of as greenskeepers and building services workers. Living in the South had taught him a great deal about being a savior for black people, who in his mind certainly needed one. Every black church he'd seen in the south had a picture of a white Jesus up on the wall somewhere. It was clear who would make a good savior.

Many male authority figures in the school building looked like saviors in that regard, but few of them had much in common with the Christian one. One teacher who did was Ray Roberts. Ray Roberts was an excellent business teacher who didn't practice what he preached. "Business is an inherently capitalist pursuit" is what he would have to say, because his text book said it. He also taught about how profit was an outcome of supply and demand and how advertising was used to stoke demand. He sometimes went outside the textbook and explained how demand wasn't always a function of need, how often it was all about wants, and wants were often easily manipulated.

He was gray on the edges and the sides and ran the school store like a young man while his students worked there for class credit. He also worked after school as a real estate agent, supplementing his teaching income by helping people find the right homes for their families. He was fluent in four languages and worked hard to be conversational in several others, so he carved out a niche in his local real estate market working with immigrants. He never passed by an opportunity to practice his second, third, and fourth languages with students at school, or with the Spanish or French language instructors at school.

He also owned his own pear orchard with a stream running through it where he also grew pawpaw trees, and in the late summer and fall he spent his weekends giving hay wagon tours on a tractor and working his own roadside fruit stand, selling varieties of delicious pears and fresh pawpaws at cost without doing any advertising to increase demand.

If he'd been a proper capitalist businessman like he taught about, then he would have been a fool. In practice, he gave away more sweet pears and pawpaws than he sold. He gave a basket of pears to each family that he helped buy a home as part of a house-warming gift for their children. Ray Roberts gave pears to hungry students who didn't have money for lunch, whether they were in his classes and in any other classes that he might have heard about. He brought bags and baskets of pears and pawpaws to school and passed them out to co-workers at meetings. It was the only thing fresh that they were given when Swamp was principal, as her offerings were usually bags of expired snack chips or stale outdated candies. She had an inexhaustible supply of expired snack foods.

Niles did the math. If he was growing pears for seven cents a piece and selling them for only five cents a piece, and then giving away nearly half of his harvest, there was no way he could make a profit. What kind of business teacher was he anyway?

All he did was share. Everyone had a share. If only there were more people working in that building like Ray Roberts, people who didn't worry about making cents, but instead concerned themselves with helping the students to make sense of the world around them, then it could have been a better place. Isn't that what teachers were supposed to be for? Niles didn't know, but everyone else seemed to have an opinion.

Ray Roberts didn't drink, so he never went to the bar down the street and around the corner that some of the other teachers went to. The bartender who worked down the street and around the corner from the high school was mystified by teachers, but especially by Niles. He didn't make sense. He didn't come in to get drunk. He didn't socialize at the bar. He didn't even have a favorite seat at the bar like the other boozy creatures of regularity. He simply showed up, ordered a beer and sat in front of it quietly while it got warm.

The bartender didn't like Niles because he was different, but he hated him him because he suspected that underneath the surface he was just the same as everyone else and was merely pretending not to be. The bartender wasn't the only one who hated Niles for pretending to be something he wasn't. Everyone hated Niles. He just tried not to think about it.

Niles wasn't there to meet new or old friends. He wasn't there to get drunk and complain to the bartender about women or work. It was hard to like someone who didn't do what he was expected to do. Everyone needed him to fit into an easily defined category. They saw his papers that he would grade sometimes and knew that he was a teacher. He wasn't like the ones on tv and in movies. He didn't say racist or sexist things over the din. In fact, he didn't seem to have much to say at all. He didn't hit on the female staff, he didn't stare blankly into a tv screen showing sports, he didn't high five with groups of similarly dressed people. He didn't fit into the category he was supposed to. Most people knew instinctively that someone who can't be easily categorized might be a threat.

That's what Niles was: an existential threat.

This inability of the bartender (as well as anyone else) to categorize Niles made him unlikeable. No one liked people they didn't understand. He would never know that Niles didn't like to drink - that he only did it because he didn't know what else to do.

Being existentially threatening was what Niles did best even though he didn't know that he did it at all. If he had known that he did, he would have tried to stop. Niles was too tall and too intimidating to be non-threatening. All of those things set off alarms in just the types of people that Niles actually liked best. He was a staunch supporter of the underdog even though he himself looked like a thug. When he became aware of how people saw him, he tried to overcompensate by being too nice. That didn't work well either. To most people, kindness was a free commodity meant to be abused by whoever could take advantage of it first.

Niles also had a regular unconscious habit of slouching to make himself appear shorter and less threatening. The slouching combined with his anxious habit of drawing his shoulders up toward his ears created an odd combination of a postmodern Christopher Reeve Clark Kent melded with comic book Lex Luthor. He was often compared to Luthor by the students in his classroom, so he made certain not to wear purple and green, lest they feel that their first impressions were closer to verisimilitude than he wanted them to be.

Even though Niles didn't enjoy drinking, he did appreciate the way that a drink would remind him to relax his shoulders and how the backless stools at the bar would force him to stop slouching. A drink now and then allowed him to feel less self-conscious than usual which was a double weight off his broad shoulders. It didn't matter how hard he tried though, people still didn't talk to him - or even worse, no one listened when he talked.

Niles felt safe at the bar, as long as he left before it got late. No one half his age was telling him to "fuck off" over a writing assignment. He was near enough people to not feel lonely and disconnected even though he rarely spoke to anyone. On the days that he didn't want to be bothered, he'd bring a stack of papers in to score. He didn't even have to grade any of them. He could simply set down a stack of papers with a sigh, throw a colored pen on top of the pile, order a drink and a sandwich, and deliberately make a pained face as he stared off into space in the general direction of his stack of papers.

Everyone avoided Niles. He wondered why it was so hard to make friends. He tried to make the most of his loneliness. His favorite thing to do there was to sit and watch while listening through the din. There were so many stories there, so many ways to feel connected without ever connecting at all. It was there that he learned that no one's life is ever really interesting, and that he wasn't missing anything at all by not having a bigger one himself.

Some days, he did grade the papers in his stack. Grading papers every day was a hassle, but it was a necessary hassle. If the didn't grade every day, the stack would become overwhelming. He couldn't be a teacher without giving the students some meaningful feedback. Just writing "Good Job" on the margin didn't cut it. Why is it a "good job"? What's good about it? What have they done well? If he didn't make it clear, then they wouldn't know how to repeat it. It took Niles back to Basic Psychology class again. "Make feedback meaningful and specific." Cook had told him that too. That was the only way to keep it from being monotonous as a teacher anyway, so why not do it the right way? If the feedback wasn't meaningful and interestingly written, why would the students even read it? Did he like to read things that weren't meaningful and interestingly written? No, he didn't. Why would he torture himself? Those were the questions that Niles tortured himself with. And that was what made grading student work so difficult. It was a lonely and arduous job.

That was the way of things. Being at work in the school was one way of running from his loneliness. Sitting at the bar was another. Surrounding himself with people was a short-cut without going all the way to the destination.

5. Swamp

Niles sighed deeply. Here was another professional development chosen by the principal seemingly to torture the ghosts of the teachers who had mistreated her, but thrust instead upon the flesh and bone teachers under her administration because they were convenient targets of her boiled-over hatred. He looked around him at the menagerie assembled in the auditorium. All of the players were there facing the stage.

Three rows down and to his left, Halverson was looking at pictures of his children on his phone, flipping from photo to photo, wishing that he were wherever they were, even if it meant sitting in day care for seven hours (which to be fair, was what most non-teachers accused him of doing at his job anyway). Halverson was a middle-aged dad, and everything that being a middle-aged dad entailed. He wore oversized polo shirts with baggy cargo shorts when he was teaching. It was a Social Studies department practice that only Bradley broke free from. He had a belly, and he ran half marathons with the sort of enthusiasm that could only exist when someone was rewarded for doing something halfway. He was quality though. He knew his material and he was passionate about working with students to improve their lives. Some teachers didn't care about the lives of their students; Niles had already gotten to know several. They were all about satisfying their ravenous egos. Halverson only had a history teacher's ego.

Halverson was his first hallway neighbor, and the Niles that he'd met at first was a mask. Niles still believed back in those days that a teacher was a public act which was completely disassociated from who that person really was. Any weakness and aspect of his true self that he allowed himself to display was something that a student was potentially going to use against him. Back in college, he had learned that being a teacher meant being in a consistently adversarial relationship with the students. That knowledge was reinforced whenever Niles turned on the news or read a website and heard about any educational proposal.

"No child left behind" was the political buzz phrase when Niles was becoming a teacher. The stunted shrub was in the White House, and his ascendancy proved beyond a shadow of a doubt that no one needed to be book smart or academically successful to become the leader of the free world. Teachers were under fire. They didn't work enough hours to justify full-time pay, they didn't do enough to make sure that students were more challenged than they would have been at a daycare, and their liberal agenda that brainwashed the children of America was the true reason that America's standing in the world was dropping.

That falling perception of America was clearly the fault of each of its teachers on a personal level, and Americans everywhere banded together online anonymously to let it be known in the comments section of every single article about education on the internet. They read like a litany of offenses from an organized crime trial. Everyone remembered their teachers and the horrible things they had done.

Remembering teachers is the exact opposite of remembering the dead. When people remembered the dead, no one brought up horrid truths, no matter how true they might have been. No one brought up alcoholism, child abuse, domestic violence, or bigotry. Everyone must be forgiven for believing that every single dead American was a saint who might have been Jesus's best friend if only Jesus had known him or her when he came to America to create Mormonism.

In contrast, remembering teachers was a game of dredging up the very worst anecdotes and comparing them with friends who took the same class. Each one tried to outdo the other with a tale of how awful the teacher was. Then, in the contest of who was the worst, the memory itself was shifted, as the mind rewrote it with each retelling until it became more fiction than fact, shifting into a parody. Granted, there were awful teachers just like there were awful ministers, awful supervisors, and awful Presidents of the United States; but none of them were taken as being so perfectly representative of the whole as bad teachers were.

Niles had heard from the students about how that young teacher next door to him had been punched in the face while trying to break up a fight on his very first day. That was daunting to him. Halverson however was not daunted. Niles knew that a good many other people who would have quit if they had been assaulted on their first day on the job. Halverson was not one of them. That was a good sign. He might have been teaching for the right reasons, even if he did scan through photos of his children during every staff meeting and ignore whoever spoke from the front.

Just to the right of Niles and parallel in the auditorium sat Trudeau, Pianosa Springs's finest doing what he always did in situations like these: assiduously taking notes. He was both a good student and a good teacher. When Niles was hired in permanently and was introducing himself to everyone in the English department, Trudeau had been the first to shake his hand firmly, to give it a good squeeze and proclaim that it was wonderful to meet him and that he looked forward to working with him.

Niles wondered at the time if Trudeau was campaigning for something. He also thought he had selective memory loss. Niles had known Trudeau for years, having been a year behind him at university but sharing many History and English classes with him.

Niles knew Trudeau, but Trudeau didn't know Niles.

Niles didn't say anything about them having shared several classrooms already. At the time, it didn't feel right to say anything beyond hello and thank you. He looked over again at Trudeau as the speaker went on. Trudeau looked anxious. He was looking for something so important in the moment that if he didn't lean forward in his seat with his eyes glued to the presenter that he would miss it and never recover.

Trudeau was struggling in the moment to be present because the person that had a magnetic pull on his mind made it painful to think about her. He was waiting for his phone to buzz in his pants pocket, for his wife to reply to his messages. She was spending the day with some people from her Kirlian Aura massage class. She talked about them a lot to Trudeau. He wondered if she talked as much about him to them, even though he felt deeply in his heart that she did - because why wouldn't she? He must have been just as important to her as she was to him and he had to admit to himself that his world revolved around her.

Still, he wondered what she was doing and why she didn't text him back. Forcing himself to pay perfect attention to the speaker about differentiated instruction meant that he could force himself not to think about how his wife wasn't putting him first right then. Trudeau knew without question that he had to "fake it 'till you make it." It was his mantra. It would carry him through anything.

Down in front, Tibbs had his laptop open, searching for whatever state rules or regulations meant that this was something that he had to sit through. As was typical, other teachers scattered throughout the auditorium kept talking through the presentation.

The irony seemed to escape them, or at least it escaped the gym teachers, math teachers, art teachers, health teachers, and science teachers who hadn't taught their students about irony and so hadn't heard the word used correctly since they were in secondary school themselves. Or maybe they heard about irony from Alanis and were still confused about the difference between irony and coincidence, just like most people were confused about the difference between "literally" and "figuratively." Niles thought that people were literally trying to be ironic when they initially figured on using "literally" when they should have used "figuratively" but that now, coincidentally, because of the lack of understanding of how to use irony, they all meant things they did not say and said things they had not meant. If only someone would hold teachers accountable for their learning. If they knew what irony was, they might be able to savor it the way Niles did - but Niles wasn't savoring this. He was in a bad mood, and Principal Swamp was happy about it.

Swamp didn't care about Niles except to hate him, so his personal moods meant nothing to her unless they were bad, which was what she wanted. He was by all tokens a bug on a windshield to her. She was happiest when her teachers were miserable.

The meeting ground on and the topic switched. The numbers on the slide on the projector screen were about student referrals and suspensions. The assistant principal was reading the script that Swamp gave him and was making it clear that there were too many referrals to the vice principals' offices for violations of classroom defiance. He told the teachers that they needed to handle their problems in their own classrooms because all of this necessary documentation was making them all look terrible. School policy said that when a student received five referrals for negative classroom conduct then the vice principal had to suspend them. The vice principals were opting not to suspend the students, instead sending them back to class, but the ones they did suspend made them look bad, so the teachers needed to stop making them look bad.

The obvious meaningless of the exercise wore Niles down quickly. He was tired. His evaluation had been negative. He was overworked. He wasn't sleeping well. He just wanted to teach the students, but he was stuck in a meeting instead of doing something that felt meaningful. Niles looked around, seeking facial expressions in the assorted faces that in some way mirrored his own, someone to feel a shared sense of camaraderie and suffering with. He saw nothing.

Niles wanted to expel them all, teachers, principals and vice principals, student counselors and deans of students, along with the school psychologist and the only school nurse in the whole district who only showed up at his school every third Thursday of the month. That literally made her the district nurse, but even though it wasn't her fault, Niles lumped her in with all the rest in that moment. She was the victim of a hiring policy. Everyone was a victim.

He'd love to give them their walking papers and tell them that they "could come back and try again in 365 days" for their foolhardy behavior. That was the joke, the one told by all the secretaries who handled the paperwork regarding the students who saw a crack in the floor of the institution and tried to dive through it like some sort of mustachioed plumber in a video game skirting moving walls.

Niles sat fuming over the absurdity of it all. This meeting wasn't about enrichment, or any sort of development, instead it was punishment. Vice Principal White droned on, tone deaf to all of the behavioral cues of the non-listeners as if he were a teacher in the latest comedy that elevated youth to the peak of intelligent culture and denigrated those rigid, unthinking robot teachers, filled with bitterness that spilled out over their classrooms like a violent volcano seventh grade science project spewing orange food dye and vinegar mixed with baking soda. His PowerPoint presentation was outdated, made with slides from the original office suite with the soft pastels and cloudy images that were so prevalent with Windows 95. Niles wanted to expel that too.

Instead, Niles escaped into his mind, thinking about how ironic the ridiculous discipline policy was. He'd believed in it all when he was a new teacher and failed miserably often because he was trying to do what the district told him to do. IDs and enforcing rules made the students hate him, and a student who hated is one who refused to learn out of spite. When Niles failed at teaching, he hated himself. His first few years were painful ones of trying and failing because he listened to his administrators instead of his students.

He learned the hard way the pointlessness of rewarding a student with time away from school for misbehaving and he was just a "ineffective educator." It was a basic thing: He couldn't reward a student who didn't want to be there with time off when he acted up at school. Almost any intervention would have had a greater impact on a creature capable of learning than being removed from the situation that they disliked. That taught them to break rules when they wanted time out of school. It wasn't a punishment. It was a reward. But White and the chattering teachers seemed incapable of learning that. They'd had their time to learn, and now it was gone. They were resistant to change and reluctant to listen to any new ideas.

His mind wandered while the presenter buzzed. Did that make him the same as the others who talked in low voices to each other non-stop through the show? No, he decided. He might not be paying attention, but at least he wasn't being rude. He gazed at the screen and daydreamed. He looked like a good student. That was how most people made it through the American public school system. They created the illusion that schoolwork was important to them by not being disrespectful during the presentation. Certainly that's how students were sorted into the honors level courses. Many of them were average scholars who were above average in understanding both social cues and cultural expectations. There was a very dog-and-pony-show aspect to being successful in school, and Niles was one of the ones who had figured it out at a young age. He saw that if anyone paraded competently to the cues of their handlers that he could win first prize. It wasn't about the skill of the dog or pony, it was about the control the handler had over the dog or pony. He didn't know that he knew it when he was a boy, but when he became a teacher himself and started asking himself why others couldn't figure it out, it became suddenly clear. The question had clarified the answer he had always known.

He looked over and saw Principal Swamp turned sideways in her auditorium seat at front, looking up at the teachers that she hated. She looked angry, like she was upset that her efforts to torture them were being thwarted by their own inability to act like polite adults. Her bejeweled hands were folded over each other on her tablet, multiple bracelets with assorted bangles and dangles reflecting a hundred points of light. The teachers continued to mumble quietly to each other or to stare into their cellular phones, hiding them in laps and behind chairs just as the students did. She loathed them all and would do anything to punish them, to control them - to avenge her own terrible classroom experiences as a child.

She was the child of immigrant parents, but she worked hard as a young girl to hide the slight Russian accent she acquired from them. Her parents left everything behind to come to America to have children, so when they arrived they latched onto the strongest thing they could find for support: the local Baptist church. Whatever they had been before was wiped away as they were born again and ready to start an American family exactly like the ones on TV. Swamp was born into and grew up in the church; she loved the spotlight she was given there when she displayed adult-like devotion. She was fine until she got to high school, but church was always her safe place. As a child, she was happy and well-adjusted. Her parents doted on her with all the attention that they could muster.

It was her ninth grade year that things started to fall apart. Her parents could no longer show up with her name on a poster board surrounded by hearts and pom-poms to celebrate her at every sporting event where she was a cheerleader. They could no longer find the time to be present to cheer her on in everything that she did. It was as if being closer to being an adult meant that she didn't need constant validation.   But worst of all were the teachers. Through middle school, she had been given permission to be herself and to do what she wanted through the school's policy of advancing students through social promotion, but the high school teachers changed all that. Suddenly, her minimum effort wasn't good enough for an A every time. Suddenly teachers didn't allow her to be the center of attention - they wanted the attention of the class for themselves! Not being allowed to be the center of the classroom was an affront to her delicate ego which she was never able to forgive. She decided when she turned fifteen that it would become her mission to right every wrong that was thrust upon her. It was the energy that drove her through her classes in educational leadership at the university, working as an attendance specialist, right up until she got the job as a principal when she quit school before finishing her degree. That could wait. The time for vengeance was nigh.

By the time she was hired by Pianosa Springs Public Schools to track student attendance, she was already running a small local church with her husband. They had splintered off her parents' larger Baptist church with a dozen other members who also felt slighted by the reverend's unwillingness to change his mass to suit their personal needs and visions of what a relationship with God looked like on Earth. They confirmed themselves both reverends after taking some free online courses in theology and reading a handful of Wikipedia pages. Their church doctrine was largely copied and pasted from a missionary church in Africa onto their AOL member page to start with, and then later her teenage son had moved it to GeoCities before they bought their own church domain page. It featured large file-sized photos of each of them smiling and wearing robes they'd bought from Amazon.com while holding on to fancy-looking plates and chalices they'd gotten at flea markets in nearby Pawsville. It was all very pious, as far as web pages went, and all of it demonstrated her drive and ambition.

It was this platform that she was able to use as a springboard into education. The stars were aligned and God's plan unfurled before her. The new superintendent of Pianosa Springs Schools was looking for a bridge to the local churches in a demonstration of unbiased religious freedom, and he saw this beefy, plucky, dusky, young woman with a barely noticeable accent as a perfect bridge over troubled waters. He could tell by her church's webpage that she was charismatic and motivational - the perfect qualities that he needed to bring his faith-based vision of public education to a place more palatable to the local throngs.

Contact was made initially when he brought his token Hispanic wife to one of their ten-hour long holiday masses and stayed through the whole prayer marathon (or "Prayerathon" as it was advertised in a low quality internet video) to tell Swamp how wonderful she was at captivating a religious crowd with a dogma that they agreed upon wholly (even though he was Jewish). Kaseman walked away from that meeting with sore feet and knees as well as a powerful certainty that this woman could be a star in the firmament that he was crafting.

With her prior experience at running a church in a vacated storefront, he knew that she would be perfect as a principal with control over one of his high schools. Those students were going to get very educated with her in charge!

It was about the time that she became principal that her mother passed away, and Swamp found among her valuable things several boxes of gaudy jewelry and baubles that seemed to be a part of her hidden cultural heritage. She gradually began adding bracelets and rings from the boxes into her daily wardrobe, cluttering her meaty paws with those souvenirs of her mother.

She successfully moved right into her new principal's office by decorating it with a subtle, small cross and large piles of unorganized paper files. By the end of the first week, she'd filled her cabinets and drawers with even more glorious files! Files and paperwork meant that she was accomplishing things, and the larger the piles that she left on top of things in the office for visitors to see, the more they would know that she meant business! By the end of the second week she had increased the amount of time spent in searching for the right document by 300 percent over her first week's numbers. This meant that she was learning quickly on the job. When Kaseman stopped by her office in her new building and saw the glorious piles of papers, he knew that he'd made a perfect choice. She'd be far too inept and disorganized to push back against any of his policies. She was a perfect marionette to dance his dance and create the illusion of a multicultural administrative team. After that, there was only one direction for her to go in his administration: up. He cultivated her like a hothouse flower, made her master of student destiny, lavished attentions on her, checked on her, always showered her with loving praise so that she would know she was a golden child, not just any golden child, but his golden child. He would work through her and she through him to glorify and lift each other up through the resplendent world of public school administration. Someday, she too would be a public school superintendent, and she would think upon her position and lavish praise on her mentor who had helped her to achieve her goals, the benevolent and righteous Dr. Kaseman.

The presentation in front of the auditorium shifted from school policy to "best practices" in the classroom and Swamp cleared her throat loudly during a lull, asking teachers to put away their cell phones and pay attention like "professionals."

This P.D. was largely meaningless to them, just as it was to her; it was simply another presentation on the same topic that had been presented five different times before that day. The problem was that teachers weren't buying in. They didn't pay attention, and even weeks after the P.D. they all pretended not to understand the hows and whys of the topic, so in the eyes of Principal Swamp more presentations on the information were necessary, and each one a carbon copy of the one before it.

It was another one of those "do as I say, not as I do" types of mandates from the top. In the classroom, if the audience wasn't learning the concepts or material that were being taught and they needed to be presented again, a teacher would be expected to change the manner or style in which he or she conveyed the material so that the students with barriers to comprehension could make material gains in knowledge, even if they were small ones. When it came down to administration presenting information to the teachers, it was the exact opposite. It was the same set of PowerPoint slides each time, and each time the presenter became more condescending and cruel in tone, treating the audience like the fools they expected them to be.

Niles was angry at the foolishness of it all, both at the administrators for organizing it and the teachers for walking into it like sheep headed for the slaughter house. If Niles had to evaluate his fellow staff members then many of them were fools, or at least acted like sheep, but almost all of them including him quickly dropped to the level of the presentation. If people were treated like idiots, they quickly became idiots, no matter how highly educated they were.

White had stepped down from the stage and there were two presenters this time, working as a team, taking turns and elaborating long and hard on the importance of crafting what they called "Activated Choice Paradigms" as a kind of "thinking tunnel" to guide students into. They were paid consultants from outside the district dressed in the pale business suits of people who believed that education should be a business.

The male presenter spoke of how many students were becoming progressively conscious of the people and the world around them; he described their burgeoning social activism as "Peer Gendered Initiatives." He didn't care that they were trying to find themselves and who they were by creative uses of language. All he did was to buzzword what they did. Then it was the female presenter of the duo's turn to talk over a slide labeled "Metacognitive Scaffolding Innovation." "Scaffolding' was all the rage in educational circles. It was loosely defined as building up to complex ideas using things that students already knew, but the added "meta-cognitive" buzzwording made it marketable, made it seem new and sexy like a bikini model leaning on a car at the Detroit Auto Show. Niles looked around and saw some of his peers now writing their words down furiously with a determination that matched the faux enthusiasm of the presenters on the stage. The presentation continued. The first speaker noticed the same thing Niles did at the same time, except he helpfully labeled it as "Close Reflective Outlined Engagement" instead of what Niles thought it actually was, which was "taking notes." The second presenter jumped on board in her special way and assured the audience of teachers that that was just first step toward "Annotated Contextual Analytics," which Niles knew was another way to say "taking notes," but Niles could no longer feel sure about what he knew. The presenters were escaping through new doors of their own construction and he was a few rooms back considering whether he would tip the bottle labeled "drink me" into his mouth or onto the floor.

Niles was running away into his head, but he was fighting that desire to hide there as they continued "Unpacking Cognitive Initiatives" in front of a wide mix of consciousnesses. If Niles had looked behind him, he would have seen other faces that recognized garbage when it was being spilled on the floor in front of them like he ostensibly did, but he would have also seen a few faces that were drinking it up, not realizing the difference between shit in a champagne glass and Dewarr's in a Dixie cup.

Young idealistic teachers were always ready to vacuum whatever was fed to them in the name of advancing their career prospects. For most teachers, that stage might last five years. Niles woke up in year three and realized that the "Professional Development" that he was being fed was being cycled every three years and that ultimately none of it was any newer than a retreaded tire that blew out on the highway after 20,000 miles.

He couldn't tell if the presenters on the stage believed in "Disruptive Parenthetical Analysis" or if they were just wearing the face paint while dancing to the man spinning the crank on the music box, but it didn't matter. He thought that once one had gazed into the abyss and it gazed back, all that a person could do was stare into her own eyes for the horrid selfie that she'd trot out on her FaceSpace page for her 10th anniversary as a teacher. It would be tagged "#10years" and she'd still be going through the new teacher movements with each cycle of administrative mandates. They would still be talking about "Differentiated Strategic Alignment" and telling everyone that they were doing it all wrong, just to pay the presenters four hundred dollars an hour for four three-hour sessions plus the thousand dollar consulting fees to put the willfully ignorant teachers on the right track. After they were on the right track, that track would soon be switched again before the train had moved a mile. Then there were a few more thousand dollar sessions to bring everyone back to life over three months or three years - whichever they could talk the district into paying for. For the district's money, everyone would get more buzzword ready phrases to use in the Professional Development crossword puzzle.

Niles looked around again. Something was developed here, but it wasn't professionalism. There was a certain something being presented when the people choosing the presenters and the material have never actually been in charge of planning and executing a system of learning and classroom management. Here it was, the same basic material on repeat, hidden behind new words, presented as if they were either brand new teachers or just completely incompetent. While yes, some of the assembled teachers were completely incompetent, the ones who weren't were rightfully offended to be treated like a classroom of seventeen-year-old ninth graders.

For the ninth graders, most of them couldn't help it. They'd been brought up in a school system and passed through by age with their cohort, not once being held accountable in a meaningful way through elementary or middle school. Then they got to high school and were clueless about how to behave. For them, school was a legal compulsion. They had no other choice according to state law. For these teachers it was a job. Unlike the incompetent students, they could be fired. Some of them should have been but weren't. It was a mystery that Niles couldn't wrap his head around. Were the administrators apathetic? Were they too busy playing tag on their phones with ghosts? Did no one notice but him? He had no idea and likely never would. For now he was simply trapped among the unwilling, the unwitting, and the unwanted.

He wanted to escape out the doors, but in an exercise yard with fewer than 90 prisoners he would not be easily missed. He'd seen how last month Geit was chased back into the meeting by an assistant principal who insisted that Geit didn't really have to go pick up his sick son from daycare and that he was just using the child as a convenient excuse to get out of a pointless meeting. Niles had to grant that the assistant principal was right, but he could not have known that. He also didn't know what Geit had been threatened with to get him to return to the meeting, but it must have been impressive. Niles hadn't spoken to him a lot, but he noticed it took a lot to redirect Geit.

He turned around to look for Geit. He was sitting toward the back, looking pale and sullen, fingers tented in front of eyes that clearly indicated his mind was elsewhere. Geit wasn't like all the rest. He was a misfit too, another hick intellectual from the backwaters of Michigan. His faith wasn't in farming though: he was the son of an illegal alien from the Ukraine who was a carpenter and an emotionally abusive second-generation Scotch immigrant mother. Or maybe she loved Scotch. Either way, Geit was an iconoclast in the body of the least popular teacher among other teachers at Hogwarts. Geit looked shorter than he was and was less pale than he looked. His hair was black, and he'd have claimed his soul was darker than the bottom of a Siberian borehole if anyone had asked. Geit was on more drugs than a whole floor of a mental ward thanks to an overly medicated medical professional who thought that more was better, and hoped that more would become less through the complicated mathematics that he performed on Geit's medicines for the modern world.

When Niles met Geit, both were very wet behind the ears. It was raining heavily that day, and neither man was wearing a hat. Geit was short-haired and Niles was shaved bald. Geit was in his second year of teaching and Niles was an intern, but they were paired together in a faux-team-building meeting at an English department professional development. They were teamed up and made "shoulder buddies" in the parlance of the facilitator who was acting more friendly than he truly was. Geit made a dirty joke that nobody else except Niles got, and then Niles responded with another but only in Geit's ear which had finally dried. Clearly their partnership had potential.

Geit was a contrarian. Most contrarians liked being against whatever anyone else is for just for the sake of being difficult, like the modern definition of a 'troll" that is so different than the one that was possible prior to when the public got access to internet message boards and found the power in anonymous antagonization. Geit was contrary because he wanted to make people think. Niles's head was more Socratic in style, as that statue seemed to show the Greek as bald on top, but Geit's style was goatish. Niles asked questions, but goats butted heads. They ran around and did odd sideways cartwheels and bumped heads on everything because it was there.

Geit was was intellectually agile and strong. Niles liked him. He made sense. Nothing else about this professional development or the people who were subjected to it did.

Niles fumed quietly, feigning involvement in the never-ending professional development, fighting inside to avoid succumbing to the dull sense of resignation that was creeping over him.

6. Fitzgerald

Jan Michael Crockett came to work at the school when a different faceless young Mechanical Turk left after one season of unsupported pain. J.M. Crockett was different. He was dressed for the wrong century by thirty years and his attitude toward women was off by two hundred.

He got his undeniable fashion sense from watching reruns of Miami Vice as a child and had all the self-awareness of a rutabaga. These things combined in his mind to make him the perfect man for any woman, or every woman, or just whichever woman was in front of him at any given moment. He pretended to like Halverson because Halverson was the department head and he knew that befriending the department head could get you special perks in the school building. He'd have gotten along well with Linn in that regard, except that he did not respect the industriousness of the Chinese and believed that blacks were responsible for their own hardships because slavery had ended more than a hundred years ago. Those were the first two strikes in their relationship which would never be, and the third strike was that he found her too old and too unattractive to be worth his effort to cultivate a sexual relationship. After all, she was a woman, and what else were women for but to have sex with?

He sexually harassed most women as often as he could, but he was only successful in sexually harassing a few repeatedly. Most women were too polite to confront him which made him think that he was doing it right. One of those women was coincidentally a former intern of Linn who was substituting around the district. He liked to give it to her when she was available for the taking but would still gleefully give it to anyone else who would accept it. Some women found his polished white shoes and his suspenders to be as attractive as the rest of him, and somehow his throwback ensemble to an 80s cop show invoked a pleasant kind of non-existent nostalgia for an era when a Phil Collins song could define a powerful sexual experience.

He was accidentally at the bar one night at the same time as Niles and Halverson but acknowledged neither of them since he was with some woman that neither of them had ever seen before instead of Linn's former intern whom he was dating at that same time.

Niles was searching for common ground with Halverson, but stumbling over rocks and uneven terrain.

"Have you ever read 'The Adventures of the Black Girl in her search for God'?"

Halverson was only half listening, so he replied with a "no" while gazing over Niles's shoulder at the more interesting people behind him.

Niles switched this tack to more historical one hoping to engage Halverson. "Do you realize that there hasn't been a meaningful student protest movement in the US since the Kent State Massacre in 1970?" Lately Niles had been obsessed with futility.

"Are you sure?" replied Halverson. "If all you have to do is shoot four people forty years ago to put a lock on student protests, then that doesn't say much for the students of today, does it?"

"I don't think it does. At least the Chinese students in Tiananmen Square protests in 1989 had the guts to get run over by tanks. Or actually, I guess they had the guts until they got run over by the tanks." Niles smirked, but Halverson did not enjoy his joke.

"That's pretty messed up."

"I agree. Who runs over people with a tank?"

"No, I mean that you made a joke about it."

Niles laughed. "Well then, I guess you can just throw me on the ground in front of a moving tank then."

Halverson frowned at him. He was patriotic, but not nationalistic. "You know that sort of thing would never happen in the US, we really are the most free nation in the world."

"Free? Free from what? The rigors of critical thinking? There are a lot of other nations in the world with much more progressive views toward liberty than what most Americans have been taught to call 'freedom.'"

"You can't deny that the average standard of living in the US is higher than any other nation in the world." Halverson patriotically asserted.

"Actually, I could, but instead I'm just going to go after your use of the word average. Do you know what it means?" Niles felt like a goat. Drinking his beer instead of warming it on the table made him bold.

"Yes."

"It means that you can have some huge outliers on the far edge of your sample that will throw your average into a zone where it's an unreliable measure of any group. It would be far more realistic when dealing with extremes to consider the mode instead."

Halverson did not give a damn about what Niles was saying and was watching Crockett across the room. "That guy's a dirty son of a bitch. He was hitting on the new math teacher on the third floor just this morning."

Niles waved his hand between them to try to bring Halverson back. "Halverson. I'm over here. My point is that he in the US we have a handful of super-rich people who throw the average way the hell off. If we have 250,000,000 people making minimum wage and five guys making 250,000,000 dollars per hour, that doesn't mean that we have the highest standard of living in the world. It just means that statistics are a tool that can be misused like any other tool."

"What do you want me to do about it?"

"I want you to teach kids that America isn't that great."

Halverson was still clearly impressed by Crockett on the other side of the bar with at least one of his hands on a spot on the woman's person that was usually regarded as "saved" for a place much more private than a table at a bar.

"Come on, Niles. America isn't just the leader of the free world in name. We've been carrying the banner since the First World War!"

"Which banner is that, the banner of oligarchy? That's pretty libertarian of you, to say that freedom equals the ability of a few to control the lives of the many via capitalism."

"Isn't that just little bit cynical?"

"No, it's a lot cynical, but that doesn't make it any less true."

"C'mon Niles, our founding fathers created a nation where an individual could have the freedom to achieve his wildest dreams."

"Halverson, I would trust you to teach my little sister, but you're oversimplifying things. Work with me here. Why did those guys rebel against English rule?"

"They wanted freedom."

"Don't give me that simplified storybook bullshit we use on elementary kids. Tell me the truth. What was the popular slogan? You know, the one from SchoolHouse Rock?"

Halverson thought for a moment, but knew the line well. "No taxation without representation?"

"Yeah, that one. They were pissed off that they were being taxed on certain items, right? Most of it import or export fees, if I remember correctly, and those only actually impacted businessmen. Not your average farmer or fishermen. They only paid more to preserve the businessman's profit margin."

Halverson thought for a minute, then replied warily, "Yeah?"

"So facts seem to indicate that the popular notion of George Washington and the rest of those wealthy white guys being worried about 'freedom' was actually more about keeping what they thought of as 'their own damn money,' right?"

"I guess you could look at it that way..."

"So the fight for American freedom was much more about personal financial gain for some prominent colonial businessmen who also controlled popular media at the time than it was ever about making sure that some poor bottom feeders felt 'free.'"

Halverson looked at him like he was crazy.

"You're crazy, you know that? You need to cut back on your Zinn."

"What's crazy is that we feed students some fairy tale about ideal "founding fathers" who were never any more real than Batman. If you look at objective history, it's obvious that American ideals of freedom that we teach in high school have about as much foundation in the real world as Bruce Wayne deciding he's going to dress up like a bat to avenge his parents' death on any petty thief who happened to be in his vicinity on any given night in Gotham."

Halverson was getting exasperated quickly. "You know Niles, people from all over the world want to live here, they want to move to America where they have the opportunity to become whatever they want to be. They can't do that in other countries."

"They can't do it here! The only people who will ever be politically powerful in this country are the people who have enough money to buy influence. People like you and I can't be anything except for in debt."

Halverson was patriotically offended. "Why are you so negative? Our democracy is the best system there is!"

"How would we know that democracy even works? When was the last time any politician at the state level or higher actually acted on behalf of his constituents' wishes?"

Halverson was getting physically tired, but Niles's questions demanded answers.

"All the time. That's how they get elected and re-elected."

"The people who win the elections are the ones who can buy name recognition. All you need to get elected is a name that people recognize."

"Don't be such a cynic!" Halverson's attention was aggressively waning.

"Don't be such a Pollyanna!"

"You're crazy. Let's talk about something that doesn't make me want to hate you." Halverson was still watching Crockett shamelessly molest some woman across the bar. Niles wasn't taking the hint.

"Freedom is just false advertising."

"Shut up."

"Everywhere on the planet has better healthcare for less money."

"Enough."

"America is a corporate oligarchy."

"If you don't stop, I'll leave."

"Fine, leave. I don't have any friends." Niles was throwing stones at windows but losing Halverson's attention.

Halverson was still looking around the bar for a reason to escape and not paying attention to Niles. He nodded in Crockett's direction.

"Did I tell you that guy stopped in to my room to talk to me the other day? He asked me what he had to do to get an AP class. Can you believe the sense of entitlement?"

"Did you tell him that he should start by attending the morning prayer meetings with the principal?"

Halverson continued speaking aloud to himself. "I mean, I've been teaching for years. I paid my dues. I earned those AP courses. I demonstrated my quality. This guy thinks he can just walk in and get his hands on an AP course."

"Did anyone accuse you of kissing ass? If not, you haven't been talking to the right people."

Halverson shook his head at himself. "I don't like this guy. He dresses like he's going to a wedding every damn day."

"Actually he dresses like a minor character from The Wedding Singer. Like he still believes that Miami Vice was the cultural high point of Western Civilization. He probably can still quote Reagan's stump speeches for his classes." Niles thought he was being witty.

Halverson still wasn't listening. He seemed to have forgotten that Niles was there. Niles took the opportunity to make inflammatory statements to get the history teacher's attention back. He furrowed his brow and tried throwing more stones.

"The housing market in Dublin, Ireland during the Celtic Tiger is the best argument against unregulated capitalism during the twentieth century. The world hasn't yet seen a true experiment in theoretical communism because such a thing would require that people be less selfish than is humanly possible. Jimmy Carter was a one-term president because he diverged from the power backers of the democratic party and they sabotaged his domestic policy program in Congress."

Halverson didn't hear him. He was daydreaming about being a decade younger and in better shape.

Niles ranted on. "For most people, drinking a pop sweetened artificially is more effective at prompting a bowel movement than a prescription laxative. What people call aliens and UFOs are actually trans-dimensional visitors from a parallel timeline." Niles paused and looked to Halverson for a reaction, but there was none.

Sensing the break in Niles's speaking merely through the vacuity of a breath, Halverson came back. "I'm getting another beer. You need one?" He rose from his stool and paused, but still didn't make eye contact with Niles. He was a ghost.

"Yeah, put it on my tab."

"Done and done."

Niles went back to contemplating the bottom of his own drinking glass. He looked up to notice that Halverson had gone over to talk to Crockett who was not on the way to the bar.

"I bet he's a better conversationalist," Niles said to no one in particular.

The waitress who was walking by stopped and said "What?"

"I'm sorry. Just talking to myself."

"Can I get you something?"

"Can I have a personality that people actually like?"

"What?" She couldn't understand Niles, with or without the noise of the bar at hand.

"I'm sorry. No thanks, I just sent my friend over to the bar to get me a beer." She nodded caustically with a grimace that would peel paint and went on her way.

Niles was great at making new friends and entertaining people. It was why he was lonely. That was just the sort of thing that Halverson was now talking about with Crockett.

Niles sat alone in the bar surrounded by people who didn't want to know him and plumbed the depths of his own memory. Was it all really as halcyon as he remembered it in the days before Swamp brought her brand of dis-ease into the realm?

Before her, the principal had been Gerald Fitzgerald. Gerald Fitzgerald had been the district's follow-up to Miles Smithson and was as quick of wit as Smithson seemed slow. He was an albino who was fond of women and had a powerful way with them, including the ones that he was not married to. He'd had his own weaknesses, but many of his strengths were weaknesses of Swamp. He had moved on, as good administrators always do, but he'd gone on to a lobbying position on the state level, working in Lansing. It was a natural fit, as he'd always been about the people side of what he'd done, schmoozing and glad-handing - not in the terribly insincere, barely-submerging-the-hatred and condescending way of Swamp, but in the old-school style of 19th century American politicians. He would have been a better fit for those days, if an albino in American politics had ever fit at all.

He'd had a most glaring weakness in his strength though, and that was his own pride. He was a self-made man who was the son of another self-made man, but he didn't try to glide on his father's making into making himself. So, of course he was proud. He had every right to be. No one could name another albino who'd done as much as he had. Niles certainly wasn't able to, not even when he was drinking with Halverson who knew his history and civics and surely could have named such a man. As any cliche-spouting English teacher would point out: pride comes before the fall and sometimes started in the Fall when students got their phone calls from the district transportation departments about where and when they would be picked up by the busses.

Fitzgerald's pride was in his accomplishments, and his accomplishments made him bigger than his position. In fact, his accomplishments combined with his position overshadowed the small petulant Dr. Kaseman, who was easily threatened by anyone who was taller than he was, but also by any one who was shorter. Gary Coleman was a threat to the fragile ego of Dr. Kaseman, and he was dead.

Kaseman had hired Fitzgerald, but Fitzgerald was a thorn in Kaseman's side, a gut-punch to the delicate man's indelicacy. He was more well-known and much more noticeably distinct as a human being. He was also much more well-liked. Fitzgerald was a local boy made good and Kaseman was an outsider who wanted very much to win any and all popularity contests that he made up in his head to satisfy his Napoleonic complexity of an ego.

Fitzgerald was everything that Kaseman wanted to be: popular with men, popular with women, popular with small babies who would try to kiss him during photo opportunities to increase their social capital with other babies who would then consider them more strongly for invitations to future birthday parties. He was even popular with high school students with whom he somehow formed an instant rapport of mutual respect.

All of these things meant that Kaseman had to get rid of him. He could not allow a building principal to outshine the district superintendent. Such a thing was inexcusable! How would he ever win the award for Handsomest Superintendent in Michigan if everyone could see every day that his tall, strong, albino building principal was more popular and more charismatic? No, he had a plan to get rid of him. He would threaten the threat, thus proving himself more threatening than that which he was threatened by. It was an inconceivably beautiful plan, and he had conceived of it, proving himself superior and more beautiful than anyone else who had ever conceived anything.

That feeling was very important to him, as it made him feel much better about being the shortest man in the room. Not only would he get rid of Fitzgerald though, he also had to punish everyone who liked Fitzgerald more than they liked him. He couldn't actually make them like him through kindness and overt acts of positive humanity. No - that would take too much time and be too far out of character. It would be a weakness to handle things that way. He had to do something else, something to truly make everyone who liked Fitzgerald more than they liked him pay by proxy for supporting Fitzgerald's likeability. He would have to get rid of them all.

Once he forced Fitzgerald out, he had to make the building pay. Those teachers who applauded louder and longer for Fitzgerald had to be punished for not liking Kaseman as much as they were supposed to. His revenge would be sweet, but it would be drawn out, punishing everyone who had given Fitzgerald more favor than Kaseman. As his resentment of Fitzgerald grew, so did his awareness of Swamp, and he saw how he could use the one to erase the other. Swamp had come to him, and he sensed in her the perfect tool with which to destroy everything about the school that Fitzgerald and his staff had built. Swamp was as egomaniacal as he was, but she was a minority woman, so she wasn't a threat to him, and she was nowhere near as intelligent as she imagined, so her own ego's need for validation made her not just a perfect photo negative for Kaseman, but also a perfect tool to use to strike back at that whole building of teachers who had liked and respected someone else more than they did him.

First he made her an attendance specialist in the high school across town. She turned out to be perfect for a management position in his district. She was a wrecking ball, a rotund sphere who could use her strengths as a minority woman coupled with her blindness to personal responsibility to smash Fitzgerald's legacy to pieces, to destroy the staff that supported him and to absolutely undermine and destroy everything that he had built there with them. Moreover, by using Swamp, Kaseman believed that he could keep his hands clean of the destruction. He could say that everyone who was chased out left because of their own sexism and racism provoked by a minority woman who was simply being strong.

His plan was perfect. He was perfect. Sometimes he simply sat in his office and congratulated himself with an expensive cup of coffee over his plan. It would get them; it would get them all; they would pay for Fitzgerald's hubris and popularity. And then he laughed with dark glee - sitting in his oversized office, legs dangling from his chair - at the thought.

As Kaseman gave himself "highly effective" across the board in his self-evaluation on a Tuesday, Niles was across town falling behind on grading and planning to make sure that all of his evaluation materials and paperwork were turned in. He had a banker's box full of copies of student assignments marked with his comments and scores, a binder full of lesson plans that he had taught, all of which had been turned into the evaluating administrator the week that they were put into place, but now had to be printed again and annotated with his own comments about success and failure with lengthy reflections. The "minimally effective with reservations" that he had been rated in his last evaluation still stung, and Niles was trying to do everything better this time, because he'd been told that the difference between effective and ineffective was in the documentation, and he believed it. Packed on top of the box were spreadsheets displaying all of his students' scores from pre and post-tests, the percent change, the standard deviation, the expected change, and the deviation from expected change with annotations regarding student attendance and discipline. Niles knew that if any of these things were missing, that he could once again face being labeled as a "non-effective" or "minimally effective" educator.

No one in the education program during his university days had told him just how important documentation and paperwork actually were to prove that he was a good teacher, so he was blindsided by the hours of work and the load of paper that it required, all of which took significant time away from his life outside of school as well as the limited time available to dedicate to actual instruction and grading. What good could he actually be to students in the classroom unless he proved it on paper? The thought of failing alone made him want to drink.

But not too much.

7. Attendance

Attendance had to be documented ad infinitum. There were many ways to record attendance, and each proved the other true. Attendance was a determinant of the amount of money public schools received from the state. A young, inexperienced teacher like Niles could not be faulted for thinking (logically) that a responsible citizenry would consider education to be the bedrock of a functional society and would want for it to be of high quality. Anyone might even reasonably associate high quality with an expenditure of financial capital, but that kind of thinking would underestimate the self-centered nature of American culture.

There was something in American society that Niles began to recognize early on when he was a child who watched the news regularly with his mother. He noticed that there was a certain sense of selfish individualism that permeated all of American culture and that most Americans were only interested in having "their" money go toward things that benefit them directly, and even then only in the short run. Their eyes couldn't see to much of anything beyond an arm's length, either materially or chronologically. People didn't want to pay to educate or provide for anyone else. They couldn't see that if the family down the street had smart, well-informed, and conscientious children that those children would then be less inclined to smash them in the back of a head with a fencepost in a dark alley for pocket change. They also couldn't believe that an educated and informed electorate would work cohesively to create the type of society that would benefit everyone and not just the few who were elevated to the status of gods by endless media propaganda and financial largesse. There was such an element of money worship in American culture whether religious or financial or some slick Prosperity Bible blend of the two, and it made Niles rather ill to think about it. When he got older and chose not to have children of his own, he'd always wonder how others could raise children in such a toxic stew of cultural influence. When he started leading his own classroom, it was increasingly clear that the answer to that question was that "they don't."

Both sides, the teachers and the students were changing their approach to school because of a lack of parenting going on. Students would try to skip. Teachers would be there to mark their attendance and call home when that student was absent. If they parent answered the phone they would express shock and promise to rectify the problem. Then, two to three weeks later, the pattern would repeat.

Taking attendance was a perfect bureaucratic four-part process: Most teachers had a seating chart that they marked down on paper printed from the program that they used to upload and record data to for the district - probably on a clipboard. They marked it there first. Then they moved over to their computer, internet-ready with the attendance program loaded, and recorded attendance data there. That program was accessible to anyone in the district office with the proper software. The next step was take those attendance numbers, break them down by grade and class and to post them on yet another sheet of paper on the outside of the classroom door for someone to pick up for a paper count that had to be submitted hourly to the office. The fourth step was that the teacher had to go down to the main office during their lunch or plan period (if they got one) to sign a sheet that verified that they had taken student attendance and committed it to paper and silicon chip in all the other ways first.

There was redundancy in the system because teachers could not be trusted in Kaseman's district.

It was drilled into Niles's consciousness in the first, second, and third days of his inaugural "New Teacher" orientation. It was just like Fight Club. The first and second rules were simply repeating an absurd absolute. After that, no one could remember what came next.

"A student is not present in the room, unless there are three forms of verification that he is in the room. Without those three forms of verification, no student can be verified as having actually been in your room."

Niles raised his hand.

"What if the student was in your room, and you forgot to mark him present?"

"Then he was not in your room and the school cannot receive state monies for the student having been in that room."

"But what if he was there, did the work, turned it in, got a grade, and you recorded that in the gradebook on that very day?"

"He wasn't there."

"What if you mark him present on two of the three forms of verification, say the computer, your paper list, and maybe even the note on the door, but at the end of the week you forget to go down to the main office and sign the verification sheet that you took daily attendance."

"If you fail to sign the weekly verification sheet, then none of the students have been there."

"What if they've all been there all week, but you just forgot to sign the sheet."

"Mr. Niles, is that your name? I can barely read your name tag from up here."

"That's my name. Unless there's another Mr. Niles here. Is my dad here? If my dad's here, then you can just call me Niles, and he's Mr. Niles because -" Niles thought he was introducing humor into an appropriate situation. He wasn't.

"-Mr. Niles," the speaker interrupted, "if you fail in any part of the attendance process, whether it be any stage of recording or verifying, then when the the state audits us, the student was not only not there, but you are guilty of committing fraud."

"Well that's illogical. That seems like I'd be guilty of forgetting, at the very worst."

"Mr. Niles. Taking correct attendance numbers might be the most important thing that you do here in your career in PSPS, however long that might be."

"I thought the most important thing that I might do here would be educating the students."

The presenter narrowed her eyes at Niles.

"We're moving on. You must take attendance every class period, within the first ten minutes of class, you must have two forms of attendance, both paper and digital, and you must post your attendance outside your door within those first ten minutes of class so that the numbers can be collected and counted in the main office. At the end of each week, you must come down to the main office and sign the verification form that proves that you have taken your attendance hourly and daily."

Niles had his hand raised again, but the assistant superintendent presenting ignored him. He put up both hands as the presenter started droning on about another topic. After a patient sixty seconds more, Niles started waving both hands. The presenter still refused to make eye contact, so Niles started swaying his body back and forth like he was in a music video. Some of the other new teachers behind him started to snort and giggle.

Finally, the assistant superintendent had to respond.

"What's your name again?" She asked to show Niles that he wasn't important enough to remember without telling him directly.

"Niles."

"Yes, Mister Niles. Can you hold your questions until the end of the presentation? We have a lot of important information to cover."

"Sure." Even though Niles wanted to make a point, he still didn't want to appear to be rude. He thought he was being funny at first but realized at her reaction that he was just being obnoxious. He was new. It was best for him to keep his head down, but he was in an absurd mood. It was also better to allow the assistant superintendent to be rude, since it was her program.

So he waited until the lunch break. When the presenter chose to allow everyone to stop for lunch, Niles approached her to bring up his question again. He stood next to her podium waiting patiently for her to finish and make eye contact so he could ask his questions. She pretended he wasn't there and simply gathered her materials into her bag, never looking up as Niles patiently tried to get her attention.

She walked past Niles and left without ever answering his question about the importance of taking attendance. He simply wanted her to justify her statement that taking attendance was more important than actually educating the students.

She did not return that afternoon. Another district presenter came into talk about assessment tools and software. Niles's question would not be answered by any of the appointed authorities.

Niles finally had to come to his own conclusion without the help of the people who made the policy. Of course the act of signing a paper simply proves that a teacher can sign a paper, just like the act of marching in unison simply means that a soldier can march in unison. Similar to how shooting clay pigeons makes one really good at shooting clay pigeons. Taking attendance means that a teacher can count heads. Posting it on a slip of paper taped to the door means that a teacher can tape a slip of paper to a door. None of these things added to the quality of the classroom environment in any meaningful way. It wasn't as though the state gave Niles the money in those moments right after he recorded student attendance - no, it was all rather mystical in a sense. And no district administrator would ever offer to dispel that mystery.

Niles was remembering all of those things when the dismissal bell for the last class of the day had rung, and students hurriedly started packing up. He moved toward the door with them to stand in the hallway when a voice interrupted him. There was a student who'd been captivated by something Niles had said in his lesson who wanted to know more.

"Hey Mr. Niles. What made you want to become a teacher? Were you like in high school and you thought, 'Hey, how can I be here forever?'"

"Believe it or not, no. When I was in high school, the last thing I ever would have wanted to be was a teacher. Some of my teachers were jerks. I didn't like many of them very much."

"So what are you doing here?"

"You know how some people tell you that high school is the best years of your life? Well, they're all full of it. Any teacher who says that to you? Get away from them fast."

The student laughed and leaned forward in his chair.

Niles went on. "When I was in high school, my life sucked. I barely had any friends, nobody liked me. I was depressed and suicidal. My teachers had to have noticed it, but none of them said anything at all about it to me. Except one. They were adults who spent more time with me than either of my parents, but only one of them felt compelled to say anything at all about it to me, and what he said was barely an acknowledgement at all."

"What do you mean? What did he say?"

"It was more like what he didn't say. It was close to the end of my senior year. My life had already been awful for a good four years. Maybe not like real world awful, but definitely "high school I-have-no-perspective-on-the-world awful." I was in my College English class, which was the closest thing we had to AP classes at my high school. I think my grade was hovering somewhere in the C+ range. Anyway, near the end of the first semester, my teacher took me out into the hallway during class and said something to the effect of "I don't know what's going in your life right now, but it won't last." Niles stretched his sore shoulders. "That was all he said that acknowledged that he knew I was having problems in my life. Then he gave me a choice. I could either quit the class and take Yearbook, which was where all of the losers were - no offense if you have friends in Yearbook - or get my act together and bring my grade up."

"So what did you do?"

"I got my stuff together in the class and brought my grade up."

"And that was what made you want to become a teacher?"

"Not really. When I thought back on it a few years after that, I realized that teachers could and should do more. If I would have had a caring adult mentor in my life at that time, literally anyone probably, but like a teacher who I spent a lot of time with who would have said something to me, it would have changed my life for the better."

"So that's why you're here? You were going to do what they didn't?"

"Somebody needs to step up and say that stuff to teenagers, don't they? Who better than a teacher?"

"I can't argue with that, Mr. Niles."

"Well, you could, but you shouldn't. I know what I'm talking about." He smirked. "I look at things this way. You could talk to your parents, but you wouldn't. I never did. I couldn't." The student nodded. "We didn't have that kind of relationship. Most high school kids hate their parents, or if they don't hate them, they at least don't get along with them, right? It's a pretty adversarial relationship that exists there. They want to treat you like a child, like you're still their baby, and you want to act like the adult that you think you are, so there's friction right? Most kids are willing to mention things to their teachers that they wouldn't share with their parents. I don't know why, that's just what I've noticed since I started teaching. I was the same way when I was a kid, or at least I might have been if I'd thought that my teachers gave a damn about me or my well-being. If I had a caring adult to point out some of the ways that my thinking was wrong, I could have been saved a lot of pain and anguish while growing up."

"Why do you think that they were like that? I mean, you said that people didn't like you. Did your teachers not like you?"

"No, they just didn't care. They weren't supposed to. They believed that they were just there to deliver content. They weren't there to invest in a student's life."

The student looked perplexed.

"That's just what it was for them to be a teacher. As a kid, I needed more than that though. A lot of people do. We need people to teach and to be the types of teachers that they wish that they had, not the types of teachers that they think they should be."

"Why is that? What type of teachers do people think that they should be?"

"Well, we've all had bad teachers. I had my fair share. For whatever reason, those seem to be the ones that people remember the most strongly. Those are the ones in movies and television. Those are what people think teachers are or should be. I don't agree with that. You don't have to be mean, or cruel, or cold, or uncaring to be a teacher. In fact, you should be the exact opposite of those things."

The student looked over to the clock anxiously. The bus drivers were not in the business of being patient. He put his chair on the table for Niles and made ready to hurry downstairs.

"I think if you're going to be a teacher, that you should be the kind of teacher that you wish you'd had."

"I'm glad you did that, Mr. Niles." And he rushed out the door and was gone.

Niles went out to stand in the hallway to watch them leave for home or work or wherever their attendance would be marked next. He wasn't sure, but he felt like he'd received a compliment. Maybe he wasn't doing as poorly at his job as he usually felt.

8. Kaseman

It was four AM and Doctor Kaseman was pacing back and forth across the enclosed veranda of the mansion that was paid for by the district as a part of his record-breaking compensation for being the state's Greatest Public School Superintendent. It was snowing hard. He could barely see through the white and drifting snow to the unattached garage where his Bentley was parked. According to the local weather service, the air temperature was negative nine degrees Fahrenheit with a wind chill of negative fifteen.

There was a difficult choice at hand with many variables to consider. Should he close the school today? He flexed his fingers and cracked his knuckles. He had immense power in these two small hands. The fate of a community rested on his small, narrow shoulders. He went to his roll top desk, grasped a pad of yellow legal paper and his favorite Tebaldi pen. He would make a list. A list would make his important decision easier.

He drew a long, crisp, flowing, beautifully etched line with his pen down the middle of the top sheet on the pad. On the left, he labeled the top "Close" and on the right, "Open." The weight of the almost perfectly balanced pen brought a prolonged sigh from his concave chest. On the one side, he wrote "cold at bus stops." On the other side opposite, he wrote "my daughters don't ride bus." Underneath "cold at bus stops" he wrote "poor children without proper winter clothes might get frostbitten." On the side opposite he wrote, "my daughters have nice coats." To the left column he added, "buses might get stuck in snow or slide on ice causing accidents." On the side opposite, he wrote "the Bentley has four-wheel drive." The list was forming up beautifully. He admired his own ability to print sharp letters. His handwriting was art.

His proper choice was becoming more clear in his mind, and he would soon be able to return to his warm bed with his minority wife. He continued his list. To the left he added "teachers driving in might have accidents resulting in need for sub pay." To the opposite side he wrote "teachers are easily replaced."

The list was shaping up marvelously indeed! He paused in creating his marvelous list to consider his own grandeur. How would the public respond to his decision? He needed to appear controlling and wise, benevolent and pernicious at the same time. He had to be the "soft mother" at the same time as the "wire mother." He was so worldly and wise, his subjects would accept nothing less. He might not have been gifted with height (for which he blamed his mother) but everyone looked up to him. He could not let them down. That was what a small person would do, and he would not be small.

Kaseman was born and raised in the power centers of the East Coast, and he knew how to be powerful. When he was contemplating taking the job as superintendent in this small Midwestern podunk town after spending years as an assistant superintendent in Boston's largest private school district, he recognized the opportunity for what it truly was: a mission to spread his own gospel of school management to the rubes in Michigan, to enlighten them and broaden their world, to show them how things were done in the prosperous and grand cities of New England where policy-makers and presidents were born and educated. He felt that the change that he would bring to Southwest Michigan would be an echo of a similarly small man whose family had left the power center of the Middle East roughly two thousand years ago to settle in a small village that wouldn't exist for another four hundred years: the town of Nazareth. Like that other small Jewish man, he would gather disciples about him, except these would be former businessmen and women, not fishermen and whores. His disciples would be influential people, not outcasts. These disciples, or "assistant superintendents" and "principals" as they would be called, would spread his gospel of school management far and wide, first throughout his district, then later throughout the country. Then his name too, would be spoken far and wide around dinner tables as newly enlightened Midwestern wives talked with their hard-working husbands, home after a challenging day in the auto factory or the corn field, about the benefits brought by Dr. Kaseman's benevolent leadership and how healthy and healing it was for their children. How Kaseman had improved their lives and made them all happier, healthier, stronger, and smarter.

Yes, that was his future, but for now, how would he handle these days of inclement weather? His mind drifted again. People would awaken to their alarms on this snow-filled, turbulently windy and icy day, look at their cellular phone alerts and say to each other, "Yes, this decision was righteous and strong. This decision was good and wise, it showed strength and good planning as well as a canny understanding for the welfare of the children. It was beneficial and considerate to all." Parents would speak of this around their water coolers and coffee machines of their plebeian Midwestern jobs and grow in their admiration of this New England scholar who was so wise and so powerful, and who had come to them to make their lives better.

The list! He returned to the list. The clock was ticking and he had to make a decision. All of the superintendents from the neighboring districts would be looking to him too. His district was the largest for almost forty miles of this backwater Midwestern state. He would send out his group email to them and they would all know it was good. He checked the weather one last time. Wind chills had dropped again and would not rise with the sun, that day hidden by thick clouds pushed from the north. Snow would continue to fall and accumulate.

School was on. He quickly sent out the message and prepared to return to his sleeping wife, but first, he would reward himself. He quietly crept into the master bathroom, locked the door and began to silently disrobe. He removed his velour nightshirt and hung it on the back of the door. He folded his pajama pants carefully and placed them on the counter. They looked like they did when he chose them off the shelf at the Brunello Cucinelli store in downtown New York City. Perfect. He pulled his step-stool out of the linen closet and stood on it in front of the mirror. The power he had just wielded had excited him. It had aroused a throbbing need that only one thing could satisfy. He took a hold of himself and flexed. The lack of demonstrable muscle tone made his pale skin look like marble in pale glow from the night light. He looked upon himself and saw that his creation was good. He began to tug at his protruding turgidity.

After a few short moments, he relaxed in exhaustion. Now he could go back to bed. The maid would have the counter cleaned before his wife woke up. It was going to be another good day.

Niles woke up to wind chills of negative thirteen and a foot of new fallen snow on his driveway. There was no message on his phone from the local news station regarding school closing. He would have to leave earlier than usual to compensate for slower traffic on the roads. Some of the other local more rural districts had closed, but not Pianosa Springs. The others had to get buses down unpaved roads. Pianosa Springs had plows and salt trucks. He shoveled the foot of new snow in the two feet in front of his garage door and backed out into the snowy oblivion. Visibility was poor, and plow trucks hadn't done anything meaningful with any roads but the most primary of the primary ones, so Niles drove slowly. Each turn seemed to be against the blowing snow and the oncoming flakes blown into the glow of his headlights gave him the impression that he was doing light speed on his way to work at the Death Star.

Niles was on time, but buses and even some other teachers slid in late, all wrapped, all bundled; some of the students were wearing layers of coats that they piled in classroom corners because they didn't fit in lockers. Some students stayed home, their parents wary of sending them out into such temperatures and depths of snow. According to the state's rules, as long as sixty-seven percent of the student body showed up, it could be counted as a "school day" and Niles's numbers tracked right around that mark all day as they all watched the wind blow more snow around through the windows in the hallway by the stairwells.

Dr. Kaseman slept well upon returning to his bed, waking satisfied and well-rested at 9:30, then working from the comfort of his home office as his station allowed. He gazed out the window at his back garden, enamored with the pure white vista, unspoiled as it was by the view of any other lights or habitation across his sizable property.

What a beautiful day to be indoors.

Niles was going to be at school for extra hours as usual, regardless of how much new work he had to do or how much snow was on the ground because he was still trying to catch up on old work, but today was special. It was a Wednesday, which meant that there was a building PD to attend after school.

This PD, like many building PDs, was being led by teachers who had attended an outside training and were now volunteering to teach their peers everything that they had learned. One of the the volunteers was Ms. Heller. She'd joined the school a couple years after Niles and hadn't yet seen the PD cycle come around again. She was a short brunette who was long on patience. She might have been a physical straw-weight, but she was heavy on enthusiasm. Niles liked her. They needed more people like her in the building.

The topic this time was "differential instruction." Heller was going to be taken under wing by Linn, but it hadn't happened yet and she and Niles got along well. "Differentiated instruction" was a phrase for a style of teaching that involved providing each different student with a different method to learn with, in terms of acquiring, processing and making meaning of whatever the material was that the teacher presented. It sounded excellent. Niles thought it was about time that that teachers began thinking in terms of how to appeal to the students who were typically left behind because the mode in the classroom didn't fit them. He listened and took notes like everyone else as Heller went through slide after slide projected from her computer, narrating them for her captive audience in the snowy frozen wasteland of West Michigan.

Niles was processing the information. Usually what happened was that two basic groups of students present in the classroom were neglected. The ones on the top end and the ones on the bottom end. Pianosa Springs being what it was meant that a lot of students were pushed through the grades in high school because there was a premium placed on the graduation rate. A higher graduation rate meant a more successful school. There had been plenty of students in Niles's classroom who by nature of their level of reading or writing skill should not have been there, but he was accustomed to doing the best that he could with them considering the amount of time and energy that was available. He'd been given the sound advice from Cook and Jobe to try to raise everyone in the class's skill by one grade level. It was all he could do given the class sizes and how much time was given to him.

115

Demarr had a different philosophy - one that she shared proudly at a department meeting: "Don't worry about the smart kids - they'll be fine no matter what. The ones that don't get it? Just pass them anyway. Pass everybody."

Niles was taken aback when she said it, but he looked around the room and most of the English department was nodding. Linn was smiling. She looked satisfied, like she was being proven right.

Differentiating instruction meant that Niles had one focus, one "lesson" that had to be presented potentially 35 different ways. It meant that he had to plan ahead to meet each of his students in their "proximal learning zones" and have everything explained step by step in his lesson plans that were due every Monday by 8 AM. When Heller was talking about it, it seemed like the best thing ever. She was enthusiastic and her enthusiasm spread to Niles easily because he appreciated her. When Niles was lying awake in bed that night thinking about all of the work that it would entail, it no longer seemed like the best thing ever.

In every class, there were students ahead of grade level and students below grade level because students were grouped by age for grade level instead of ability. The students above grade level could typically be quantified as being one to four levels ahead. The students behind would be anywhere between one and eleven grade levels behind. He had seniors in his English 12 class that were illiterate beyond making sense of sports scores and Stop signs. Truly differentiating his instructional materials to meet all of his students meant that there would college-level assignments at the peak of Bloom's Taxonomy and assignments at much lower levels for students who could barely read let alone comprehend some of the bigger ideas that Niles wanted them to take home.

For the students who had been left behind by the other teachers but who still showed up, Niles could start with information retention. It was basic, but that was the most that some teachers ever did. All Niles could actually do was to provide opportunities. That was what he did anyway, even before it was called "differentiated instruction."

Kaseman liked Differentiated Instruction too, but for a different reason than Niles did. Kaseman liked any shift in the paradigm that came through education because as a manager, he was always looking to cut costs. Each shift meant that there was a need for new teachers who hadn't learned the older ways and could be paid less.

Every new teacher who came through the university system heard the same stories about older teachers who created problems and held students back because they were rigid and unchanging in their pedagogy. "Old teachers" were a dead weight, an anchor on a system that was trying to rise. If it wasn't true, it was still true. Kaseman needed a high rate of teacher turnover to keep costs low. Every district manager knew that. Few people supported the idea that old teachers were bad teachers as strongly as Kaseman did. He was excellent at his job, after all -- he was paid more than than any other superintendent in the state.

He was highly effective.

9. Wein

For his first two years in Pianosa Springs High School, Niles was part of a team of teachers on the third floor. It was part of an initiative that lasted three years called "Small Learning Communities." These Small Learning Communities were going to change the school for the better. One of the four teachers that Niles was partnered with was almost a literal ray of sunshine. Her name was Luna Pogodzinski and her skin was the tone of a cool summer night under a full moon.

Everyone, even the students just called her "Luna" because "Pogodzinski" was too much and "Misses P" didn't sound right. Her parents were also hippies who lived on an island in Michigan's U.P. after fleeing California in the mid seventies. They were the only black people for 250 miles and the island in Lake Superior ended up being the best place for them. She was the first person that Niles ever met who could pull off a mohawk. It wasn't the kind of look that anyone could put back on, but she grew her hair out and did what it took to make it happen. Her dogged persistence and unique haircut were reflected in her teaching style, and Niles looked up to her even though she was a good foot shorter.

She'd overcome a lot in her life. She lost her father and two siblings when she was a child and was raised by her mother alone from the age of 12. Her father, Marshall, her brother Will, and her younger sister, Holly, had been on a routine rafting expedition in Canada when they disappeared. Niles didn't know the whole story, only a bit of what he'd heard on television when he was a child. Something about an earthquake that was "the greatest ever known" at that time in Canada, and how not even a bit of their raft was found in the aftermath. Searchers combed the river and the surrounding forest for weeks, but three-fifths of her family were lost in those lands north of the border forever. No one would ever know what happened to them,

She was however, in spite of those tragedies, or perhaps due to them, a highly excellent teacher. She understood loss. So many of the students had lost something, or never had something in the first place but understood absence. That sort of empathy was difficult to find, even in teachers, and impossible to teach.

She wasn't the only great teacher that Niles got to know during his first few years. The old guard was still there in some degree, although they'd be gone long before Niles would. John Jobe was one of the good ones, he was part of the team with Niles and Luna and had already been teaching for almost twenty-eight years by then.

Some teachers calcify with time, some went hollow on the inside like a diseased tree. Jobe did neither as was as fresh and kind as a new teacher. He was a giant among men, an inch above Niles and broader as well. He taught Special Ed and had a lot of special children because he treated all of them with the same kindness and love that he directed toward his own offspring. They were all Jobe's kids and when Niles was put in their group, he became one too. If M.A. Cook was Niles's School Mom, then Jobe was Niles's School Dad. Like all great teachers, he taught through example and worked hard to be the kind of teacher that he himself wished he had grown up with. Jobe hardly ever said an unkind word, but if he did it was clear that the person had earned it through hard work and dedication to being awful. Jobe knew that words could hit like hammers.

Working closely with those teachers for his first two years reminded Niles of his time in the building as an intern under Cook. Both periods had given him lots of experienced support from good teachers. The internship was something that Niles couldn't have been reasonably prepared for. There were no classes to take that could put him in a classroom. There was no lecture to hear and no assignments to complete. The internship was the only thing that could prepare anyone, and if someone were placed with a poor teacher, all it did was compound the difficulty of coming to a classroom to teach for the first time. Niles was fortunate in working during his internship with someone who knew and understood how an ideal school would work, and how to treat people like the best versions of themselves. If he knew the ideal one, then he could work to bridge the divide between that and the actual one in realistic and effective ways, and if he could see the best in people that they could become, he could treat them that way, and pull some of their best selves through to the surface. People like Cook, Jobe, and Luna were all exceptionally good at teaching through being teachers. They knew the tools of the trade and spent every year working to improve their skill with those tools.

Niles learned early in his own education that a classroom was a tool as well, one that was used to try to effect a cultural change in the people who were being socialized there. Tibbs, Geit, Halverson, and many of the others knew that too - on some level. Like any tool, a hammer, a screwdriver, a jackhammer - it could be used to create or to destroy.

If only one could simply insert brass screws into the students' hips and elbows to make them move all at the same time. If only students were more like consistent raw materials, then they could be effectively measured at the end of a school day or the end of a lesson. A classroom wasn't like boot camp or basic training, the students weren't conscripted. They were compelled by the law to be there in body, but there was nothing that anyone could do to make them present in mind. The true difficulty in educating students was to get them to be present in their minds.

Niles figured part of it out early on after failing a few times, and he was no stranger to failure. At first, he treated his students the way he was treated when he was a student: as an ignorant passerby. Most teachers treated their students as if they were temporary visitors to life, as if their existence didn't move beyond the walls of the classroom. Niles remembered how disconnected that made him feel, as if he didn't matter. He could see the same feelings in the bright eyes of his students. He didn't like it. Most of them didn't like him. He didn't matter. The problem was that if he didn't matter to them, then he couldn't teach them anything they didn't already believe that they knew.

He decided to treat the students the way that he would want to be treated by a teacher, the way that few of his teachers in high school did for him. He treated them like people with feelings and emotions. People who had hurts and cares and worries that they carried with them at all times. When he was a teen, he had wanted to be treated like a meaningful human being, but few adults were willing to do that, as if doing that meant that they would sacrifice a part of their own value in themselves. Niles decided he wasn't going to be that way; he tried to be the teacher that he had wished he had when he was their age.

It was slow at first, and it took him a while to grow into it, but he thought if he gave up some part of the wall of defensive apathy that most teachers built, that he could become a better teacher. For most people that apathy was a significant part of their identity, so he sacrificed a part of himself for his students, and in return they became more human to him. Once he allowed them to see how vulnerable he was, they made themselves vulnerable too. Human interaction was often like a conversation involving a give and take of information. Depending on the players and the information, it could lead to increased trust and intimacy. Being taken into confidence could make a person feel safe at the same time that they felt vulnerable, but only if they knew that they could trust the people they were with. When people felt safe, they were more likely to listen than to talk. Talking was carving out space, taking territory and laying claim in conversation. If someone could listen, they also learn to watch. Body language changed and opened up. People disengaged from the shells of rounded shoulders and defiant jutting chins.

Niles discovered by trial and error that the only way to get students to be mentally present was to help them to invest in the moment by seeing class time as meaningful, and helping them to see that he could offer something that could benefit them. He did that by investing himself in them and in their moments. He gave them attention and experience. He shared what he had learned and how he learned it, even talking about some of his own struggles with anxiety and depression in school. He asked them questions about their lives. That was the only way to get them to exist in there in the classroom, to not run and hide in daydreams and fantasies, and to invest in listening and being present in the moments that they could share to become a functional community.

There weren't any classes that taught that, but that was part of what Niles learned from working with those quality, experienced teachers. If he'd been placed with different people, if he'd had no Cook, no Jobe, no Luna, then he'd have probably gone wrong at some point. Fortunately, grace and luck had given him a sound roll of the dice early on in his career. Nothing that was good lasted though, and the small group of teachers was dissolved when the winds of change swept a new educational paradigm in to fix everything that was wrong with the system.

There was no handbook for grading either. Certainly, the wrong things get marked wrong and things that needed correcting got corrected, but there was more to consider than just that. Niles took grading seriously; it was work. Non-stop work that often became tedious.

When grading grammar got monotonous, Niles tried to go deeper and find the students' manner of thought and to write comments that would help them to see new things or to look at what they knew in a different way. After all, the biggest obstacle that young people had to overcome was their own inability to think outside of themselves. They had to learn empathy, and no one learned empathy by being lectured. Niles had to get them to read in order to write better, but his aim was more complex. By getting them to actually read and consider the perspectives of the characters, he could also teach them empathy quietly without them even guessing at it. He couldn't say, "Today, you will learn how to empathize with people who don't look like you," because that would force the students to be reactive, maybe even defensive. Many of them with strongly held prejudices would shut down if they were told that was the point of their reading. For many people, understanding others on a meaningful or deep level feels threatening - as if they might lose some part of their own carefully constructed identity by letting someone else's have space and compassion in their brain.

Niles learned the hard way when writing feedback on student papers that he had to do more than just write "good job!" or "nice work." The students were numb to that sort of bland feedback that meant nothing. They didn't read it and would just make all of the same mistakes over and over again. It was all that most of them had gotten from teachers for years. Those kinds of meaningless phrases lost their significance somewhere around third grade when the students started to be self-aware. By the time they were in high school, it was difficult to get their attention and keep it. Why would they bother to read the teacher's comments on their papers? After all, few of them had any motivation for improvement; they were accustomed to being rewarded no matter what and most of them liked who they were -- at least on the surface. He had to find some way to give them a reward for reading the teacher's comments, and then a reason to honestly think about them instead of merely blowing them off.

A few times, he had gone too far in his quest for relevance. One time, after a weekend *Evil Dead* marathon, he'd written at the end of an AP student's summer assignment that the thesis (or rather the lack thereof) had "swallowed his soul." He found out later that the student read that comment and cried. There was a delicate line to manage. A teacher wasn't an editor of those papers, a teacher was meant to be guide, and the comments left on the sheets should have been a guide to forward progress, not a judgment on someone's value. Part of that process to Niles was a starting point of asking the students to disassociate their personal self worth from the grades that they received. For the high achievers that was very difficult. A large part of what made them into high achievers was that belief that their grades were an indicator of their value as people. "Good student equals good person" or similar nonsense had become a part of their identity or just another part of how they defined themselves.

Niles knew that he had to guide the students toward forming an vision of self that was independent of their grades without necessarily trying to tell them that what they did in class didn't matter at all. It was a thin tightrope over a very deep crevasse. A good teacher would consciously help them to break that association by separating their output from their self-image through carefully constructed feedback that was specifically targeting their writing, not through comments that were so generic as to be easily mistaken for commentary on that student's character and value as a human being.

If only it were so easy for them to find real meaning in their lives. That would have been a good topic for a professional development with several departments in the building being lacking in the ways and means of giving meaningful grades and responsible feedback. After Cook retired, the remaining English department outside of Niles wasn't well known for giving significant feedback that would make the writers better if they took a chance and followed it. Doing something with a dedication to purpose like making lessons and development meaningful was a foreign language to the people pulling the strings for the teachers in the district.

The focus of that Wednesday's professional development was on adjusting teaching methodology to better assist the young black men in the school. It started by focusing on the "othering" of black men and illustrated that concept with an unrelated YouTube video that Swamp had heard about at her church. It was a heavy-handed product of a white congregation in Mississippi that was caught in the midst of community-wide gentrification. The religious overtones seemed to be lost on everyone but Niles. The speakers in the video might as well have been offering black salvation to King Leopold's Congo. The video ended and the nice white ladies in the audience nodded with energetic validation and applause that warmed Swamp's heart.

The start was horrible, but it degenerated as always into a twisted game of one-upmanship led by certain people within the English department. It usually began with Wein and/or Kringe at this point in the game, as both had learned well at the heels of Demarr and Linn about how to make others feel small. Wein stood up and congratulated Swamp on her choice of "such a powerful and meaningful video" and elaborated on how those white members of the Mississippi church had captured the essence of the experience of a young black man in southwestern Michigan without a hint of awareness or irony. Kringe then stood up and seconded Wein's effusive praise for the video and Swamp and then added a little praise and some undercarriage stroking for Wein before explaining how awful it was that so many people in the building still didn't understand young black men the way that she and Wein did. From there, it only spiraled downward.

Their behavior wouldn't have been out of place in a classroom full of teaching pre-interns, a group of people who were sharing their experiences from their first short and relatively meaningless forays into the world of education; here, with experienced teachers it was a pathetic attempt to make themselves look high quality by talking about how everyone else was terrible. Niles thought it was a good deal like being a unfunny comedian: when you have to tell people how funny you are compared to everyone else, then you're not funny.

If it wasn't Wein or Kringe, then it began with some younger or more inexperienced teacher saying something like, "I can't get 'Trevor' to pay attention in my classroom. He's got an F, and he just doesn't care about anything."

That was a question to which the proper answer lay somewhere along where "talk to the student like a human being with thoughts and feelings" and "check. on the home situation by contacting someone there" intersected, but too many teachers weren't thoughtful enough to go there. What it became was a policy of "I'll put my foot down harder here, and if I can, I put your face underneath it." Whenever a teacher started speaking in formulas such as: "Well, I try to put A with B and react as C," then the audience is nothing more than a prop to boost their ego. That person is fishing for compliments about their manner or their personality. It's a basic way to feed their starving egos at unsophisticated levels. That's why Linn and Demar didn't have to lead the way into those types of ego-boosting exercises anymore because they had advanced so far beyond into other power games. Wein and Kringe were just understudies in their twisted practice of education.

Wein was the more experienced of the two, so she usually took the lead, but Kringe was quick to follow. They would raise their hands to speak like any good mindless product of the American education system. Then they would launch into their practiced spiel about "this is how I do it and it always works for me." It always gave them the attention that they craved.

Other heads in the audience would look at them and nod, and the younger, inexperienced teachers would respond, "I didn't think of that" or "I'll try what Kringe mentioned. Thank you," and the duo's egos would puff a little bit larger each time. Sometimes the sessions became all about one topping the other, and the two went back and forth for as long as the speaker would let them about their own practices and prejudices. They were simply taking turns pleasuring themselves.

Niles saw through it. The thing that Wein and Kringe and Linn and Demarr had either forgotten or never known in the first place about being a teacher was that it was not about the teacher's ego. That even though there was a performative element in what the teacher was doing, that she was not supposed to be a "star." A star used a performance to feed her ego, which made it difficult to keep it in check. Each of those women had an ego that demanded everything be about her. If ego was what mattered, then hurting others to feel good was okay. A good teacher didn't do that. A good teacher didn't belittle or bully to elevate her status with the class or with the other teachers.

The English department coven had no idea about what a good teacher really was, but they felt free to speak about it as often as a floor was offered and because of Swamp's loose vision of how meetings were structured there was always a floor for them to take control of so long as she could see their goal was to make the other teachers feel bad. That was something that Swamp always supported.

10. Creative Writing

Niles was crazy and the rest of his department knew it. Or some of them knew it. The rest didn't care. Trudeau was indifferent. He was busy being crazy differently. Geit didn't care because it didn't matter either way. Linn and Demarr cared if they could use something to their benefit. Kringe and Wein cared because Niles didn't like them. Niles had to be stopped. What kind of English teacher would try to get books for his minority students to read with positive minority characters? What kind of English teacher would try to steer a curriculum away from Shakespeare and his Golden Phallus?

Niles knew that he was crazy too, but by then he didn't care. He was sent off to another AP training far away across the great state of Michigan to Livonia Hills. There, surrounded by the suburban sprawl of Detroit's White Flight, he would be trained better and perhaps even be fixed by being surrounded by the superior teachers from those schools with higher tax bases and stronger funding than his.

He showed up to his appointed room on the third floor of the learning annex, the last of the thirty-four teachers to arrive. Every single one of them was white. They were not quite as white as the paint on the walls which seemed to be the right white, almost the "optic white" of Liberty Paints, but white enough to be right.

Niles took his seat in the back corner at the only seat that was left after just seconds before he arrived the proctor had asked the person in the back corner to "please come to the empty seat in the front and join the rest of the group." Now Niles was in that chair that had not been "a part of the group." He looked around at the cornucopia in front of him. Each of the assembled teachers had a laptop in front of them on their desk. Niles noticed that they were all different brands and models, but he still whispered lightly to the dyed blonde next to him "Where do we get the laptops?"

"You didn't bring your own? The email that was sent out with your confirmation information said to bring your own laptop."

Niles didn't get a confirmation email. Everything had been handled by Swamp's secretary.

The instructor asked everyone in the room to introduce themselves to the rest of the group in the time-honored tradition of education and started with the last guy who just walked in.

Niles stood up.

"I'm Joe Niles. I'm from Pianosa Springs Schools."

"You've come a long way to be here." The instructor was impressed.

"I did?

The rest of the class introduced themselves and revealed that none of them had driven more than a half hour that morning. Niles had left his school parking lot at 5 AM to be there for the start of the program at 8.

Niles also noticed that every laptop computer that he could see had a label or an engraving from the district that each person represented. The blonde dye job next to him complained to him that hers was old and slow, and that she wished her district would get with the program and replace it since it was almost three years old and clearly a "dinosaur compared with the other laptops" that were assembled around the room. Niles didn't have a school-provided laptop. He'd had to provide his own mouse and his own speakers for the desktop computer in his classroom that he'd inherited along with his desk. Both of those things came from his own home for a desktop computer that was almost old enough to be required to take Freshman English itself.

Niles took notes on his smartphone while the rest did the dilly part of dilly-dallying on their laptops.

Just before lunch, the instructor thought it best to go around the room again and have each member of the group share one thing that worked successfully and well for them in their own AP instruction. This time Niles went sixth, since to be diplomatic the instructor started with the other back corner. There was a cascade of Shakespeare references and tableau exercises, self-congratulatory praise and sentences starting with the same stem, "In my classroom, I..." and Niles, like the crazy misfit that he was interrupted it all.

"In our classroom, we like to start off some of our bigger books with a dramatic reading of a first chapter or a first section. I've seen that it can really get the students excited and into a piece if they can hear the emotion that's sometimes otherwise locked away in the words." He paused and looked at the pale, blank faces in front of him. "For example, I do a dramatic reading of the Prologue of Ellison's *Invisible Man*. I read it angrily, so they can get the tone of Ellison's narrator right away."

His statement was me by blank stares and silence.

Niles felt compelled to attempt to justify his practice.

"It's such a powerful and emotional book. It's told in the first person because Ellison wants the reader to feel the rage of the *Invisible Man* at the society around him, and if the students don't key in on the anger immediately they can misread the character and just think him 'crazy' and paranoid."

The instructor grimaced. Niles listened for crickets but heard none. They moved on.

"And how about you?" The grimace softened and the proctor focused on the woman just in front of Niles. Then the litany continued. Shakespeare, British authors, self-congratulatory bragging, art projects, and each speaker after Niles tried to one-up all the others. Each one added to their statements to try to outdo the others who had gone before, except for what Niles had said. They ignored what Niles had said. "...and my students came back to me later and told me what a perfect shining star I was, and how I had changed their lives forever with this assignment that I designed." Their assignments were all the same. Niles listened to each of them in turn. He might have been the only one in the room who was listening instead of simply planning out what he or she was going to say, so inwardly focused on being outwardly impressive were the whole lot of them. He was crazy.

At lunch, one of the dyed blondes sympathetically spoke to him as he drew back alone to his spot in the corner with his sandwich and bottled water.

"That's pretty bold. I've never heard of anyone using *Invisible Man* in AP. What do you do with Shakespeare in your class?"

"Not much. I try to focus on minority authors that are more modern and accessible to my students," was what Niles said, but what she heard by the look on her face was, "Can I piss in your coffee?"

"You don't think you're putting them at a disadvantage?"

"Well, given that we're supposed to be teaching them skills and not necessarily Shakespeare, no I don't."

The look on her face spelled disapproval with a capital "D" which is also the first letter of "dick" which is what she thought Niles was.

Niles caught her look and understood. He had to travel to a new place to get it, but he got it. His thoughts ran a marathon around an Olympic park, out into the countryside, and then back coming in fifth. She was a nice white lady from a nice white school with nice white students who had nice white parents who had nice white collar jobs making nice white money. None of her students had ever felt any more like an outsider than the realization that all the other people on the playground had more expensive brands of shoes in the fifth grade. It would have done her class some good to read Invisible Man, but under her guidance, none of them would have understood a thing about it. Her students read Shakespeare at her feet, and she had them writing love letters in modern voice and vernacular from Beatrice and Benedick, and had them composing modern playlists of popular music in "mixtape" form to give each other to prove their feelings. It was all much ado about nothing in her class, but her students could walk out every day feeling like they'd been validated, not challenged or changed by the readings assigned. If they read Shakespeare they didn't understand a thing about it.

It hit Niles like a gut-punch. All of these teachers had actually come to the program today to be validated, not to be enlightened or to have their pedagogy broadened. They would bring what they had done, hear about others doing the same thing, then take hold of a couple of variations on a theme to bring home to their classroom and horizontally build into what they'd already been doing. There was nothing there that would elevate students intellectually, nothing there that challenge critical thinking, but everyone else in the room besides Niles looked around and saw that it was good enough. It would maintain the status quo both inside and outside the classroom. That was all they wanted. To keep doing the same thing in the same way. Routine and repetition were inherently satisfying and self-rewarding. Niles wanted something different. He wanted the exhilaration of forging a different path that was at least slightly less worn, even if his walking upon it did leave it looking quite the same as the other.

Niles felt like he was in the wrong place. Something about being there was familiar for him. Sometimes even in his own classroom, he felt like people were telling him he was doing it all wrong.

It was a dark and chilly Thursday in Creative Writing. It was time to workshop. Niles had a different approach to teaching the class than the other teachers in the building who had taught it. He didn't treat it as a "blow-off" class for either himself or the students. He'd decided early on in his teaching career to actually teach, and he had no interest in not being a good teacher.

The class was too big to workshop with, but he found ways to make it work and to get students engaged with each other's material. He prepped them all beforehand, talked to the classes about all the opportunities to make money as a writer, told them how all of their favorite tv shows, video games, songs, movies, and literally everything else they consumed started as an idea that someone somewhere wrote down and worked to develop until it became good enough to sell. A good song could start as a poem, a video game plot could start as a short story idea. Every superhero movie that they loved started off with (usually) some Jewish boys in New York writing their power fantasies down for costumed alter-egos. Niles's students could do that too.

In the workshop, one of the things that Niles harped on was the process of giving each piece a unique and fitting title that could draw their peers in.

"How do you pick which things you're going to use your disposable income on?" He asked them.

"If it looks cool." Was the umbrella student response to the question.

"Yes, you all like things that look cool. But 'cool' is a bit of a problematic concept to tackle because everyone's opinions on that are different, so let's break that idea down into some constituent pieces."

Niles pulled a few book covers up on the projector. "Let's consider these." Projected on the whiteboard were four different covers of the same book. It was *One Flew Over the Cuckoo's Nest.* There was the original cover in green, pink, yellow, and brown with the off-kilter font meant to look "crazy," the cover that Niles's class sets were in with what appeared to be a detail of a painting with a short, fat, suited man peering off an orange roof at a yellow sky, another version with orange cuckoo clocks on a white background, and the last with the title in black on orange over a photo of the actor who had played McMurphy in the award-winning movie based on the book.

"Which of these covers looks the coolest? Like if you were going to buy this video game, which of these covers would draw you in?"

"Are we making book covers Mister Niles?"

"No, I'm getting to a point about something else."

"We should do book covers. They did those in Demarr's class."

"Maybe we'll do something like that if we have time one of these days." Said Niles, even though he knew for sure that he would not assign an art project in his writing class.

"That looks like a stupid video game." Another student piped up.

Niles hesitated and looked over at the whiteboard. "Yeah, you're probably right. It's no Grand Theft Auto 7: Selling Crack for Blood or whatever." He looked out at his audience. There were thirty-six apathetic faces, and he was losing this battle.

"Why did you ask us about video games if this is a book?"

"I wasn't going to ask you about books. None of you are going to buy any books, are you?"

The question was rhetorical, but one student raised her hand.

"I might."

"Thank you, you've given me some hope for the future of America. Let's take another tack here. Let's look at the title. At least with this title, it might engage your curiosity a little bit, eh? You might say to yourself, 'Huh, that seems mysterious and intriguing, what does that even mean?'"

"Mister Niles, that title is lame, I wouldn't buy that game."

"Hey, it sounds cooler than Mario Kart if you ask me. But consider these instead..."

Niles flipped the slide to the same four covers but with hastily altered titles. The book was now called alternatively, *Crazy White Guys, Big Indian Flips Out, Mean Nurse Battle Ward III*, and *Let's Bet Who Dies First*.

"Take a look at any of these titles." A few more student heads popped up. They were usually curious to see what Niles would come up with when left to his own devices. "Each of these four new titles has something to do with the plot or theme of the book. Do any of them appeal to you more than the original?"

One student raised her hand. Niles gestured toward her. "My mom is a nurse, so I'd kind of want to see what *Mean Nurse Battle Ward III* was about."

"Thank you. That's what I mean, choosing a title is all about piquing your audience's interests. She knows a nurse, so that title grabbed her. If you had an interest in Native Americans, you might pick the second one."

A hand shot up on the side, Niles nodded to the student to talk.

"Actually, they prefer the term 'First Nations' now, not 'Indians' which was really a misnomer attributed to them by Columbus who was lost." She looked very smug with her statement.

"Yes, you are correct, thank you for pointing out my politically incorrect terminology. They call him an 'Indian' in the book since in the 1960s Kesey didn't foresee that forty years later he'd look like an inconsiderate horse's butt. Also, 'First Nations' is technically a phrase since it has more than one word and is not a term. Thank you." Niles segued away quickly, leaving the self-satisfied student feeling better about herself. He looked around the room gauging interest again and did his best to try to draw the wandering minds back. "I personally like *Let's Bet Who Dies First* because I'm morbid and I think death is funny."

As usual, four students out of the thirty-six got his joke and laughed. The rest looked at him as if he'd just suggested suicide.

"My point is this: For all of your pieces, make sure to try to come up with an engaging title. Think about someday trying to get paid for what you're doing instead of just writing anything to satisfy your teacher's stupid assignment. If you have no questions about this story, I'll give you some time in class to work on it. Any questions?" He scanned the room again. No one had a hand up. "Excellent. Begin writing.. Now." He phrased the last sentence as if it were a timed writing test to see if anyone was listening.

From the back he heard: "Wait, is this a timed write?" and "No, he's just messing with us." A girl near the front of the class put her hand up as he walked by. Niles stopped.

"Yes?"

"Mister Niles, why are you so morbid?" She smiled at him, gazing up from her seat innocently.

Niles scratched his chin.

"I blame my mother. She would take me to the library every two weeks when I was a child and allowed me to pick out any books I wanted to read. I rarely grabbed children's books."

He wagged his finger in the direction of his mother several dozen miles away. "Yup. It's all her fault."

"If I read a lot, can I be morbid like you?" Still she smiled sweetly.

"Well, you can sure try, can't you?" and he returned to his desk to double check and update his attendance. He felt a little crazy, but it was a good kind of crazy, like maybe he wasn't the only one.

Niles was wandering during lunch down the hallway on the other side of the building toward the stinky staff bathroom when Halverson grabbed him by the eyes and pulled him into his room.

"Hey. You're good with words and stuff, right?"

"Well, as an English teacher, I feel obligated to present that appearance, so yes after a fashion."

All that Halverson heard was "Yes."

"I need your help to figure this out." Halverson was serious. "Yesterday I got a phone call during one of my classes, and this was all they said." He held up a slip of paper with 'T S Elliot' written on it. Niles smirked quizzically and bit his tongue to let Halverson speak. "I think it's a name, right?" Niles nodded. "What was the first name of that French teacher that used to work here? Her last name was Elliot, right?"

"I think so. She wasn't really on my radar. We should ask Geit. I think he was a fan." Halverson was about to stand back up with a granola bar in his mouth before Niles added, "He's got a class right now. I think he has third lunch."

Halverson returned to his comfortably broken chair. "So do you remember that email that we got from outside the system? When somehow someone managed to hack the school email and send a group message to the whole staff that accused her of having an affair with the attendance specialist?"

"No, I think that was about the secretary that was having an affair with the security guard. You're thinking of the the other email that was sent out with a link to video that showed her wearing a wig working as a stripper."

"Yeah. That's what I mean. Did you watch that video?"

"I watched it at home. It was baloney. Some woman walking into a nightclub from fifty feet away. It was so grainy and blurry that it could have been you. I deleted it."

"Anyway, do you think this was about her?"

"I don't know," said Niles, even though he knew. "Do you think someone would be trying to contact you directly about her? She quit a year and a half ago. Were you 'special friends' with her or something?" Niles winked awkwardly in way that looked like a stroke victim caught in a squint.

"No. But I would have liked to have been. She was way too hot to be a teacher." Halverson momentarily gazed into the distance, as if he was remembering a dog that understood his deepest feelings and had sacrificed its life to save his.

Niles had to interrupt his revelry. "That's why she left. She got a better offer. A much better offer than a high school history teacher."

"Okay. So it's not about her. What is it then?" He pondered the slip of paper with the name on it. "Could it be an anagram for something? He put the slip down on his desk and started writing on it.

Niles started thinking aloud. "Well, T.S. Eliot was a famous poet in the early twentieth century. One of the few poets in modern history who ever got paid well to be a poet."

Halverson was barely listening.

"Look at this. I figure if you rearrange the letters it spells out 'toilets.'" He lifted the paper from his desk that now said 'T S Elliot' and 'toilets' on it "Do you think someone is trying to tell me something about the bathrooms? My room is right across the hall. Do you think there's something going on in there? Should we check it out, maybe have one of our female teachers investigate the women's restrooms?"

"I think if you ask a teacher to investigate the women's bathrooms because someone called you on the phone and said 'T.S. Eliot' that she will know you are crazy."

"I'm not crazy, Niles. Why would someone call my room just to say this and then hang up? You have to admit, it's kind of mysterious."

"I have to admit. It's kind of mysterious."

"I know, right?" Halverson knew it. He was right. He thoughtfully put the rest of the granola bar in his mouth and looked again at Niles for an answer. "You haven't gotten any weird phone calls, have you?"

"No, I haven't gotten any calls at all. No one wants to talk to me. Even in code." Niles tried to look regretfully neglected as he said it. Halverson didn't bite.

"Speaking of toilets, I have to use it. Should I look for more clues while I'm in there?"

Halverson pointed to him with the granola bar wrapper. "Let me know what you find." Niles had almost turned to go when Halverson had reconsidered. "On second thought. Don't let me know what you find. Some things are better kept secret."

Niles gritted his teeth and nodded. He knew what Halverson meant.

11. Pep Rally

"What would the pep rally be like if the cheer team captain was in charge of them?" was a question that no one asked.

This question that was never asked was emphatically answered as soon as Swamp took control of the school. The cheerleaders became the star athletic attraction and all other student sports became tertiary. With a little (tripled) extra budget money pushed in their direction, the cheer team doubled in size. A professional choreographer was brought in to design routines that became decreasingly less about building team spirit or encouraging players toward victory and became increasingly more about writhing. The uniform budget increased, but the material used in them became more expensive so it was cut from the middle of the uniform and the bottom edge of the skirt. They were odd choices given that Swamp was behind them all in her manipulative and overly controlling way, and yet in her role as Women's Ministry Leader, she would shame and denigrate immodest women in her church sermons.

The football and basketball teams were asked to stand from their place on the bleachers where they sat with the rest of the students for brief applause and that was the sum total of their participation. Some of the drama students were enlisted to stand at the gym light switches and to control extra spotlights which were placed on the upper transom to create more dramatic effects during the dance routines.

Another new element was added. One of the security guards began roaming the gym in a circular fashion with a digital video camera to record student reactions. Initially, the students and teachers thought it was about catching students violating school rules and tried not to overtly break any when the cameraman moved past. When the full homecoming video was released a week after the pep assembly on Swamp's new school online video channel, they learned that the crowd footage had been skillfully edited and cut into a video of the cheer team dance routine. The footage was edited to resemble a music montage from a reality show. From then forward, the students knew it was about getting a few extra seconds of screen time with a chance of going viral. It became a competition to see who could generate the most buzz for their clip when the video was released online.

The scene on the gym floor was every dance video on MTV that Swamp had wanted to be a part of when she was a young attention-starved cheerleader. There were now more than fifty cheerleaders. There was a new freshman cheer team, differently garbed than both the varsity and JV teams, and each of the three three groups had their own routines that were going on simultaneously. When the music dropped the three groups of girls ran together to coalesce into one giant dance routine from the different sides of the floor. That went on for an uncomfortable ninety seconds, then everything stopped. The girls froze in their places on the floor. Then the music started up again with a short dance track that threatened to deafen the assembly. The three teams separated, switched sides and continued their three pronged attack on the sensibilities of staff and student alike.

They somersaulted through pyramids of bodies, running, jumping, sliding, sweating, shaking; teen girls in tight clothes krumping, stanky legging, Dougie-ing, cranking, whipping nae nae, and then finally culminating into a full-on twerking booty-clap that drove the pubescent teens wild. Swamp turned from the girls dancing to the students crammed into the bleachers, smiling without teeth the whole time. This was her dominion, and she was in control of every aspect of it. The thrall was one of her own creation, under her power, and it demonstrated her mastery of the school building.

It was a three-ring circus sideshow of idiocy and the ringmaster was Swamp. She stood in the center of it all clutching a wireless microphone, her rings and bracelets glinting in the lights, shouting and gesticulating like an burned-over twice evangelist out to save the souls of the damned from their own lack of school spirit. Niles could only sigh and sit on the bleachers with his beard in his hands watching and trying to hide his full-body cringe.

To Swamp, administrating was about control and micromanagement whether it was in sitting in the back of the lesbian teacher's classroom undercutting her authority by interrupting her lessons or steering a pep rally into a pile of pointlessness. Controlling everything was how she justified her own existence to her version of God. Authority was power and power was control. There were authentic ways to get it, even honest ways to earn it, but they were far too slow to satisfy her lust for control. In Pianosa Springs Public Schools, the less qualified the administrative candidate was, then the better that Kaseman liked it. He considered putting people into positions which they had no qualifications for as a way to make people grow into those qualities. That did not happen. Instead it degraded the position that the individual was unqualified for. Department head was one of those positions that was often degraded.

It was true until Swamp took control of the school that department heads were elected without interference or even any interest from the principals in charge, but as soon as she could she began to insert her fingers into the process. She interrupted department meetings to make strong suggestions that a particular person within each department should become the head, extolling their leadership virtues whether they existed or not. It didn't matter to Swamp that her politicking was convenient fiction; she always believed that the voice in her head was divine inspiration and that God was truly steering her ship. Niles would never be God's choice for department head. That suited him just fine.

At no point in his teaching career did Niles ever consider becoming a department head. In movies and people's imaginations, high school department heads held some profound power over those in their department, telling them what to do and how to do it while also acting like a brave commander of a battleship tossed in stormy seas while enemy planes and ships attacked it from all sides. Some teachers even thought of department heads as heroes, as leaders of men, and aspired to be one. Niles however knew better. He could read between the lines. A department head held on to the bottom of the purse that the principal held the strings too. That was it. They handled supply distribution to their department. There was no extra power or command over other teachers. It was a powerless arrangement that added seven percent of base pay for an additional two hundred and fifty percent increase in frustration and wasted time.

A department head couldn't legally tell anyone what to do or how to do it, because they were all members of the same teacher's union and by that token all had the same rights and responsibilities to other members. To be in charge of a teacher was to manage them, and the only people in the building with a right to manage teachers were the administrators who were not part of the union. Still, it was the poorly annointed department heads who imagined that their posting gave them many powers over their peers.

The first department head that Niles had to deal with was his own mentor teacher, M.A. Cook, so that was a straightforward affair with no meddling on the part of administrators allowed. She had an impressive grip on what the title actually entailed. She set department meeting agendas and procured supplies. She also handled most interactions between the department and the principal at the time,

Miles Smithson. That was more pragmatism than anything else at the time because Smithson couldn't or wouldn't remember anyone's name except hers. He thought that Niles was an intern even after he had been hired in full-time until he finally eased into his retirement by not doing anything at all besides waddling around the building confusedly for his last several months.

As Niles's mentor prepared to retire, she had asked Geit to take on the role. He accepted and ran for department head. He was duly democratically elected and continued the same sane dedication to the role, but at the same time threw his weight into it with the sort of soulful cynicism that he was so very good at for two years. At that point it was decided among most everyone who cared that anyone who wanted to should take a turn at being department head for two years because there was arcane language in the employment contract that stated that retirement pay was related to the two highest years of salary and the addition of the seven percent of base pay that a teacher could receive for being department head might cover the cost of half an extra medication in retirement. So it was that everyone else who was fit for the job declined to run for after Geit's turn in spite of the pay increase and it landed with Demarr. Demarr was Linn's number one acolyte. She would pave the way for a comfortable transition from Geit to Linn in due time.

Doo Linn was a white nationalist in the body of a black Chinese woman. She hated Cook and Geit as well, but she held a profound hatred for Niles. The only thing that she hated more than Niles was herself, and she truly hated Niles with a passion. Her self-loathing was manifest in the way that she treated others. She did everything with hatred. It was the kind of hate that no one would believe unless they were the target. If someone simply told the story of

146

the depths of her hatred second hand, it would have felt like they were exaggerating it for effect.

Everyone has had a bad teacher during their time as a student. It's just endemic to the system, but Linn went out of her way to be the absolute worst. She couldn't be the best at teaching because that would have required a degree of kindness or softness of heart, and she felt nothing but animosity toward the students in her classroom. It was much easier to be the best at being the worst. All that required of her was that she utilize the hatred that was such a significant part of her self-identity. She took every imagined slight against her for her ethnicity or skin color and turned it to use against others whenever she could. In being the worst that she could, she hated anyone who was good at teaching. If there were good teachers around her, it would be obvious how awful she actually was, so she worked diligently to make good teachers around her worse.

At first it was innocuous. She'd say things. She offered a myriad of little backhanded compliments dripping with disdain and condescension. "Hmm, that's nice" was accompanied by an act of dismissal that would drive all attention and focus back on her and the things that she did. It escalated to whispers in the ears of teachers who were vulnerable about how other teachers were working against them. Before long it became a story of how some teachers she did not like had backroom deals with the administration to give them "all the good classes." Those inflammatory statements did more to create an isolating and combative environment among teachers than any administrator or any real-world event could have. It was ironic because after Swamp took over the principal's office, Linn was the one making secret deals to benefit herself to the detriment of the rest of the staff and the English department in particular. She was out to destroy anyone and anything that made her look bad before she could convince her students and her disciples that bad was actually good and good was bad. After that, it didn't matter how bad she was.

Demarr was an disciple of Linn. Linn's hatreds dictated Demarr's spite. She had no spine of her own, no gray matter in her skull to design her own hatreds, so she became a container of Linn's negativity. She was little more than a venomous ball of ego, an echo chamber that took hatred in and spewed vile, hateful behavior and language out. She was the embodiment of the evil teacher seen in kid's movies where all adults are terrorists simply manipulating their heroic young charges through fear and intimidation until that dramatic climax when the tables are turned and the bully loses her grip not only on the children, but on herself. She could be and was sometimes brought to tears by being forced to confront her own awfulness, but she never changed. She only put more effort in being worse.

Mara Demarr was the unwashed child of dirty hippies who raised her in an unclean and Godforsaken commune. All children in the commune were considered to be everyone's children, but that meant that no one bothered to care for any of them. Demarr was fortunate in one way though - she was not a pretty child. That spared her from some of the attentions of the men in the commune who considered the young women and female children to be their sexual playthings. She wasn't molested in the way the other girls in the commune were. She still learned some terrible things in that place though, things that she applied to the children in her care when she became a teacher.

She learned that power was for adults. Mara Demarr wanted power, and power over children was still power. At first when she started teaching she hid her true nature, her true belief that everything was all for her own gratification, but then she found the wing of Linn to take shelter under. Linn carefully fed and sheltered her ego while she trained her to be subservient while still encouraging all of her worst, most selfish beliefs. She would never consider her an equal, but she'd lead her to believe that they could see eye to eye.

Linn and Demarr had formed a clique with other members of the English Department who came later after Niles. Together they reminded Niles of the witches from Macbeth. The strongest difference between them and the witches was that none of them (despite their career choices) knew what iambic octameter was. Kringe and Wein were the second pair. They were twins of the bleach-bottle blonde and hard on the eyes. Both had spent far too much time in the sun in their salad days and had wilted accordingly. Each were weaker versions of their more experienced sisters in dishonor, but each was still caustic and burning in her passive-aggression.

Kringe was the slimmer of the two. She was a dried-out husk of a high school drama queen long past her prime. She was Niles's age, but long hours spent smoking while cocooned in the tanning bed she got from her well-meaning parents for her eleventh birthday had aged her drastically. Her skin was a shiny Oompa-Loompa orange with cracks and wrinkles beneath layers of makeup. Her engine ran purely on carbohydrates and nitrates, and despite her claims to being a certified holistic master chef she never ate anything but candy and beef jerky from the variety of open bowls and bags that she kept at her desk. If Niles could find one kind thing to say about her (and one kind thing was all that was available) it was that she shared her candy with everyone. Her candy wasn't all she shared.

She claimed she never was a stripper in those hard-candy Christmas years of college, but she went out of her way to dress like one because she found that being an anorexically thin and bleached blonde blended well with shirts that showed more skin than ought to have been worn in a secondary school and gave her an edge against people like Niles that she instinctively hated. She wore clothing that showed the cleavage of her withered dugs in defiance of all good sense as a teacher, and sprinkled that crease with sparkles so that it would draw pubescent boys' eyes like crows drawn to shiny gewgaws tossed in the dust to lift her massive ego up out of the dust that drifted off of her in even a weak breeze.

She was hateful of people like Niles who had skills, abilities, and knowledge. She loathed people who had made themselves through hard work and character instead of using hair dye and push-up bras to achieve recognition. They were stupid for doing things the hard way. Everything she received while at school she received from male administrators who were simple-minded enough to fall into a vacant smile, to accept chewy sour gummies, homemade dehydrated beef, and free long, hard looks at her disturbingly bony frame. Niles had never seen a real whore who sold her body to pay for crystal methamphetamine, but thanks to Kringe he knew what one looked like. She looked like she was on year five of the four-year addiction plan. She was a disturbingly emaciated poster model for young girls everywhere about the dangers of self-loathing and anorexia.

Wein was different but the same. Somehow a man had put three children in her and even though she had given birth, she looked like the bulk of each child had remained within her. She was on the track to be a principal herself, so she threw any colleague except for her friends under the school bus at every opportunity, trying to show that she was principal material. She was useless in the classroom, assigning dioramas to high school juniors in honors level classes and spending most of her time at her desk texting a mysterious man that she wasn't married to on her cellphone while claiming that she "had to be connected to her children." That was hardly the most mysterious thing that she'd been involved with at the school. She had also managed to make nearly two thousand dollars of charity money that the students had collected for water in Flint disappear into her own brand new top of the line tablet computer without any member of the administration turning their heads. She was as dishonest as she was unlikeable, and she was as unlikeable as she was ugly.

Niles didn't care for her either way, choosing to ignore her unless she confronted him. She, however, would not be ignored. She made sure that Niles knew who and what she was because she was proud of it, and he and everyone like him had better pay attention to her because she was the best. Of course, what she was best at had nothing to do with teaching, but that didn't stop her from trying to blow her own horn at every opportunity. She and Kringe both hated Niles.

The significant thing that those four English department stalwarts had in common was that they all played favorites with students in the classroom and didn't make the slightest effort to hide it from anyone. They were adolescents gone sour with age and fallen into psychological rot. They picked out the popular students and allied with them in classroom, going so far as to not just condone the bullying of the weaker students, but also to be themselves the biggest bullies in the classroom gaining size by making unpopular students feel smaller in the quest to fatten their already overfed egos.

They would all elect each other department head in good time. Niles wanted no part of it or them.

12. French

The heat was a real problem, one that was touchable and fragrantly unavoidable. It went far above and beyond mere classroom temperature, wafting over bodies that were more distracted by simply the temperature of their own skin. Adolescents in the grip of hormonal changes and base drives that they could not understand were sometimes more dangerous than anything else in the classroom. Every year there were news stories spread across the country of teachers who'd succumbed to the heat, and there were likely many more tales untold of young teachers who'd given in to the the temptation of raging unfiltered sexual drives bursting like flowers in the spring.

Being a young man in a classroom full of pubescence was a trap, or at least that's what Niles was told through much of his preparation to become a teacher. If he'd made a dollar each time he was warned never to be alone in a classroom with a student and had wisely invested that dollar, he'd have been able to retire comfortably well off and five years early. Men were sex criminals waiting to happen in educational circles. Few men joined the ranks of elementary teachers because every one of them was suspect. Even though the positive impact of male role models on young children from fatherless homes was immeasurable there would never be enough of them working in elementary education.

The key to being someone meaningful was to be something different to each student. Something desirably safe and yet undesirable. To some students Niles could be the fun uncle, to others the caring father figure, or an older, wiser brother of sorts. To some he could be the "cool" teacher who was sensitive to the struggles of being a teen like Trudeau, whom every student loved and admired. The most challenging complication was trying to be what each one needed while also teaching the content and material. It was fortunate in that regard that some students didn't need him at all and that some didn't want anything to do with him. For those, he just brought content and patience. They were much less trying than the others but were also necessary for the classroom environment to function. Students like the last ones were the norm according to television and movies and even in districts outside of where Niles worked, but in his the numbers of students who needed more than just a content lecturer were a strong majority.

Niles knew all of these things because he watched and listened. He was self-aware and watched the students in his classes and observed the other teachers when he could. He heard the things that students said to each other because they didn't know how to temper their own tone or volume. An observer like Niles who studied and wanted to learn could know things. He knew about the assistant girls' volleyball coach who was far too excited about hugging as many of the girls as he could and gave all of them his personal phone number. He knew which teachers rode to school together in the mornings and then rode together to other places before going home each night.

Anytime a young teacher was surrounded by sweating adolescents there was an element of danger for both parties. Scents triggered drives, and drives triggered emotions, and emotions made both sexes susceptible to miscues and errors in judgment that could kill careers. and torpedo plans for the future. The female teachers he knew always seemed to display better judgment than the males. The boys were always cast as the predators, hitting on nubile young interns as though they were hunters shooting deer in a pen, feeling so certain of success as to ignore any sense of propriety that had ever before taken root in their hormone-addled brains.

Sometimes the young women working in the school had been too eagerly man-like in their reactions to the flirtations of their young male charges. Niles recalled painfully the young red-haired teacher who'd foolishly allowed some members of the varsity basketball team to record her with a mouthful of the team's star player. That was more than just a lapse of judgment. That was an error of conscience, and one that should have brought her career to a crashing halt in a courtroom of outraged parents. Perhaps it would have if the sexes had been reversed, but she was protected by people higher than she was on the chain of responsibility whom she'd also had a mouthful of. So cash was transferred and threats regarding silence were made and the videos and photos only surfaced when the holders were secure that only rumors would spread and not facts.

Most of the students didn't care about rumors or facts when the heat caught them. Part of the forebrain was switched off. The frontal lobes were drowned in hormones and the teens become slaves to their own ascending libidos. A good teacher could illustrate healthy boundaries for them: how to be close without being too close, how to be proper in the context of propriety, and even how to be discreet when they were overwhelmed.

The poor teens caught in the throes of new, intense, and consuming drives would not be able to learn through observation. Desire created a tunnel vision that didn't allow the obvious through. Niles would pull a student aside after class and speak with him or her in an oblique fashion to let that student know what he and others around them could see and how it might be interpreted. Oftentimes, getting caught being indiscreet was enough to bring their senses back for a few moments or days. The student would apologize for having been so obvious and make adjustments. That was all that it took. Sometimes. Pointing out the obvious to people who were so caught up in their secrets that they overlooked it was usually enough to bring them back to a certain indefinable sense of self-awareness.

And yet none of these things mattered in the heat of the moment, in the heat of a classroom filled with unwashed bodies, sweating scents pungently embedded in the carpets and cinder block walls, scents too close to sex and too far from religion and guilt to lead character to better choices because no choice seemed better than to indulge one's desires when the painfully hungry throb in the back of the skull and the base of the spine kept beating in time to a faster heartbeat than was carried in the chest of a hungry beast that was less god than devil and less devil than animal hungry for a short taste of connective bliss. That was where ego and desire had met churning in a maelstrom of passion, and people were swallowed up. That was the heat of a classroom. Awareness and discipline were Niles's twin rod and staff of righteousness, and they protected him as he walked through the valley of the shadow of sex.

It was always worst in the spring, as the atmosphere churned with pent-up frustrations, it became a broiling pot of conflicted emotions, a pressure cooker filled with hormones and flesh and feelings that students didn't know how to process or refine into something sweeter or more nutritious than pure unadulterated lust and all of it was always driven by the heat. There were thirty-five seething personalities jammed together into too tight a space and their tempers were far from the only thing that flared. There were fights surely, but other things too, more potent and less dangerous to the immediate bystanders. It was one thing to get caught by a chair that was thrown by an angry teen, but it was another painful thing to get caught in the chemical bath, the pheromone stew of spring.

The building heat was always on long past the point where spring in Michigan required it. Then, it took several weeks before the air conditioning was turned on, always only after two weeks of early May ninety degree days - a weather phenomenon that was all too regular each year. There was a period where it was hellish, where the unfiltered air inside was a musty broth of humid repellence. Building services responded to the yearly complaints and multiple work orders with "the system takes time to switch over" and Niles had to imagine that it took multiple giant levers pulled and pushed simultaneously in cavernous underground machine spaces, giant tracks on which cyclopean pneumatic-powered temperature elements were changed over, huge chemical bath pools were emptied and refilled, all of this requiring hundreds of man hours, like some sort of childhood fever dream born of Fritz Lang's Metropolis.

The truth was beyond Niles's imaginings. When the school was first constructed in the 1970s there was a "Building Engineer" whose job included monitoring the school's temperature and changing the air filters, as well as supervising in real time all of the building services staff who were unionized employees of the school district. He was "let go" in the early 80s in a cost saving measure, and since then not only had none of the building's air filters ever been checked or changed, but also there was no one to adjust the temperature using the simple thermostat that was locked in a wall box just outside the room that had been his office in the bowels of the building. In Niles's time, it took weeks for one of the superintendents downtown to find the key that was necessary then take the three mile drive to the school building to make the adjustment. In the meantime the students suffered, the staff suffered, and everyone was pushed to their psychological extremes.

It was foolish and short-sighted to believe that men and women were immune to biological urges based on scent, and Niles's undergraduate psychology books barely gave such a notion a passing mention. "Humans have no known response to pheromone cues as the olfactory apparatus which corresponds to certain mammalian sensory inputs is either atrophied or non-existent..." Even before he had his own classroom Niles knew that statement wasn't true. He had evidence - granted, it was all anecdotal, but powerful nonetheless. He remembered his own reactions well: months stuck in the overheated classrooms of his youth. He had thought that his years spent in the barns growing up would have deadened his sense of smell, but it was as powerful as ever even though cow manure no longer offended his nose. His sense of smell had lost its delicacy at the same pace he had lost his youth.

There was the ever-present stench of the boys' locker room. It was always the same. Never a pleasant odor, merely one that had to be accepted because it was everywhere that young men sweated. Niles never had the chance to ask any of the girls if it smelled as awful to them as it did to him. The girls' locker room didn't smell at all - not that he'd ever gotten close enough to it to catch the lightest odor. It was on the other side of the gym and as taboo to him in his teens as it was as an adult. Other people in the building didn't handle the situation as Niles did.

Niles was a teacher. A good teacher always tried to teach whatever needed to be taught in the hours in the classroom while also attending to the dangers around him. Not all of those things were specifically related to the academic discipline. Not all of the dangers to be avoided were from other adults, and not all of the threats to professional life and limb were intentional.

Niles was sitting in his classroom during his fourth block planning period at the end of the day, grading student work. His classroom at the time was right across the hallway from the Freshman Principal's office on the third floor. He kept his door open most of the time unless things in the hallway were too rowdy, and so far that day it was quiet.

He was too absorbed in grading to notice as a student named Alice popped in the door. She was in his first period Honors English class. She carried a large piece of poster board and a package of watercolor paints in one hand and a pass from her art teacher in the other.

"What's up, Mr. Niles?"

He looked up in surprise. "You snuck up on me! Same old same old - grading papers. What are you doing back up here on the third floor?"

"Too many obnoxious kids down in my art class, so I asked the teacher if I could come up here to work. Is that okay?"

"Absolutely. I like people who want to work quietly."

She sat down at a desk facing Niles and laid her paper down flat.

"I need some water. Do you have a cup?"

Yep, over there in that gray cabinet is a bag of styrofoam cups. Just grab one."

"I didn't know you were a coffee drinker, Mr. Niles."

"I'm not. Stuff tastes like mud." It's a waste of perfectly good water."

"Then why do you have to the cups?"

"That is a good question." He leaned back in his chair, stretched his shoulders and straightened his neck "They were here when I inherited the room, and I kept them in case some diligent student like you needed them for her watercolor assignment."

"Really?"

"Close enough."

"Can I borrow one to get some water for these paints?"

"I'll do you one better. I'll let you have the cup." He grinned at her avuncularly. She smiled back and walked out to fill the cup with water.

As she walked across the hall to the fountain, a noise that had been building in the distance grew more urgent and near. Two students who were still engaging in a profanity-filled argument were being brought down the hallway toward the principal's office by campus security guards. Alice ducked back in the door just as they reached the principal's office.

"Jeez. Is it okay if I shut the door?"

Niles thought about that for a long second. That was not an easy decision. He'd been told as an intern and as a young teacher to never let himself be alone in a classroom with a closed door with just one student. There was a logical reason for that, but the logic was based on a cultural assumption that any male authority figure would use his power to take advantage of a situation with a young naive student. Niles had no desire to take advantage of anything or anyone except perhaps an opportunity to work in peace and quiet shut away from the violent language that the principal could not control across the hallway. Alice was a straight A student whose mother was a teacher in another building in the district. She was actually a rare triple threat: an A student, all-conference athlete, and budding artist with exceptional talent for her age.

Naively, Niles said, "Sure." She shut the door and went back to her seat, still facing him. He continued to focus on his grading, gradually moving papers from one stack to the other as he made comments and notes with one hand and typed grades in the online grade book with the other. The room was quiet, and the cursing outside was muffled by the door.

Niles would only glance up as Alice made artist-in-action noises, like smoothing the paper, sighing and dipping her watercolor brush. Fifteen quiet minutes passed that way, and the noise outside in the hallway died back down to nothing as he was absorbed in his grading.

Alice stood up and stretched, raising her arms high above her head and did a backbend. She was dressed well that day - it must have been an away game day for her team thought Niles. She was wearing a black dress ending two inches above the knees with finger-width straps and uncovered shoulders. She kicked off her black dress flats and wandered around the fringes of the room opposite, seemingly searching for inspiration for her art. Niles looked back down and focused on his work. She came back to her desk and sat on the top of it, still facing him.

"How's grading going?"

Niles looked up at her. She was sitting in a masculine power pose, legs spread, body back slouching, hands on the desk. His eyes instinctively trailed up from the paper on his desk to her bare feet and then up her exposed legs and his heart skipped a beat. He glimpsed the shadow where he could not ever look and turned pale white as he shot his attention directly to her eyes. He was speechless for what seemed like an eternity, but locked on to her eyes with laser intensity. Suddenly his absent mind came back and brought the scene into focus.

"Almost done" passed out of his suddenly parched throat.

He quickly assessed the situation. Clearly this innocent girl had no idea about the not-so-subtle message of her body language. The door was closed. Niles tried not to make his sense of panic obvious. "Only eyes, only eyes" kept echoing in his head on a parallel track to the conversation that she engaged him in. This was neither a

Humbert vision of Dolores, nor was it a bewitching Lolita. It was just a child, a child trying on metaphorical clothes that were too big for her. Just a kid. Niles knew what to do with children who played with fire that they didn't understand. Protect them. Always protect them.

He took a drink from his water bottle and went back to grading the papers, cleared his still dry throat and continued on as if he hadn't just dodged a speeding bus driven by a driver too young to reach the pedals and the steering wheel at the same time. She lost interest in that moment too, sat down in a chair facing the window and continued to paint. Mr. Niles had proven to be just another boring teacher. He got up and opened the door, walked out to pretend to be interested in hearing more about something he had not actually heard in the hallway. Alice took no notice.

Later, after the school day was over and Alice had gone to get on the bus, Niles took time to reflect on that explosive situation that he had just dodged. He knew that he was right about her. There was no way a fifteen-year-old girl was out to seduce her English teacher twice her age. Not this one, anyway. He'd made a mistake by allowing her to close the door, and he'd handled the rest of the situation as well as he could given that first mistake.

She did know part of what she was doing though. She was playing with her power, testing it on an older man - as a young woman might want to do, as any young person stretching their growing arms and legs might do. She was smart enough to know what she was doing, but also trusting and confident enough to know that she could depend on Mr. Niles to do the right thing. He was safe. She'd gotten what she wanted from him even though he was a bit too naive for his own good. He had acknowledged the power that she had, even when the state still considered her to be legally a child. She was validated, and she wouldn't have to test it again in an unsafe situation where things could go wrong quickly.

Niles could have done something stupid and naively put himself into a position where he lost his job and more. It was one of those places where without knowing it, he'd allowed someone else to push the boundaries a bit too far. He learned about his own discipline and self-control and about the importance of always looking into people's eyes to gauge their intent. Eyes weren't just the gateway to the soul, they were also the gateway to the mind and keeping his mind focused on the fact that he worked with children was going to be one of the most important things he could do. Not everyone saw things as Niles did.

Henry "Hungry" Lee was a fixture in the building for over thirty years. He'd been a student there and went right to the local college and then from there right back to the school as a teacher. After that, it had become a local tradition to avoid ever allowing a student to matriculate into a teacher in the same district because Lee had not stopped dating high school girls from the building. As the years passed even after he married a woman ten years his junior, he never stopping trying to treat all of the high school girls in the building as if he were a sixteen-year-old boy seeking dates, or to staring at their bodies as if trying to evaluate their reproductive potential.

Lee was never not looking. The girls knew that he was looking. Sometimes they told other teachers or the principal that he made them feel uncomfortable, but no one in authority trusted teenage girls to understand when they were being objectified. Still, administration knew that he was looking. But Lee came from a great local family. A family of educators. His father was a teacher and the school's football coach for thirty-five years, his mother was a teacher. Lee had a local pedigree.

It wasn't tenure that protected him, it was the complacence of the administrators that allowed him and his rapacious eyes to continue to feast. His wife had been a victim of his eyes when she was a student, but she thought she would change him, that she could save him from himself and his hunger. She couldn't, so she also followed suit with the school administration and turned a blind eye.

Even after Lee had found the internet and started using it at school to find more long-lasting images of teenage girls, the administration kept looking away as if that would make him stop. After all, it could have been worse. He could have been printing off the pictures he'd found using the school printer, using the expensive colored ink that the school provided.

Of course, the situation escalated because it went unchecked and because his urges grew. He began printing the pictures he found on Facebook of his students on the school printer. Then one afternoon he forgot to pick up his pictures from the tray. Some students found them and were caught by the librarian at a dark table in the library.

The photos were tracked back to Lee's computer. The time of printing was tracked back to before school before the students had even gotten off the bus. It was inevitable that the boys would have to be disciplined, but what about Lee?

An administrator from the district office downtown came to address Lee before his building administrator did, to talk to him specifically about how he could better protect his computer from the students who must have hacked it and put those things in his browser history dating back months in order to try to incriminate him. He got a full course on covering his own tracks on the computer and about using a password that wasn't written on a sticky note on the top left of the computer monitor.

Lee did change his password, but he kept forgetting it, so he had to have it reset four times by IT before he just wrote it down on a sticky note that he taped to his desk next to his computer. Then one day when he was taking one of his many mental health days, the substitute teacher found the note and guessed correctly that it was the computer password. He used it to access his personal email at lunch and then forgot about it. The computer was still logged in when he left the room at the end of the day and forgot to close the door, when a couple of students dropped in to use it to update their social media accounts. When they discovered that it was left open on Lee's login they decided to look through all of his files, looking for answer keys or upcoming tests. They didn't find any upcoming tests, but they did find files on a flash drive left plugged in to the back of the computer containing photos of several female students that had been downloaded from social media.

After sending all of the photos they found (including some swimsuit photos) to themselves, they reported their find to their parents who took it to some of the parents of the girls. It took two weeks, but as the stink started to rise Lee was finally called into the office where he stated that "clearly the flash drive was the work of the substitute teacher who'd been in that day to 'hack' his computer."

The substitute was tracked down at home and questioned by the police that evening, who found his long-term involvement in a committed gay relationship to be less than convincing in their investigation. He was invited to never work in education again, but the hammer had dropped a little too close to home again for Lee. He was already thinking of taking some paid "administrative leave" when another clandestine visit from an unnamed downtown district administrator convinced him that such a thing was an excellent idea.

It was good to have friends in the downtown administrative offices.

Henry "Hungry" Lee took his pay and benefits for his final five years from PSPS in a severance package and ended up somewhere else. Where that was, Niles would never know, but he hoped it wasn't in another classroom. The next year, Niles moved downstairs to the second floor to teach upperclassmen.

Taryn French was the Canadian transplant with the French last name who taught Spanish and had a flair for the mediocre that often dipped below mediocre in terms of effectiveness. She was tall, aged, white, and as polite as a Calgary debutante -- which for some reason meant that she didn't mesh well with her black students, even though she had been married thrice to three black American men and had six children that resulted from those marriages, keeping a perfect average of two children per husband as if it were that and not time or something else that drove them apart.

By the time that Niles met her, she was divorced again and on the prowl for younger men. It made for awkward interactions at best, especially when a young black man started teaching next door to her and across from Niles. He'd grown up in Pianosa Springs as well, and had spent time working in the segregated schools of the deep south during his internship. His specialty was math, but he was also highly effective at working with the school's young black men as a role model and mentor. All of the girls in Niles's English classes thought that he was quite fine and so did French. She started wearing low-cut blouses that displayed a cleavage that resembled nothing else so much as a box of candles left on the heater. It was difficult for Niles to look her in the eye in the same way that it was impossible not to look at an interstate car crash.

On her sixtieth birthday, she wore tight leather pants and purposely dropped a stack of copies on the floor in the hallway between Niles and the new teacher. She then huffed, puffed, and almost passed out as she shimmied and shook across the floor to pick up the papers, making sure that her posterior was aimed at the young teacher. It was the most frightening thing Niles had seen in ages from his spot in the hallway. The young teacher looked at Niles for guidance on what to do as she paraded her goods in front of him. Niles shrugged his shoulders and furrowed his brow. What should anyone do when confronted with such an inappropriate vision? As scarring as it was for Niles, he felt that there was more scarring going on in her classroom. She was a flesh and blood Peggy Hill in ill fitting clothes and was only on par for excellence with a substitute for a substitute.

She gathered the papers up and shuffled toward her classroom, looking back at the new teacher seductively over her shoulder with all the sexual power of a dairy cow in heat. He shuddered visibly and dipped into his classroom. The rude energy was more than he could bear.

Niles laughed in spite of himself. "Have you guessed the riddle yet?" He said quietly to no one at all.

"No, I give it up," he replied to himself. "What's the answer?'

"I haven't the slightest idea." He said and turned back through his classroom door.

French didn't win the young man's heart, but she didn't have time to as he left for greener pastures out west when summer came.

The cold each autumn and winter was as dangerous as the heat of spring and summer, but the effects upon the staff couldn't have been more different. Heat made people ill-mannered and ill-tempered. Cold just made them ill.

Everyone got sick. Students got sick and kept coming to school. Teachers got sick and couldn't take a day off. Classrooms became cacophonies of sniffles, sneezes, and coughs. Tissues were consumed by the crate. Fevers, so different from the fevers of spring, raged.

Niles slid down the door on his back and crouched on the floor. The last students of the last class before the winter holiday break were noisily breaking for the exits to the bus. Across the hallway on the Freshman floor, Duckett took notice.

"Are you okay?" She asked with apparent concern.

"I'm okay. Just utterly exhausted."

Niles had walked the halls and classroom for over a week with lungs that made the sound of rice cereal popping in milk, and it got louder with each passing day. He couldn't afford to take a day off for being ill, let alone the three or four that was needed to feel nearly well again. The students were already mentally deleting files containing information that they were taught in class to make room for the truly important things they were going to focus on for the next two weeks: video games, reality television, and social media. He wasn't going to give them a substitute teacher and Christmas-themed videos during the last week that they were supposed to be learning. That would have been an unforgivable waste of everyone's time. The curriculum had enough material in it to last far beyond the weeks that they actually had remaining in the semester, and every day before the break counted double toward his efforts.

"Any plans for your break?" She was polite and well-meaning. Niles thought she cared.

"I'm probably going to sleep and try to get well. That is, if it's not too late." He brought up a wet cough from deep in his chest to punctuate his statements.

"Are you always so dramatic?" She frowned.

"Well, I do teach English. And anyone who has known me for longer than a month will testify that I have a great gift for hyperbole. I can exaggerate anything, anytime, anyplace."

"Is that a useful skill?"

Niles cleared his throat.

"I believe that it is. Most people are numb to basic information due to the overwhelming amount that is available, so in order to have an impact on the ways that people think and feel, I believe that I have to punch them in the face with exaggeration."

"Did you come up with that yourself or did you read it somewhere?"

"I believe that it was Aristotle who said to punch people in the face with hyperbole when they don't agree with you. I might be paraphrasing that, but I'm sure that's what he meant if he didn't say it that explicitly."

"So are you really as sick as you seem, or is that more hyperbole?"

"Oh, I really feel like a cold bag of garbage. That's not an exaggeration. That's a simile."

Niles was still crouched on the floor, but his quadriceps were beginning to ache. He didn't have the energy to stand up fully yet. "How about you, what are you doing over break? Working on math?" Niles's nose was plugged with mucus. The "math" sounded like "meth" from his chapped lips.

She smiled and uncrossed her arms. She was clearly excited that he'd asked.

"Well, my husband and I will be working with our church to offer twenty-four hour prayer services at our facility. If you're feeling better, perhaps you could stop by. Some of our masses last twelve hours."

"Well, if you keep talking like that, you're going to really sell me on this. Does it include lots of standing and kneeling in increments like a Catholic mass?"

She laughed shrilly. "No, no! Catholics are apostates! We're real Christians."

"Oh, "real Christians! You guys actually talk about who's real and who's not at your church? Sounds really holy." Niles chuckled and pressed his hands to his knees to lift himself up, sliding back up the door in an inverse of how he'd slid down a few minutes earlier at the beginning of this delightful conversation. "Do you still do the 'gift' thing, or is that too Catholic? I really don't know. I was kind of sheltered, you know? Everybody at my church growing up was Catholic."

"Oh, I'm sorry." She said, but whether she was sorry that he had grown up Catholic, or sorry that she'd just insulted a whole section of Christianity in a very un-Christian way was very unclear to Niles.

"We do gifts too, even though Catholics aren't really Christians." She added, without even the barest hint of irony. It was her naive faith which ran counter to obvious attacks of reason that made Niles fall in love with her when they first met. She was sheepish without being sheepish about it. She had no guile. It made Niles feel sick.

"We're also sponsoring a little African boy for Christmas."

"You're sponsoring him? Sponsoring him for what?"

She pulled her cell phone from a hidden pocket in her smartly tailored vest and brought up a photo of a widely grinning African boy in a New England Patriots 2008 NFL Championship t-shirt holding a thick black leather Bible.

"His care and education, silly."

"It looks like you're educating him silly. Are you making sure they teach him that books filled with symbolism are meant to be taken at literal value?"

She ignored Niles's question and walked back into her classroom to answer the ringing landline on her desk. He already knew what the answer was before he asked, but he wanted to ask to hear her response. The way she ignored him made him think about the origin of the word "ignorance."

Niles wasn't the only one in the building who was sick. There were many teachers who were getting sick, too sick to work in the building. Their maladies ran the gamut from intractable back pain to deep and unremitting ennui. There was a certain outbreak of post-traumatic stress syndrome that was unreliably traced to no specific event or series of small events which forced one special ed teacher to retreat to a career of selling diet patches online. Teachers were falling apart. Tibbs had been acting strange lately so when he was missing without warning leaving an unprepared substitute in his room, Niles was not surprised. Tibbs had gone to his doctor with an ache in his heart that the doctors thought was a bad case of gas in his bowel and been diagnosed with an advanced case of Kalamazoo shingles. He'd gotten a medical leave of absence.

"What the hell are Kalamazoo shingles?' asked Niles.

"That's exactly what the doctors wanted to know!' blurted out Tibbs proudly, and then burst into laughter. No one had ever seen him so effervescent, or so joyous. "There's no such thing as Kalamazoo shingles. Don't you understand? I lied. I made a deal with the doctor. I promised that I would let him know when my Kalamazoo shingles went away if he would promise not to do anything to cure them. He gave me a prescription for antibiotics and sent me home." Tibbs's grin felt infectious. Niles couldn't help but smile. "I never told a lie before. Isn't it wonderful?"

Tibbs had made it up, and it was good. His common sense told him that telling lies and pretending to be too sick to work were bad things to do. Everyone knew that lying was a sin, and sin was evil, and that no good could come from evil. But Tibbs did feel good; he felt positively wonderful. Consequently, it followed with a sort of mathematical logic that telling lies and pretending to be too sick to work could not be sins. The positive numbers had more real-world mass than the negative ones. The math was sound. Tibbs had mastered in a moment of mathematical problem-solving the handy technique of protective rationalization, and he was exhilarated by his discovery. It was pure math: positive over negative.

This all felt strangely familiar to Niles, as if he were living in *Catch 22*: "It was almost no trick at all... to turn vice into virtue and slander into truth, impotence into abstinence, arrogance into humility, greed into philanthropy, theft into honor, blasphemy into knowledge, nationalism into patriotism, and sadism into justice. Anybody could do it; it required no brains at all. It merely required no character." And now Niles was seeing it outside of the book. Except Tibbs had character, and his was based in math.

Any other day of the week, Tibbs was a good teacher. He was getting worn down. Anyone with any logical ability should have been able to see that if a good person were caught in a negative place that they should do whatever they could to escape.

Not every teacher was a Tibbs, though. There was a low bar for being a teacher, and few gatekeepers along the way to say "No. You're not cut for this. Try business instead." Niles could remember one would-be teacher in the university classes when he was little more than a would-be teacher himself. That pre-service teacher was always overflowing with stories of drunken pleasures and epic tales of never-ending parties which blended with accounts of two-day hangovers. He asked one day in a class about teaching practicums if the other people there were "cool" with his plan to be a friend to the students instead of being an authority figure as if it were the most natural thing in the world to want to hang out with teenagers when you were an adult. He wasn't concerned with what the instructor thought about his plan, he simply wanted validation from his peers. Niles lost touch with him after that class but had no doubt that somehow the questionable young teacher had gone on to make many inappropriate friends.

Teachers were humans, and like any random sample of humans there were always poor and ineffective ones mixed with teachers of high quality. Low quality and high quality varied from month to month based on a hundred variables, just like the students' ability to learn. One math teacher fell heavily into the bottle when his wife served him with divorce papers on account of her affair with a police officer. One art teacher used an oversized steaming travel mug of half whisky/ half coffee to get himself going in the morning just to steel himself for the inevitable wads of clay that he was pelted with daily. Then he took a nap at his desk during his plan period whenever the effects of the alcohol overwhelmed the effects of the caffeine. When Niles found that out, he was sad. The art teacher seemed like a good person who didn't know how else to protect himself in the classroom. There was another art teacher who was forced out just as Niles was coming in because she started off each morning by raising her blood alcohol level to a point where she shouldn't have driven to work. It took a year to get her out of the building, but it wasn't due to the efforts of the weak teacher's union. It was due to a lack of diligence on the part of an administrator who felt his time was better spent elsewhere than in working to remove a mess. Apparently, the key to successful alcoholism was to drink on the job and not before.

Niles knew before he became a teacher that truth was always in degrees: by degree of compassion, by degree of fact, by degree of complicity in whichever lie seemed most likely in the moment. That was the only truth of being a human -- that each man and woman had to figure out for him or herself what was right in that particular moment for them. Sometimes the lines between right and wrong were thin or transparent. They seemed to move to one side or the other for certain people. Everyone was a villain, and everyone was a saint - it just depended on who was looking.

Niles was confused by the complexity that seemed to overwhelm what should have been a simple proposition. Everyone was sick, everyone was "good." Everyone was damaged, everyone was fine. The only thing that mattered was the moment in time which was captured by the viewer. In the absence of observation, everyone could have been awful and wonderful all at once. Could have been -- in any place but Pianosa Springs. In Pianosa Springs, every teacher was ineffective and needed constant micro-management.

13. Dr. Conway

Doctor Conway sat in his office in the center of the ground floor and considered how appropriately placed he was. In the very center, close to the foundation. At the heart, or rather, the brainstem of the school. He was the school's overqualified psychologist, actually a psychiatrist and thus able to prescribe medicine by the letter of the law. He was a real doctor, a doctor of medicine, not a doctor of philosophy like Dr. Kaseman, and thusly he was smarter and more able. His medical degree came from the open air classrooms of the University of Trinidad and Tobago. Despite their lack of reputation, he knew that the school was one of the best on the planet, and that he was the man who would make their reputation -- just as soon as his was fully complete.

If all things were decided by brain power alone, he knew that should have been in charge of the district, but he didn't want to be. There were too many pieces and parts to control and manipulate, too many variables that couldn't be controlled. A district superintendent didn't have the means available that he had - didn't have the control. Oh yes, Kaseman's office had the funding, but money was money, and money was beholden to corporate or state interests. Conway considered himself beholden to no one. There in the basement of the high school he could successfully manipulate the meaningful variables in the district: the children.

In a theoretically perfect world, every variable would be controlled in order to create the society that America needed to remain the greatest country in the world. In the messy and complicated real world, there was no way to control for all of the variables that had a strong impact on human academic achievement like poverty, quality of food, sleep, comfort, shelter, emotional connections, and safety. Those things were outside the power of the school psychologist.

Within the power of the school psychologist were things that he could influence on the outside, like children's interactions with teachers and parents.

He leaned back in his chair and imagined a utopia where he controlled the students' lives and made them into whatever they would be. He was a Geppetto without a workshop, a Svengali who needed a Trilby, but one Trilby would never be enough. He needed hundreds, then thousands, and they would help his power grow exponentially.

He'd tried to make his move before, when he first came to the school, replacing the previous school psychologist who'd been excused from his position by being caught with a married special education teacher in a compromised position: She'd savagely had him bent over a table in the copy room with his pants down after hours by a member of the cleaning crew who was searching for a missing broom. She had found more than the broom, and the school psychologist found that he quietly had to update his resume at the end of the school year.

Niles and Geit had found out about the incident through the school grapevine and spent one day's planning period together talking about how fortunate he was to work for this school district where such things were swept under the rug aggressively, and he would only suffer from rumors about how his time at the school had not killed his career, but merely "wrecked him" for a short time.

At Conway's interview when he had been hired, he told Swamp right away that he was interested in methods of control. It was a moment of instantaneous bonding, and they both recognized immediately that they would have exactly the sort of relationship that would benefit the building and the whole staff.

175

"Who cares about controlling the children, what about controlling the teachers? Is there some way we can put them all on drugs so that we can control them? Can we lace some of this stale candy I keep in my office with pills and give it to them on Teacher Appreciation Day?"

Her short-sightedness would have offended Conway if he hadn't seen that her office resembled nothing so much as a enclosed chamber ravaged by a mini-tornado of slovenliness. She was without vision, without comprehension of the importance of order and of the means by which one achieves such a grandiose concept as he had conceived of in the darkness of his office at the brainstem of the school.

"First of all, I don't just have psychoactive drugs on hand, and secondly, do you really think all of the teachers are going to eat your spoiled candy? Some of them are not so stupid as you think... possibly."

But she hadn't heard him. She was busy plotting in her head ways to feed her family tonight, since she was a proper family woman and knew that it was up to her to serve dinner no matter what. Could she feed her family the candy? Perhaps. She unwrapped two pieces of taffy and threw them in her mouth at once. She'd be better able to answer things more clearly with the grace of God and some sugar.

And she'd almost forgotten! "When can you start, Mr. Mindbender?"

"I am Dr. Conway. I can start right away."

"You can? That's wonderful Mr. Conway! It will be a pleasure to have you on the team here where we believe in all of the children, all of the time."

"Please, I'm a doctor--"

"--would you like some of this candy?" She purposely interrupted him without listening. She had to let him know the power structure of the building immediately, and this was clearly the best way to do it. She held out a handful of sticky, aged Jolly Farmer candy inches from his face like the wicked queen stepmother disguised as the poor farmer who proffered the poisoned apple to Snow White after failing to kill her with a comb.

"No thank you, I'm on a sugar-free juice cleanse right now." He eyed the corn syrup product wrapped in petroleum warily. He also saw the moment as an opportunity to make a strong ally: perhaps their goals could coincide. "Which teachers here are ones that are having issues of control? As your new school psychologist, our goals may overlap a bit."

"Control? I don't know. Ask the kids."

She was now tapping furiously on her phone, still attempting to ignore him in a vulgar display of power. He decided that if he only had half or less of her attention that he should speak as directly and plainly as possible.

"May I speak directly and plainly to you, as your new school psychologist?"

"You're the new school psychologist? Who said so? I still have more people to interview."

"You just asked me when I could start and told me it would be a pleasure to have me on the team."

"I did? She seemed genuinely puzzled. "What's your name again?" She fished through a pile of papers on her desk and found a dog-eared sheet that had names and times printed on it.

"Doctor Conway."

"Doctor Conway? Sounds shady..."

Just then her phone buzzed heavily on the desk, causing a small avalanche of plastic binders to slide to the floor to join a pile of cast away candy wrappers. She lurched bodily toward the phone, seizing it before it hit the floor and started tapping furiously on it again.

"You're on the list? You're hired." She turned and then yelled out to her secretary in the next room. "Fatima? Cancel the rest of my psychologist interviews. There's no time."

"Yes, Mrs. Swamp," Fatima responded.

Conway seized the moment. "Excellent, now that that is settled, let's talk about where our goals for the school might overlap."

"Do you know our motto, Mr. Odd?"

"Dr. Conway-"

She interrupted him breathlessly, candy rattling against her teeth. "It's 'Punctuality, attentiveness, decorum, dedica-'"

"Yes, I remember that --" He interrupted her, even though he didn't.

She interrupted him again, candy clicking against her teeth. "My goal is these teachers. I've got to get these teachers in line. These teachers aren't treating the best students with the proper care. I was mistreated as a student, and I'm here to make sure these teachers don't do it again to my children."

His eyes lit up. Revenge. He could work with that.

"Which of your staff in particular? I could begin to talk with them, schedule some sessions, have them put on antidepressants or antipsychotics or anti-anxiety medications."

"Not these teachers, my teachers."

Conway needed clarification. "Your teachers that you had thirty years ago?"

"Yes, all teachers."

"Are you talking about these teachers here on your staff, or about your teachers that you had when you were a girl."

"I'm talking about teachers. They all need to know." Her eyes grew moist and steely at the same time. "They need to know that what they did to me was wrong."

"Yes, I can see that now."

"Dr. Conway, do you know Jesus?"

Dr. Conway had to pause to think about that before he answered. He did know Jesus. He went to school with him in Trinidad. He pronounced Jesus with the anglo-English "J" sound instead of the Caribbean-Spanish "H" and he had long stringy, dirty hair and tattoos of the stigmata on both sides of each hand. The likelihood of her also knowing this same man was remote, so he carefully weighed a "yes" before letting it slip out. She noted his pause and lack of religious fervor.

"I do know him, Doctor. I speak to him everyday. And he speaks to me." Tears welled in her eyes as she leaned toward him, invading his personal space in a show of power. Conway was taken aback, but tried harder not to show it in this moment as he unwittingly had in the one before. He looked around at her office, thinking that it resembled nothing so much as the dumpster in front of the University of Trinidad and Tobago on the last day of classes as reams of paper, mountains of notebooks, and boxes of files were all unceremoniously tossed into the bin.

"That's beautiful, Mrs. Swamp. And this, this is your divine mission?" He lifted his eyes toward heaven, to show that he was on the same page of her particular Bible.

"Yes, yes, I am here to show these teachers the way, to guide them toward a heavenly retribution for the way that teachers always fail to recognize the greatness of people like me who are chosen by

God for special things." She clasped her hands as if in prayer, and gazed heavenward with him as he mirrored her prayerful pose. He felt like making the sign of the cross, but he didn't. Maybe next time. He would build toward that.

"When can I move into my office?" He didn't want to ruin the moment, but his patience for psychosis was wearing thin. Her manner changed on a dime. Her faced snapped into Blue Steel. Her cellular phone was vibrating wildly again in her breast pocket, making her bosom look possessed.

"The office is open. I blessed it this morning to rid it of the Satanic influences of the former occupant who believed in science. Before you move any of your things in, I think that we should pray together in the room. I can't do it now though, I have important matters to attend to." She took her phone from her pocket and resumed violently tapping on it.

"Very well. I will return to my home to gather my necessary things and return soon. I will let you know when I arrive so that we can pray together before I install myself."

She was no longer paying attention to him but did manage to wish him a "blessed day" on his way out of the office. This was perfect. He'd have to be cautious, but he could easily play her to his advantage. He could find a way for their goals to coincide. He could manipulate her and everyone here to achieve his goals.

Here, everything would be made perfect.

Pianosa Springs Central High School had several functions, both legitimate and illegitimate. One of the legitimate functions was the socialization of the younger members of the community. One of the ways to certify that a society endured was to inculcate deeply into the young a mindless loyalty to particular symbols. Those symbols could be money or something more nationalistic, like a flag. That socialization kicked into overdrive in the US after the events of 9/11 and the after-effects of those heady days of flag-waving spending money to "defeat the terrorists" lingered through several generations of public attention span. One of those effects was a sort of publicly mandated admiration for the flag, and an outgrowth of that was a new state law that said that every teacher in every public school classroom had to "make time" for students to recite the Pledge of Allegiance.

In the minds of the state legislators, that couldn't be done unless extra taxpayer money were thrown into the winds of blind patriotism, so they settled on granting tens of thousands of those dollars to the schools to make sure that they had brand new flags. Of course, the flags that most of the classrooms had were still in fine condition because most of the teachers were aces at following the rules regarding handling those flags.

When the new flag arrived in Niles's room during one of his classes, he tried to return it. "I still have the old one. Maybe you can give this one to a more deserving classroom?"

"Nope. We got a couple hundred of these. The district received the money to be spent only on flags. We have a lot of flags. Everyone gets a new flag." The security guard who brought it in was less than enthusiastic about his task for the day.

Niles took the flag and added it to his flag collection, which he had just increased by 100 percent in one day! He had 200 percent more flags than most people who didn't have a classroom had, and that surely resulted in 200 percent more nationalism.

At the same time that the political ruckus was going on about putting more flags in classrooms so that children wouldn't forget where they were, there was another concurrent flag themed attention-getter on news channels and in public media: flag burning. Every few years when some elected buffoon needed a bump in the polls, they fabricated a new media fascination with flag burning and loudly took a stand against it. Niles felt that there was only one way to intelligently protest. He had to draw some kind of attention to the absurdity of the whole situation.

The next day, there was a fire drill. On the way out the door after the last of the students, Niles took both of this flags. Bradley from across the hall asked Niles what he was doing.

"I can't let these burn, that would be disrespecting the flag."

Niles walked out to the student parking lot in a mock goose step, waving a flag high and straight in each arm.

Ray Roberts walked up to him, "What's with the flags?"

"I can't let them burn."

"It's just a fire drill."

"I have to practice keeping them safe. Isn't the point of a fire drill to run through all of the procedures that you'd have to employ in the event of an actual fire?"

"Well, yeah, but-"

"But intentionally allowing a flag to burn is virtually the same thing as setting it aflame yourself, isn't it?"

Roberts shook his head and walked away. Niles just continued to wave his twin flags as if he were some sort of hyper-patriotic and demented color guard while his students looked on, mildly amused at the banality of his absurdity.

No one understood why he did it. They just looked at each other and said, "He's crazy."

Most people misunderstood Niles and his sense of humor, but that was hardly the only thing they misunderstood. Niles was surrounded by people who misunderstood basic kindness and how it worked. Linn and Demarr for example. At least they weren't religious in their condemnation of Niles. Theirs came from a deeper and much more profound place. Sometimes people had their prejudices bred so deeply into their foundations that they had no idea they were awful.

Niles's first several department meetings with the ELA facilitator were all the same those first few years. He was wide-eyed and bushy-tailed as they say, and fresh for the grinder. She was a component of that grinder.

Mrs. Daisy was a product of a southern college, a fair alumnus of a grand system cultivated in the soils of slavery and share-cropping. She was a perfect southern dame, a true debutante who blossomed like a flower in the segregated south, the institutions of Jim Crow singing the song that made the background music for her own education.

"We have a population that cannot read or write at grade level. We need to provide these students with alternative methods to show what they know" was a constant refrain of her song of the south.

Niles was young and inexperienced. All of the people with more age and experience than he were nodding their heads in agreement with the speaker.

"Our assessment protocols need to change to meet our learners where they are at."

Niles looked at the people with him, who should have known what they were all doing.

"Failing our students or labeling them as failures will not help them."

Niles thought that made a lot of sense. After all, they were tasked with helping the students. That would clearly be helping the students to pass their classes.

"We have to shift away from straight writing to doing performance-based assessments. Not all of our kids are going to become writers," she said. Niles didn't realize at the time that she meant "our minority students won't become writers, so don't try to teach them." He hadn't yet learned the truth of the institutionalized racism built into the system that he was laboring in. He didn't yet see that the Southern Belle didn't know it either. She wasn't self-aware enough to know, and so she was teaching those teachers to lower their expectations for their black students too, just as she had been taught to all those years ago in the Southern college.

Niles looked at these assembled teachers here, so many years of experience. So many years of working as teachers. Surely this must be the correct thing.

And it was. Niles worked hard to follow the established patterns of the building, to fit into the culture. He watched as the older, more experienced teachers would assign "multi-genre projects" to avoid asking students to write, every year that he was there.

"Let's break into groups of three and brainstorm some ways together for students to show their knowledge without writing. There are markers on your tables, and let's use these large pieces of poster paper to assemble your groups' ideas visually so that we can present them to the larger group," said Mrs. Daisy.

That was the pattern that Niles was to use. Students could be artists, they didn't have to be writers. They could express their knowledge through posters and art. This would make them whole, complete adults who could function as contributors to a better world. Many ideas came spilling out onto the table. Students could make dioramas out of shoeboxes, they could cut pictures from magazines to create collages, they could craft multi-genre pieces of art using clay, paint, and barbie dolls to express the themes of the books that they found on online. They would have to think hard, except that they wouldn't.

They used their phones to look for what other people had posted online about what the themes of the books were and then thumbed through old magazines looking for pictures they thought were "cool" to cut and paste onto their collages, effectively taking other peoples' art and photos, throwing them together and claiming the piece as an original act. High school students used sculpting clay and markers to copy ideas that they found online with nary an original process in mind, and taped and glued them into old shoeboxes. It was like pouring cereal and milk into a bowl and claiming that it was an original creation. And the English department loved it. It was so easy to grade. Linn and Demarr and the others looked upon each collection of unoriginal breakfast in a bowl and saw that it was good and so easy to "grade."

"I like this one. I'll give it an A." "This student got a bit mouthy in class and didn't give me the respect I felt that I deserved. He failed." "This student made me cookies, she gets a B." This seemed to be the rubric with which Linn and Demarr scored their students.

Niles looked at it all when he was doing it too and said to himself, "This is not what we should be doing. There is no deeper level thinking going on here. There is no synthesis or evaluation, or even in some cases, comprehension going on here. A student doesn't have to read a book or even listen to classroom discussion, let alone take part in it to look for a few highlighted phrases on a webpage and then cut and paste someone else's work together to call their own." It was the equivalent of copying and pasting from two or more different web pages into a word processing document and then claiming it as one's own personal work. Students did that all of the time too, and none of the other teachers seemed to catch them. Or care. Niles did though, even though he wasn't supposed to by Daisy's method.

Niles felt a certain way about writing though, a way that some philosophers and teachers had thought before him, that it was a necessary step toward processing thoughts and feelings on a level that transcended the more basic reactive animal reasoning.

A feeling is felt, not reasoned, not rationalized, or thought. A feeling is a start. Animals have feelings, sensations and responses. People do too, but they're not supposed to stop there. Many do stop there because they don't know any more than that. An English teacher, more than any other high school teacher is supposed to teach students how to think. A multi-genre collage doesn't get a student to parse out and examine his thoughts, doesn't get her to trace the lines to ask herself why she feels what she feels. A diorama can't prepare a human for a lifetime of being assaulted from all directions by lies and half-truths, advertising and propaganda.

A poster or a collage in English class taught a student how to make a poster or a diorama because the teacher herself didn't have any idea about what skills cutting and pasting actually cultivated. That was the bailiwick of the art teacher. Niles wondered why he was the only one who thought that.

14. Kaseman

The knock on the door came ten minutes after Niles had settled down at his desk during his plan period to grade essays and just ten seconds after his head hit the desk the first time in frustration. He sighed hard and leapt up and sprinted across the room to answer the energetic knocking.

"Whoa!" Niles almost hit the student who was standing within the compass swing of the door, sending the boy rocking back on his heels. "Mr. Niles, can I hang out here for a while?"

Niles's right eyebrow rocked upward as if a spring snapped.

"Uh, why?"

"Because Mr. Freyburger is showing Forrest Gump again, and I can't sit through it anymore."

"Does he know you're here? Did he give you a pass?"

"I don't know."

"What do you mean, 'you don't know' if he gave you a pass? It's a little slip of paper with his name and your name on it that—"

"No, I didn't get a pass. He was too busy explaining how Jenny probably had gonorrhea or something at the end."

"What?" Niles replied incredulously, "He spoiled the ending? That lousy spoiler!"

"Well only kinda. I mean he has shown the movie in class four times now."

"In that case, get in here. I am grading your papers though. If you distract me too much, I might accidentally give you a worse grade than you deserve."

The student dashed through the doorway eagerly almost before Niles had even moved out of his way. Niles had compassion for the student's suffering. The movie was an ordeal after the first viewing. Niles wondered how any teacher could submit students to so much unnecessary pain. For some, a movie was the only way to make it through the week. Freyburger was that kind of educator.

Freyburger was part of the Social Studies department, but he may not have actually been a teacher. Nobody could seem to remember when he was hired in. He had just been there the whole time like a tree in the yard that didn't seem to grow. He had to have been old, but he didn't look like it. He was a man-child perpetually stuck in mid-life crisis mode.

He was average in height, but above average in width around the midsection. His belly bubbled out like a dollar store balloon from China with a weak spot, and Niles often wondered how he could walk down a hill without tumbling over with such a pregnant center of gravity. He somehow managed to buy only polo shirts for extra short men so that the bottom of his belly would protrude above his belt line like an inverted hairy cleavage. And he wore khaki cargo pants that looked like the pockets were filled with sand. He was the uncle that everyone had but no one could remember. What was it with the Social Studies department and polo shirts and cargo shorts anyway?

He was a good teacher when people were watching, but sometimes people didn't watch enough. When no one was watching, he'd discovered that he would have more time to devote to his six children at home and his second job if he did all of his grading and planning while he was still at school, so showing movies became a standard part of his lesson plans. Movies were easy. There were always plenty of them in the dollar bins of the second-hand stores around town and they required almost as little an investment of time as they did money. Perhaps most importantly though, students would usually sit quietly and watch. If the only measure of teaching success was that students were quietly seated, then showing a film was an easy path to a meaningful victory.

In his second year as superintendent, Dr. Kaseman took a stand against those easy victories. It was his best policy move. The memorandum prohibited whole films being shown in class and said that twenty-minute clips of relevant films could be shown if and only if the lesson plans of that teacher could tie each movie clip to a minimum of four different State Standards in that particular content area. The memorandum didn't impact Niles at all, as he was too idealistic to have resorted to the "No one gives a damn, show a movie" lesson plan, but some of the other teachers panicked. Having to suddenly replace thirty percent of their lesson plans on short notice added a great deal of stress to the lives of people who were already highly stressed.

That elevated level of stress lasted for two weeks and four days. Within those fourteen school days a handful of the movie-showing teachers went ahead with their normal lesson plans, "policy memorandum be damned!" They continued turning in those same lesson plans the next two weeks without a peep of protest or any sign from the building administrators that they were going to be put in check or even monitored. This cemented as fact the suspicion that "no one in administration cared" and a general sigh of relief washed over the staff as the loud clear message was once again to continue the standard operating procedure as it was. To Niles, it was a clear SNAFU.

"Mr. Niles? Can I get a pass to come here whenever he shows a movie? I promise I'll just sit quietly and do my homework."

"Yes. Anytime."

Wasting time was a necessity in education, but Niles could find no reason to waste more time than was being wasted anyway by all of the things that teachers were required to do. Many meetings were scheduled to meet a state requirement regarding teacher train-

189

ing hours, but no administrative planning went into making sure that those mandated training hours were more than wasted time. For most of the staff, being at the meeting was just as edifying as not being at the meeting and much less meaningful.

Geit and Niles were both dawdling that day. Both exhausted and ground down by the wheels of the machinery to which they pledged their service. The "Professional Development" was scheduled directly after school, but instead of following the rest of the staff like cattle to their appointed pens they both left immediately in Niles's pickup.

Earlier that day, between second and third periods, Geit shuffled in a crowd past Niles's door: "Hey, can I ask a favor?"

"Sure. What's up?"

"I had to drop my car off at the mechanic this morning, and my wife brought me to work. I have to pick up the car tonight, and the shop closes at 4. My wife can't come get me. I don't want to ride the bus. Can you give me a quick ride over there?"

"Absolutely. Any reason to miss another worthless P.D."

"Great. I need you to drive me to Texas. Maybe Mexico. It depends on how quickly they find the hooker in the trunk." Geit smirked at him.

Niles pumped his fist. "I'd always wanted to be a fugitive! I'm so glad we're friends."

And then Geit was swept away in the crowd of students.

Niles liked Geit. They had that similar dark sense of humor, and Geit reminded him often not to take things too seriously. Niles wondered what Geit was like outside of school, outside of that building that made sane people say and do insane things. He looked forward to having a little time to talk to him after work and outside of school.

As they swept out of the parking lot directly on the tail of the buses laden with students, Geit was already talking about the Collingsworth writing program being pushed into the building.

"So what do you mean you're not interested in hearing how other people in the department use the expensive writing program in the their own classroom?" Niles asked.

"The first three times, I might have cared. For the last two, I've been totally checked out. I understand the program. I can't believe the district paid for it. It's a lot of easily managed stuff that should be obvious if you have any stake at all in teaching writing anyway. We have to keep going over it again and again because everybody who is not in the English department doesn't want anything to do with it, and they pretend not to understand it. Or maybe they don't get it, but they could easily if they gave any effort at all. Half of the English department gets it, and half doesn't get it. The half that doesn't get it thinks they got it and keep volunteering to lead the P.D.s. All they're doing is muddying the water for everyone else." Geit had a way of seeing the truth.

"As usual. Isn't that how society actually functions? The ones who know are quiet, and the ones who don't keep begging for attention and pretending they do." Niles changed lanes as the road narrowed.

"If you're so wise, why don't you lead the P.D.?" Geit was looking out the passenger window, waving his hand against the wind. He didn't look like he gave the slightest damn, but he did. He was good at that.

Niles settled in his seat and checked his passenger side mirror. He was actually sneaking a look to see if Geit was being ironic, but he already knew the answer.

"Ha. Could you imagine? It's one thing to deal with true ignorance, and it's another thing to deal with people pretending to be more stupid than they actually are. I can take it when teenagers do that. I can handle that. Hell, I handle it every day. Adults on the other hand? I can't handle adults pretending to be stupid. Or even adults who are actually stupid, but should know better. I just want to choke them. I'm not the one to stand up in front of faculty about this or anything else for that matter."

"So you're saying that you're better than them."

"If you want to phrase it that way, sure."

"You're probably right." Geit smirked from the passenger seat.

"Speaking of being right, where are we going anyway? I was just driving."

"You're a good driver when you don't know where you're going. Anyone ever tell you that?"

"No. My wife says I do it wrong. All the time."

"You know where that foreign car shop is over by campus?" Geit gestured vaguely toward the direction Niles was going already.

"Yeah, the one right around the corner from the fraternity neighborhood?"

"Well, the only foreign car place in town, but yeah."

"Wow, your car is pretty special. I bet they charge a pound or two of flesh for service. I can't afford to drive a foreign car."

"Actually, I had to promise them my first born son."

"You and your wife better get busy then. What if it's a female child? Then you're screwed."

"Not really. We just go Chinese One Child Policy on her and try again."

As Niles was turning left into the car lot, Geit turned to him. "You don't have to wait or anything, I just have to pay them and pick it up."

"What if the car isn't ready? Then you'd just have to walk home and miss the P.D. I couldn't sleep tonight if that happened. Besides, if I leave now and you're not behind me, I might just give in to my worst impulses and go home to take a nap. If I know that you're going back to school, then I'll have to go back too. If I don't go back and you show up there in 15 minutes, then I look like the lazy bastard. I can't have you making me look bad."

"Suit yourself." Geit jumped out of the pickup clutching his messenger bag and went in. Niles backed into a parking spot but kept the motor running. Geit was fast and efficient. He didn't bother with incompetence in or out of his classroom. He came back out quickly, flashed the keys and waved to Niles. "See you back at school." Niles nodded and turned the radio up as he pulled out into the traffic fleeing the university.

Fifteen minutes later both vehicles pulled into the parking lot back at the school, one after the other. Neither man was willing to shirk the meeting, pointless though it may have been and neither Niles nor Geit knew where they were supposed to meet. They re-entered the building hurriedly and headed for Demarr's classroom thinking it might be there as it was supposed to have broken down into departments by the halfway mark and they had just passed it. The room was empty and dark. They exchanged looks and headed toward the library. It was empty too.

"Listen." Geit called their attention to the silence. Had everyone gone home already? No. The staff parking lot was still almost as full as it was during the school day. There were no sounds. Wherever everyone else was, they were being quiet. Niles and Geit made a quick circuit of the second floor hallways and found no one. Not even a Foreign Languages meeting.

"They must be down in the 2000 wing." Niles was trying to imagine where else everyone could be.

The 2000 wing was where the skilled trades classes were when the school was built. All of those classes had been gotten rid of during the race to the top, and now the oversized classrooms that once held woodworking and metals shop classes and an automotive repair and maintenance class had been repurposed for classes that were more in keeping with the enlightened new millennium. There was a dance studio where the twerk group met, a photo lab where students could practice their darkroom skills with film even though they were already well into the digital camera age and every student held one in his or her pocket. When art classes were eliminated from the curriculum all across the state to save money, Pianosa Springs just pushed theirs into the dark corner and cut their funding to attempt to strangle them into submission. In the very last corner of the wing, in what had formerly been a welding classroom, Hippy was given room to hold his drama classes.

Geit and Niles made their way quietly through the halls, past the cafeteria and down into the former shop wing. They were quiet so as not to disturb the rare silence of the building.

Finally, in one of the Art classrooms there was the small pod of Art teachers splayed around a table as the department head gesticulated to her own whiteboard covered with esoteric scribbles. There was further noise coming from Hippy's room. Both men peered through the small rectangular window into the cavernous space. The room lights were out, but jerry-rigged stage lights illuminated Hippy on his makeshift stage, surrounded by the rest of the department on risers.

As they entered the darkened room and slunk to the back of the emptiest riser, Hippy went on about using a tableau with the students as means to teach drama, using it to illustrate blocking and character placement with Trudeau as his assistant. Both men were engaged and engaging, but Linn and her coven were visibly tuned out and demonstrating an unmistakable attitude of condescension toward the proceedings.

Linn was facing down, arms crossed as Demarr was talking in her ear. Niles couldn't make out what she was saying, but he didn't need to to understand the message that they were sending: Trudeau and Hippy were stupid, and whatever they were doing deserved to be ignored. That was Linn's attitude when anyone else had anything to say about teaching.

She was an expert on everything in the classroom and if she didn't do it, then it didn't need to be done. She didn't like poetry, so she didn't teach it. She didn't have time to grade writing, so she didn't assign it. She taken hold of the Southern Belle District English Coordinator's subtle institutionally racist ideas of what black teens were capable of and ran with it.

She was a firm believer in the outdated and disproven notion of Gardner's Multiple Intelligences. It was her gospel, and she leaned heavily on "multi-genre" projects to "prove" it with her students. The end result was that not only did they learn from her a hatred of poetry but also a devalued opinion of writing. They didn't write in her classroom and couldn't write when they came from her classroom, and she'd convinced them all that it didn't matter just as long as they could cut pictures from magazines and paste them into shapes they had drawn or craft a paper mache phallus painted with shoe polish and glued into a shoebox with some disheveled Barbie Dolls. That was her way of preparing them for college.

Half of the English department were her acolytes: bullied, groomed, or coerced into following her leadership and adopting her same practices so that a student in four years might never have to write more than a page at a time and might never have constructive criticism offered that would help to improve their writing or thinking processes.

Linn believed that she and every student that she taught were simply born a certain way with certain skills and probabilities, and that they had to work in those directions instead of working toward any growth in others. It was concrete mindset: what you were born with was what you had and that's all you were going to have. Linn's brain was nothing but what it was, and it had the steel rebar sticking out of the edges waiting to hook and gouge. She was skilled at hurting people and at teaching her students how to hurt others through her example.

A great teacher didn't simply teach content. Linn knew she was great. She would proudly tell everyone how great she was, and she taught apathy, condescension and bullying right along with egotism.

Niles was deep in thought pondering her awfulness and other of life's mysteries as Trudeau and Hippy continued their presentation when Geit leaned over and asked, "Since when is it a good idea as a teacher to cover your tits in glitter?"

As in all other aspects of civilization, incompetence was shrouded at times by appearance. Famous pop stars could molest youngsters as long as they kept up the surface appearance of someone who would never think of such things. Presidents could hire porn stars for private service as long as they denied it to the press. Both Niles and Geit strove for competency first, then allowed the appearance of professionalism to follow organically. They worked hard at being as good at teaching as life would allow them to be.

Just as some teachers were born to greatness, some teachers were doomed to mediocrity by events beyond their control, and some were damaged from the start. Some evil was in the very material crafted in the forge, and some came later in the darkness far from light and reason.

"Every student deserved an opportunity, a chance to be whatever he or she should be, or could be." That seemed right to Niles. He thought about it, but he didn't need to in order to agree with it. It read very progressively and gave great satisfaction to anyone who was critical of public education. Niles had often heard that already in his first five years of teaching. He also learned that it wasn't always true.

There was the boy who'd tried to drown his younger sister when he was seven and she was four. The incident was stopped by the intercession of a watchful adult lifeguard who showed up two steps beyond sibling roughhousing and one step before the point of no return.

Niles didn't learn that story until years after the fact, years after the boy had shown up in Niles's freshman classroom, angry and subtly predatory. He was gone already when that victim sister arrived in his classroom years later and wrote stories of growing up that included that sad anecdote. In Niles's classroom every student wrote about things that they might otherwise have kept hidden. It was a safe place for them.

Some boys were out of control reacting to hormones without any reserve at all, but Biff wasn't like that. He had gazed upon the Christian math teacher Duckett with a sort of hungry malice, watching closely for her unguarded moments. He had harassed his female classmates under the radar, out of Niles's sight, drawing up just short instantly when his attention turned toward him. He hated Niles passionately and did everything he could to try to undermine his authority in the classroom, but that was manageable. It was his eyes and his manner toward the females in the vicinity that worried Niles. He had seen the animal look in the eyes before. He knew what it meant from the farm.

Sometimes, young heifers would go into heat before they were grown enough to bear a calf without complications. They were kept separated from the herd's bulls until they were old enough for that reason. Sometimes the bull got in the pen with the heifers, breaking the gate or the chain that held him in his animal lust. Any heifers that he got to were either doomed to a very difficult delivery that needed human intervention to save both her and their offspring or to having a premature undersized calf who would struggle for the first two months of its life. Either one was an unnecessary cost to the farmer and an unnecessary strain on the heifer. It was that lust that Niles recognized in this boy. The look in his eye was like that of the bull straining at the gate, driven nearly mad by the scent of the heifers in heat. It was frightening and he was worried for the girls in his classroom.

Biff was removed from the school by his single mother before the end of that school year after several altercations and sent to a private academy for troubled youth for private family reasons that Niles would never know. Niles thought of him and wondered where he was, hoping that he and everyone around him was safe. When he discovered that he had that younger sister in his senior class years later, he learned a little more of the story.

She'd had a different surname from a different father, but Niles made the connection when she wrote about her brother in the journals that she turned in. She had written of what he had done to her when they were children, about the near drowning that she could remember strongly out of the haze of early childhood and of a hundred other frightening events in their sibling relationship. But she didn't know that she was a victim. She didn't write with fear or regret, only facts that Niles knew were predatory abuse. She was lucky to be alive and certainly much more lucky than she even knew. Niles asked her politely about her brother and confirmed for himself that he'd had him in his freshman class all those years ago. His name was unmistakably unique and she remembered her brother talking about Niles, saying cruel things about the hapless English teacher.

She also revealed that she was happy that he was about to be released from his institution for troubled young men as he had aged out. Niles admonished her to be careful around her brother. There was no more that he could do. She wouldn't follow a warm-hearted direction to avoid him. It was her older brother that Niles wanted to warn her away from. She already loved him more for their blood ties than any harm could subtract from.

There were some threats to the safety of the students that were out of his hands. Dangerous or annoying teens became dangerous or annoying adults. If no one put them in check, they grew to influence others in negative ways. Jake Howell was one of those who had escaped check.

The gelatinous beast that was the high school librarian came harrumphing out of the staff's men's restroom followed unfailingly by a scent that was somewhere between a feline dumpster carcass and a bag of sugared potato crisps. He was diabetic, but he was one of those diabetics who could have made a stronger effort to control his diabetes through diet and exercise. Instead, he bragged about spending all day editing Wikipedia and drinking Diet Coke from consecutive 2 liter bottles while books that students returned piled up horizontally like coats of partygoers in a closet with no hooks. His lunch was often a vegetable, but potato chips and nacho cheese flavored tortilla chips rarely combined with diet cola to make a balanced diet.

If life was a salad then his was awash in the creamiest of ranch dressings. When Howell left the men's restroom, it was marked by scent, but no one needed the nose of a bloodhound to track the perpetrator. Howell's territorial boundaries were available at a distance to anyone with any nose at all.

He also started an after-school anime club for the students. They came in once a week and watched DVDs on a cart tv in the library while Howell worked on the Wikipedia pages for the anime series that they watched. Somehow, no other adult was watching, and it slipped past everyone for weeks that most of the anime that he was watching with them was much less than "school appropriate." Niles didn't know how far it went, but he was kind of glad of that, and the activity of the group happened to peter down to almost nothing by the end of the school year. Teens with short attention spans went outside after school to do what teenagers did.

It was during those same days that as the weather got warmer Howell began to wear shorts to work exposing his swollen, scabby legs. Geit had caught him more than once sitting in his chair picking his scabs under the desk when he thought no one was looking. Geit had an awful way of noticing terrible things.

There were few fans of Jake Howell, and they were all young boys who were on their way to being miniature versions of him. They wanted to drink diet cola from a 2 liter bottle between mouthfuls of chips while clutching manga with their free fingers with eyes glued to animated pages and screens. They looked up to him because he had everything they wanted: a job where he sat all day and the freedom to make rude remarks to people who were powerless to respond in kind without penalty. He was an exceptional role model in that regard.

There was one good thing to say about Howell. He didn't allow students who looked like they might cause problems to just "hang out" in the library, either at lunch or when they might be skipping class. Of course, he always overstepped and tried to run out those who meant no harm to anyone else, those who were having a bad day and trying not to make it worse, but at least there were no fights in the library. There couldn't be if he was the only one there.

The same wasn't true in other places in the building. There were many different levels of tolerance practiced by many different people, and each of those tolerances was conditional and based on several conditions that were not ruled by objectivity. Some days were better than others, some were worse than that. Some days were marked by fights, some days were calm and cool and collected. Back in Leinster Hills, the story was told that it was connected to the cereal being made across the river at the factory, but there in Pianosa Springs it was a matter of the phases of the moon according to some of the more superstitious folk that Niles worked with.

Swamp wasn't good at dealing with fights. Fights removed her from the center of attention that she hungered for voraciously, whether she was spending lunch hour in the cafeteria during homecoming week to tell students to vote for her nephew for king, or running out of breath down the hallway to chase students to class after campus safety has broken up an altercation over misplaced affection.

If the fight happened at lunch while she was eating hers, she would get on the PA system breathlessly and shout into the phone "Everyone go to class!"

She shouted into the phone as if raising her voice to teenagers made a difference. She made threats about suspensions and calls home until she was red in the face while Niles and the other teachers taught in their classrooms, and her breathless interruptions put the brakes on their work. Niles tried not to roll his eyes in front of the students, but they caught him time after time. They knew he resented her and her interruptions. They all did. It was impossible to take her seriously, and it was getting more and more impossible each time she did the same thing. Yet it was her unfailing response to come over the PA system and shout breathlessly about the importance of being in class.

Swamp was tone deaf to the response. Her closest subordinates came to her upon hearing the unhinged rant over the school's speakers and assured her that it was the "appropriate response" and the "right thing," but it wasn't and they lied. They were sycophants, seeking only to ingratiate themselves with Swamp because she was seen by all as a rising star thanks to Kaseman's blind loyalty to her and all that she brought to the job. All of her threats meant nothing. Suspensions couldn't be handed out for such trivial matters to the district as tardiness and even if they were, which student would argue against an extra day off school? And who was going to call home? She didn't. There was no time in her schedule. The vice principals didn't. They had too much to do. It fell on the teachers with all of their spare time and energy.

It was always the same and it would always be that way as long as Swamp was running her show. Whether it was a policy against student violence in school or a policy for student literacy, the district had it covered beautifully on paper. The PR man could type out press releases day and night that went through the local news service about how PSPS was doing magical things for the youth enrolled, but the real practice inside the district had very little actual follow through.

The district had a fine policy regarding literacy. There was an outreach program to get the public libraries into the children and the children into the public libraries. It made great press. There was even a photo op for the local paper where Kaseman and his assistants all signed promises stating that "Literacy is the number one priority" and smiled prettily for the cameras like beauty queens on pageant display. The public libraries in town were aglow with bright posters that encouraged the students to read and commended them for coming to the public library. Everyone who saw them was duly impressed by the efforts to increase literacy that the district was making under Kaseman's sure hand.

In the schools themselves the story was very different. All of the elementary librarians except for one had been cut for financial reasons. The one librarian now split time between each of the ten elementary schools in the district spending a morning or an afternoon once every two weeks at each of the libraries. The rest of the time, they were closed to the students. Students were able to check out books once every two weeks. There were no middle school librarians at all - they were staffed one day a week by teachers who would volunteer to be at the desk during their plan periods for a bit of extra pay. Each high school had one librarian who then also worked as copy clerks in the teachers' centralized print and copy rooms. This was all done to cut costs due to the shrinking state budgets offered to the public schools, but it struck Niles as an odd statement about priorities that his district also had the highest paid superintendent in the state for seven years running. That would have been more sensical if it were the largest public school district in the state or if it had the highest tax base of any district, but it didn't. It wasn't even in the top ten for taxes. Kaseman was well compensated for his PR skills.

It wasn't just that the district heads made themselves look like literacy heroes while truthfully being literacy enemy number one in practice. The hypocritical take on the topic filtered down to the building principals throughout the district as well. They were at best apathetic about the topic and at worst belligerent when the opportunity arose.

Twice each school year all of the building principals coalesced for a meeting. One year, well-remembered and often complained about by Niles to anyone who would listen, Principal Swamp hosted the meeting in their library and pulled several students out of their first period classes to line the hallways from the entrance door to the library door to clap for each of the arriving principals. Because surely no one deserved applause for showing up to a meeting like a high school principal. She also closed the library both days of the planned meeting, choosing to ignore her own principal's conference room that had been built just two years before in a new addition to the building right next to her office for meetings just like that one.

She could have even chosen to have the meeting in the storage room kitchenette back room of the library where there were plenty of tables and space for twelve people to meet up and talk about very important school matters. That was where some of the intern meetings were held when Niles was learning to teach through experience in the building just a few short years before. There were literally buildings within the district that had been purposed specifically just for Professional Development and administrative meetings, but the principals' meetings never used them.

It was an ego trip for Swamp. She crowed in private about bringing the meeting to "Her school" as if that were a new feather in her cap which she imagined to be a peacock's tail. Closing the library and making those resources unavailable to students was the very least of her concerns so long as she could make herself the ringleader of a ridiculous circus and feed her own rapacious ego.

15. Linn

For Swamp, drills were a toy to play with. Drills were an excuse to show everyone that she was in charge. The many drills that she was given command over gave her more opportunities to exercise control. There were several types of drills that were mandated annually by the state. Tornado drills were the least liked and shooter drills were the most eagerly anticipated, but the most drilled drills were for fire. Fire drills were also the most well thought out and executed of all the drills. Usually. They required little in the way of thought or execution, only that everyone exit the building quickly in an orderly fashion. It was simple: first, the alarm; second, the exit. It was difficult to screw up, but more difficult to monitor for success unless there was top down accountability. A successful fire drill was easy to define: initially, according to those administrators running the show when Niles started teaching, it involved getting the students out of the building as quickly as possible.

When Smithson was principal, Niles was told that all students had to be accounted for outside the building. So, ever after (thanks to Cook's advice,) Niles always took a class list with him as he headed out the door. If it were a real fire and he had to be accountable for his students, then his paperwork was proof of doing his job. If working as a teacher had taught him anything, it was that paperwork counted more than anything else. The students could walk halfway down to the grocery store but if they were marked present in the paperwork, then he was doing his job.

When Swamp took over, the emphasis was no longer on accountability but on speed. Speed was a metric where she could potentially outshine her predecessors. Records weren't kept on how quickly Smithson or Fitzgerald had the building emptied, but she could make some be "found" in her hoarder's den of an office. She prepped and seeded the soil carefully then cultivated believable exit times by putting them in the heads of the secretaries in casual conversation.

"Fatima, do you remember the times for Fitzgerald clearing the building? Wasn't it something like four minutes and fifty-four seconds?" Fatima, the principal's secretary who could remember many things quite well couldn't quite remember that, but just under five minutes sounded good. She confirmed that it was likely. The number was repeated around the office to make it stick, and Swamp told her assistant principals to mark it down. The number she had created started to spread like a virus and before the teachers knew anything, it was a concrete fact. It was the time to beat, and Swamp could beat it easily by standing in the way at the main exit and screaming that the fire was "real!" So she did.

She topped "the record" on her second fire drill and made it official. She sent a mass email out the staff thanking them for "breaking the record" and included Kaseman and his assistants in the CC line. That was how she made a lie into a truth. Kaseman lauded her excellence. She was no doubt saving lives. After that, it became even more important each successive fire drill was another chance for Swamp to get another gold star. She would have whipped the students and staff out the door if it were allowed. The drill times crept downward with each drill. New records were set each each time, and Swamp was doing well at making her star shine brighter than her predecessors who had no idea that they would be judged so harshly and so retroactively after they had moved on to bigger and better things than being high school principals.

Niles did his duty regardless of who was in charge. He told all of his classes which door to go out and where to meet him in the event of a fire on the very first day of class. Some of the time some of the students listened to him but sometimes not. What was he to do if they decided to hide in the bathroom on the way out of the building? Could he truly hold them responsible if they didn't go immediately to the right spot in the parking lot? Sometimes they were barely outside long enough for him to go through the whole attendance roll before students were being waved back inside, having satisfied Swamp's ego for quick building clear times. Niles would not give out detentions for not following his guidelines during the fire drills as Swamp instructed all of them to. The danger likely wouldn't ever be real, but if it were, he knew most of them would stick to him anyway. Students in uncertain situations tended to cling to people who looked certain. Niles could feign certainty. Not every drill was as certain as a fire drill.

Tornado drills became overtly ridiculous during Niles's time in Boiling Pot. First of all, shortly after Swamp became principal the alarm system was revamped and "updated," but lost functionality. The official "Tornado Drill" sound went away. Swamp took the initiative to replace it in the most cost effective manner possible. She did not warn teachers of the switch over before triggering the drill, and when class was interrupted by an inarticulate honk over the PA, Niles's thought it was a prank by students who had gotten an airhorn and the code to use the PA over the phone. It wasn't though. It was Swamp. Her new tornado drill alarm came from the dollar store.

Drills were meant to prepare students and teachers for dealing with potentially dangerous situations. Niles knew that you had to have children when you were young enough to be unaware of the horrors that you would consign them to. It was already too late for him. No drill would prepare him for being a parent.

He was creeping toward his forties at a rate that he was barely aware of. His life was flying by as he spent his days leading classroom discussions and teaching literature. Teaching was like that. Days coalesced into weeks, weeks into semesters, and semesters into years. By the end of each school year Niles was used up, ground down, and exhausted. The summers were mere heartbeats in the life of a teacher, and those two and a half months were barely enough time to recover from the extreme emotional exhaustion that was the cost of dedicating himself to being the best teacher that he could be for the students that needed him to be more than just a teacher.

Niles was not going to have his own biological children, He had already chosen to doom himself to a lifetime of caring for other people's children, people who had learned too late that life was drudgery and too late to save their progeny from being born and were then crushed by the weight of the terrible truths that everyone had lied to them about until it was too late.

He watched the other teachers too. He saw how they stumbled and fell. He saw how they hesitated and followed through. He saw how the ones who had their own children at home made difficult choices that impacted all of their children. Someone always lost. An extra hour or two of doing work or at school was an hour or two less that their biological children got to have. All of the extra time and energy given to children and students meant less for themselves. There was never enough time or energy to go around. Niles had seen plenty of teachers have their breakdowns and fall apart. Niles was not a father and he still felt crushed by the weight of all that was on his shoulders. The responsibility of being a teacher was so much bigger than just teaching content.

It was his fourth year of teaching British Literature that a light came on in his head after years of mediocre or poor results while trying to teach the books to students who didn't look like him. Yes, he loved *Brave New World* and *The Lord of the Flies*, and

George Orwell in general - but why? There were good writers behind all of the books in the curriculum especially now that they had been given the Seamus Heaney version of *Beowulf* to work with, but there were plenty of good writers with bad books and even some good writing from bad writers out there that could have been read in class. He wondered why the books that they used were considered the bedrock of an American student's education.

"Mr. Niles, why do we have to read this?"

"Because these books give us insight into the culture that had the largest influence on American culture. These books are also part of the foundation of the language which we all speak here. Because we can learn important things from them if we give them a chance."

That explanation never met with approval from the assembled multicultural mass that sat in front of Niles every day. Sure, there were a couple of "good students" who took what their neck-tied educator had to say as truth, but others were unconvinced or uncaring. After he realized that explanation carried no meaningful weight in changing hearts and/or minds, Niles's narrative slipped a bit.

"Mr. Niles, why do we have to read this?"

"Because even though these books don't reflect upon or show who we are as a people, they have universal themes that every human being can easily relate to."

That explanation didn't work well enough either. He could see a light come on in some students' eyes, but it wasn't getting the traction that he wanted it to in order to change the way they saw the books that he had to put in front of them. It wasn't until he ran through another writing assignment where the students were comparing the culture of the Celts and Scandinavians in *Beowulf* to their own that a new understanding hit him like a bucket of cold brine. He pulled out the photo seating chart and looked at his students. This section had thirty-five students. Two of them were white.

That meant that there were only two students who were assigned books about people who looked like them. The gears started moving the day earlier when he showed them BBC produced clips on the origins and writing of *Beowulf*. The talking heads were white. The characters in the re-enactments were white. They talked about marrying daughters off to create alliances and hoarded gold. Black people in the stories they knew never did that. In fact, they never heard stories about black people that didn't involve some aspect of subjugation to white people. Black people in the stories they read only talked about escaping slavery, murder, and jail.

They'd read *Black Boy* in tenth grade. It was a powerful book that contained many great ideas, but if it was not taught well, then it was just a book about a black kid who burned down his house, was beaten by his parents, and went through all kinds of hell just to survive. When did that happen to their white characters?

It wasn't taught well at Niles's school. Linn had the students making "Wanted" posters of the main character to show things they had learned from the book. It was "artistic" and it was easy to grade. Linn's practiced subjectivity meant that if she liked the student and or the piece, then it received a good grade. If she did not like the student or consider their art to be aesthetically pleasing, then it received a bad grade. She continued to make being a teacher look easy.

Looking around at how his peers were teaching got Niles to start thinking about how people of color and minority backgrounds were shown in those books that he liked to read and teach. Brave New World repeated racist ideas about African fertility and sexuality near the beginning and in the rest of the book the descending caste structure was partially described in terms of skin color with the whitest being the Alphas and the Epsilons having the characteristics of darker skin along with a host of other "deformities" ascribed to non-whites, including some terms used institutionally in academic circles that were racially charged like "mongoloidism." The most prominent minority character was Mustafa Mond, but Huxley used him as a mouthpiece for the notions of white racial supremacy that were in vogue in Europe at the time. No one else of consequence in the story was anything but white.

And then there was Shakespeare. That bedrock, that pillar of English Literature as it was taught in America. Those plays typically read in public high school included *The Merchant of Venice* where the Jews are greedy and selfish, and *The Tempest* where Caliban the dark and monstrous rapist beast was interpreted by scholars as a non-white example of the indigenous faces that were brought to heel by the kind benevolent whip of colonialism. Then there was that favorite of high school teachers everywhere: *Othello*. It was the story of a black man of power, fooled by the ridiculous lies of a white traitor whom he trusted as his best friend and confidant, who then murdered his own white wife in a jealous rage whipped to a froth by the manipulations of that "friend" before committing suicide. There was no one of color at all in *Romeo and Juliet* or *Hamlet* or *Macbeth* because of where they took place historically. Was Shakespeare supposed to be a progressive 600 years ahead of his time and throw a few token Moors into Scotland or Denmark? William Golding didn't make blacks into the villains of *The Lord of the Flies*, but they couldn't even reasonably exist in the white upper class English world that he had constructed in his text. These were wonderfully written stories with powerful morals if they were taught well and the classroom was open to them, but when they weren't, they were terribly problematic.

They were books that a non-white student could not see themselves in. And if they could not see themselves in the story and embroiled in the conflict facing the same problems, then they could not internalize the theme. Niles could see when students arrived in his classroom that books were not being taught well around him.

To empathize better with his students, Niles pushed himself into a thought experiment. He inverted his privilege. He imagined a world where in all of the books he read when he was in school had only a few characters who looked like him, but those who did were criminally inferior to the Asian or African characters presented in those books. He asked himself, would he have loved reading if those were what his teachers taught him about his people?

The sad and true answer was that no one wanted to see a reflection of themselves that threatened or demeaned their positive self-image. To reject those stories and characters that were unlike them was a very reasonable and realistic response. That not-so-secret message was what his minority students were trying to tell him time after time when they asked "why?"

Man is an animal that defines himself and interprets his world with stories. Words are the tool with which man created his place in the world. When Niles pushed himself out of his own head-space and into that of his students, it became no great wonder that his minority charges could not connect with characters in stories who did not look like them and came from places that they could not conceive of being from. How could he in any good conscience offer them the biased, hateful world-view that saw them as less than equal or greater than in evil because of the color of their skin?

If he had to teach those books, then he had to teach them differently. He couldn't teach them the way that the other teachers had always taught them, the way that he had been taught them. A minority student, even one who had been born and raised in America, would never be able to see those stories the same way as a white student who had never encountered any casual dismissal, hatred, or violence due to the color of their skin.

"Mr. Niles, why do we have to read this?

"Because the white people who run the district think that reading these books will teach you your real place in our society."

"That's some bullshit."

"You're darn right it is. We're going to do something different."

Niles was hamstrung by a district policy that was reinforced and concretized by the the prejudices of his peers. His students were not just his students. The British Literature Class was a two semester class, and one-third to one-quarter of his students would be switched out for the second semester. When the students who had been in his first semester class switched to Kringe or Wein and mentioned that they hadn't been shackled to the district curriculum, they both went berserk with indignation. They attacked Niles in front of the students, calling him a bad teacher and worse before taking their complaints to Linn or directly to Swamp, demanding audience in her cluttered and cavernous office before finally being met outside the door.

"You have to do something about that Niles! He's not following the curriculum! He's not doing what he's supposed to do! He's making our jobs more challenging!"

"Niles?"

"Niles!"

They hated him regardless, but the manner in which he taught that effortlessly exposed how awful they were was too much to bear!

"You have to get that Niles!"

"I have to get that Niles," said Swamp, and then she oozed back into her grotto, slid between boxes of incomplete paperwork and bags of candy that were well past expiration date and sat in her overworked chair to further contemplate ways to make Niles pay, to make all of them pay. It was Niles's fault that these two had come to whine and moan and complain, to interrupt her plotting with their pleading. She'd make them pay, but she had to make Niles pay first.

"Do something!" they said.

Oh, she'd do something all right. She'd get all of them back for not treating her like she deserved to be treated.

She scowled. "That Niles."

Meanwhile, Niles was looking for African or Asian narratives that would parallel and complement Beowulf and the other stories. There were problems involved in that search. Most of the fiction published in the US by minority authors about the struggles of not being in the majority were written after Reconstruction began. All of them were heavily influenced by American ideals of slavery and race relations. Niles wanted a parallel to *Beowulf* that was African in nature and showed a pre-colonial state of being. Those books were few and far between for a handful of reasons, but two of those reasons dictated the rest.

First and foremost, the market for those books in the US or other English speaking countries was very small as far as publishers were concerned. Economics determined what was published and there was not enough of a market for them to justify spending the capital. The second major factor was the impact of colonialism on the origin nations of the Atlantic slave trade. For hundreds of years anything that came from the African continent that wasn't generated by whites was considered garbage and culturally irrelevant. It didn't help matters that those cultures supplanted by the whites were large-ly oral as well, with everything passed down from generation to gen-eration by word of mouth. The indigenous peoples weren't anti-liter-ate as most European histories of the continent would tell you, but were instead aliterate. Things were done differently in way that worked well for the indigenes for thousands of years until the Euro-peans came in their tall-masted ships and impressed their cultural norms on the locals. Hence, most of those stories were never printed and could never make it into the hands of their cultural descendants who had ridden the slave ships to America.

One year, Niles had made enough noise about the lack of cul-tural significance in the texts he taught to get Kaseman's attention and a meeting was called to reassess the quality of the text list by the district's new head of curriculum development who had just replaced Miss Daisy. The new coordinator was young, black, under-qualified, and overwhelmed by the job. It was a perfect set-up for Linn and Demarr on the one end, and Kaseman on the other. On the top side, Kaseman could be certain that nothing would happen in the High School English curriculum because his new coordinator wouldn't have a clue how to do anything without running it past him first. On the bottom side, Linn and Demarr would retain their complete con-trol over what they considered to be "their" curriculum even though neither of them taught it because Daisy's replacement had no experi-ence doing her job.

Niles went to the meeting. Linn and Demarr skipped it be-cause it was beneath them and sent Wein, their deeply indoctrinated proxy, to it instead. As the meeting was entirely optional, only three teachers showed up, the third being a mid-year hire from the dis-trict's alternative school who was trying to still make a good impres-sion by going to every meeting and doing anything that might make her look like a good long-term hire for the regular high school. She was only one step beyond what Niles had been in his first year, but he had traveled far in the intervening time.

"Mr. Niles, I've heard that you believe that the curriculum is due for some changes, is that true?" asked the new coordinator.

Niles took a deep breath. He knew that he was tossing seeds to the wind, but someone, sometime had to say something. Now that he had a chance to speak, everything spilled out of him at once.

"Look, I know that every English teacher everywhere in the US and in every other country that the British colonized is taught that "Shakespeare" is a synonym for "good writing," but we should be considering whether or not using it as a foundation for a whole year of language and literature study is making for a meaningful and positive experience for our minority students, especially those who are not planning on going to college." The words had barely fallen from Niles's lips when Wein jumped in to share her small mind even though no one had addressed her.

"I have a lot of poor black kids in my classes who hate English, but I make sure that we read at least one Shakespeare play every year. I have them read the whole thing. That way, when they're older and appreciate it, they can say, "I read a whole Shakespeare play in high school."

Niles's head exploded in confused frustration showering the meeting room in an arterial red mist. The gray matter of his mind that could not comprehend the blindness and privilege of her unasked-for comment painted the walls like a cheap Pollack copy. The echo of the explosion reverberated through the hallways of the mostly unused building like a ghostly firecracker.

In the physical world, his jaw simply dropped. The words that came from his mouth next were his, but he'd have been more careful if reflex hadn't won the moment.

"What future are you preparing them for? A white privilege quiz bowl at a charter school where knowing about Benvolio gets them a minimum wage job working for their dad?"

Wein's face contorted darkly in shock.

The overwhelmed subject coordinator decided at that very moment that whatever Niles said going forward was going to be sexist and that she was going to politely ignore him because Niles was a man, and men were the most fragile beings on the planet. Whatever he had to say about race or privilege was already lost because he'd reacted poorly to Wein's blind white privilege. If he couldn't be civil, then he wouldn't be heard. She'd been taught well herself because she'd grown up a black woman: either you be polite or you keep your mouth shut.

Niles had made a mistake. If he were Linn, what he said and how he said it would have gotten a positive reaction from the women. Linn enjoyed a license that Niles did not. Niles was the kind of person to simply avoid conflict, but his fatigue combined with the obvious stupidity of Wein's comment forced the words out of his mouth before his frontal lobe could stop them. Niles screwed up. The meeting changed nothing. He was further marked as a troublemaker beyond the walls of his own school building now when the coordinator reported the results of the meeting back to Kaseman.

Niles couldn't speak as freely as Linn could. Some animals marked their territory by pissing on things literally, Linn marked her territory by pissing on things metaphorically. Her cackle that rang through the halls was her way to mark her territory and her territory was everywhere. She interrupted staff meetings with it, she used it like a weapon during other teachers' classes when she was in the hallway, and she used it to demean students, mocking them any time she felt like it.

Niles was standing in the hallway outside his classroom during passing time as was his custom and directive from Swamp. A student passed in front of him, clearly eight or so months pregnant, a very visible belly peeking out from ill-fitting clothes. Such things were commonplace because the local community's version of acceptable sexual education in school had only two bullet points to present: The first - Don't do it, and the second - You're too young to know.

The pregnant girl's clothes were very tight, and Linn took the opportunity to cackle loudly and shout down the hallway for everyone to hear, "Girl, you look like 10 pounds of sausage stuffed into a 5 pound casing!"

The girl took offense, drew in a sharp breath, set her jaw and put her head down. There was nothing she could say to Linn that would not escalate the bullying, so she continued walking. Linn never considered that the student and her family were too poor to buy her new clothes that would fit better during her unplanned pregnancy. Linn didn't care.

Linn would not consider even for a moment the weight that the girl was carrying in addition to the baby weight: the weight of failed expectation, the weight of social disapproval and the girl's own knowledge of the burden that she was about to become on her family. None of that mattered to Linn who was only out to increase her own power. It didn't matter to her that she was a teacher, it didn't matter to her that she was supposed to be a role model. All that mattered to her is that she would wield increased power in the building because everyone who witnessed this incident would do all they could to avoid being the next to receive her antagonization. Bullies created silence among those who could oppose them by exaggerating weaknesses and flaws in front of an audience. That was how people like Linn got and maintained power in such a dysfunctional place.

That was her territory, not Niles's.

16. Collins

"All right teachers, I'm Cal Collins and I'm here to work with you on learning how to implement our Collingsworth writing program."

Niles nudged Geit with his elbow. "Collingsworth again? Jesus."

Geit jokingly replied back in a much louder voice than he'd thought, "Tom Collins? I'll have one!"

Cal Collins, who was joyfully passing out folders that his company sold for a huge mark-up to the district heard Geit indistinctly, replied with no small amount of glee, "Your name is Tom Collins, maybe we're related?"

"No, my name is Geit. I was making a joke."

Cal Collins who hadn't paid any attention to what was being said to him went on with his program, "What can I get for you, Tom Collins? An extra folder?"

It was too early for Geit to tolerate his new name that had been agreed upon by a party of one. "What I said was, 'can I get a Tom Collins instead of this garbage?' If I have to go through this again, I'm going to need to be intoxicated.'"

Cal Collins immediately went from seventy miles per hour in one direction to two-hundred and ten in the exact opposite. All the amiability left him in an instant. If Cal Collins could have served his anger toward Geit for breakfast, there would have been enough for the whole room. Apparently he had already started his morning on a bad note and would not brook Geit making it worse.

"No. You're going to get this wonderful folder and you're going to like it. He added an audible "goddamn it" under his breath. Cal Collins had some rage all packed up for someone else, and Geit was going to get a hot package of steaming furiousness that was incorrectly addressed.

Niles and Geit made eye contact with each other in perfect synchrony. Geit grinned and his eyes flashed light. The game was on.

As Cal Collins stopped passing out folders and glared at him from four feet away, Geit responded. "That's an awful lot of hostility that just came shooting out there." He playfully pointed at Collins and said to Niles for everyone to hear, "He just ejaculated hostility at me."

Niles guffawed. Collins came unglued.

"You shut up!" He thrust his hand toward Geit.

Geit remained cool as an ice tray and said, "Hey, don't take it out on me, I wasn't the one who screwed your wife. That was him." He gave a twist of his upturned hand with the thumb at Niles.

Niles's head jerked back in shock.

"Uh, I don't know his wife," Niles stammered.

"You're Crockett? You son of a bitch! How dare you!" Collins's face twisted in rage.

Niles couldn't tell now if he was talking to him or Geit. Cal Collins clumsily lunged from behind his overhead projector toward Niles and attempted to pummel him, but Geit was swiftly on him and pulled him away. As he held the struggling man back, he winked at Niles who was climbing out of his chair and moving away from the infuriated Collins and asked, "Dude, why did you screw his wife?"

"I didn't screw anyone! Are you crazy?"

This redoubled Collins's efforts to break free of Geit's hold. He was winning the impromptu grappling match.

"I think you should probably get out of here, this guy's got some kind of retard strength!" Geit gasped.

Niles was grabbing his bag when the building principal and a security guard came in the door. One of the other English teachers had pulled them in from just outside the door.

"What is going on in here? What is this?"

The red-faced, panting presenter broke free of Geit's grip and pointed at both him and Niles, unable to speak, shaking with rage.

"Mr. Niles and Mr. Geit? Join me in my office right now please. Bring your things."

Collins straightened his tie and glared. Geit and Niles gathered their things from where they had fallen on the floor. The principal waited until both Niles and Geit had left the room and followed them out.

In the hallway, Niles regrouped. "How did you know that his wife had cheated on him?"

"I didn't. That was just a shot in the dark." His grin was deep and profound. "Look at the bright side. We don't have to sit through that again."

Niles and Geit marched toward the principal's office, followed by the already weary principal who shook his head and mumbled "Fucking English teachers" under his breath.

Cal Collins had a bad night and it came crashing down on Niles and Geit. Geit may have pushed a button or two, but Niles found himself drawn in.

To Geit, it was improvisational comedy, another act in the farce that all of the teachers were complicit in. He just wanted to push some buttons and see what happened. Geit had no malice. There was just something in the moment that he went with. Even though he was shocked at first, Niles saw the smile on Geit's face and went with the farce. If Geit was guilty, then Niles was willing to be guilty by association. He was starting to understand that everything was going to be evaluated on the same rubric whether or not it fit.

Later that month, Niles had just settled down and in with his Creative Writing class in the 2000 wing computer lab when another act played out. The students were working on their final drafts of creation myths. He'd gone over some of the shorter ones that were available for free like thumbnails of Norse gods along with a bit from *Indaba, My Children* so the students weren't focused on writing in the European style. They were now on the final draft stage of their assignments. Their stories were focused mainly on the more mundane things that were geared toward their age group like shoes and phones, and some of them still trailing childhood behind them wrote about unicorns and elves - overall, the topics they chose tended toward being a pretty entertaining mixed bag, and the freedom he granted them gave them permission to be goofy. After all, writing was supposed to be fun, not a chore.

It was a peaceful day to that point, marked only by the sounds of typing and students chuckling excitedly as they shared their attempts to make each other laugh in the assignment when Wein stormed in from the side door. The lab was next to her classroom and interconnected by a shared office from the days when vocational classes were still taught in the wing and the drafting instructor would sit and smoke during class with the Home Economics teacher.

She was upset.

Niles had hit "reply all" to an email that she had sent to the entire staff wherein she had strongly suggested that her problems with a particular student in her classroom were due to the other teachers on the student's schedule being overly permissive with his behavior. She had called out Niles by name. Niles's reply was simple:

"Thank you for sharing your personal problems with classroom management with the rest of the staff, now does anyone have any ideas that can help Wein improve in the classroom?"

She stormed up to Niles at the desk and demanded, "Who do you think you are, responding to my email like that?" Her voice was loud and curt - she was making no effort to be subtle on behalf of a classroom full of students.

"I'm just a teacher trying to help another teacher out," he said, unable to conceal his smile.

"That was an attempt to embarrass me!"

"I"m pretty sure you embarrassed yourself, just like you are now in front of these kids." The front half of the class was looking unashamedly over the tops of their screens at the bloated mass of Wein blotting out their teacher sitting behind the desk.

"Do you know who I am in this school?" she asked, as if to imply that she were some central pillar of the school's precarious prestige.

Niles, who to this point had been leaning backwards a bit lazily in his chair leaned forward, put his hands on the desk and glared into the bleached, wrinkled mass in front of him.

"I know exactly who and what you are. You are an affront to every professional rule of conduct that exists for professional educators. You are a ridiculous shambling mess on an ego trip, and you think I'm going to let you get away with throwing other teachers under the wheels so you can try to make yourself look better to your buddies in administration. But I won't have it. Not now and not ever. Now get out of my classroom before you show all the students what you really are, too."

Her eyes bulged with rage at Niles.

"Well I never -" and she turned on her heels and strode back out of the hole in the wall that she'd crawled in from. Some of the students laughed. A handful who knew her in from their own schedules rolled their eyes.

One walked up to Niles and asked him, "What was that?"

"That, my child, was a small, petty person getting even smaller."

Niles didn't always have such promising material to work with in making light of certain situations. There were things that even he and Geit couldn't joke about. There were plenty of days that were dark and heavy and that threatened to crush, and those days offered different challenges. Niles tried to navigate them all by following his heart, whether it made him want to laugh or cry.

Sometimes, the only thing left to do was cry. Niles knew that too. He was at his desk after school when three of his AP students shuffled quietly from the empty hallway into the dark side of his classroom. He put down his pen and went to them in his avuncular way.

One of their classmates who'd been struggling with childhood leukemia had succumbed after three years of struggle. She'd been a cheerleader when she could and a hospital patient when she couldn't. Now she was neither, and family and friends were preparing to bury her. The news had broken in waves through social media after lunch and even though the girls had been in Niles's class earlier in the day, they returned there after school instead of getting on a bus and going home.

The lights were on in the back part of the room over his desk, and the girls had come in and sat on the floor in the front where it was dark. He knew what grieving looked like. When enough years accumulated, grief became familiar - like the kid who came in for class every day and never said a word. He sat there in his spot, never asking questions, never talking to the other students, but he always did what he was supposed to do so the teacher didn't need to address him when the other thirty-four students were having issues of every other color under the sky. That was grief.

It was there all the time, like a lost sock underneath the bed sheet. Niles had lost aunts and uncles to various cancers, three grandparents to old age, and a friend to childhood leukemia when he was eight. Life was like that. Those numbers accelerated with age, and the more people that he knew, the more people that he lost - more friends and acquaintances, more illnesses and more unexpected accidents. Lives of all shapes and sizes began and ended around Niles it seemed, and at some point that he didn't notice, the scales tipped toward loss and then fell over, solidifying there like baby shoes dipped in bronze.

The girls sat on the carpet, heads tilted down, mumbled and wept. Niles left his desk and moved respectfully toward them. Body language would tell him if they needed him to stay back or move close.

He remembered his own discomfort with sharing the loss of his grandfather when he was an intern. Grandpa Niles had passed away after a drawn out struggle with dementia. He'd told young Niles in one of his lucid moments that he felt like there was a wall separating him from his wife and other friends that had passed, and that he'd have to climb up and over in order to join them. His passing was quicker than expected though. Niles and his sister had been on the highway riding to see him to say their last sets of "thank you" and "I love you" when the cell phone buzzed in his breast pocket and his mom told him, "He's gone." That was a Friday in November and the dirt they laid him in three days later was already cold and hard.

One of the texts he was working through with the students in one of the classes at the time was *Tuesdays with Morrie* by Mitch Albom, and they were near to where Morrie was going to pass away. On the day he came back, his mentor teacher Cook offered without hesitation to take the class back into her hands to finish the book. She knew instinctively that Niles couldn't do it. She told him he could leave the room and that he didn't have to be there as they finished the book. He was stunned. He hadn't considered that he would be given an option to do anything but persevere. He accepted her kindness with a relieved lack of hesitation.

When those times came in class he left to wander the hallways. There was no place to sit and reflect or to gather himself, so he just walked. That whole book was about taking the chance to say the things you wanted or needed to say to someone who was going away, and Niles hadn't gotten to do that. His grandfather had been lost for too long, mistaking him at one point for his own long-passed brother fifty years in the grave. Then on that final chance, that last day, Niles was an hour too late.

He wandered around the halls for a few days while Cook taught, unable to see any of the other people who were in the halls with him because he was so absorbed in processing his own grief. He thought of those times when he had to deal with other deaths that followed.

As he quietly approached the girls, the first saw him, turned and raised her arms up. He knelt to her and caught her solidly. As a high school teacher, he didn't look to hug his female students, but neither did he look away when they look to him. He hugged her and she let a wet sob escape, her tears darkening his shoulder. She released him from her arms and sat back on the floor, legs crossed. Niles joined them, forming a third point of a triangle. The second girl looked to him, and he reached a hand to her, squeezed her shoulder and looked into her teary eyes. "I am here."

She nodded. Niles's own eyes were clouding and he felt that odd pressure in the bridge of his nose that always marked the onset of his own tears. They all sat there in their triangular circle wordlessly, until he realized that the box of tissues from his desk would work much better in this space and rose to get it. After girls wiped their noses and cheeks, the words started to spill out. He listened. All of their frustration and loss came out. They were hurt that their prayers and well-wishes, medical treatments and all else had come to naught. They spoke of last words and final goodbyes, but then their stories shifted without prompting. They shared with him their joyful memories, the good times and the laughter that they'd shared with their lost friend.

The girls' tears were a chorus, intermixed with verses of words of loss and anguish, punctuated by a sob. Niles listened until he had to speak because his quiet felt like powerlessness, and he didn't want the girls to sense that he was truly powerless in the face of death as everyone was. It was the same motivation that brought words out of adults when events in life pounded down the doors and they were forced to explain the violence of the world to young people who were just getting their first taste of heartache and suffering. He told them, "Grief is a monster that will devour everything, absolutely everything unless you bring it to heel. You can't let these things eat you up every single night. You can't keep resurrecting every morning just to go back and take the same damage over again. You have to say, 'Today is the last day that I will die for this.' You have to take control back from the things that will otherwise mean destruction for you. Grief will never have its fill unless you are dead."

Niles listened, and he cried and laughed with them until they could stand again on their own. And when they were done for the time they left, each giving Niles a hug before they headed out the door to rejoin other friends to continue to find ways to live through their grief that like his, would be that quiet kid in the class who showed up every day and did exactly what he was supposed to do.

Shakespeare hadn't said it in as many words, but it was still in his plays. Beckett's and Ford's too. "To live is to suffer, and to suffer is to endure pain and loss that youth cannot yet imagine." The saying didn't make anything true, like so many things that old people say to young ones. Niles knew it but didn't always know how to say it. To close off from pain was to close off from connection, and to close off from connection was to be dead. It was true that people had to lose to fully appreciate what they had, but that was just an empty aphorism that gave cold comfort. Only by losing did anyone know what it was like not to have something they thought was theirs forever, and only through that deprivation did anyone understand what it truly meant to have. It was a math that wasn't taught in school, but people had to understand how that simple math worked to appreciate it. It was beautifully uncomplicated: Losing made having better. Niles knew that on some level but hadn't yet applied it to all the places where it fit. There were many things that were lost to him before he ever understood that they were gone. That was how a lot of change took place.

The next morning Niles was in early as usual, but he made a detour down to the main office. He was concerned about the lack of support measures being taken in the building to support students in grief. He went through the back doors into the counseling office and found the person he was looking for: Dr. Conway the school psychologist.

Conway was hunched over his desk in his office eating cake for breakfast. Niles knocked on his door frame shyly apologetic about interrupting the meal. Conway jumped as if he'd been interrupted while talking to himself and lifted his plate to his chest as if to run away.

"Yes, hmmm?" his mouth full of food. "Who are you?"

"My name is Mr. Niles. I don't think we've met." Niles stepped in and offered a hand to shake, but Conway looked at him strangely, as if he were covered in mud. Conway set his plate on his desk and brushed crumbs off his chest. Niles noticed that his dress shirt had what appeared to be food stains on the front of it.

"What do you want, Niles?" He seemed to make a point of dropping the honorific. Niles was confused by what felt to him like hostility.

"I've had some interactions with some students who were powerfully impacted by the death of one of their friends. I'm worried about them. I was going to ask if there was anything in place to support them."

"Just what makes you think you're able to determine what students need or want?"

Niles drew back. "I don't think anything. I just know that they were in my room yesterday crying after school"

"That's right. You're not qualified to think about those things. You're not a psychologist."

Niles stepped backward out of the office pushed out by the size of Conway's ego.

"And Niles? If you have something you need to have brought to my attention, take it to the counselors first, all right? Protocols about this sort of thing are established for a reason. Thanks."

Conway went back to devoting his entire attention to the remnants of his cake, indicating to Niles that his audience was over. Niles walked back to his classroom while confusedly pondering just how he had so clearly stepped on Conway's toes without meaning to. He returned to his desk and wrote an email about the grieving girls to one of the counselors hoping to create a forward avenue for some meaningful interventions to be put in place.

His response came a week later. The counselor told him that she would "for sure talk to Dr. Conway about it" after the upcoming round of standardized tests which were only a month away. By then, Niles and every other staff member forgot that anyone had died. School went on. There were too many other things to take care of and no one else to take care of them. It fell on Niles and the rest of the teaching staff to keep doing their jobs.

Teaching was based on socializing young people to be contributing members of society In the historical past, it was usually for the the farm or the factory. That was changing during Niles's time on the front line. There were tests to consider. Niles learned more about the importance of tests every month that he worked as a teacher.

The news was out: the state of Michigan had made a deal with the largest standardized testing company in the United States. Change was coming and everyone would benefit from the change. Formerly, the tests were administered on weekends and proctored by employees of the testing company. That meant that the testing company had to compensate the school districts for the operational costs of the building during the testing period, as well as paying its own employees for administering it.

The new agreement meant that testing would happen during regular school days and be proctored by the teachers. This removed the testing company's liability for paying for the operating costs and the overhead of paying for its own employees to proctor. It also meant that regular school content instruction time would be used to administer the test instead of placing the testing during a weekend or some other out of school time. Now the school district absorbed all the costs! Every one, including the teachers and students benefited according to the the press releases.

During administration of the tests, teachers were not allowed to do anything else except watch the students test. If the teachers failed to watch the students during the testing process, all of the results of each student's test in that room could be invalidated. It was a benefit to everyone and very fair.

The state-mandated tests were all that mattered. All progress in the classroom could only be measured by a test created by a corporation for profit. There were no sections for "wisdom" or "citizenship" on the test. No sections labeled "thinking autonomously" or "ability to accept that previously held beliefs were wrong." Administration made it clear that anything that wasn't on the test wasn't acceptable to be included in teachers' lesson plans when those test scores were average or below average. Lesson plans changed accordingly. If the lesson plans weren't up to snuff, it was another large nail in the coffin of the teacher's career.

In Niles's first year of testing, he was working in his own classroom. He took down all of his materials on the walls that could have been of any assistance to students during the test. Teachers were assigned in three person teams. A "Test Administrator" in each room with two "proctors" or room supervisors. One of the proctors was assigned to the hallway maintaining the quiet environment in the hallway and providing respite in turns to the proctors stuck in the room. During the first years of this new testing protocol that benefited everyone, two teachers were required to be in the room during testing. Later on that changed due to other requirements imposed by the testing company, but at the start it was about making sure that students had supervision, that testing materials were kept sacred by each individual like the secret formula for the colonel's chicken. Tests were prayers from God meant for only one person. Three years after the public schools took over the testing they mandated only one room supervisor because to have two cost the district too much.

Michigan's governor had issued the statement via press release through the State Secretary of Education on a Friday afternoon two months before the testing was scheduled to take place, and on the following Wednesday the focus of the after school staff meeting was already on the test. The announcement came as a relief to Swamp because she had no idea what to put on the agenda for the staff meeting and was waiting until the last possible moment to fabricate something. Early that day she'd put her Dean of Students at the time, Sue Shuhorn, in charge of the meeting to disseminate the testing information, but Shuhorn was out of her league. She'd have had to have been a master of improvisation to carry the meeting on her back without time to prepare or information to share. When Swamp passed the microphone to Shuhorn's bony hand swinging from her hollow frame, she simply froze staring up into the space above the library bookshelves. All she could do was look out at the assembled teachers with a hollow grin like that of an Alzheimer's patient who'd forgotten how to speak.

Swamp nodded lamely at Vice Principal White and signaled for him to push the confused Dean of Students out of the library. She'd clearly lost her nerve. With Shuhorn gone though, there was no one left to lead the meeting about preparing for the standardized state test. Swamp looked out over the teachers she hated. She wished she could just get rid of all of them, but that would take too much work. She would actually have to fill out paperwork regarding the reasons why instead of just throwing them out of the building like she imagined every night before she fell asleep. The staff looked around at each other as if one of them had secret key and if they could just figure out who it was, all would be revealed. Swamp didn't care what happened next. Vice Principal White was utterly confused about what to do without someone telling him. Swamp knew that she could have handled the situation, but she didn't feel like it. Dr. Conway stood up and came to the rescue by taking control. He wasn't required to be at the meeting but he'd come anyway because the email announcing it had been mistakenly sent to him.

"Ladies and Gentlemen, here behind me are boxes filled with testing materials. They are labeled with room numbers, and the materials in that box are the ones that will be used in those classrooms come testing day. The tests themselves are still in a locked room across from my office, but everything else you need is there in those boxes already." He gestured to a stack of banker's boxes behind him as if they were the prizes behind door number one.

He paused and looked at the assembled staff whose eyes were on him. He felt very satisfied with himself for taking control and putting the train that had derailed back on the tracks. "Now ladies and gentlemen, inside the boxes that you're going to receive are stopwatches that we're going to use to time the test. It is imperative that we synchronize those stopwatches so that each test is started and ended simultaneously, or else you're going to invalidate the test results for everyone." Conway was highly skilled in creating the illusion of purpose. After all, he was a school psychologist.

"In order to facilitate this in the most efficient way possible, we're going to synchronize our watches right now. That way if testing doesn't begin and end at exactly the same time in every classroom on the first day of testing, Mrs. Swamp and I are going to know exactly who to hold responsible." He looked quickly to Swamp for approval but only saw her dead lizard-like glare in response. "Let's set our watches for 2:45 PM on my mark." It was five minutes to three. Teachers looked around at each other for confirmation, but there was none to be found. Half of the staff present didn't wear watches. Everyone was confused, but said nothing. That did little to deter Conway. He had found a purpose in this meeting and he was going to purpose the hell out of it. Niles looked across the room and saw Geit by the door smiling like the bearded lady's bikini top had fallen off. Clearly he was enjoying the sideshow.

"On my mark," continued Conway. "At zero, mark the time on your watches. 10... 9... 8... 7... 6..." and then more quickly, " 5, 4, 3, 2, 1." He paused for effect. Looked around the room at the teachers. Only one had his fingers on his watch. Vice Principal White did too. The look on his face said that he was in for both a penny and a pound. "Zero. Excellent." The room had dipped into the surreal and only Niles and Geit seemed to notice. "When you get your boxes next week on the day of the test, take care to make certain that your stopwatches are synchronized with your time on your watch, which is now synchronized with mine. Swamp, White, Shuhorn, and I are going to make sure that this is our best testing year ever. Thank you. You're dismissed."

Niles looked over at Geit again. He was laughing into his hand. Everyone rose to leave, a murmuring crowd shuffled through the library doors and into the hallways spreading out like metastasizing cancer cells. Niles walked over to Geit who was stretching like the Cheshire Cat on a tree branch, grinning just as widely.

"What the hell did we just witness?"

"Theater of the Absurd stirred with Kafka."

"That sounds like a mixed coffee."

"It's just another day, my friend, just another day." Geit rose and adjusted his tie. "You should go home before the alien virus gets inside you too. If that happens, the only way I'll know it's not you is if you start saying things that don't make any sense."

"I'm starting to think that will happen to anyone who is here for too long anyway. Except you. You manage to avoid the madness pretty well."

"Jo-Jo, just do whatever it takes to survive. Okay? Whatever it takes. Even if it means escaping."

Niles wrinkled his forehead as he tried to understand. Geit sighed, smiled and disappeared through the door. Niles stood alone trying to figure out just what he was supposed to be synchronized with.

17. Halverson

Niles was proud that he worked in a building that had a lounge in it.

It wasn't a lounge originally. It was just a part of the cafeteria. When the school was built, the district argued there was no reason for a teachers' lounge. The teachers' union argued otherwise and two years after the building was completed, the drywallers were called back to wall off a small portion of the cafeteria to be separated for the teachers' use.

It wasn't like the factory he'd worked in where there was a fenced off area for breaks (due only to the efforts of the UAW). The spacious factory was structured as a zoo with gates and locks and cages. The school had an actual room. It became the teachers' cafeteria when the district was forced to admit that teachers might just deserve a duty-free lunch, but when further budget cuts put the teachers into the students' lunch lines due to lack of food services staff, the room was repurposed. When the announcement went out, an overly excited teacher invited other teachers to take advantage of this newly unused space for their own designs. Niles ignored the call to action in much the same fashion that he ignored most things that his peers emailed out. He'd been trained well.

The email asked for donations of cash or objects for decorating the room to make it more comfortable and "friendly." Some teachers offered furniture in the form of garage sale pick-ups or dentist waiting room cast-offs. The art department painted the room. Several missives were sent out to encourage participation by fellow teachers to engage in a type of community building event, but Niles ignored them all. He had never used the teachers' cafeteria and never had time to "lounge." He was proud of his lack of involvement because he believed that it proved his dedication to the students, almost as proud as he was of the other teachers who'd actually gotten involved and done something to create community in the building. After all, there was almost no sense of community in the building, and no effort in that direction would ever be taken by administration. They wanted to destroy the community.

Sadly but not unexpectedly, the effort failed. Shortly thereafter, the building's "Comfort Committee" disbanded too. The committee had formed in the late 70s and had run all the way into the 21st century, but Niles's lack of commitment had been its death knell. The group had originally come together to serve the purpose of community, providing both celebration and comfort, both of which happened with some regularity given the age cohort. It wasn't that there was no need for the group, it was that putting community-building activities together became too time consuming for the members, and with all of the other things they were compelled to do to be highly effective, a comfort committee had to fall by the wayside. When it did, the administration was pleased to see it go so they could return the space to its original purpose.

When Niles did stop by the "teacher's lounge," it was to get a cherry cola from the building's sole vending machine. It was always devoid of teachers when he went there because he deliberately avoided being there when anyone else was. Once he accidentally walked in on a member of the building services crew taking a nap on a couch, but Niles never saw it being used otherwise. Not long after, the vending machine was pulled out of the building and he no longer had any reason at all to stop by the dusty room.

When the lounge lost its last motivating factor for teachers to visit, Swamp decided to convert it into a "quiet lunch space" for students to escape the insanity that was permitted in the general cafeteria. She texted that change of usage directly to a handful of her favorite students and failed to inform the teaching staff. The following Monday at lunch, Halverson and Tibbs went there to find the room filled with members of the cheer team making out with their boyfriends from the football and basketball teams. The room smelled like a combination of fish sticks and the waiting room at the local cryo clinic where men showed up to exchange genetic material for cash. The pair backed out quickly before they could interrupt and retreated back to their own classrooms. They had to find a new place to talk about soccer.

Halverson and Tibbs were crazy. They didn't understand how to maintain safe boundaries between themselves and the students despite the fact that they knew to avoid the new student make-out room. For example, breaking up fights. Every young male teacher wanted to jump in the middle and show his strength and force of will, but most of them would have had enough adrenaline to duck punches. Not Halverson. When Niles first started, being in the hallway next to a teacher who was already known for taking a punch seemed to lend him some credibility merely by geographic association. Students didn't want to fight in that hallway anymore. They went to other ones where a teacher was less likely to leave his face in the path of their fists. Like Tibbs's hallway. Tibbs was quick and known to both dodge punches and engage in witty banter in a caffeinated frenzy.

One fine Friday, Tibbs and Halverson showed up at Niles's pub with Geit. Niles was hiding behind his stack of grading, but Geit made eye contact and invited him to join them in a cold drink. The three friends and Niles were seated together at an outdoor table at the brewpub. Each had a drink down and a drink on the table. They were discussing the things that they were asked to do at the school that felt crazy. Niles was mostly listening until Geit started talking about all the "special considerations" that Linn and Demarr were able take advantage of since Swamp had become principal - like the "extra" planning period and several days where they were able to work as a "committee of two" to do the planning and paperwork for the school certification process that Swamp had applied for.

"I hate those bitches." Niles interjected, both offering and seeking validation. He hated anyone who made backdoor deals that benefitted only themselves. To Niles, if you had some kind of privilege, then you also had a duty to use it on behalf of people who didn't have the same privilege. Neither Linn nor Demarr felt that way.

"You see what I mean?' asked Halverson to the rest of the group looking at Niles. "He has anti-social aggressions."

"Obviously," Tibbs agreed. "Niles, you're usually pretty quiet. That must have touched a nerve?"

"Sorry. I just strongly dislike people who are so transparently only out for themselves." He liked Halverson because he was willing to get punched in the face. He liked Tibbs because Tibbs would help anyone, regardless of the quality of their character. Tibbs didn't discriminate. He liked Geit too. Geit understood the line between what was meaningful and what wasn't.

"Well, fortunately, neither of them is here," Tibbs pointed out triumphantly to Niles.

"Who said anything about them being here?" Niles wanted to know.

"Swamp isn't here, either. You should just let it go. Leave it at work." Geit advised.

'Who said anything about Swamp?' asked Niles.

"What bitches do you hate, then?" said Geit.

"Don't be a son of a bitch,' was Niles's sublime response.

Geit laughed. "I'm not going to argue with you," Geit decided aloud. "You don't know who you hate. Even worse, you seem to hate just about everyone."

"Just whoever's only out for themselves," Niles told him.

"Everybody's only out for themselves. You just have to watch for the ones that are out to get you," Tibbs asserted.

"He's a pragmatist," said Halverson, pointing with his thumb at Tibbs. Niles's tongue felt loose. Like an old man at the rest home who finally had an audience.

"Everybody hates me. The kids don't like me. You guys don't even like me."

"We don't really like anyone," Halverson explained.

Tibbs wrinkled his brow and nodded in agreement.

"And what difference does it make whether anyone likes you or not?" asked Geit.

Niles reflected on the wisdom held in that question.

"You're right," he said. Even though he wanted to be liked, it wasn't meaningful in the bigger picture of things in the building, or perhaps even in life in general.

"You're going to be all right." Geit winked at Niles. He had been right about some things. This last statement was going to require time and effort to validate. Other things were validated in a more efficient fashion with little reason to engage in deeper contemplation. Niles had potential. How that potential was expressed needed some guidance.

"You know, you've got to be careful who you hate in that building if you don't want to look like a racist." Geit offered advice.

Halverson interjected. "He already looks like a racist," indicating Niles's bald head with his eyes.

"You know that she's not really black, she just looks black."

"Who?"

242

"Who do you think I mean? Who do you hate?"

"Everyone."

Geit smirked at Niles's jest. "Who do you hate the most or maybe second most?" Clearly he meant Linn or Swamp.

"Well, I know that Linn is half Asian - that's pretty obvious, so you must mean Swamp."

"Yup. Swamp's parents came here from Russia. Her mom's family was from the Caucasus region there. She's actually Roma."

Niles looked confused. "You mean she's a gypsy?"

Geit laughed at his surprise. "Easy there, Hate Crime! If you don't want to look racist, you call them "Roma" or "Travelers.""

Niles was still confused, trying to do the skin tone math in his head. There were a lot of mixed race students at the school, but somehow Swamp being Russian still didn't compute.

Geit filled in the gaps in Niles's thoughts. "There are actually a lot of dark skinned people living the Caucasus region, ironically enough. There are even old stories around there of 'Almas' or 'wild ape men' that were derived from the way the whites living there saw African immigrants."

Halverson, who had been drinking and listening offered a salient, if drunk question: "How the Hell do you know all this, Geit? Are you her biographer?"

Niles pondered the appropriate irony of his principal being a true 'Caucasian.'

Geit raised both hands as if in supplication. "My dad was from the Ukraine. The community tends to stick together in weird ways." He tented his fingers like a cartoon villain. "I know things." He smiled playfully at the rest of the men. Geit did know many things. "Actually, have you ever talked to Jobe? He grew up around here too. He lived right down the street from Swamp's family when they first moved here. He's known her since she was a girl."

"She was a girl?" said Tibbs, trying to be funny. Niles shrugged. He was unconvinced. Geit knew meaningful things. The things he knew probably saved Niles more than once.

Months later, Niles and Geit and Trudeau had the ill fortune of riding to a English AP conference near Detroit with Demarr. They rode together in Demarr's car since none of the young poor men had vehicles that suitable to drive from one side of the state to the other.

There were always concessions to make while living on a teacher's salary when starting in the profession. A reliable car was the first and easiest major sacrifice. A teacher could carpool, bike, or even go from seven hundred dollar junker to seven hundred dollar junker always cobbling parts together and substituting old shoestrings and used nylons for whatever auto part he couldn't afford. Niles had picked up Trudeau twice on the way to work next to a broken down automobile. It would happen again. Demarr didn't have to worry about it. She'd been teaching for more than twenty years, and she was married to a tenured professor at the local college. She could afford a nice reliable car. The boys rode with her.

Mara Demarr was a storybook troll in the flesh. If there were a bridge that weren't already occupied by homeless people, she would have lived there and tried to eat every goat that trod above. She took power through manipulating others, and the simplest way for her to manipulate others was to make them intensely uncomfortable.

With the boys trapped in her car on the long road to the conference, she had them where she could easily control the conversation in the car. She was older than them all by twenty years and that was a major part of the authority that she held over them.

She subjected them to stories that made them cringe, stories about her life that may or may not have been true. The point of her story wasn't related to its truthfulness, it was related to how she could use it to make them feel uncomfortable and thus assert her power over them.

Her favorite story, one that Trudeau and Geit had both heard before on the way to another conference, was specifically told to make people uncomfortable and to manipulate them through discomfort and unease. She was going to use it again, this time on Niles. She had them captive in her automobile, trapped at 74 mph on the highway.

"Did I ever tell you guys my best parenting story?" asked Demarr. Niles looked at Geit across the back seat from him and noticed him tense like a deer caught in headlights. Trudeau stared straight ahead in the passenger seat, seemingly absorbed by the ribbon of darkness stretching through the Michigan countryside in front of them.

Geit knew the key phrase "best parenting story" so he spoke. "I know the story. Trudeau knows the story. Nobody needs to hear it again or maybe not even for the first time." He looked at Niles.

Trudeau only nodded, still staring straight ahead.

Demarr looked back at Niles in the rear view mirror, making eye contact for an uncomfortably long time for someone driving at a high rate of speed. She wanted Niles to ask for the story, to give her license to have her power over him. Niles thought of Geit's reaction, but didn't take his eyes off of Demarr's. He simply shook his head and said:

"No."

Demarr huffed disappointedly, wrinkled her nose at Niles and turned the radio up.

They arrived at the hotel for the conference to find that the school had booked two singles and a double room for the four of them. Demarr took one of the rooms by fact of nature; she was a married woman and would not share a room. Two of the three men would have to share a room. Which two though? None of them would say that they were taking the single. They went around and around at first, and although all of them wanted the solo room, none of them would claim it outright until Trudeau broke the uncomfortable truce.

"I'm going to need some privacy to talk to my wife on the phone," claimed Trudeau.

"None of you are sleeping with me. I'm a happily married woman," declared Demarr as if there were a question.

"I have night terrors and once tried to choke my wife to death while sleeping," announced Geit.

Trudeau and Demarr thought he was joking. Niles believed it was a rare moment of honesty in the conversation.

"My wife doesn't care," Niles responded.

"Well, you boys figure that out. I'm going to go have a wet push and lie around my room in my underwear." Demarr had struck again, making at least one of them visualize her plan.

"On that note, I guess I'll see you guys in the morning?" asked Trudeau in a way that much more a statement than a question. Before either of the remaining men could answer he turned on his heel and swept with the key into the room next to Demarr's.

"I guess it's you and me now, new best friend. At least we won't have to hear Demarr's bowel movement through the wall if we're across the hallway."

Geit's face hung. He gave Niles a pale resigned sigh. "You can't say I didn't warn you. I was totally serious about waking up screaming in the middle of the night." Geit couldn't make eye contact. It was too odd to admit something like that to Niles, but if they were spending the night together he'd know it for certain regardless. Niles found his eyes and grinned at him.

"If it happens tonight, I'll come over and spoon with you."

Geit was silent, but a tiny smile gave him away.

Niles tried to lighten the mood as the two men entered the darkened hotel room.

"So what do you think? Pay-per-view porn before or after dinner?" It was exactly the sort of awkward joke that unsocialized men make to break awkward.

Geit hit the light switch and walked to the curtains to open them overlooking the parking lot. "Actually, I was thinking I might read for a while. You can do what you want to."

He flopped onto his bed. Immediately he put his comment in context and added a caveat: "Within reason. I don't want to glance over to your side of the room to see you flogging yourself like some kind of unwanted stepchild." Geit said it as if it had happened to him before.

"I won't if you won't. However, if I wake up and you're sleep masturbating, don't be offended if I join in."

"What is this, junior high summer camp? We don't have to do everything together, you know." Geit wanted to laugh, it was in his eyes, struggling to make it down his face.

"What? So you're saying you don't want to hold hands on the toilet? Okay. Fair enough, but don't complain when I don't give you flowers on your birthday then."

There was a pause as both men arranged their belongings on their sides of the room. Geit was putting some of his clothes in the room's dresser.

"You actually use that thing?"

"Yeah. That's what it was made for for. It's for clothes storage."

"Exactly." Niles put his finger in the air and waved it, pointing at Geit to emphasize. "That's why I've never used those things. You don't know what the last person shoved in there. Do you think the maids clean the insides of those drawers? The last people in here might have filled that drawer with used condoms. Or maybe they put garbage in sandwich bags and stored it in there for a week while they toured scenic Detroit. Like what Demarr would do. You know? Save it and sleep with it."

"You just gave me some ideas for the extra drawers. You're a bit twisted, aren't you?"

"Yeah. It definitely takes one to recognize another that quickly. I can see that I'm in good company."

Geit laughed. "Yup, you pegged me."

"Nope. That comes later. After you fall asleep."

The dam broke and Geit laughed. Niles laughed with him, and the tension was shattered. Geit still turned the shower on when he used the bathroom, but neither he nor Niles seemed anymore bothered by sharing the room.

Niles fell into a troubled sleep that night and dreamed that he was a pastor in a church reciting a sermon that he didn't believe in. He awoke troubled and sweating. The ghostly parking lot lights filtered past the edges of the sleep shades in the hotel room. Geit was sleeping corpse-like across the room, facing away. The dim hotel alarm clock read 3:22 in red blocks. The only sleep terrors to be found were not his that night.

Niles wondered if Geit would be willing to spoon if he awoke. The idea didn't seem as weird as it had earlier. He laid his head back on the coarse cotton pillow and drifted off again into a troubled sleep.

18. Conferences

If Niles were not crazy, he'd have owed his good mental health to a rigorous routine of physical exercise and sunlight combined with a healthy diet and a strong social network of supportive friends and peers. But he was crazy, so he had none of those things. Ten to twelve hour days at the school combined with a generally lazy attitude toward lifting himself up by his own bootstraps kept him inside during Michigan's few sunny hours. It was easy to be too tired to exercise when he was constantly surrounded by people who looked like they bought all their meals pre-cooked at the convenience store. Working at Pianosa Springs High School meant that there was no supportive community available to teachers either in the building or in the community.

Conferences made those days even longer.

The first parent in for conferences that day was also a local psychologist.

"Good morning." Niles reached across the table to shake her hand.

"You look like hell."

"Well, I do try to dress up a little bit more than usual for conferences, thanks for noticing. Now which student are you here about?"

"You should really take better care of yourself."

"Is that a professional diagnosis or a polite observation?"

"First one, then the other -- the latter shifting into the former."

"What's your child's name again?"

"You don't have my child as a student. I just wanted to let you know how you looked."

She stood up, pushed her chair in and nodded. Niles watched her uncertainly wander off with surety. He furrowed his brow. He looked over at Geit who was just sixteen feet ahead and to the right across the aisle between the library tables where conferences were located.

Geit shrugged at him, and gave him the facial expression that clearly meant "Who cares?" even in the aboriginal cultures that were just now being discovered in the depths of the Amazon river basin where in five years they would all be dead and bulldozed over in the name of cheap beef.

Niles and Geit shared that look often.

A few weeks before, they had both been called down for a 505 meeting by the Dean of Students. Shuhorn had been replaced, and the Dean that faced them now was a top-heavy brunette past her prime named Susan Middleson. Other than a penchant for giggling when she was talking to men in positions of authority, Middleson was as mediocre as her name. Like most of the people in the building she was just passing through on her way to someplace else. She didn't care. Neither Geit nor Niles had the student in class and it didn't matter.

"I need you to come down the counseling office at three o'clock today to take part in a 505 meeting."

"For whom, and why am I just now being notified on the day of the meeting?"

"It doesn't matter, you have to be there at three."

"It matters at least a little bit. I usually like to be prepared for these things."

"Just bring your clipboard, your grades, and be ready to talk about their student." She was clearly trying to hang up the phone.

"Wait a minute. Today is the last day before Thanksgiving. What if I have to get on a plane right after school and fly across the country to be at my dear grandmother's who is about to die?"

"You have to be here at the meeting at three today or else you'll be in violation of state law regarding teacher participation in 505 meetings. You've been notified. If you don't comply, we'll have to put you on a Corrective Action Plan and the Assistant Principal will have to watch over everything you do. If you don't comply, we'll have no choice but to take tenure away from you."

"You can't take tenure away from me. Tenure is based on years of service."

"Not anymore it isn't."

"Tenure in the dictionary is "a period during which something is held, like a job." You can't change the definition."

"If you're not at the meeting at three, we'll find someone who will be, and then we'll give them your job."

"That's not how that works."

"That's how that works. Be there at three."

The phone disconnected from the other end and Niles sank into his chair like a bag of cement.

The students went home for the day, and Niles rushed through grading papers as quickly as he could before the meeting started since there was no guarantee of how long the meeting would last.

At five minutes to three, his phone rang again. It was Middleson.

"The parents are here to see you. Don't worry about bringing grades. It's not your student."

"If it's not my student, then they're not here to see me. Where is a teacher who actually has the student?"

"They're just here to see a teacher. It doesn't matter which teacher. As far as we're concerned, you're just as good or as bad as any other teacher. They're waiting for you. Don't keep them waiting."

Niles scrambled out into the hallway just in time to nearly collide with Geit who was hustling past from his own classroom farther down the hallway.

"Where are you going?

"505 meeting."

"Do you have the student?"

"Nope."

"Me neither. Who is it?"

"I don't know. I was just told that I had to be down there or else I would lose tenure."

As both men approached the door to the counseling office, the dean of students jumped out at them and closed the door behind her, leaning against it.

Middleson was spilling out of her top. Niles looked away. "Make sure you're ready for this. These people took a day off work to come here to talk about their son and you'd better not disappoint them."

Niles was still confused. "Won't they be disappointed that we don't know who their child is?"

"Look. We're all in this together, and if you make me look bad, I'll make you look worse. How's it going to look to these concerned parents when they took a day off work and drove all the way over here just to talk to you about their child and you don't have anything nice to say? It's not going to look good for either of you." She seemed tense. Like a startled cat.

Niles and Geit were two points on a plane, between which a line representing the hypotenuse of a clear look of confusion was plotted between them. The right angle opposite them was all wrong: The ninety degree angle went in exactly the wrong direction.

Geit took a deep breath. "Just follow my lead, Niles."

Middleson glared at both of them one last time and opened the door.

The parents were sitting there, disconsolate, grieving even. They were both sere, short, and proud. The father, with his curling silver mustache looked like he had been a sailor, ruddy and thick of complexion, like he'd been scrubbed overly hard over and over. The mother was a hair model from a wall poster in a hair salon in 1970. Her coif was severely parted and combed without flair or ornamentation. It shone like a duck's feathers and looked just as waterproof. They both looked powerfully timid. Niles sat down next to Geit and folded his hands on the table.

"Which one of you is the English teacher?" asked the old sailor.

"I am." Both men replied in unison. Everyone was confused.

"I mean which of you is Ms. Linn?"

"He is. Er, I mean she is." Niles thumbed toward Geit before he could react.

"We expected a woman."

"Must be a typo." Geit expertly deflected.

"Then who are you?" asked the mother, staring painfully at Niles.

"I'm the math teacher, Mr. English. That's why I was confused by your question. Sorry."

"My son doesn't have Mr. English for math, he has Mr. Browning."

"I'm sorry, Browning is my maiden name. The school hasn't changed it yet in their database."

Middleson looked murderously at Niles as Geit leaned away from him as to avoid an explosion.

"You changed your last name when you got married? That's odd for a man."

"Well, it was all very last minute, like this meeting. Anyway, enough about me, let's talk about you. We're all here to talk about your son." He looked over at Geit. "Ms.Linn here is going to go first."

"No, you go first. I want to hear from you, Mr. Browning, how is my son doing in your math class?"

The old sailor interrupted his wife. "It's Mr. English. His name is English now."

"Actually, it's German. Or Latin. I'm not sure," Niles interrupted.

"You look terrible, Mr. English. Are you okay?"

"Thank you for noticing. It's a permanent condition brought on by a temporary situation. My grandmother is dying in another state."

"I'm sorry to hear that," said the mother softly.

"Me too," Geit chimed in.

"How is our son doing in your class?" interrupted the father.

"Yes, I want to know too," said Geit, stroking his chin bemusedly.

Niles scrambled. "Well, he knows his right triangles from his wrong ones, and he's doing very well in figuring his hypotenuses."

"You're working on triangles? In Algebra Two?"

"Well, yes. I like to make my instruction very inclusive. We bring a little bit of everything in to play, especially for students like your son who display different intelligences. I like to make my instruction proactive instead of reactive when it comes to differentiating pedagogical paradigms. I'm very progressive."

"He is," Geit nodded. "Everyone says so."

Middleson just glared at them both, stone-faced and red, like she was holding her breath underwater.

They shifted their gaze to Geit.

"What about his English class, Ms. Linn? How is his behavior in your room?"

"Mr. Linn." Corrected the husband.

"Mr. Linn," said the wife.

"Well, he comes directly from Mr. English's math class into my room, so his behavior is pretty much the same. He looked to Niles for confirmation.

"Yes, he does. He's saintly. I tell him he's a saint. So well-behaved."

"We're Third Reformed Episcopalian."

"Yes, yes, and he's gaining lots of ground in math class. Right up there with his peers. Great behavior. Just great."

"What's next in each of your classes. What kind of homework should we expect to come home. We haven't actually seen any English homework at all, all year. Do you not assign homework, Ms. Linn?"

"Mr. Linn." The husband corrected her.

Geit improvised. "Well, for your son, I like to keep close tabs on how he's doing with our assignments, so I work with him in class on our dioramas and collages. I work with him one on one as much as I can to make sure that he's getting the differentiation that he needs. If he were to take a lot of work home, I wouldn't be able to monitor him as closely for his comprehension and multi-genre capabilities."

The parents looked surprisingly satisfied with Geit's answer. Niles looked at him, impressed by his ability to make up nonsense on the fly. The parents both looked at Middleson, and Geit winked at Niles. The meeting was going beautifully.

By the sixth year of teaching, Niles had seen it all. That was eighteen sessions of parent-teacher conferencing that had gone off the rails, gone on the rails, flown over the rails crossways without ever touching rails and gone every which way but loose. At least there were no trained apes to account for.

Some parent teacher conferences started happy, some started sad, but only a few started with the threat of physical violence. The threat didn't have to be spoken, although sometimes it was. It was Niles's very first conference ever as a full teacher. It was forty miles down the highway and fifty miles down the river back in Leinster Hills.

Leinster Hills was a Midwestern town that had collapsed under the weight of expensive infrastructure after the manufacturing tax base pulled out to move production overseas. If wafer cookies and air conditioners were more easily produced in Mexico by ten-year-old children working in 120 degree heat for twelve pesos a day, then who could blame the owners of the company for trying to increase their profits? It was the American way.

Unfortunately, the American way meant that without the tax base those manufacturers provided, the public school system had largely gone from mediocre to less than mediocre. It started as money was pulled out, then class sizes increased as teacher compensation took a hit, resulting in less-qualified, less-experienced instructors having more students in each class. They couldn't get supplies or updated texts, and parents started to notice that textbooks couldn't come home for homework because there weren't enough of them for every section of the class that the school had to run. Then, parents pulled their children out of the inner city school to go to the suburban districts, and that resulted in another drop in the money coming into the school from the state due to the reduced headcount. Then the school laid off more staff targeting the high priced ones first - the experienced teachers who had done enough time to have mastery by evaluating the them as ineffective. The district replaced them with less experienced younger teachers or with older teachers who had bounced around from district to district because they were awful. Niles was hired in as a long-term substitute for an English teacher who was on an unpaid maternity leave, so he was one of the former, but not the latter.

Leinster Hills suffered in many ways, and all of that suffering pooled toward the bottom, and at the bottom of every American town were the public school students. If the parents were affluent enough, they left the district for the outskirts when the school started going down the tubes. It was always the poor families who were left to deal with the economic fallout; then when those families fell apart, it all landed on the teachers' laps.

Niles's first full parent-teacher conference experience was a memorable one, not because it was wonderful and joyful, but instead because it was excruciating and painful. The principal had a wonderful idea: each of the teachers would be in their classrooms, receiving parents in the same environment that they taught their children in. There was a small problem with that though. The teachers being alone in their rooms had no guarantee of safety or security in a bad situation. And like Murphy's law states, all things that can go wrong must go wrong, and usually at the worst possible time. Niles was destined to be at school for conferences from 3:00 PM until 9:30 PM - so as to give parents the most time possible to come in and talk with them, despite however many part-time jobs they had to juggle, and most of the parents in Leinster Hills did have to juggle multiple minimum wage jobs. The long schedule was great for the concerned part-time parent - not so great for Niles and his co-workers. Niles was in a wing hallway, isolated and disconnected from most of the other teachers on his floor.

His classroom overlooked the old cereal factory. The day's second shift was working hard, and the smell wafting through the windows reminded him of crazy cartoon birds shouting about chocolate. Students had all gone home, and it was the parents' turn to talk to the teachers as adults. Or it should have been.

It was always the angry parents that came first. They'd been grinding their bones to pick all day (sometimes even for days) and chomping at the bit to lay down their own private versions of the law to the insolent teachers who didn't understand that their children were beautiful unique snowflakes to be nurtured and preserved in amber as the innocent wide-eyed wondrous beings of myth that they were.

So it was that Niles's first visitors showed up twelve minutes early and would not wait to tear into him.

Their child was white, the product of wealthy parents - upper-middle class and with the same sense of entitlement that echoed around in the wealthier districts on the edge of town. The student was not motivated to do homework or classwork because he knew that it didn't matter. He never did anything that he didn't feel like doing at home, and he could see no reason to treat school differently. He didn't accomplish anything in class other than to create a vision of perfect boredom surrounded by things that he should have been doing.

Student motivation was one of those things that mystified both new and experienced teachers alike. A teacher would have to get to know a student better than he might be comfortable to. It would require a greater investment in time than the one or two minutes per period that he had to talk to a student when there were almost forty in the room for seventy minutes, but that was not one of the things taught to young teaching interns.

Niles didn't know how to motivate this boy. He tried asking, he tried telling, he tried walking through an assignment with the boy. None of those actions got the boy to turn anything in. He coasted into the conferences with a six percent.

Progress reports had been mailed to each student's home, and if the students weren't crafty enough to get to the mail first on the right day, then their parents knew the grade. From what Niles could put together in his mind's eye after the conference, this young boy had been confronted by a very angry father. The mother wasn't the power in this house, he could tell by the interactions at the conference. She was behind him and on his left at all times. The two walked in early as Niles was still trying to get some papers graded before his day took a turn. The father was aggressive in posture and tone from the start, entering the room with his head first. He could hardly wait to put Niles in his place for what he had done to his pride and joy.

Niles looked up with surprise and rose to greet and shake the parents' hands from across his desk where the man had stopped, chest puffed out and arms akimbo. He made eye contact with a face whose jaw was set and whose eyes were stern, and no hand was offered in return. He glanced to the mother whose eyes were set to the floor in front of his desk.

"Well, hello..." Niles spoke uncertainly, wondering why the conference had started so early and had gone off the rails so quickly. "Have a seat." He gestured to the desks that he had moved in front of his, hoping for parents to seat themselves as comfortably as the classroom would allow for their business. "It's a bit early, but I think we can start..."

Neither parent sat, but Niles confusedly went back to his chair as both mother and father stared at him silently. The tension was almost unbearable. He did his best to not contribute to building it higher. He glanced back and forth between the two parents waiting for them to say something as the father tried to bore holes in Niles's skull with his eyes.

Finally, it was the mother who spoke, still looking down at the floor.

"My husband would like to speak to you about your conduct and treatment regarding our child, Perry...." She spoke hesitatingly, almost painfully.

Her husband leaned forward, putting his knuckles on Niles's desk and leaning over so he could appear threatening. Niles sat up straighter in his chair in an automatic response.

The man was shaking. "My son told me how you humiliated him in class. You went out of your way to try to embarrass him, to try to make him look stupid. What kind of teacher are you?"

Niles's heart stopped. Instantly he started shuffling memories in his head, trying to think of when and how he might have embarrassed a student in class.   "You're lucky that my wife is here or I would come across this desk and teach you a lesson..."

Niles was stunned. Why would anyone talk to him that way? Surely this father didn't think that he would do anything so awful to a child.

But he did. The son had told him that Niles had called on him in class, and that when he admitted not knowing the answer, that Niles had mocked him. Niles's mind raced. What did he do? He must have done something. Certainly he was at fault. He was young, he was fallible, and there's no way that the student would make up a story that blamed the teacher for his own failure. Niles knew that he'd screwed up. He didn't know what he had done in those moments, but he had to have been the one at fault.

He stammered out an apology while admitting that he didn't know what he had done.

"Mr. and Mrs. Hall, I apologize profusely for anything that I might have done in the classroom that might have impacted your son in such a negative fashion. I assure that whatever I did was unintentional, as I would never seek to humiliate or bully a student in any fashion."

And he wouldn't have, either.

Niles had been bullied himself by a teacher while he was in the fifth grade at his parochial school and knew how horrible it felt. But the parents didn't buy it. The father continued glaring at Niles as if he wanted to tear his embarrassed and apologetic head from his shoulders to then defecate in the stump of a neck that would remain.

It was as painful a twenty minutes as any spent by a Muslim or Jew caught in the hands of the Inquisitors, but would only be truly comparable if one traded the physical torments for the psychological. Niles was only here bound by the constraints of his job, sitting behind his desk, believing the worst about himself.

He was left feeling like utter and complete human garbage as the parents strode out the door after gaining some measure of satisfaction by verbally dressing down and humiliating Niles. From there the evening was better, but he had been knocked so far down that anything at all fit under the description of "better." He repeatedly wracked his brain in between meetings trying to figure how and when he had wounded the boy so deeply because he had to make sure that he never did anything like that to a student again. After conferences he drove home quickly in the dark. He resolved that night to be more aware of his students and to be more sensitive to their needs in the classroom.

Early the next morning, Niles was back, dreading the day and still feeling exhausted from the night before. He had barely slept and not deeply. He beat himself up all night for having been the one thing that he had not wanted to be as a teacher - a bully. His plan was to apologize to the boy in person as quickly and as sincerely as he could.

When the boy's class period rolled around the next day, Niles was waiting in the hallway at the door to greet students. He looked for the boy but he was nowhere to be seen. Niles went about business doing his best to welcome the students to class and police the hallway for problems. The boy wasn't there. Something was up.

The tardy bell rang, and Niles ducked into the boys' bathroom across the hallway to check for stragglers while his students began their bellwork. Empty. He went back to his classroom to take attendance. The boy was there. He'd snuck in after the bell, in those mere moments when Niles was checking the restroom. That showed planning and precision on his part which was more than he'd ever shown in class. The boy was sharpening his pencil and acting more engaged than he'd ever shown before. Niles wandered over to where he was and stood next to him, speaking softly.

"I can't help but notice that you were a bit late today. I think we can let it slide." He was offering an olive branch to him, but the boy wouldn't look at him. He acknowledged Niles with a blank "thanks."

The boy returned to his desk, and Niles went about his lesson. Niles watched him hold on to his pencil and paper as if he intended to do something with it, but he didn't. He didn't write a word.

Niles scanned around the room checking for student engagement and with each pass, the boy looked away. His conduct was different than usual; his pattern had been to put his head down and completely disengage, but today he was sitting upright the whole time - not looking at Niles but creating an illusion of engagement.

Something was up. Niles was puzzled.

The realization hit Niles suddenly, taking the wind out of him. The boy had lied. Niles hadn't humiliated him accidentally. The child had lied to his father to make Niles the villain and to save himself. It was shocking, but there could be no other reason for why he was acting that way in class on the day after the conference. Whether he had done it to save himself from violence or just out of malice, the boy had lied and made himself into a victim in his father's eyes. His behavior on the day after seemed to indicate that he felt guilty about it. If he had not lied, there would be no reason to avoid Niles, to demonstrate shame. That was the only reason he was compelled to break from his usual classroom routine.

The next day, the student skipped. Niles saw him in the hallway, but he didn't come to class. Niles called home and left a message about the boy missing class, but it was not answered.

A week later, the boy was playing in traffic while waiting for the bus and got hit by a semi-tractor. His friends said that they were playing a game running back and forth across the street between speeding cars in the dawn's low light. Fortunately for the boy, the truck had only been going 45 miles per hour and instead of being detonated upon impact like so many deer caught in the headlights, he was only severely and critically injured. He was in a coma for three weeks and when he woke up he'd suffered severe brain damage. He spent three months after that in in-patient rehabilitation attempting to learn to walk again. Beyond that, Niles had lost the job due to declining enrollment and then lost track of the boy.

The boy forgot about Niles and his class along with much of his life to that day due to the trauma of his temporal lobe bouncing against his skull off the truck grill, but he wasn't the only one to forget Niles. Three weeks later, as he departed from Leinster Hills for the last time, Niles was merely someone to never be remembered again.

19. The Texan

Niles was taking his uninterested juniors through the intricacies of Beowulf when there was a knock on the door. As usual a fifth of the class was missing, so potentially it was a student arriving. He nodded to the student closest the door to open it and in burst Linn and Wein.

Several boxes of old out-of-date and never-used textbooks sat in a closet in the back corner, dusty and forgotten - at least until now. Linn and Wein had to have them immediately. He was accustomed to fellow English teachers coming through the room during his planning period and lunch to get things that were stored in the adjacent rooms and closets. Usually they didn't interrupt Niles's class to get books. Today was special.

On Kringe's first day in the building, she came in with Linn and accused Niles of having blown someone to get assigned the room. Linn laughed. It was a slight that he'd never forgotten nor forgiven. Now Wein and Linn were making a point of dragging out a bunch of books that no one would use while Niles was trying to teach a class. It was bad enough that he was teaching an epic poem about ancient northern Europe to minority students who fancied themselves as hard-ass inner city kids, but these were also the same students who went after any distraction like a pack of dogs on a walk at a squirrel park. Some of them even woke up to watch the two carry books back and forth from the closet to the hallway door. As Niles went on shifting from reading the material aloud to differentiate his instruction for the students who wouldn't read and asking them Socratic seminar style questions, he continued moving around the room, making eye contact and trying to capture the attention of his class. Meanwhile, the two who should have known better continued to slowly make themselves as obnoxious as possible.

The clock ticked. Niles tried to teach. Twenty-five minutes passed since the pair had first shown up to make themselves the focus of attention. It was clear to Niles and his students that they were simply there to be obnoxious, walking in and out of the door with a few books at a time in the middle of his classroom, splitting the class cleanly and inconveniencing not only Niles but also the students sitting in those seats nearest where the books were stored. They moved slowly and spoke loudly to each other in the book storage room.

Niles tried to be professional around the distraction, but his hand was forced.

"Pardon me, Ms. Linn and Mrs. Wein. I'm teaching right now, and it's difficult enough to keep students focused on the book without two of their favorite teachers going in and out through the middle of the classroom non-stop for a half an hour. Can I ask that you please come back sometime not during class and finish your necessary task?"

Linn glared at him with the power of her own fictional perfection. "I'm sorry Mr. Niles, we didn't realize we were interrupting anything important." She smiled at Wein. Wein then seized the cart filled with books and noisily banged it into the metal doorframe as they oozed out like slugs under Niles's narrowed gaze. The door clicked shut behind them and Niles continued his lesson after apologizing to the students for the unprofessional display.

It was never the students that drove Niles to drink. He didn't even like drinking. It was always the staff, his co-workers who behaved with less empathy and compassion than the hateful and sullen teenager who made him contemplate pitching himself off the roof or down a flight of stairs.

The end of the semester was the marking point. The routine was set after the very first time when Niles found the perspective he needed to keep going. The walk up the main stairwell and to the third floor was brisk, then to the door. Niles looked around to make sure that the way was clear, then inserted his key into the door that led to the roof. The stairwell was narrow and dark. Niles let the door close behind him quickly and quietly when he snuck in, and now he was uncertain of how to light the path before him. He fumbled at the walls next to the door where a switch would normally be, but found no switch, so he took baby steps toward where he knew the stairs lay before him and found them rather easily.

He found the switch at the top of the stairs and turned it on. Now he could clearly see the step which he'd have to make to clear the doorway onto the roof. When the door popped open with a metallic echo he thought he'd be caught -- just for a moment, but the bright light streaming through the rectangle before him reaffirmed his priorities. He stepped out into the bright sunlight and breathed deeply. From the rooftop, he could see many things that were not visible from the building regularly, not even from the third floor windows. It was striking how adopting a slightly different perspective could change his eyes.

The building was almost empty except for him. Students had a half day to mark the end of the semester. Teachers had a full day. Swamp had taken a day away for a "Principal's Conference" that was marketed heavily to administrators of private and Christian schools, so it was "God's hand" telling her to go. The day was warm and bright for early spring, and most of the staff, including the assistant principals who'd been trapped otherwise, took advantage of their liberty to "work from home." Not Niles. He graded exams, loaded final paper grades into the grade book and set to work making copies and planning out his next week of reading and writing for all of his courses.

There were only two other cars left in the lot when he ascended the steps to the roof. He propped the door open behind him and slowly spun in a circle. He closed his eyes and savored the moment. Here he was, alone, feeling the wind blow over his shorn scalp, feeling the warm sun. Down in his classroom, he could feel neither. It was a cave except for his own efforts to brighten it up and make it inviting for the students.

He leisurely wandered around the edges of the roof watching the traffic below. From the roof he could see that the school wasn't actually "urban" like everyone claimed. "Urban" for people in Education was a codeword for "black" when they didn't want to say that a school had mostly students who were descendants of slaves. Of course, for all Niles knew there was former slave in his DNA even if he didn't look like it. Such was the nature of America.

To the east was a housing development that was still developing. To the south were homes with huge yards that stretched out to the merchant corridor on the main road. To the west were actual farms surrounded by field and horse pasture. Niles wondered why he couldn't take his students across the road and behind the "retirement village" to experience the real world. It was the real world as he knew it when he was their age: manure and cornfields. He could smell both on the wind.

Manure was something that Niles was too familiar with. The first weekend he worked on the neighbor's farm he got to be knee deep in it. The apron chain had broken on the manure spreader, and Niles was perfect for the job. He was handed a three-tined pitchfork and left with the manure spreader in a gravel pit filled with sand. He had to pitch it out. On the ironically bright side, it was cloudy so it wasn't as hot as it could have been. On the darker side, he was pretty far up the field from the nearest road and a long walk from anywhere.

"You're leaving me here alone to shovel this?"

His boss who owned the farm, Jethro, grinned and bared his tobacco-stained teeth, "Fuck you."

Jethro's simpering ape-buddy Bobby half-snuffled/ half-chuckled and grinned from just behind him like the inbred sociopath that he was. The two then jumped into Jethro's two-toned purple pick-up and sped off spinning the wheels and spraying the manure spreader with fresh wet dirt. Niles found out later that the two had driven off to inject expired pig tranquilizers and get high, but that day he felt abandoned. Abandoned on top of a gargantuan load of manure by two semi-epsilon morons who thought it was the funniest thing since the Volume 1: Truck Stop Comedy cassette tape that Jethro had inherited from his uncle when he was in high school which they could repeat word-for-word in between warm bottles of cheap beer.

Niles felt like he was again standing on top of a cyclopean pile of manure with only a three-tined fork.

He paced around the roof, walking from side to side and corner to corner. He was overwhelmed. The drivers passing by on the road were immune to the one-man show on top of the school. All they saw was a building filled with hormonal teens on the one side and the assisted living facility filled with dying old men and women across the road. It was perfect juxtaposition.

Niles thought about how some things in life were universal, how they transcended time and place and how some beings always seemed to be magnets for misfortune. He felt depressingly alone.

His walk around the roof had brought him almost full circle. He was looking over the teachers' parking lot. He saw his own pickup truck. It was a holdover from his years on the farm. It stood out. Other teachers might have had a truck, but his looked like it belonged to someone who'd spent a lifetime on a farm. It was dirty, scratched, rusty, even a bit banged-up.

He was like that too. He never quite fit in. No one had groomed him to blend and meld with the group. The behavior of grooming took place in many classrooms. Grooming was supposed to happen. It is a part of a process of socialization of cultural norms and values. Teachers "groom" students to become good citizens in a similar way to trainers grooming a horse for riding to work well with people. School was about socialization. Niles was not well-socialized.

Linn and Demarr liked to "groom" their students with food. They started with food and moved on to grades. In polite society, gifts were a part of grooming behaviors in everyday encounters. If a man or a woman wanted to date someone, then gifts were expected. Flowers, jewelry, clothing - all of those things might flow from one partner to another if they were seeking a romantic partnership. No one batted an eye. For Linn and Demarr, grades were similar currency. Grades were gifts used to curry favor as well, and they expected to get something back in return from the students.

A higher grade was associated with a more positive outcome: a student who was effectively socialized sought a higher grade by changing his or her behaviors to achieve that A. That was a form of grooming. For students who weren't socialized to think of grades as motivators, food worked even better. Humans had used food as a trading card for millennia in gaining favors and training behaviors.

Linn and Demarr had no qualms about being open in trading food for behavior, using it as a reward, turning classtime into potlucks so that they wouldn't have to provide any of the food but would still benefit from feeding the class. They would tell students to bring in food for "bonus points" and watch the snacks roll in. That created a friendly atmosphere during the potluck meal by incorporating the norms of a shared meal that most students innately understood. They feigned community by talking to students as equals or as an enlightened mentor, one who "understood" and "got it" at the same time that they gave leeway to "special" students. Linn and Demarr did it often. Every holiday was an opportunity. Students felt like they benefitted. They had a day off class and the possibility of eating some homemade food, but Demarr and Linn were using the whole setup for their own selfish gain. They got days off from teaching. They got free food. They used the students themselves to create a hospitable classroom environment for the others without giving anything of themselves. Students did the heavy lifting of creating community and Linn and Demarr were parasites who leeched off whatever positivity was generated and then twisted it to make themselves stronger.

Linn and Demarr would also make deals with certain favored students who were popular and athletic. They cut them deals in grading under the table that were not offered to other less favored students. Once they had the popular ones on their side with special favors then the rest fell into line. They also set up back-door channels for communication with certain students that they hid from other teachers and administrators, giving out their personal phone numbers for texting, or using classroom technologies as modes to establish the same links under the guise of supportive teaching strategies. The students who weren't popular or who didn't kneel before them in the classroom were brought low in other ways. They couldn't get an answer right when called upon in class.   Linn in particular would find something about the student to attack or criticize even if the student could provide a response that was correct. She would attack their hair, their clothes, their voice, anything to weaken them in front of the other students. "Oh, at least you know what a metaphor is, even though you didn't know you wore those same clothes to school all week." Her pedagogy was bullying, and the students who were subjected to it day after day came to accept it as normal behavior from a teacher.

Teaching always happened whether or not the teacher was actively attempting to teach. Linn and Demarr were teaching their students that teachers were bullies, that bullying was normal, and that education was meant to be something painful. Other teachers taught other things. Some were school appropriate and some were not. Rarely did Niles find himself with an opportunity to challenge a fellow teacher on what they taught because he was so busy with teaching and preparing for evaluations.

One day Dallas Austin the computer drafting teacher who was originally from Fort Worth had dropped by the local bar for a drink on the way home while Niles was there talking to Halverson about politics. Austin was polite and amiable, and he was willing to talk to almost everyone. The "almost" was the reason that people didn't like him. Dallas Austin, when he was being friendly and talkative would get a little too friendly and talk too much about certain topics. He was like the army veteran uncle on the right wing of the family tree, who would be recounting a trip to the grocery store when a bit about stopping the car in the parking lot to let an Asian woman pass with a shopping cart full of children and two bags of groceries would lead to him assuming that his listeners had the same keen bigotry toward the "orientals" or the "slant eyes" that led to an inevitable rant about how two bombs weren't enough. Dallas Austin had a keen bigotry toward the certain cultural and racial demographic that made up two-thirds of the student population. He also had either a complete lack of understanding or an uncanny level of indifference to the cues from whoever he was speaking to when they had no interest in what he said.

Niles hated being too polite to tell him off whenever he was pinned like a moth to styrofoam board, but politeness could only last so long under the withering hate of Dallas Austin.

The Texan was three beers deep when he started talking to Niles and Halverson as if they were old buddies bumping into each other at the Klan Rally after-party.

"I'm glad that I can come here, relax and not have to worry about seeing any of my "problem" kids or their parents. You know what I mean? This place doesn't exactly cater to their kind." He gave Niles and Halverson a knowing look and chuckled into his glass.

Niles's head jerked back slightly during the second sentence that dropped from the Texan's lips, and for the third, he tipped his glass to block the Texan's view and gave Halverson a cringing side-eye look that said "God damn it." He sat his beer back on the counter and took a deep breath. Halverson's jaw dropped a bit because he knew what was coming.

"That's probably because there's a bit of a different demographic that this place caters to, you know? Like how it's situated in a mostly upper-middle and mid-middle class neighborhood with higher property taxes. People mostly hit their own neighborhood places when they want a public beer."

The Texan misunderstood his statements and body language, just like always.

"Yeah, that's one way to keep them out!" He laughed loudly and tipped his glass to Niles.

Niles got angrier. "Look, I'm not saying that it's good or it's bad, I'm just saying that it is a thing, and it's because of bigger issues than someone actively trying to keep people separated. Besides, why are you scared of running into some of your kid's parents if you're having problems? Aren't you trying to talk to them anyway to get that worked out? I mean we're supposed to be partnering with parents in helping the students."

Dallas Austin looked like a big sloppy baby with scant long hair that was combed over a bald spot that rubbed on the bedding too much while he slept. Now, three and a half beers deep, he started to make his twisted-up upset face, that one that the infant made when he had been wrapped in his own creamy bowel movement for too long and it had gone cold on his baby-soft skin.

"Those parents don't want to talk about their kids - if they're even in the kid's life. Those people don't give a shit about their kids, they just shit them out. They even look like shit, you know what I mean?"

The Texan was looking not just for validation, but for an ally in his ideological war. Niles knew it, and he wanted to make it politely clear that he wasn't an ally. After all, the Texan might have been an utter racist, but Niles still had to work with him. He wasn't compelled to be friends, but he was compelled to be friendly by the work environment.

He winked at Halverson, whose jaw was now set incredulously.

"What do you mean by 'those people'? Do you mean poor people, because I have a lot of poor students who work hard both in and out of school."

"Well, some of them sure are poor! The Texan laughed and pounded the rest of his beer.

If the Texan knew or cared that Niles didn't approve of his racism, he didn't show it. Like many overweight, balding, short-sighted, middle-aged white men, he couldn't be compelled to care about anyone or anything beyond himself.

Niles's polite tone was used up. "You wouldn't say that if they were white, would you? You might as well call them what you want to, and then complain about how they can say it and you can't. You know you want to. You know that you yearn to say it."

Dallas Austin was feeling heady from the beer.

"I will say it. Fucking niggers. Slavery's been over for almost a hundred and fifty years. Why can't they just get over it?" He shrugged at the question he didn't want answered. "You know who the real racists are..?"

The question was purely rhetorical. Niles bit his tongue.

"They're the people who keep bringing it up! I look at the kids in my classes, and I don't see color. I see personalities. If they act like shit, I treat them like shit!" He smiled at Niles. He looked around the room nodding. "You know if they let those fuckers in here, they'd ruin the place. They don't respect anything."

Niles couldn't resist, the alcohol was in him. His face went red and he fought to keep his volume low enough to only be heard by Austin and Halverson.

"I think the thing they don't respect is the unashamed and blatant racism of people like you. By the time our students hit your classroom, they've met hundreds of stupid assholes like you. They've met you in the streets, in the stores and restaurants, and they've met you in the schools. You and every other dumb son of a bitch who thinks that your whiteness entitles you to ignore their blackness, the very essence of their American identity. You think that racism ended when your ancestors were forced to free their slaves? How goddamn stupid are you? Have you ever listened to a black kid?" Niles moved closer and closer to Austin's flabby pale face. "I take that question

276

back, because it wouldn't matter if you did. They'd be stupid if they ever trusted you for a second to listen without hatred and resentment. You can't get over the fact that there is one word in the English language that you can't say, and you think that displays a bias against people who look like you? You know what our students do around dumb-shits like you? They let you see what you want to see. They tell you what you want to hear so you won't make their lives any harder for them than they already are. That's what they have to do around people like you who've crawled so far up inside their own ass that they can't see light."

Niles was poised inches away from Austin, straining against the urge to violence that bubbled at his very core. The Texan was speechless. His saggy-cheeked mouth gawped. His eyes darted from Niles to Halverson and back again. He got no apology from Niles and no support from Halverson. He stepped back from the bar and looked around for anyone who'd heard Niles go off and was willing to stand with him. He was alone. The bartender was busy at the other end. Nobody in the bar was paying attention because Niles and the Texan were teachers and teachers didn't matter. Finding that no one was on his side, the Texan simpered and pushed back from his stool. He turned away and shuffled out of the building like an overweight emperor penguin.

The two teachers watched him go.

Niles gritted his teeth. "And fuck that guy."

Halverson raised his glass in Niles's direction and nodded, "Amen."

20. Tibbs

Everyone was on their way out the door for a three day weekend. Memorial Day meant that the school year was in the home stretch and Niles could finally feel safe to think about the end of the school year. Niles had even manipulated his Friday schedule to be able to get out of the building at a reasonable time instead of staying hours later than everyone else like he usually did.

Geit was preparing to leave as well. Niles stopped in his doorway on the way to the exit.

"Geit, what kind of plans do you have for the weekend? Grading papers, and then grading papers when you're done with those?"

"Some of that and then I'm going to shoot some stuff."

Niles's eyebrows shot up. "Shoot some stuff? Like 'The Most Dangerous Game'?"

Geit nodded. "No, more like the movie with Ice T that was based on the story."

"I never figured you for the gun owner. You seem pretty liberal."

"Socially liberal, firearm conservative. I like guns. Shooting stuff keeps me sane. Besides, I'm from Alpena. I'm surprised you don't love to shoot things, farmboy."

"Did you know that wounded rabbits sound like squealing babies?"

"Enough trying to guilt me. I just go to a shooting range. Paper targets."

"White hot lead downrange at white hot male rage? What do you shoot at the paper targets with? Got yourself one of those semi-automatics that more auto than semi?"

"Revolvers or pistols." Geit calmly answered.

"Revolvers? Sam Spade? I hope you wear a fedora and a trench coat when you pull the trigger."

Geit ignored the suggestion and had a suggestion for Niles instead.

"You should shoot with me. You'd like it."

"Thanks for the offer, but no thanks. I'm going to have to shoot you down." Niles chuckled. "I have a therapist."

"Guns are cheaper."

"I'd rather buy a first person shooter from the clearance video game bin at Meijer than support the gun industry. And nobody is going to break into my house and use my own therapist to kill me." Niles smiled with self-satisfaction, but Geit had a rejoinder.

"You hope. Your address is public you know."

"Yeah, but here's my real thing with guns. Hear me out, it's convoluted because I think way too much and I see connections and cause and effect everywhere. Here's what I see: men make more money than women in America, something like twenty to twenty-five percent more, so we have more disposable income. We're not teenage boys, so we're not going to spend it on clothing with labels all over it or bad junk food. But, capitalism only works if they can get people to give up their money in exchange for stuff they don't need because once all basic needs are met, there's not a lot of reasons to part with our savings, right?"

Geit sat with his arms folded but his hand on his chin. He was thinking about Niles's train of thought so far. "Go on. I want to hear where you're going with this."

"Conflict creates need. Men in conflict spend more money. Happy men don't consume large amounts of alcohol. They don't buy drugs, go to the therapist or buy guns. Happy and satisfied men don't buy diet pills and energy shakes and penile enhancement drugs. Men who are satisfied don't buy a new car every few years or spend thousands of dollars customizing or upgrading the ones they have."

"I notice you're not saying 'we'."

"Nope, I know what I am. So, to get men to spend money, they have to be made to feel conflicted, diminished, or emasculated - made to feel threatened all of the time. They have to feel small and insufficient. That's what successful capitalism needs.

"Oh, you want to be comrades, is that it?" Geit laughed.

"I'm serious. Stay with me here. They want to cut us off from support structures, to make us feel the constant gnaw of want. The core of this world we live in feeds on conflict. Now, the peak form of capitalism is weapons dealing. You remember what Eisenhower said in his farewell address about preparing for a constant state of war?"

"Well, I wasn't there, but I think I read it. Something about the abuse of power and the potential of the military-industrial complex to abuse its power in connection with government..?" Geit already knew where Niles was going with his train of thought.

"Weapon manufacturers need constant sales to stay profitable. They need a constant state of war. And guns have to be made to last, because if they fail on the field, well, you lose your market. So guns don't really have a range of planned obsolescence. Once the market is full of guns, what do they do? If they're making guns and bullets they need people to keep shooting the bullets and buying the guns, right? So they have to make the average Joe feel frightened, like he's less of a man if he doesn't have the ready ability to spill hot death semi-automatically from his hands. The average American man who owns weapons has almost 12 guns. That's more than one trigger per finger. The only way to use that many guns is to have more arms - pun intended!" He winked. Geit was not amused. "Why are arms called arms? Which arms came first? The limbs for conflict or the tools of conflict as limbs? Either way, make no mistake what your arms are for."

Geit gave a bemused chuckle for Niles's benefit. "I think you took Goldstein and the Brotherhood a bit too seriously."

"No, just seriously enough. Orwell might have been writing fiction, but he was trying to make a point about the real world. He saw war first-hand during the Spanish Civil War. He knew that if he tried to tell people about the nature of war in a non-fictional text that the powerful people he was exposing would bury the book. Of course, the danger in couching his message in a work of literature is that people are in danger of missing it. That's why you and I are in this business of teaching people how to actually read and understand it."

Geit was a bit nonplussed. "Are you sure you're not over-analyzing this?"

"Probably."

"Do you ever do anything fun? What do you do for fun?" Geit was pulling him back down to earth and Niles looked confused. He was simultaneously trying to figure out why Geit thought he didn't have fun just because he didn't like shooting guns and trying to think of what he did that Geit might agree was fun. "You look like a runner, but you don't run. Do you play sports?"

"No."

"Do you even watch any sports?"

"Martial arts. I like MMA."

"Me too. Who's your favorite fighter?"

"I don't really play favorites. I just like guys who can show skill and determination."

"Do you have any plans for Saturday night? Do you want to come over to my place and watch sweaty guys try to beat each other up until 2AM? I was thinking of getting the pay per view."

The invitation caught Niles off guard. Nobody that he worked with had ever invited him anywhere. He was always the odd man out at every job he'd ever had. Here he'd just recited his own conspiracy theory about weapons manufacturers and conflict and Geit was inviting him over.

"Are you inviting me over after dark so you can shoot me?"

Geit laughed. It was an unprotected laugh, deep and hearty, with the head tipping back that gave way to a real smile. Niles blushed.

"I hadn't thought of that. No. Bring a six pack. We'll order pizza. I'll tell my wife to put out the fine china. The card starts at eight. Are you in?

"Yeah, that'd be great. But not this weekend. One of these days, I promise we will." Niles could hardly believe it. He was invited to to hang out with a co-worker instead of just showing up at the same place near the same time by chance.

A few weeks before that, Niles was up on the roof of the school again.

Whenever it was a rough week at the end of the semester, he plotted and planned to get perspective. Whenever the administrative bureaucracy got to be too much, he fled to higher ground to avoid being washed away in the flood. He looked forward to it. It was a benchmark. For Niles, it was a simple matter of rebellion that he'd never outgrown. He wasn't supposed to be up on the roof. Other people rebelled in other ways, they drank themselves into numbness or sought out pills to dull the pain of existence. Niles knew that from a bit of first hand experience.

Niles had used alcohol to undercut negative emotions before. When he was young and stupid, he was the high school senior chugging a beer on the way to school while driving. Teenagers did stupid things because they lacked foresight. Niles had lacked postsight sometimes too back then, but he grew out of those days.

Some people considered the effects of their actions in a long-term view. Geit did. He'd been around, done the stupid things when he was young and learned from them. It was another key concept that Niles and he had in common. It was rough being an employee with long-term visions working in a bureaucracy with myopia.

The district was run like a business, chasing short-term gains in exchange for long-term benefits. Lowest level employees were contracted out of existence, with the number of building custodians being cut by half when a new outside contractor stepped in to save money for the district. Teachers were swappable cogs, and when the substituting for the district was also contracted out, the pay for substituting dropped coincidentally as the district saved money. No one with a degree wanted to teach for a day or two for so little coin on the dollar, so the regular teachers who did show up for work were forced to substitute and never received their planning periods because they were pulled to work in other classrooms whether or not they had even a basic knowledge of the content. They were treated as interchangeable parts even though they weren't. They were tiles of poly-topic tessellations being thrust into spaces where nothing matched up, causing patterns to be destroyed and lost. And like sprockets in the Commandant's Apparatus in Kafka's story, being spread too thin and going too long without repairs meant that the machine would break down on its way to achieving an unreasonable goal.

Not everything was terrible by design, something were simply terrible by accident and Niles could appreciate the things and people that weren't designed to ruin everything. Good people came into the building by accident, but they always left by design.

Tibbs was all-American. He was a privileged gifted child and had been scouted for men's field hockey by all the big men's' field hockey schools. He had turned down a scholarship to play for Harvard's team. He was introduced to social justice by a black girl that he had a crush on in high school. He was always worried about a cop shooting her on a traffic stop when she tried to reach into her purse for her ID. He once told her that if she was going to drive to his house that she should pin her license and registration to her chest just in case a white cop thought she looked suspicious. She didn't date him long after that. It wasn't a good match. He felt like he had to prove himself outside of his privilege and familial wealth.

Niles was poor, but he knew his own privilege. He'd been pulled over for speeding three times by the age of 30 for speeding, but had never been ticketed because he looked like a nice guy. None of his minority friends could say that. One had even been assaulted and thrown in jail for speeding.

Niles had studied to be a police officer for two semesters before the statistics presented in his Criminology classes changed his life. He wanted to use his privilege to help people who weren't as fortunate as he was. Privilege couldn't be rejected. People were born with it. Niles figured that if you had it, you had to use it on behalf of people who had no power. It seemed like a basic proposition, but it escaped Tibbs. He was honest and straightforward. He was reasonable and likeable, and like a lot of other culture warriors he meant well but didn't have a handle on exactly what he meant well.

Niles called Tibbs for help with computers. Tibbs was the T.A.S.T.E. person. The acronym stood for "Technology Assistant Specialization in Technical Electronics." Volunteering for the position meant that Tibbs was responsible for all of the technology in the building for an extra six percent of base pay. It also meant that his email and phone messages were filled daily with almost one hundred other people's problems with technology. If someone's 1970s era phone didn't work, they emailed Tibbs. If their computer speakers didn't work, they called him; if Microsoft XL froze and lost a file, they sent him a text. If a light bulb went out in their classroom, they knocked on his door in the middle of his Statistics class, even though that was a building services issue. For an extra $1642 dollars a year, Tibbs had allowed himself to be the Sisyphus of technology in the building.

On that morning classes didn't start for another half hour, and Tibbs answered his phone on the second ring. It was Niles.

"Tibbs. My computer won't boot. I need help."

"Have you tried turning it on and then off and then on again?"

"Tibbs, I'm serious. I need help."

"I'm serious. Did you try that?"

"Of course I did. I did everything but pray for it."

"Try that too, it's usually the last thing you try."

"Tibbs, I have things that I need to do to get ready for class today. Things to print and copy. Things to set up for class presentations. I need my computer."

"I'll be right there."

Tibbs also had things to do to get ready for class today, things to print and copy, things to set up for class presentations, but as Technology Assistant Specializing in Technical Electronics, he had a responsibility to his co-workers. On his way out his classroom door he walked by two more teachers who were already coming to him to ask him to fix their problems. He told them he'd be right back.

Tibbs swept into Niles's room with the speed and proportionate strength of a giant bee clutching a mug of coffee. He was already on his second cup. He was "Bee-Man" the Fawcett Comics superhero that never was.

"What's up?" He buzzed. Niles was already fretting. Niles was Captain Anxiety, the superhero who was so consumed by worry that he only saved one-third as many people as he would have if he had confidence in his own abilities. No one would have bought ten copies of his first issue even if the covers were printed in 3-D holographic foil.

"Tibbs, my computer is trying to sabotage me. Remember how five years ago they told us we all going to get new computers, and then four years ago told us that they had the computers in a warehouse and were just waiting for the paperwork to replace the old ones, and then three years ago told us that they were starting in the elementary buildings first, and then two years ago said that they'd replace the ones in the high schools that summer, and then last year said that they were replacing ours?"

Tibbs nodded and sipped from his oversized cup.

"Well, mine was never replaced. Was yours replaced?"

Tibbs ignored the question and examined the exterior of Niles's equipment.

"That sucks. What was that thing running?"

"XP? I don't know... The Office suite was from '04."

"No kidding?" He buzzed.

"I kid you not. What am I supposed to do?"

Tibbs's left hand had never shifted from his pocket, and his right hand had never put down the coffee cup. The caffeine calmed him as it sped him up.

"I think everyone else had their computer replaced already. I'll put a call into Tech Services and ask why yours wasn't."

"Thanks, but what do I do in the meantime? I mean, I could pray, but I think this is Lazarus and Jesus is not coming back for at least a few years yet."

"I'll get you a laptop from one of the student carts. You can plug that into the projector and take your attendance on it."

Niles's heart dropped.

"A student laptop? Missing keys, and unable to reliably connect to the wireless?"

"I think they might have fixed the connectivity issue since you last had to use those to teach the Collegiate Preparation courses."

"Tibbs. That was a mess. If I have to put up with those computers again, I may as well out of my own pocket buy every student a small board of slate and a piece of chalk. If I go *Little House on the Prairie* at least I know that things will work, and I can follow through on my lesson plans instead of having to make it up as I go."

"That's what I like about you, Niles. You're so optimistic." Tibbs tilted his head beguilingly and inhaled his coffee. Niles could almost hear the buzz as he left the room.

Niles had many reasons to be optimistic - in an ironic way. One of the classes that both he and Geit often got to tackle on their schedules was "College Preparation." They both referred to the class as "Preparation C." The joke was that "Preparation H" had become the name of a medicine sold for hemorrhoid treatment after the corporate lab had experimented with seven other treatments for the condition. "Preparation C" caused a slow death by pain in the ass.

Niles knew too, that a long time ago, when the corporate oligarchy was just a gleam in the eye of the emergent colonial merchant middle class in America, that their country was one of the places where the unwanted and unneeded inhabitants of many of the other continents could find a way out from under the heel of others who sought to increase their personal material gains by climbing on the backs of those they disadvantaged. They brought with them an ideal forged in the crucible of ancient monarchies, hammered and tempered in Feudal aristocracies and Papal theocracies, and then brought to muscular refinement in modern Federal and so-called Democratic governments. This ideal, so deeply hardwired into modern culture as to be considered merely a part of the societal machine, was that people who had wealth deserved to be in charge. The quest for material holdings was a sacred pilgrimage, and he who had the most gold was clearly closest to the divine creator. "People with wealth should be put in charge of everything" thought everyone, especially in America which by the late twentieth century had built this concept into its institutional DNA. It didn't matter what those people did to have the money, all that mattered was that they had money. Americans believed that by putting them in charge of how society worked, they would help everyone to become as rich as they were.

By the time Niles became a teacher it was a strongly held core American value that putting people with money in charge would benefit everyone and everything. Education was no exception. Educational policy was handled by elected officials who were elected because they had the most wealth and the most wealthy financial sponsors. They had the best name recognition, and therefore, when the average voter (who had hated school and hated his teachers and therefore had rejected learning critical thinking skills in favor of demonstrating the purest form of adolescent rebellion) saw a name that he'd heard before and it wasn't associated with communism or fascism (which were the same thing as far as he knew), he voted for that person.

That's how the tradition of educational leadership was formed in America. Elected officials who had no experience in the field of education beyond sitting in a room as a student were tasked with dictating educational policy that formed curriculum and set managerial procedures for how classrooms operated. Gradually, as public education took shape and matured, what little inroads into school management were made by professionally educated educators in the early to mid-twentieth century were eroded and worn away until they had become more transparent than Wells's Invisible Man. Whereas at one point, it might have been common for a district superintendent to have worked his way up from a lowly classroom teacher, now business and money interests had pushed back until only a handful of experienced teachers were admitted to or even had the desire to be admitted to the ranks of school administration. It was much more common for a district superintendent to have a background in business law than it was for him to have had any experience in education, much less time as a teacher in a classroom with the ability to understand the dynamics of adolescents and education. Certainly there was no elected official who could make a claim to classroom experience beyond being a student. That was a Venn diagram with teacher on one side and politician on the other in which there was no overlap.

So it was that at the same time that state legislators made it possible for public high schools to get money for technology updates, they made receiving that money dependent on a class with no curriculum which was a requirement for graduation. Seniors who were starting that final year in position to squeak through at the graduation podium could not be made exceptions to the rule.

Niles's Collegiate Preparation classes were a hodgepodge of seniors through sophomores with freshman sprinkled in. Even though the class was designated a sophomore class, it was always a case of "we've got nowhere else to put them!" made by counselors who hadn't tried to put them in classes that were made for them, but who had now short windows of time in which to complete scheduling and were entirely happy to put them in any room no matter how poorly they fit.

Niles looked at the Master Schedule printed in his new teacher handbook and groaned. In addition to the usual battery of English courses, he'd been saddled with two sections of the new state-mandated course toward college readiness. Some geniuses in the legislature decided that since Michigan students were so very ill-prepared for college that some tax money could be given to public schools to spend on technology, specifically computers for students to use, but only if the schools created and taught a course that was specifically designed to get students "ready" for college using those computers. The district had no more idea about what that class would be like than the politicians, but they wanted the money and the technology so it was done.

It was the first year of the class and Niles and Geit were given nothing but a very bare bones directive to use class time and re-sources to prepare the students for the springtime standardized tests that would get them into their colleges and to use the rest of the class time for a "career technology" website created by the state a few years prior. It was a hurried mess using outdated graphics and interfaces.

Niles hated the lack of curriculum for the class with a pas-sion. There was nothing he could do. Literally nothing some days due to a shortage of available computers in the building. Niles's College Preparation classes were based out of laptop carts that used a wire-less connection for the online component of the class. It was a great idea on paper but the execution was full of holes.

The internet connection that the school bought from Spectra Communications was for a lower data cap than what the school was consistently using. Only so much data per month was allocated to the building based on the amount the district paid for it, and once that data cap was exceeded (usually on the eighth day) the level was throttled back and the school was charged for overages that tripled the amount charged in the basic package. Once the speed and data were choked off, Niles's and Geit's classes would be unable to get online and access the websites they needed to use as mandated by the curriculum.

Since the whole curriculum was based on those websites and those alone, once they were inaccessible, the laptops were useless, just like whatever lesson plan was based on the curriculum. Both teachers found ways to cope, but only after Niles spent several days working with the building parapro who was in charge of technology for minimum wage and part-time hours. He'd call her, and she'd troubleshoot, not knowing yet that the school had neither the services nor the infrastructure in place to support the class from the very start. There was a great deal of time wasted. The students both loved and hated the class. They loved it, because since Niles and Geit were both creating their own content for the class in addition to all of their English classes, it meant that assignments and materials were being tried for the first time with little in the way of experience in terms of meeting the course's nebulous requirements. Some flew, some didn't. When things didn't fly, the students got to engage in their favorite methods of wasting time. Both teachers did everything they could to make the classes take wing, but sometimes there just weren't enough hours in the day.

There were many times when Niles could flap his wings all day, but he could just never seem to get off the ground.

21. Cook

There were many things that were wrong. Niles was growing increasingly frustrated with his own ability to make them right, but the worst frustration of all was how deeply ingrained into the system the wrongs were. It was a wall wherein every fifth brick in the layer was replaced with a bologna sandwich. The gravity of the situation hit home for Niles when he was sharing his frustrations with the summative evaluation for juniors with his retired mentor teacher, M.A. Cook, one day over lunch.

"On their final exam they're asked to give either a definition or an example of consonance or assonance. They're also asked to break the word "language" into syllables and mark them as stressed or unstressed."

"That's the junior final semester exam?" She looked non-plussed and taken aback. "That was on the test for my grandson in second grade." Her grandchildren lived in the next town over and went to school there.

Things had changed a great deal in Pianosa Springs schools since she'd retired. The curriculum had been made much more friendly to students who couldn't reasonably be asked to work at grade level. Daisy's philosophy of education for minorities had taken a firm hold. That exam and the junior curriculum had been re-written by Linn and Demarr.

"Is that the test you give to your students?" Her face held a look of concern.

"Well, I have to give the same test, I can't change those materials. When I go off course and the other department teachers hear about it, they complain to Swamp because I'm not following the mandated curriculum. So what I do is leave it on the test, but then I add a great deal of my own material on the back end since what we're given takes the students less than a half hour to complete."

She frowned. "Why do the other teachers complain about what you're doing?"

Niles thought hard before answering. Why did another adult act that way in a professional setting? "They don't like me personally. When I point out issues in pedagogy in the department that they see it as a personal attack."

"Is it?" Cook knew him well enough to know the answer already.

"Yes. I think some of the things they do and the ways that they do them make the whole profession look bad. Teachers are under fire enough without actually being as worthless as we're accused." Niles pushed his food around the plate with his fork making a neat pile. "Like that junior curriculum. It's garbage. Pure garbage. Or something worse. I'd be embarrassed to have to show it to parents or other teachers outside the school district. Hell, I'd even be embarrassed by the lack of academic rigor in it if I turned it in as a practice sample when I was an undergrad trying to get my shit together."

"So you're saying it's shit, and it's not together?"

"Oh, it's together all right. Two people made up a lot of shit, then scraped it into a pile, put it in a binder, and now it's our curriculum."

The curriculum failed to make meaning in Nile's eyes -- either objectively or in the minds of the students it was supposed to be cultivating. In Niles's elective course he felt more freedom to innovate.

It was day two of the Adventure Story workshop in Creative Writing. Students trudged on, blood-shod and weary, heads on hands balancing on their desks. It was as if the snow outside had engulfed them, its weight covering all. Niles fought to keep their heads above the icy chill and off their phones. Day one had seen adventure stories with insipid titles that had no zing, like "Jerry was a Race Car Driver" and "Tommy the Cat." Niles could feel the life draining away.

His lesson on interesting titles had seemingly fallen on deaf ears. Almost a quarter of the pieces were turned in untitled, so Niles had tried to arm those nameless pieces with powerful, evocative names before copying and pasting the stories into the workshop booklets with the word processor. A short piece about an elf queen being rescued by a green hero named Segment was now titled "No Scrubs." Niles was nimbly pulling magic spells from his memory, spells that would resonate with an audience and capture their imaginations screaming like dying seagulls into nets of narrative construction. A tale set in the 15th century, somewhere in Italy (the writer was not sure) that featured a highly trained assassin struggling against a church conspiracy was now titled "What about your Friends?" A story set on race tracks with friends competing against each other and obstacles on the course became known as "Ain't 2 Proud 2 Beg." Niles was delighted with each new title that he assigned on the untitled stories. His fingers danced across the keyboard as he leaned forward in his chair with each one. In between, he leaned heavily backwards in his chair, hand on chin, eyes scanning the ceiling for universal truths that he could bestow in these slots left empty by apathetic students.

He ran out of slots. There were only so many untitled stories. Some students had listened and tried their most mediocre. He couldn't re-title those. It would be disrespectful. Almost as disrespectful as ignoring a teacher's directions on an assignment.

And so it went, on and on, punctuated only by things that always became so much more deeply depressing than they should have been. Like department meetings.

The next department meeting began like all the rest since Demarr took over from Geit. Linn had been the de facto face since Geit let go of the reins to be a father, Demarr was just taking a turn to up her pay by that insubstantial department head sum. Niles walked in right as the meeting was scheduled to start, mostly to avoid awkward pleasantries at which he was never good at, but also to avoid spending more time than necessary around people who made him feel physically ill. Geit was already there, texting his wife with plans regarding their child or dinner or whatever Geit was doing those days. Trudeau was taking notes on something esoteric going on in his head in his ever-present journal. The coven was already cackling and participating in their group ego grooming session, petting each other with comments on their outfits and sharing banalities at twelve decibels too high for their conversations to be private. Hippy was late, as usual, seven minutes after Niles. He had better things to do. Niles, Geit, and Trudeau had better things to do too, but Hippy was the only one of them with head far enough in the clouds to not give a damn about being the last man in the door after the meeting started.

This meeting, unlike one of Swamp's, had an agenda, but just like Swamp's these department meetings also had a tendency to drift wherever the egomaniacal person in charge gathered the most ego gratification. Everything was focused on one person and her inflated sense of self and how she wielded it as a weapon. Somewhere in her story, someone had made her feel unimportant, and now everyone else who wouldn't kiss her rings had Hell to pay. The message was often the same as Swamp's, but only to a degree. In the close quarters of the English department there was an addendum to the "all teachers are awful" rhetoric, and it was that Linn and Demarr in particular but also Kringe and Wein were shining standard bearers of all that was good, and that the obvious failure of the rest of the staff to teach didn't pollute or diminish their obvious shine of excellence.

Niles knew the difference between shit and Shinola even in the most challenging of circumstances. He also found less challenge than most people in discerning plain stupidity from belligerent ignorance, and then again the differences in those two standard human conditions from different types of evil that were almost as common as brown eyes and birthmarks. There was an ordinary evil in the ignorant or stupid, an evil that wanted to set fire to good useful things just to watch them burn down to ash, but there was another evil, more insidious and even more destructive. It was an evil that required an intellect and some foresight, an evil that sought to enrich and grow itself at the cost of goodness.

In these meetings, the cruelty was of a very distinctly negative quality. She liked to pretend that she was the heroic protector of students, but she was not. Anyone who didn't gush with admiration for her was just fuel for the fires she started. She would burn the building and every student in it to feed her ego. She held none of the false religious compunctions of Swamp. Swamp would stand on the top of a hill overlooking her own destruction with a cross and claim it was all for Jesus. Linn would proudly look at what she'd wrought and admit it was all for her own ego. Linn could have poured raw, untreated sewage in a cupcake tray in front of the department and told them to eat it. For their parts, Kringe, Wein, and Demarr would have gobbled it down. They'd have wolfed it down and then complimented Linn on the flavor and the texture, asked her what she'd used in order to make the cupcakes so wonderful, and then tried to push them on Niles and the others as if they were the finest royal European delicacies.

Niles doodled skulls on the agenda sheet and focused on grading papers that he'd brought with him. He was attentive enough to turn and nod if someone said his name, but he knew that no one would. The meeting wasn't about him. Few of the meetings that Niles was required to attend actually required his presence. There were plenty of other times that Niles showed up on a required basis that no one needed him. Meetings demanded attendance, and attendance was one of the most important things in Pianosa Springs Public Schools. Every meeting demanded his body, but few meetings required his brain. Parent meetings were among the few that did.

Niles walked into the conference room late because he was having so much fun writing feedback on his students' papers that he lost track of time. It was three minutes that he regretted. Punctuality was a hallmark of his that he liked to brag about.

"Mr. Niles, thank you for joining us. This is Rudyard's mother, Victoria."

He nodded at the principal and then shook Victoria's hand apologetically before taking a seat that was covered in breadcrumbs for some reason. Niles decided against brushing it off as all of the eyes, including those of the other four teachers in his "Learning Community," were on him. He hoped the bread was dry and would brush off his dress pants on the way out.

"We are meeting here today to discuss an intervention for one of our students here at Pianosa Springs Central High School. Now, Mr. Niles, your referral here for Rudyard is the most recent one, so let's start with you. Will you please tell his mother exactly what was going on in your classroom that moved you to write this referral?"

Niles clasped his hands together on the table and leaned forward. This required deep effort to keep a straight face.

"Well, Mrs. Brown, I was attempting to talk with the students about our current text, The Odyssey, and as I was looking around the room checking for engagement, I noticed that Rudyard was..."

Here he paused. As he relived the incident in his mind's eye, the words to describe it seemed to run away.

"Well, he appeared to be... simulating... sexual intercourse with the desk."

Rudyard's mother's eyes doubled in size and she suddenly shrank back from the table.

"You're not serious." She clutched her chest over her heart in incredulity. "What do you mean? Like how was simulating intercourse? Like humping the desk?" Niles's eyes were locked on hers as he nodded. "You can't be serious. You must be making this up?"

Her eyes scanned each of the other teachers eyes in turn as she looked for some kind of confirmation that she was the butt of some absurd practical joke.

"I sincerely wish that I was, Mrs. Brown. At first I tried to ignore it, as he was seated behind most of the other students and none of them seemed to notice it, but when he saw that I saw what he was doing, he... intensified his.. uh, actions."

"No!" Her mouth dropped further in astonishment.

"And then the other students started to notice, so I had to address it."

"And..?"

"He refused to stop and instead started audibly moaning and humping the desk so hard that he was banging it into the desk of the girl in front of him."

"No!" Her hands slapped down on the table to punctuate it and her face was as pale as it could have gotten. Niles was trying not to laugh, but a smile was slipping through. Mrs. Brown was either smiling or grimacing at the absurdity of it all.

Her head dropped to her hands.

"I am so sorry. I do not know what is wrong with that boy. I've tried. I've really tried."

Niles nodded. "We've all been trying." He looked around the room at his peers including the godly math teacher, Duckett, who began to speak.

"You know Mrs. Brown, we've all been praying for him... even before this last referral." Niles hadn't been praying at all, but he bit his tongue.

"Lord help us all!" Mrs. Brown was on the edge of apoplexy. Here she had found a Christian ally in the fight for her child's soul. Fortunately, the dean of students intervened before a praise conference could be convened.

"Be that as it may, we need to work together on a real intervention here and now to get this young man to the proper place for school."

"What do you want to do with him?" asked his mother. Her jaw was set and hard, but she was almost pleading. "You want to suspend him? I'm okay with that."

"Well, we've done that before. We've done in-school suspension before. We've done meetings and interventions. This is his fourteenth intervention in eight weeks."

"Yes, I know."

"What we're saying is that the things we're trying to do here at school aren't working. They're not having a meaningful effect on his behavior. I want to talk to you about what's going on at home." Mrs. Brown was frightened by the prospect of being held accountable for her son's behavior. She was enthusiastic about the school punishing him more, but reluctant to address her own role in her child's life. She looked nervously at the four teachers there.

"We've been trying some things at home," she said uncertainly, as if teachers hadn't tried anything at school. She hesitated. "Can we talk about these things privately? I'm worried about biasing these teachers against my son. There are some things that I think we should keep private." The dean looked around at the assembled teachers. Niles nodded.

"I think that whatever we need to do in order to move forward is agreeable to everyone here." She looked to the rest of the team for affirmation and received it. They rose from their chairs to leave Brown and the dean alone.

Duckett paused on the way out to clasp hands with a grateful Mrs. Brown, "I'll keep praying for Rudyard." She smiled her best Christian smile, dead from the nose up, before rushing out the door.

Niles went back to his classroom and closed the door to resume grading. He could use his brain for that. It felt like he was using it for something meaningful then.

22. Teacher Appreciation Day

If Principal Swamp had been an educated reader of more than the Bible, she might have learned that her motto regarding teachers had already been succinctly stated by Oscar Wilde. She'd only ever heard that Oscar Wilde was homosexual, and that was all she needed to know. She thought that she was the only one who said that "Everyone who is incapable of learning has taken to teaching." She hated teachers. She also didn't understand irony. Why didn't people just say exactly what they meant all of the time like the Bible did?

She knew that "Professional Development" and "Teacher Education" were false notions that were used by educated fools to justify taking paid breaks. Every teacher was a finished book - some of them novels, some of them picture books, but all of them finished and done and nothing could be added or changed - just like the Bible (which she'd only heard read). Except the Bible was good because it was made by God, and teachers were bad because they were made by books which were not the Bible. She "knew" those things, but she didn't know that the Bible she used had been carefully selected by the pastor at her previous church because it aligned most closely with his personal beliefs out of the seventy versions that were available. Neither he nor she knew about the Council of Nicaea or any of the the other councils that edited and trimmed books from the canon that they believed was divine. They thought God edited it.

She needed only her Bible as guidance in working in education. She knew what a vocation was, and she was following hers by punishing the intellectually arrogant who thought themselves fit to teach without her guidance. An intellectual was anyone who did not allow herself to be guided by faith, and as she well knew whatever that does not proceed from faith is sin. She knew many important things that liberal elites could not learn from secular colleges: she knew that bad company corrupts good morals, and that the companions of fools will suffer harm, and that one must keep an eye on those who cause dissensions and hindrances contrary to the learned teachings and that one must turn away from them. She knew also that one must keep away from every brother who leads an unruly and untraditional life and that faith was the Lord's proof of absolute loyalty. She couldn't see why the teachers did not have faith in her. She knew her reason for existence was to be as Christ-like as possible, and that Christ is Lord, so then she was destined to be the lord of her vocation to shepherd the faithless sheep of her staff lest they mislead the children into troubles and misadventure.

She knew to distrust anyone who wore glasses because glasses were a sign of intellectualism in young people. Intellectualism was a disease that led people away from the righteous truth. She knew that God's perfectly and divinely miraculous human eye which could only come about through his intelligent design was designed to stop working well after the age of forty, and so it was part of God's divine plan that his shepherds memorized the Bible quotes that were needed to control the behavior of the flock, or else one must bring its divinely radiant knowledge and wisdom closer to the face to better bathe in it.

She knew that intellectualism was passive and that only faith was truly active, because a proud and learned man was guilty of introspection instead of self-flagellation which was intrinsically demanded of all who had faith. Except that if one truly had faith as she did, then she could tell a mountain to go throw itself into the sea and it would be done. Or even if If she had faith as small as a mustard seed, she could command a mulberry tree to be "Be uprooted and planted in the sea," and it would have obeyed. That was why she was so sure that most teachers had no faith in the savior who died on the cross so that their sins might be forgiven, because if they could not train a child to refrain from using the electric pencil sharpener when they were speaking to the class, then surely they were without favor in the house of the Lord.

She did not appreciate teachers at all.

Teacher Appreciation day was a made-up social media/greeting card holiday that came around just often enough to inconvenience people like her. It wasn't an official holiday, but the liberal media had created such a storm about it that if someone like Principal Swamp ignored it, it might create bad press. Bad press was something she couldn't have. Her image was very carefully and craftily controlled. She had to give them something or make a show of "support" for the teachers in her building.

It was easy for her to manage despite her discomfort. There was no challenge that she could not surmount with the help of her lord. Swamp had bought several bags of candy on clearance after Halloween a few years before and then lost them under the piles of paper and assorted miscellanea in her office. One day while navigating piles of forms and paperwork she knocked over a mound and found the candy. Normally candy didn't last long at school. Everyone wanted some of it. She told everyone that she bought it for the students, but she ate much of it herself. She inflated with extra calories like a slow balloon over many months. It was for the best that those bags of candy had been lost - quite likely God's will, though she replaced them the very next week.

She had too much expired candy. Could candy expire? Did sugar go bad? Those were questions which she couldn't be bothered with. The labels on the packages of taffy said they had "expired" a year ago, but weren't expiration dates just a corporate ploy to get people to throw away perfectly good candy and buy more like they did with canned food and medicine? Regardless of those answers, this was the answer to both questions of how she could show her "appreciation" to the teachers on her staff and take care of the candy so that she wouldn't be tempted to eat it. She called in her secretary to divide all the different dollar store candies equally to pass out to the staff on Teacher Appreciation Day.

The sense of satisfaction she felt was palpable. This was executive decision making at its finest. She had solved two problems at once, or perhaps even three! It was surely God's miraculous hand at work guiding her to success. She was creating a world in her image.

Niles appreciated the teachers that he worked with. When Niles first started teaching, he'd gotten to work with some great ones. Many of them had been driven away or simply left over the years. Six had opted out through retirement, one had left the district to teach elsewhere, three had left for private business careers, five of them had moved cross country. One was dead. There were few left. Most of the new teachers that had come in to replace them had little to no understanding of how to behave in a professional manner.

There was one new math teacher, short on height and tact that was across the hallway from Niles for three years. Her name was Kyder, and she was a simulacrum of a math teacher. As personable as a vegetable, she was an alien caricature of a human. She liked horses and worked with them during the summertime. Niles hoped that the horses got more out of her than her students did. She didn't decorate the classroom at all; it was as barren and dry as her personality and wit.

She would arrive just before the students each morning, robotically open her door and stand next to it as if she were an elevator operator waiting to pull the lever for passengers. She did not interact with the students or with Niles who stood in the hallway opposite her greeting teachers and students as they came down the hallway toward their classroom destinations each morning. She made no faces of recognition for good or ill, and after the first few days the students stopped attempting to interact with her any more than they would attempt to interact with a doorstop. Every so often just as a lark, Niles would try to get a reaction from her, offering a loud and presumptive "Good morning!" or an engaged and interactive "How are you this morning?" She never evinced a reaction that showed that she'd even heard him. Was she deaf? Was she unable to speak of anything beyond mathematics? Niles would never know.

The students knew but didn't consider their knowledge worth sharing. She was rooted in a tradition of teaching that no longer had any meaningful relevance in a world where the students expected interaction and entertainment. According to student opinions shared with Niles, she had fewer tones than one, lectured about math without demonstrating equations, and couldn't effectively answer the simplest of questions that were posed to her. She was a robot with programming that couldn't adapt to the local environment. Students didn't like her, but more importantly for the job they couldn't respect her. She had no idea about how to deal with difficulties in the classroom beyond sending the student out of class or ignoring them in the same way that she ignored Niles across the hallway.

When Niles first came back to PSPS as a full-time teacher they had just begun with their "Small Learning Communities" program. The school had received a large grant to implement the latest in educational reforms meant to increase levels of student achievement. It was a program meant to make cross-curricular connections between teachers of various disciplines, to allow them to work and plan together in small units of nine to twelve teachers to monitor and discuss student achievement. It was a great idea in theory and perhaps even in practice, but no one would ever know in Pianosa Springs. The money was taken and used for other purposes not made known to the teachers in the district. Perhaps those dollars had gone into the pocket of the superintendent as part of his record-breaking compensation.

The SLCs did nothing that they were meant to do as designed by the consulting team. They created more mandatory meetings that looked meaningful from the outside, but on the inside each was only another unproductive waste of time and resources when the teachers already had so much to do.

They were "small learning communities" in name only. Small yes, but only in relation to the very largest of public schools; learning yes, but only in the tradition of learning how to skirt the rules and create illusions that were meaningful from far away; communities yes, but only in the manner in which they were localized in one geographic location. The meetings turned into a festival of complaints for teachers who had been minimized as human beings. They had no healthy release valve for the stress, so the meetings were a symphony of squeaky wheels that received no grease and rattling lids on overheated pots abandoned on the stovetop.

The end of one semester was about to melt into the beginning of another. Grades were going in the book, and Niles had an afternoon to finish them and put things together for the start of the next semester. It was quiet and everyone was wrapped up in trying to finish things that were now due. People were working quietly and concealed around the building.

When the building was constructed in the early seventies, it came complete with small personal offices for administrators and counselors on every floor. Within a few years each of the offices had become smoking lounges due to the large "smoke eater" devices suspended in the ceiling of each office space. Niles didn't smoke and could hardly imagine an environment that needed smoking lounges, but that was how things went. After smoking indoors was finally banned throughout the state in public buildings, those smoking lounges had been converted into offices, book storage rooms or kitchenettes with giant vintage microwaves.

The rumor was that the building designer had made his career in designing prisons, but Niles considered it just as likely that he smoked three packs a day and had tumors for lungs. It was hard to imagine people smoking so much without drinking. Everywhere that Niles found smokers in his life, he found drinkers, and he also found that they were one and the same. A person could drink without smoking, but they could not smoke without drinking. It didn't matter what they drank, it could have been hard liquor or beer, wine or champagne, window cleaner or rubbing alcohol, but there was typically a glass or a bottle in one hand and a cigarette in the other.

Some teachers still smoked. Demarr for one. She'd charge out to her car during her plan period and peel out of the parking lot. She spent an easy forty-five minutes of each plan period power-inhaling a chained pack of unfiltered cigarettes. She found that she could easily smoke eighteen during her plan if she only inhaled through the cigarette and lit each from the one previous. Niles couldn't imagine how her voice did not already sound like she ate balls of crumpled tin foil, but he figured that perhaps all the damage went straight to her physical appearance. Some days she resembled nothing so much as the burnt ash of one her cigarettes, hair askew and falling out, her pale mottled skin looking like a pack of Marlboros left in the rain too long.

Niles wasn't an extremist in relation to trying to cope. A lot of teachers drank. Niles didn't know what else to do, so he drank too. He didn't enjoy it as much as other people seemed to. He saw drinking as little more than adult obligation - a way to fit in. People went to the bar to be with other people. For Niles, there was simply no other place to go to avoid being alone. Some of his peers were already filtering out of the building for a drink to celebrate the end of the semester.

Niles ate his sandwich at his desk while grading exams and research papers. He went on grading all afternoon, just finishing his last score input ten minutes before the four o'clock deadline. Then he took a lap around the school building on the second floor to stretch his shoulders and legs after spending most of his day hunched over his desk bathing in fluorescent light. The building was deserted already. Contractually, he was only obligated to be in the building until 2:30, but Niles never left that early.

Niles had been buried for weeks in paperwork, planning, grading, and documenting. He needed to push his head above the surface and fix his perspective. Niles found the door to the roof had been left unlocked by maintenance who often stored their tools and supplies under the metal steps. Niles slipped through the door smoothly and climbed up the dark stairwell to the upper door. He unlatched it and propped a broom in the hinge so it didn't close, locking him on the roof automatically.

Cool autumn breezes swept around him on the top of the building, and he zipped his coat to the collar. Currents and eddies spun dry brown leaves, making visible devils in the parking lots and yards across the road. Farmers were taking in some of the corn on distant fields, and he could see a combine slowly marching, devouring another row. Cars wailed by on the highway, just barely visible on a hill to the west. The varsity football team was practicing dropping passes on the field to the south, near the cemetery almost to the road. Niles made a square circuit on the roof, savoring the view. From up there, the wind coursing around him, he could almost imagine flying like he did in all of his favorite dreams. He felt free from the weight that threatened to suffocate him.

23. Evaluation

Sven Bobsdottir was an Icelandic giant. If he were a Viking, he would have been king, but instead he was a math teacher. King of math teachers. With his powerful lanky arms, he could have swung an axe so mightily that heads would have bounced forcefully for meters. All of the plunder taken by the math department fell under his purview. Fortunately for the rest of the teachers he was as funny and as awkward as he was gentle, and as gentle as he was good at teaching math.

Sven's last name was either a sign of good fortune or bad luck. It depended entirely on how one chose to see it. His maternal grandparents had settled in Michigan's upper lower peninsula where the weather felt like home after moving from Keflavik, Iceland. By tradition every Icelander took the name of his or her father combined with the noun "son" or "daughter" as a surname. Bobsdottir got the "dottir" suffix from his single mother because his father was a drifter who had invested only one night in his future offspring. Sven kept his mother's name and her Viking genetic heritage while his American father blew off into the nethers of the American midwest.

Sven strode the halls of the school like a giant out of the Sagas, but his myth was a comic epic. He was a giant who noticed everything because everything noticed him. He had an adult attention deficit disorder that manifested as a series of herky-jerky body language and rapid-fire utterances about math that both riveted and dismayed the students in his care. They loved him and would have followed him on the epic raids and pillages of his foremothers if he'd asked. The younger teachers in the building held him in awe, Niles included. He was as tall as Niles had wanted to be and had an odd charisma that was as awkward as it was entrancing. Geit did a dead-on impression of his mannerisms even though he was a full foot shorter. He admired Bobsdottir. Like almost everyone else, he looked up to him more than literally. When Bobsdottor retired to spend his 60s sailing Lake Michigan, everyone was sad to see him go.

While Geit became department head, he took on the task of being department supply manager as well. When Linn ordered a new printer, Geit kept it hidden under his desk for an extra two months because she was so obnoxiously and unnecessarily rude to him. Niles was in his room during their plan period one day seeking ideas for linking texts to teach when Geit took his feet off his desk to point under it and said, "Check this out." Niles couldn't believe it at the time because he didn't yet realize the games that adults could play at work. It was perfectly in character with Geit's trickster aspect. Geit was the smartest kid in the room most of the time, and he didn't give a damn what people thought of him. The truth behind his attitude wasn't revealed until later, when Niles finally figured out that the reason he played as being so apathetic was that he was firmly convinced that everyone actually hated him.

Of course some people did hate him, like Linn and Demarr, but more people loved him. The ones that hated him were simply just awful people, so their hatred had to be expected. That didn't make it hurt any less. Geit seemed to simply roll with whatever people did around him. Niles was still the opposite. He rolled into a ball.

Niles was staggering one morning. The weight of everything had toppled and fallen on him completely the night before. He was telling his wife about the challenges he faced each day at school: the struggles with unsupportive administration, the hateful coworkers, and the students who all too often behaved like they forgot that teachers were only humans. Her terse response was, "All you do is complain, I don't want to hear it any more." Niles was dumbfounded. He didn't think it was complaining. He thought he was just talking about work and looking for support from his spouse. He was wounded. After that, he no longer talked to her about work. She was the only person he talked to about serious, meaningful things, and he hadn't talked about the stresses of teaching with anyone else in longer than he cared to remember. Keeping it all inside was too much and that morning felt particularly overwhelming. He was a weak, weary, and spent Atlas with the world on his shoulders.

The bells rang that morning and the halls emptied. It was his and Geit's plan period during first block, so he went down the hallway and knocked on Geit's door as soon as it was clear. Geit was sitting at his desk, feet up, reading student work.

"What's going on, Niles?"

Niles was shaking, his eyes were red. He was fighting back the pain in the nose that led directly to tears.

"I don't know if I can do this today, man. My last evaluation was awful. My unit on Beowulf is not going well. The kids hate the book and literally everything I'm trying to engage them is failing. I've got so much grading to do that I'm getting crushed, and everything else pretty much feels like garbage right now too."

Geit looked up at Niles. "You've been taking this home, haven't you?"

"Well yeah, there's just not enough hours in the day..." Tears welled in Niles's eyes.

"Not the grading, although you can't carry that everywhere with you either. This place. This place and all of the bullshit that gets shoveled on us here. You've been wearing it. You've been walking around with a few hundred extra pounds on your shoulders for weeks." A tear rolled down Niles's cheek. His back did hurt. "You've got to stop thinking about this place, even when you're here. You can't think about it. It will eat you up." He paused to consider Niles's face. "It is eating you up, isn't it?" Niles nodded. The tear dripped from his cheek to his shirt, creating a small dark dot on Niles's blue.

"You have to stop thinking about it. You have to stop thinking about all the stuff that goes wrong, all the stuff that can go wrong, all of the stuff that's out of your control."

Niles looked down at his shoes, leaned forward, rubbed his shaved head and nodded. "I know."

Geit didn't overthink. He was in the moment. Overthinking was Niles's thing.

"These places, they're not so terrible. Now isn't the worst time to be in. I think I've seen you inhabit some far worse moments. Join the rest of us, just for a little bit. Give us a chance." Geit paused and then reset while Niles was still looking for a switch locked on the floor in front of his shoes.

"Look up, Jo-Jo. Look at me. Do you see me here?"

Niles looked up and nodded.

"Now look out the window. What do you see from there, from that spot right where you are, what do you see from here?"

Niles sniffled to draw the tears back up inside and the words came tumbling out of his mouth. "I see clouds, cumulo-nimbus clouds refracting the light from the sun that is slightly southeast. I see five geese or ducks, I can't tell from here, flying somewhere in a short v. I see the leaves on the trees in the courtyard. They're green and gold scales on a rattlesnake's tail, like waves in an ocean of green." Niles paused dreamily out the window, caught in the leaves with the breeze. He finally caught his breath and breathed.

Geit nodded. "You're a good person, and a good teacher. You're probably the smartest person here on any given day. I tell you to tell me what you see, and you speak in metaphors without even thinking about them. You and maybe five other people in this city know exactly what kind of clouds those are. You're not that bad. Why are you always in your head? Are you five minutes ago trying to say something smarter? Are you twenty-five years ago trying not to be a dumb kid? Or are you in the future? Are you trying to figure out what to say to me when the bell rings and we have to go to work? Are you trying to plan what to do if your wife leaves you for another man? Take a few minutes each day and be in these moments, okay? You don't get these back. No matter how many times you go back to them in your head, you don't get these moments back. Live in the present, Jo-Jo. Live in the now. Stop worrying about tomorrow or the next day. Whatever comes, you can handle it."

Niles didn't know if Geit was right or wrong. Things had to be objectively evaluated and paperwork wouldn't suffice to prove whether Geit was effective. Teachers had a great history of being wrong and then doubling or tripling down on being wrong to protect their egos. If there were a marker between the two sides of teachers in Niles's mind, that was it. Linn and Demarr would hammer away at being wrong until the students thought it was right. Bullies had that sort of power, practiced on playgrounds from an early age to change reality, to make wrong into right and weakness into strength. It was how they survived. He thought he and Geit were on the other side.

Forming friendships was difficult as an adult, because friendships required a lack of effort. Children formed friendships from proximity and shared experiences, but as adults, people were rarely allowed to share experiences. Adults rarely made new friends, particularly teachers who were locked in rooms with piles of paperwork. It was very lonely even though hundreds of children were cycled through those classrooms every day.

Some adults preyed on children for some of their basic needs. It was not a newsflash requiring the world to stop spinning and the superheroes of the the world to unite to thwart the insidious threat, it was simply a deviance from the boundaries of adulthood and childhood that went so far back into prehistory that it was a normal event without labels or notice. Sometimes it went too far, and it made the news. Usually it didn't.

Sometimes Niles thought about having children of his own, but the thought frightened him terribly. What were adults who conceived children thinking? How many adults had formed an alliance with other adults to conceive children because they felt "ready" or as though there was something "missing from their lives"? It seemed to him that having children was often used to fill an emotional need and no one thought twice about that. Niles listened to his own students, and he'd heard more than a few girls admitting a desire to have a baby just for that reason. The girl would say, "A baby would have to love me" and Niles would shake his head. A child could fulfill a desire to be loved or needed, which was a very basic human need and even though he'd counsel against having a child to get love, there was no denying that the humanity behind it was real.

There was something undeniably insidious and repugnant about a man seeking self-completion or friendship in children, and the fear or expectation of that behavior in men was one of the things that kept so many otherwise quality men out of the teaching profession. It was terrifying to think of one's own self as being regarded as a potential villain simply because he was a man and men were typically predators. But there was no doubt too, in watching from the inside that some women did worse things in different ways than any man would have an opportunity to do.

Niles thought back to the playground: boys were physical bullies. They'd push and shove or punch and kick, gather a team of betas around them to find and diminish a younger or smaller boy, an outcast with no friends, and use those things to boost their childish egos. Girls, on the other hand, whether through nature or nurture used more psychological or emotional methods. Girls rarely punched and kicked, largely because that was considered aberrant for such "pretty little things" and they were socialized at an early age to be more subtle, to be more covert, to be more psychological in their victimization to hide it from disapproving parents. Girls might deceive another girl who was lower on the social ladder, pretend to be her friend, invite her in, and then make her a willing participant in her own subjugation by leading her to believe that being dominated by other girls was a normal part of friendship, or that cruelty was something special that created a "real" bond between the people involved.

Other teachers that Niles knew had their ways and means to achieve trust from a student for less than pure motivations. Linn was locally famous for winning the "Most Inspiring Teacher" award year after year. Naive young Niles saw that and thought, "She must actually be highly effective!" She was effective at gaming the system. Every year, she'd ask a counselor who liked her for a list of the seniors - one that included their class rankings and G.P.A. She'd then ask for a "favor" to get the students put into her classes who were on the borderline for graduating. Those were the students who at the end of the year picked the teachers for the "inspiring" award if they graduated. Then she'd wheel and deal with them on their first major assignments. She pulled them aside and gave them a lecture about how much she "wanted to see them graduate" and how she'd "do what she could to make sure" they walked across the podium at the end of the year. She pretended to be their advocate and friend while using them to get the award.

"I understand that other teachers have given you problems" was where she would often start. By putting herself on the side of the students against other teachers she was ensuring that they saw her united with them against a common enemy: other teachers who had not coddled or enabled them. Throughout the semester when they failed or did poorly on an assignment, she'd pull them aside again.

"I know that you're having problems with those other teachers, so I'll go easy on you here, but just this one time, because I know that you could do better..." And each time the student did poorly and got pulled aside, she'd give him or a her wink to solidify the trusting relationship that was there without teaching the student anything useful that could help him or her to be successful in school or in life. But Linn got what she wanted. That was the only thing that mattered.

Linn worked hard to intimidate her students too, putting more effort into mocking and bullying them than actually teaching them.

Every year she won awards that were decided by the senior class. Niles should have learned from her what it took to be "highly effective" in Pianosa Springs. Instead, he found himself being the "anti-Linn."

Niles was often asked for advice about things that he had no power to impact. He did the best he could.

"Mr. Niles, I need help."

"I know you do. I'm not a licensed therapist, but I'll do what I can."

"Not that kind of help. I'm trying to do this multi-genre artsy-fartsy thing for Ms. Linn and I keep messing it up. I'm so frustrated." The student gritted his teeth in mock anger and real resignation.

"What's the problem?" Niles paused before continuing. "I mean, besides the fact that whipping together some Barbie Dolls, paper mache, and craft store pipe cleaners doesn't prove you can write or understand what you've read." He paused again for dramatic effect. "Or that requiring students of potentially impoverished means to purchase craft materials in order to earn a grade is just blatantly unfair?"

The student clearly was too focused on his own misery to catch Niles's thinly veiled attack on Linn's practices.

"I'm not supposed to have anything 'cliche' about my piece, and she says it's cliche and trite and that I have to fix it before I can turn it in."

"That's funny. A walking, talking cliche is insisting that you avoid cliches."

"She says my project might as well belong to someone else. She's seen it all before."

"Probably because the assignment is cliche." Niles said. He thought he was being funny.

The boy dropped his head to the desk, just lightly enough to not slam it in frustration but strongly enough to make a point.

"Mr. Niles, I need help. Please stop making jokes and help me."

Niles sat up straight and reconfigured his tie to cultivate a more serious mood.

"Okay. First, let's consider the real definition of cliche. If something is cliche, it's overused, unoriginal, and trite..."

"What does 'trite' mean?"

"Dull and overused.' So basically calling something trite and cliche is saying the same thing twice."

"Her mouth is trite."

Niles chuckled at the student's accusation. He was glad to see the young man put his new vocabulary word into use immediately. "Probably, but there's a problem with her calling your work cliche. Can you see it? Obviously, you've never seen anything else like your work that you're trying to turn in, right? Otherwise you wouldn't be so frustrated because you're actually trying to meet the requirements of the assignment, right? I mean you're not just trying to fudge your way through it?" The last part was a question that required an affirmation, so Niles waited for the nod before continuing. "The problem is that whether something is "original" or not has to do with the creator's exposure to similar things. 'Cliche' is a conditional situation, depending on a person's own bias. If you've seen it before, it's cliche, if you haven't, then it's not. She's demanding that you use her perspective of what cliche is, but she's not defining it along with the assignment. She's just waiting until she sees what you're doing and then calls it cliche. Get it? Her idea of cliche is her own personal bias, and that's inherently unfair of her to ask that you obey her mental image of what cliche is. You and she have entirely different ideas of what that word means because each of you is carrying a different variety of experiences and cultural references. Something that's cliche to you isn't necessarily cliche to her. A cliche isn't a culturally standard thing, and even if it were, you and she are from different cultures. A middle-aged black Chinese woman who is filled with self-loathing is a lot different than a seventeen year old who grew up watching every episode of a cartoon starring an anthropomorphic sponge twice."

"I get that now, but how does that help me?"

"Ask her how the heck you're supposed to come up with something new when her criteria is so personally biased. That's not even a fair assignment, and she shouldn't be attempting to grade you based on her biases, she's supposed to be teaching you objective truths and analytical skills. Has she even provided you with a list of cliches to avoid? Did she even try to teach you what a cliche was?"

"I don't remember..." He seemed uncertain.

"Well, you had to ask me, so I'm assuming that the answer is no." Niles tried to teach instead of bully. Linn bullied.

Two weeks later, the student was back in Niles's room at lunch.

"Hey Mister Niles, I got that assignment back from Linn."

"What did you get on it?"

"I got a D-. She said I didn't even try to be original."

"Did she then give you any examples of what 'original' was?

"No, she said that was my job and that I failed."

"Really? I think she might be forgetting what a teacher is supposed to do. Teach."

"Oh well. Whatever. As long as I pass her class, I don't care. I just need the credit."

Niles frowned. "That makes me kind of sad to hear you say that. The point shouldn't be the grade or the credit. It should be learning something new and coming away from the experience with more than you had before, not just with a sense of resignation that you can't meet someone else's arbitrary and impossible standards."

"Whatever, Mister Niles."

Whatever was exactly what it was.

Children went in many different directions. Niles grew up with a lot of religious families up and down the cross-sectional farm township who went to the same church as he did. The religious students always seemed to go one of two ways: If a family told a boy that he was born bad, a defective product that had to be fixed through divine intercession, then he believed it and became what they predicted he would be. If he was told that he was good, a divinely crafted work of beauty gifted to his family by a loving omnipotence, then he became that more often than not. His self-image was set early on, and whether he knew it or not, he became exactly what his parents told him he was.

Sometimes, people could do meaningful things, even if they'd been told that they were meaningless.

Niles ran into Hippy in the copy room at lunch. Hippy's real name wasn't "Hippy" but no one in the building could remember what it was anymore, so everyone just called him what he looked like.

"Did you submit your lesson plans?"

"Damn it! I forgot! Shoot, today is Wednesday, isn't it? He paused for a moment, reflecting. "You know what? Now that I think about it, I didn't submit them last week either. I'm not even sure if I submitted them the week before. I just know that I sent them in at some point." Hippy was briefly lost in thought trying to remember whether he remembered or was simply imagining remembering.

Niles brought him back to the moment. "I submit them every week. At least every week that I remember. My evaluator has been on me if they're even an hour late"

"I don't have the time, man." Hippy furrowed his brow in false disdain for the idea.

"I don't either," Niles admitted cautiously. "I just change the date and submit the same one every week." He smiled at Hippy knowingly.

"No way! Are you serious?" Hippy looked around the empty room like they were going to get caught stealing. "And nobody's caught you?"

"Do you think these administrators are going to take the time out of their days to read your lesson plans? Do you think they'd even understand your lesson plans? They just want to get their boxes checked off on the list."

"Dang..." Hippy was incredulous. It hadn't occurred to him yet that other people in positions of authority didn't do their jobs. It wasn't that he was naive, it was just that he'd never taken the time to let his mind wander to where the people in place to make sure that he did his job didn't do their jobs. After all, that was the bureaucracy of education.

Administration was there to make sure that people lower on the ladder of importance were doing their jobs. Swamp was just like all the rest of the administrators. None of them had ever been in a classroom as a teacher, but they were the ones who had to judge if the teacher was effective. Niles had heard from Cook and the retired teachers that principals at one point had been experienced teachers in the district, but that practice had died long before Kaseman had come to power. The rules of the school were just like the laws of the land. They were made by people who could afford the trappings of power and only applied to the people who could not or would not seize power for themselves. There were no rules in place to make certain that the people making the rules followed their own rules if they didn't have the decency, knowledge, or dedication to be as "effective" as they demanded their subordinates to be.

Part of every teacher's evaluation was his lesson plans. Every minute had to be spelled out, every moment delineated and bulleted so an administrator could glance over the document fleetingly and know whether or not the teacher was effective at selling his own performance.

Niles was good with problem solving, but he was also depressed. It was an ongoing problem that he couldn't solve. It wasn't a sort of depression where he could just go and check himself into a mental hospital without some sort of unbearable social censure, but it was more unbearable than he could bear without some sort of medication. So he went to the doctor and asked to be put on drugs.

If it became a severe depression, he could climb on a desk in the middle of one of his classes and start shouting about bugs in his brain and then get paid time off while the community clucked their tongues at him in low public voices and mocked him in private. If it didn't reach that level of unbearability, he would have to continue to masquerade as a well-adjusted educator who people wanted to trust their children with for seven and a half hours a day. Anyone would have had to be a bit insane to be a high school teacher, but just the right level of insane. Any less, and they were incapable of the job and also incapable of convincing people that they were capable of the job. Any more and they'd lose whatever modicum of respect the public allowed them. For Niles, it was just a moderately severe depression that always kept him on the edge of contemplating suicide. He thought of thinking about it, but never allowed it to get to the point where he was standing on the back deck with a firearm in one hand and a bottle of booze in the other contemplating the taste of the former rather than the latter. It was probably a good thing that he didn't own a gun.

A little depression could make him a better teacher. After all, wasn't that why his administrators told him he was ineffective? A little self-loathing could make him doubt everything he did enough so that he was constantly driven to do better in the classroom. Just enough depression could make him focus perfectly on the nonverbal feedback he got from his students and change his method right there in the middle of the process effectively. Too much depression would make him slouch back in his chair behind his desk while staring glassily off in to an invisible distance while chaos bloomed around him. So he medicated just enough to keep him mildly to moderately depressed, and thus he could be at best "mildly ineffective" according to the district's metric.

The thing that all teachers in the district wanted, that biggest, most beautiful gold star was to be rated "highly effective" in their evaluations. No amount of antidepressants could wrangle Niles the coveted "highly effective." As they were told repeatedly in staff meetings, the difference between "effective" and "highly effective" was solely in the documentation. To get the highest rated effectiveness, one had to build a cohesive file that proved it: student work, including photos, videos, and various types of "documentation" to prove beyond the shadow of a doubt that one was truly "highly effective." Niles suspected that all the time spent collecting data about himself and his own teaching could be much better served by simply creating the data that he wanted to show and spending all the time he saved actually being a good teacher.

Niles walked into Halverson's empty room. His computer was unlocked and opened to the grade book program. He was planning on coming back immediately. Niles felt it. He was looking at the framed picture of Geit with Halverson that sat on the bookcase just above his desk when Halverson popped back through the door.

"What's up Niles?"

"Not a lot. How's the evaluation process coming for you?"

"Mine is fine, as far as I know. I just talked to Watters though. He got burned to the ground on his." Halverson's evaluator was the hapless dean of the students, Middleson. Middleson had become Dean of Students when Kaseman pushed her out from behind her guidance counselor's desk telling her that he "needed her to make things better" when Shuhorn fell apart at a staff meeting. She was completely overwhelmed and totally out of her element in a position of management, particularly when it came to evaluating teachers because she had never been one. All she could do was rubber-stamp Halverson and move on to the rest of the job that was overwhelming her while she giggled about it.

"What do you mean, Watters got nailed?" Niles was confused. The situation surrounding him looked clear-cut when Niles thought about it. Watters had made the local news a few months before when he was assaulted by a student and choked into unconsciousness as other students recorded the incident on their cellular phones. When he passed out, another student kindly pushed the assailant off of him. The perpetrator had a history of violence against authority, and wasn't even assigned to Watters's class. He had friends in the room and had decided that spending time with them was more important than being where he was supposed to be. When Watters asked him to leave, he was violently rejected. The video hit Facebook, YouTube, Reddit, and even Instagram. There were seven different versions from nascent young filmmakers going around the internet and the district's attempts to sweep the incident under the rug were doomed to failure. Watters was out for three weeks to recover from his injuries, both physical and psychological, but the student who was already classified as "special needs" for his anger management issues was only suspended for a day until public outcry forced the hand of the Department of Public Safety and Watters himself started mentioning pressing charges for battery.

In response to the incident, every White Flight passenger in the suburban communities for miles around who had moved away from Pianosa Springs patted themselves on the back for solid decision making and went on to criticize the district as being an "urban shithole."

"Watters got 'Ineffective - recommended for dismissal' on his evaluation because for the three weeks he was out they ran a merry-go-round of incapable morons through, a different face every day. Then he had to spend weeks after he came back trying to get his classes back to where they were before he was choked out." Halverson was incredulous but only slightly angry because he was already so benumbed by what went on in the building.

Niles could only say, "I'm not surprised."

"And get this: his evaluator is the AD, and he wanted to let it slide, but Swamp told him that if he let Watters slide on this, that it was going to be his head on the platter instead."

"Why does anyone's head have to be on a platter?" Niles asked even though there was no answer.

"I know the kid that choked him. He's got issues. He shouldn't even be in a regular school building, but the district doesn't have a program to put him in that fits. They just shoved him in here and put it all on us. So when he went berserk, they either had to throw Watters under the bus or look bad themselves for putting him here. The assistant superintendent's line is that Watters provoked the kid."

"Okay, so asking the kid to leave when he's not supposed to be there is provoking him? How does that work? I mean the whole interaction's out in public and on YouTube with six thousand views. How do they blame Watters?"

"I don't know, but that's their line. Watters is pissed. He's looking for another job."

"If he isn't, he's an idiot," Niles said, while actually thinking that he himself might be an idiot.

"Hey, did you see Geit today?"

"No. I guess his son's sick again. I talked to him last week after he missed a couple days. Their daycare won't take a sick kid, all of their family lives in different parts of the state, and his wife's job won't give her any more sick days to take care of a sick baby."

"Well, Swamp was asking me about him today. Apparently he's out of sick days too, and she's taking it personally."

"Well that's drivel."

"Yeah, well he's about to get screwed over on his evaluation. Everybody knows it. If you see him, you'd better let him know."

"Geit's a smart guy. I'm sure he knows. I think his priorities are in the right place."

"Priorities or not, Swamp's got an axe to grind, and both he and Watters are on the block." He paused. "Actually, everybody's on the block."

Niles's evaluation hadn't gone much better. In fact, he may as well have been assaulted by a student. Niles gathered his evaluation materials into a cardboard banking box and stamped up the steps to the vice principal's office. This was another vice principal doing a short tour of the building on his way to greener pastures without Swamp or Kaseman.

Walter Woodley was a genius who'd taught physical education in Canada for two years before emigrating to America to make good on his American dream. He was young, younger than Niles by a full internet generation and shorter by a half a foot. He was a self-made man crafted by the Canadian education system who had fallen for an American girl and ended up in Michigan making sure that no child was left behind. He meant well, but all's well that ends well, and he wasn't going to end up in Pianosa Springs.

Woodley, who hadn't been able to make it down to Niles's room for an observation opened with a question. "Mr. Niles, did you bring your 54B plan sheet?"

Niles opened his box, pulled a folder from the top of the banker's box into his lap, then leafed through a handful of documents, pulled out his 54B plan and set it on the desk. Niles then proceeded to pull out necessary document after necessary document and put on on top of Woodley's desk.

"You know that every form that I fill out and put on your desk could be fictional, right?"

Woodley looked at Niles with the tilted head of a confused dog. "All of your scores come from the assessments."

"I know that. That's where they're from. I could have made up these scores that I'm turning into you. Anyone could. How do you know that they're legitimate?"

Woodley still looked at Niles with a dog's eyes, uncomprehending. "These scores make up a large part of your evaluation."

"And how could you know whether or not someone was trying to load their evaluation?"

Woodley paused and thought, edging closer to Niles's Socratic questions. "I can check anyone's grade book. All administrators have access to your grade book to check that your scores which you submit here are the same as the ones there."

Niles shrugged his shoulders. "How do you know that those scores are real scores? Maybe the teacher just runs through the papers, glancing over them before tossing them in the recycling bin, typing in grades based on how much they like each student, or the food they brought in, or something arbitrary like that?"

Woodley's eyebrows arched and narrowed like a suspicious dog's. "Are you saying that teachers would be dishonest?"

"What if the test was dishonest? What if instead of showing student growth, it showed levels of apathy and nothing more than the ability to memorize simple information?"

Woodley looked alarmed. As a former physical education teacher, complex synthesis of meaning wasn't something he was accustomed to looking for in evaluating tasks related to physical fitness. He didn't know what to say. Niles felt compelled to fill the awkward silence.

"A lot of teachers use multiple choice tests. The most common number of choices is 4 or 5. A student who guesses has a 20-25 percent chance of getting a correct answer regardless of whether or not he has any knowledge at all of the material on the exam. Most teachers will game that by simply offering two or three answers of the four or five available that are obviously wrong to the student if they have any cultural or self awareness at all, making the probability of guessing a correct answer something more like one in three. Mathematically, we're assessing how good they are at guessing instead instead of how much they know about the subject matter. A multiple choice test is more like gambling than demonstrating knowledge."

Woodley only half listened to Niles, but he knew he needed help.

"Hold that thought, Mr. Niles." He reached over his desk to where his walkie-talkie had sat silent, flashing a green light on mute. "Mrs. Swamp, Mrs. Swamp, do you copy?"

Both men waited in silence for a response. Woodley uncomfortably shuffled through the papers that Niles brought.

Swamp's reluctant voice came out of the machine on the desk. An overdrawn and disinvested "Yes."

Woodley was apologetic. "I've got Mr. Niles here in my office and we're having some questions that I don't know how to answer."

Swamp hit the "talk" button early so that Woodley and Niles could hear her drawn-out exasperated sigh. "Mr. Niles, are you having trouble meeting the documentation requirements?" Woodley gave her an extra few seconds before pressing the "talk" button on his device and nodding at Niles to speak.

"Oh, I've got the required forms. I have a different kind of problem with the process. All that paperwork proves is that we can do paperwork. It doesn't prove that I'm an effective teacher."

There was an extended pause

"Is this man serious, Woodley?" Swamp asked, either not knowing or not caring that Niles could hear her.

"He seems serious. He claims that a teacher could falsify information on the forms that are required for evaluation and that multiple choice tests are measures of luck."

"Mr. Niles. The difference between an effective teacher and a highly effective teacher is documentation." Niles held out his hand to Woodley and received the walkie-talkie. Woodley passed it off like it was a chemically unstable explosive.

Niles gritted his teeth for the unpleasantness to come. "No, that's not true at all. The difference between you and someone who knows what effective teaching actually is, is years of experience, of which you have none." She ignored him. Swamp never seemed to hear what Niles said.

"Mr. Niles, if you can't provide us with written evidence that best practice instruction is taking place, then it's not taking place."

"I thought you were supposed to observe us to make sure that we were doing our jobs?'

"Mr. Niles, we've been over this. It's difficult to tell what best practice looks like."

"It's not if you've got any actual experience teaching."

"Are you implying that Dr. Kaseman has given us bad instructions?"

"I'm saying that documentation can lie a hell of a lot easier than being in a classroom, or superintendent forbid, actually asking students."

"We can't trust students to be evaluators of their own learning. They're easily manipulated by teachers." Swamp's reply was terse. She wanted out of the conversation.

Niles was quick to reply, "I can't trust a principal to be an evaluator of a teacher, they're manipulated by their own self-interests."

"Mr. Woodley, can I speak to you for a moment, without Mr. Niles?"

Woodley reached across his desk, indicating that Niles hand him the walkie-talkie. Niles declined and pressed the button to talk. Woodley reclined back into his chair and tented his fingers pensively.

"Look, if we're doing what we're supposed to be doing, then we're creating self-aware learners who should be good and able to be honest in the evaluations of teachers. Aren't we supposed to be creating a 'college-going culture'? And isn't every college professor over at WMU evaluated based on his or her student's feedback at the end of a semester?"

"Mr. Niles, you and I both know that we can't trust students to be honest in their evaluations of teachers because of the power that teachers wield over them."

"What you're actually saying is that teachers are so dishonest that you think they'd tell their students to bias the evaluations, right? But yet you think the teachers are honest enough to provide you with truthful data when you don't go in the classrooms to get it yourself?"

"Paperwork is proof, Mr. Niles."

"Proof of what? It's proof of the ability to do paperwork and nothing more, but nothing less. In fact, nothing at all but exactly what it is."

"Mr. Niles, teachers like you are the exact reason why there has to be documentation that proves effectiveness in the classroom."

"That's a lie. First of all, there are no other teachers like me, and second of all, if there were, someone would have called you all out on this farce a long time ago instead of bending over backwards and taking it like every teacher in this district is doing."

"Mr. Niles, why are you so intent on causing problems and being a troublemaker? Is it because you've been ineffective, over and over again?"

Niles couldn't help but laugh in spite of himself. "I haven't been, but I guess you're the one making up the official story."

"You're very flip, Mr. Niles. Mr. Woodley, put that in Niles's file. He's 'flip.'"

"You can't put that in my file. That's meaningless."

"Oh, it's meaningful, Niles. I'm in charge here so I say what goes and what stays." She paused and Woodley looked away. "Woodley? Take the walkie-talkie back and come down to my office right now. We need to have a talk."

Woodley put the walkie-talkie face down on the table.

"I'd like to give you 'highly effective" Niles, but I can't."

"Why not?"

"Because you don't have the paperwork. The difference between minimally effective and "highly effective" rating is the documentation."

"But if I spend all my time building the paperwork collection that you're asking for, I won't be "highly effective."

"That doesn't matter. If you provide the paperwork, I can give you "highly effective.""

"I'd rather be a good teacher."

"Then I can't give you 'highly effective.'"

"That's some catch, Woodley."

Woodley was visibly confused. "What does that mean?"

"If I have to tell you, you won't understand."

Niles was excused rather impolitely. Woodley had an important meeting to get to.

Later that day, after the students went home, he walked by Duckett's room and found that she was staying late too, almost as late as he was, which was remarkable for a math teacher. He peeked through the door and made eye contact with a Duckett who looked even more dejected than usual, and making eye contact incidentally he was compelled to ask why she was so late in the building.

"Hey. How is it going?" Even though she had no use for Niles, he still felt the odd, ill-fitting love that compelled him to care about her. The dark bags that he saw around her dark eyes told him more than her lips would.

"It's going good," was her curt reply. Niles wanted her to love him in the pointless, meaningless way that he loved her, but she never could. No one could.

He smiled his most gentle smile and replied, "Do you remember what I told you about that answer when we first met?"

She wearily rolled her eyes and declined with a no that said both "no" and "leave me alone." Niles understood both, but wanted to help. Like always, he was never the right person. He simply stood in her doorway, his head tilted and balefully aimed at the floor as his eyes sought hers.

A sad moment passed before he responded. "It doesn't matter anyway." He was turning to leave as she spoke up again. She was not understanding, just letting the words slip out of her lips as if saying them would cast out some kind of demon.

"My evaluation didn't go well." She paused again as Niles looked at her from across the room. "I'm too new at this. I had this dream when I was in school that I was going to be the teacher of the year as soon as I got a job. I'm not. I can't do anything right in here." She looked at the stack of papers on her desk, then back to Niles.

He wanted to quote both Shakespeare and Peter Gabriel to her, "Is that a dagger or a crucifix I see, clenched so tightly in your hand?" before seeing that the thing held so closely to her own breast was nothing more than a red pen.

"I'm sorry. Mine didn't go well either." He sighed fitfully. "I think perhaps we're both putting too much personal weight on an impersonal process."

She ignored him and continued.

"I just wish that I could find something good in all of this. I've prayed on it... " She paused to see the effect on Niles and then went on. "And I realized that God is testing me." Niles moved closer to her, sat in a student's desk near hers as she gazed downward at her tented fingers on her desk. "How do you handle it, Niles, being awful all the time?"

Niles bit his tongue. He believed that she didn't mean to be cruel, but she couldn't help herself. Her Christ-centered world that revolved around her meant that everyone around her was just a pawn in her personal test against evil moderated by Jesus. No one was a human worthy of consideration but her. All the rest of the teeming masses of the human race were just as meaningful as Job's children. Niles was a prop in her show.

"I never stop trying to be a better teacher. Just because someone who has never seen me teach doesn't see that doesn't make it untrue."

She looked thoughtfully as him, but she was thinking of only what someone else had once said to her. "I guess I just have to have faith."

Niles suppressed an eye roll and sucked his teeth. He wanted to slam his head into a wall to make a statement, but settled on standing up instead.

"If faith were the only thing that mattered, then the power of belief would make Santa Claus real. Just keep putting work into your goals instead."

"Like my 22 C on the state evaluation? Raising the scores of my African-American boys on my summative assessment by twenty percent over their pre-test scores while accounting for a standard deviation?"

Niles was already walking out the door, looking away from her. "No. By teaching them things that are going to help them successfully navigate the complicated world that they live in. Worry about that instead."

Duckett always felt like she had a bad taste in her mouth after talking with Niles. Something was off. It left her feeling dirty all the time, but especially her mouth, as if some of the things he said entered through her lips and polluted her. She drank on occasion, even more than Niles did, but it always left her feeling dirty in some odd way, though not as dirty as being around Niles and talking to him. Wine was not as much of an issue to her, as wine was in the Bible, and wasn't it wine that was transformed into the blood of the Savior every mass at church?

The New International Version of the Bible (which she knew was the most correct version, having been edited and revised by American Bible scholars who were filled with the best, most American Holy Spirit) had little to no mention of people like Niles or how to deal with them. He was just a misguided human being who thought he was more meaningful than he actually was. What was wrong with him, anyway? Why was he so forward and hardly a gentleman at all towards her? Maybe it was because he was a false Christian: a Catholic. He was the only one of those she had ever met and she was not impressed. What did he think gave him the right to talk to her at all about Jesus or faith? These were all questions that echoed in her head. Sometimes being a good, friendly Christian was more trouble than it was worth if it meant that you had to witness for your faith to people like Niles.

At least Niles was good for something though. After talking to him that day, she decided that Niles was God's way of telling her to find another job. She felt she had done enough missionary work with the colored people, and that now it was time to get back to white society. Niles's last conversation with her had been short but painful. She'd grown tired of hiding her intolerance for homosexuals, Catholics, and lesser races.

It was her last day. She'd be replaced midyear by a succession of substitutes in typical fashion.

"Mr. Niles, I won't see you anymore after tomorrow."

"So you are leaving, eh? The kids were asking me if you were quitting, and I had told them that if you were going to quit, that you'd have told me because we have a good working relationship."

"But we don't. I don't like you."

"I thought we were at least work friends."

"I tried to be your friend." She sighed. "I just can't be friends with someone who doesn't know Christ like I do." Niles's mouth fell open a little. "You're going to Hell, and I just can't have negative influences like you in my life." Niles's jaw fell a little more. "You've been a negative influence on me here. You've pressured me into hiding my faith." Niles closed his mouth before responding with as much calmness as he could muster.

"I've pressured you into not saying awful things to our students. You can't tell them that they need to be saved because they're black, or that they're going to Hell because some of them are Baptist, or just because they're mixed up teenagers who don't know what they feel about anything yet and they're trying to figure it out."

"That's what I mean. You don't understand Christ. I have to be a witness for him everyday."

"I understand that Christ was supposedly a pretty accepting guy who hung out with prostitutes and other people that the church officials didn't like."

She sighed at Niles like he was a silly child and rolled her eyes. "I'll pray for you. I have been praying for you."

Niles couldn't hold back any longer. "You know what? Don't waste your time. If you really wanted to make a positive change in anything, you'd work on it here with these kids who need change instead of asking some magical guy in the sky to fix things as if he was your personal genie who responded to the right ritual catchphrases."

"Why are you always so flippant?" "Flippant" was a word she'd heard her pastor use when describing atheists, so she wanted to use it on Niles.

Niles was angry. Why did so many religious people use the word "flippant"? He had seriously considered joining the priesthood before graduating high school and believed the basic tenets of the

New Testament to be straightforward and easy to follow. It was always people like Duckett who were confused. "Why do you flaunt a basic misunderstanding about what it actually means to be "Christlike?"

She smiled again at the idiot-child Niles and walked away. She was right. He was a bad influence who didn't walk with Jesus. The sooner she got away from this place the better. She left and didn't look back.

Niles's problem was that he couldn't be serious and be taken seriously. He was learning that in order to not have his realistic concerns negated by the ignorant use of logical fallacies and the conservative rubber/glue defense, that he had to create the illusion of light-mindedness or a lack of seriousness. Either way, no one took him seriously. He felt that if he at least couched his critical ideas in a joke that the people he was talking too wouldn't crystalize into a hard shell immediately. With humor he could try to provoke a response that wasn't immediately hateful.

He was broken hearted that it didn't work with Duckett. He wanted her to love him. She didn't and never looked back.

24. Ellis

It was the first day back in the building after summer break for most of the teaching staff. Niles hadn't seen Geit for more than two months. Geit, as always, was the coolest looking guy in the room. He had let his hair grow shaggy and looked to have not shaved in three weeks. For Geit, whose beard seemed to grow with the speed of Kudzu in a humid climate, it was pretty full. It framed his pale face well, the contrast making him look like a calmer version of a suffering sinner in a Gustave Dore painting. Niles was the exact opposite. He was clean shaven from whorl to neck except for the cusp of hair on his chin that he grew to create the illusion of a stronger jawline. He'd also gotten too much sun, soaking up Geit's share as well as his own over the summer. Niles looked like a dirty hairless thumb.

"Geit. How the heck are you?" Niles was trying to hide his enthusiasm because he didn't want Geit to know that he wasn't nearly as cool as Geit was.

"Great. Glad to be back." Geit's reply was clearly ironic. His face was flat and he didn't even bother to take off his sunglasses even though it was much darker inside than out on that deceptively bright morning. "You look good."

"Yeah, I skipped Kaseman's speech and went to the gym instead."

Niles flexed his pecs imperceptibly like a skinny Schwarzenegger and laughed at himself. Geit seemed unamused. He looked around at the teachers gathered in the vestibule and lobby of the auditorium. "Wow. There are a lot of new people here this year." He gazed up and over some of the assembled faces. "You've been here a few years longer than me. This isn't normal, right?"

Geit craned his neck slightly. "Nope. I thought maybe some of these people ended up at the wrong building after the meeting this morning. You think they all work here now?"

"I think if they went to the wrong building they're probably too stupid to be teachers, so I guess by default they must be ours." Niles's logic was faulty, but in the moment it seemed to fit. "Now we can make a guessing game. We'll figure out who's gone and plug these new faces in. It'll be a good way to test my theory that you can tell someone's discipline by their face." He paused to look some more through the throng. "None of these new faces are wearing sunglasses inside, so I think we can discount them from being English teachers." It had been a few months. Niles had to poke Geit in his gut and test him to see if he was knowingly pretentious.

Geit unglassed and wrinkled his nose. "I thought your head was the sun."

"Are you saying I'm a star?"

Geit was amused. A smile escaped through the beard. "I don't see your little buddy from across the hallway. The math teacher. What was her name? Turnip?"

"Carrot? I don't see her either." He looked around. "She is kind of short though. Maybe her horse got stuck in traffic."

"So if she's gone, who's her replacement?"

"Hmm. Math teachers." Niles thoughtfully scanned the room.

"Well, that dude there is clearly a history teacher."

"Which one?"

"The one over there that looks like a coach. With the cargo shorts and the polo shirt. I saw both our gym teachers already, so I know he's not replacing one of them."

"History? Then who left?"

"I bet it was Nightenhelser. He didn't seem to get along with our students. I heard some stuff about him."

"Like what?"

"Like he didn't care for people who weren't white."

"Really? That's pretty stupid. Why would you apply to teach at a school that's majority minority if you don't like minorities?"

"That, my friend, is a good question. I don't see him though, so I bet I'm right."

"So if the history teachers all look like slightly smarter gym teachers, and the gym teachers all look like they play in a recreational softball league, how do you know who's a math teacher?"

Niles laughed. "Well, math teachers all look a little jumpy, like they enjoy coffee. Often they look like they spend more time sitting than standing, so one side of them is kind of flat, but their eyes are active. English teachers have active eyes too, but they're different than math teachers because most of the time English teachers look like someone just pissed in their coffee and they haven't quite figured it out yet. They're thinking about why the coffee tastes kind of pissy."

Geit looked like someone had polluted his coffee. He and Niles continued to scan the auditorium looking for the new math teacher.

"I think I've locked in on her. See that big girl over there? The one built like an offensive lineman? I think that's a new math teacher."

Geit was impressed by Niles's ability to pick out people who enjoyed arithmetic.

"I think you're right. She's wearing a sweater and it's supposed to be eighty degrees today. Maybe more of a defensive lineman though. She looks like she can move her feet."

They laughed, but the rate of turnover wasn't a joke. In a staff of seventy-six teachers, losing eleven to fourteen teachers at the end of each year with three to five leaving during the school year itself was crippling for any sense of camaraderie or unity. Too many good people were leaving for too many good reasons.

During the new staff introductions, Niles was proven correct. It was a pattern that would form as staff cycled in and out of the building at an abnormally high rate. Teachers who might stay were harder to pick out, because they rarely fit into stereotypes at the start. It was after they made their decision to stay through thick and thin that the stress and pressure started to form them into the stereotypes as though there were molds that had to be conformed to. To stay in such an unhealthy place, you had to fit into the the dysfunctional system that reduced each component into a mere easily replaced form.

This teacher didn't stick around either though, even though she knew her content. Niles heard from her students that she improved greatly over the course of her year there, as all people new to any job should. She was friendly and willing to learn. The students noticed that she was okay with being wrong and making changes on the fly when they challenged her. She won them over by the beginning of the second trimester. They were used to a vegetable in the room, so having an actual human who treated them like people was a pleasant change for everyone. She was even cordial in the hallway with Niles, and he looked forward to seeing her in the morning. Her smile was genuine and the students liked her, even staying after school to work with her.

Niles hoped she'd stay, but she didn't. A week before the end of that school year she'd come into Niles's room before the students arrived and announced that she was leaving the district and going to one farther north, closer to where she lived in Grand Rapids. She was taking a pay and benefit cut to work in a private charter school. It was the sort of district that she'd gone to herself as a student and it was where she wanted to go back to. Niles was sad to see her go, but he understood. Sometimes it didn't matter if you were good where you were if you weren't truly happy there. At the end of the last week, he'd helped her carry the last of her goods to her car and given her a hug goodbye. He wished her the best. A couple of tearful girls who'd connected with her were there too, girls who were good at math and needed a woman they felt similar to, and he'd watched them give her strong hugs in the hallway. It was sad, but it was routine. More good people left than stayed. More bad people stayed than left.

He'd heard later through the grapevine that she'd left and gone to the private school because she didn't like working with black students, but he knew that wasn't true. He'd seen her interact with them. There was none of the cold distance or visible disdain turning to bitter animosity such as he'd seen with the Texan. She actually loved all of them, and he could see it in how they interacted with and talked about her. She'd smiled genuinely and had gotten close to many of her students. She'd taught them without condescension and they felt it. There were other forces at play in her decision to leave, but people on the outside were always looking to oversimplify every teacher who left and toss them into a single category because it suited their agenda. Scapegoating teachers was a simple, straightforward con that distracted the public from making any real lasting and positive changes in themselves or in the way that their society operated.

Maybe she hadn't turned her lesson plans in on time.

Geit and Niles looked around for friendly faces. Heller was still there. She was at the side of the room, captured by Linn and Demarr. Every year brought changes. Niles couldn't always see the changes before it was too late.

It was a Thursday in November, and a student Niles knew well walked into his classroom looking even more disturbed than usual.

"Mr. Niles, this place is terrible." She looked disgustedly heart-broken or heartbreakingly disgusted. "Remember that kid from last trimester, that one from our Creative Writing class that was really gross?"

"Uh... You're going to have narrow it down some more, dear. Sorry. That's most of the boys in this school when you get down to brass tacks."

"The one that never did any work?"

"Again, you've got to narrow it down a bit more. Those are like completely overlapping Venn Diagrams."

"The one that looked like Michael Jackson!"

"Young Michael or old Michael?"

"Oh my God. You are are terrible!" She rolled her eyes and feigned a swoon. Niles couldn't resist.

"No, no, I know who you mean. What about him?"

"He was masturbating in class."

"No way. You are lying."

"Mr. Niles. I would not be facetious about that."

Niles gave her a weak scowl. "Do you even know that that word means?"

"It means joking or kidding, right?"

"How do you know?"

"I've heard you use it in class. Some of us listen you know."

"Wow. You are awesome. Anyway, you're serious about this kid. Where was the teacher? How does a class even reach a point where a kid can do that?"

"It was in Kringe's film class."

"Okay. Not surprised so far. Why didn't she do anything about it?"

"We were watching Fast and Furious 7 and he was complaining that he'd already seen it and wanted to go to the library to use the internet. She told him no, and he said that he was just going to sit there in the dark and play with himself."

"So she started that movie, which is a terrible movie by the way, has nothing to do with any sort of book, and is also so poorly made as to have no relevance when talking about the craft of film, and then she just ignored him?" Niles clarified.

"Yup. She just sat at her desk eating candy."

"First of all, I want to go on record here and now that masturbating in class is never a good response to feelings of boredom. Feel free to write that down and share it with your friends. Second of all, she's a terrible excuse for a teacher three different ways from Thursday, so I'm not impressed; and thirdly, why didn't the rest of you in the room at the time complain about it?"

"We did. She didn't care."

"I hope that she thought you were all joking. Either way, that's awful. I'm sorry. That's sexual harassment, criminal, and just plain gross. That kid is lucky he's not with me anymore. I might have to hurt him."

She looked at him hopefully. "Would you really?

"No, legally I can't touch him, but I would do everything in my power to make him regret this rather poor life choice. I feel for the kid that has that seat this period.

Students weren't the only ones making poor choices in the building. Sometimes, their role models were caught up, still stuck in the egocentrism of their own teenage years.

Mr. Ellis was the new math teacher down the hall from Niles and Bradley. He was young, fit, and attractive. All of the female students noticed what a young, fit, and handsome teacher he was, but as they started watching him closely as all teens do when they're impressed with someone, they also noticed that he had some behaviors that weren't as dreamy as his blue eyes.

He had large groups of girls staying after school each day with him to get tutoring, but they quickly noticed how preoccupied he was with his computer while he was supposed to be showing them how to do mathematics.

He had also invited the new English teacher to send him some photos and gave her the okay to make them clothed or unclothed, in case she felt like sharing a little bit more of herself than was absolutely necessary to make an impression. He wasn't exactly the right man for the job in front of him. He too, had problems making the right choice in the heat of the moment.

There was a hot moment in late April when he'd had a choice to grope a young Special Education teacher's buttocks or not to, and he chose to go full grope. She turned around and punched him when she saw that it was a teacher and not student. There was no excuse for that boundary being thrown to the ground and taken advantage of. Several students witnessed the event, but Ellis claimed no wrong-doing, that he was falling and had tried to maintain his balance by grabbing at the only thing within reach. The Special Education teacher, despite having no past history of crying wolf about sexual assault was told to calm down and let it go by both Swamp and the appropriate chairs from the Human Resources department down-town.

Niles knew both of them, and he was mystified by the re-sponse from the people in charge. They were condoning sexual as-sault in the school building, choosing to believe a perpetrator instead of a victim. The Special Education teacher left after that school year, purportedly for a district that didn't pay as well, but would perhaps do more to protect her from predators in the workplace. As for Mr. Ellis, he stayed on in the building for two years, leaving the district when he was hired to be principal in the largest city in Michigan's Bible Belt just to the north of Pianosa Springs. It seemed to Niles to prove that conservatives really do like a man to be in charge who is willing to openly grab what he wants from women.

"Well," Geit said when they were talking about it, "if you can't do what's right, you can always do what's left."

Sometimes in the act of discussing and writing about the thematic and cultural elements of the texts that he asked the students to read, Niles had to talk about God. It would have been impossible to fully explore the books without discussing everything that the au-thors included, and almost all of them - from the scops of *Beowulf*, up through Alice Walker and Yann Martel - have written about God. It is necessary to put all of those things in context with modern life and perceptions to create the type of understanding that students needed to be successful in the meaningful business of living.

In one of these conversations generated by chapter 25 of Catch 22, Niles was talking with the students, sharing his own perceptions of God after being asked by the students to explain the chaplain's literary allusions and his own understanding of faith and how it worked. Niles took those kinds of opportunities seriously, not as chances to proselytize, but as chances to be honest with students about difficult topics that they had a right to ask older people about.

The student walked up to Niles's desk timidly at lunch, first apologizing for coming during his lunch, and then asking if he had time to talk. Niles didn't care. He always ate his lunch with his students. After all, they were his children.

"Mr. Niles, aren't you worried about your soul in the afterlife?"

"I'm as worried about my soul in the afterlife as I am about my soul in the prelife. I'm quite convinced that the two will be virtually if not completely identical."

Her eyes widened with surprise. "You remember what that was like?"

"No. No one does. That's kind of my point."

"That it doesn't matter?"

"No, not necessarily. If you want it to matter, then it can matter to you. I'm just saying that I'm sure I'll be just as aware of this life in the next as I am now of the last."

"So it doesn't matter to you?"

"No, no more than my current memories of my existence before birth."

"Oh." She paused for a moment, looking down at the floor as Niles rocked in his chair. "Well, what about your immortal soul?"

"What about your pre-mortal soul?"

She twisted her head and narrowed her eyes. "What do you mean? I didn't have a soul until I existed."

"You don't have one until you exist? How do you exist after you are dead?"

"Are you trying to confuse me?"

"I'm not trying to confuse you, just trying to help you parse out your thoughts. It doesn't sound as if you've been doing a very good job of that yourself."

"Parsing them? What does that mean?

"Parsing means cutting them into their constituent parts and examining them and how they are are related to each other.

"Oh."

"You know how when we have writers that use very long and complex sentence structures, like Ralph Ellison in the *Invisible Man*, and you sometimes have to stop, re-read them, and break them into sections and compare those sections to each other to understand what he is saying?"

A light came on behind her eyes. "Yes."

"You should do that with your thoughts too. Your thoughts and beliefs are very complex structures. You're not a child anymore and now you're learning that everything isn't a binary dichotomy of either one thing or its opposite. Hopefully. Even if you disagree with the chaplain in the book, or your teacher standing in front of you, you should always seek to fully understand how both you yourself and other people find their meanings in religion or anything else for that matter. After all, how can you debate someone you don't agree with if you don't fully understand your own positions on a topic and how you arrived there?"

"That's a good point, Mr. Niles."

"I agree with you."

349

"That it's important?"

"Yes."

Sometimes the questions were more personal and less theological. There were plenty of times and plenty of reasons for students to ask questions, and Niles was more amiable than most when it came to answering them.

"Hey Mister Niles, can I ask you a question?"

"Sure. I may or may not answer it depending on a variety of different conditions, but you're always free to ask a question."

"Did you always want to do this?"

"Well, I just met you a few months ago, but I've always liked answering questions. I guess you could say that I've always wanted to answer your question."

"Not this, I mean teaching, did you always want to teach, like when you were in high school?"

"No way. My teachers were not my role models. I did not want to be like them."

"Why not, ain't all teachers smart?"

"C'mon. You go to school here. We both know the answer to that. But no, mine might have been good at their subjects, and a couple of them might have been kind people, but I never connected with them or their jobs in a way that made me say, "I want to do what you do." Besides, what kid likes teachers? We're buzzkills, we ruin your fun time with friends at the only place you might get to see them, and we make you do stuff that you hate. Like literature and grammar."

"When did you figure out you wanted to do this?"

"It wasn't until I was older, until I took some classes in Psychology and Criminal Justice that I saw that if I wanted to make a positive impact on the world, being a teacher might be the best way to do it.

"You think so?"

"Well, I look at it this way. I was going to be a cop for a while, but cops don't do crime prevention. They're a response to the problem after the fact. And not a very good one."

"I agree with that."

"I had to get older and understand how the world ought to work before I could understand how important teachers are."

"What do you mean by that? Doesn't the world work the way it's supposed to?"

"Well that's pretty subjective, right? I mean the guy who's elected to the Senate or something like that probably figures that the world is working the way it is supposed to, but what about the guy who has to steal to feed his family? Or what about the guy who just hates his job so much that it makes him sick, but he has to keep doing it because he's got kids and a family to take care of? And certainly people your age, right? If there is any group in America that has absolutely no rights, it's teenagers, right? Do you think the world works the way it ought to?"

She didn't have to think about it. "No. I hate it."

"I understand why you hate it. I hated it too. I'm still convinced it's awful, but I'm doing what I can to try to change the little bit of it that's around me. I don't think throwing people in prison after they've done something is the answer. I think we've got to do something on the front end of this society to make it better, but I didn't see that when I was a kid. I couldn't see that far forward. That's why I keep telling you guys that you don't have to figure your lives out right now. You've got time. Heck, I know people older than me who still don't have it figured out yet. Sometimes I'm not even sure if I do."

The student agreed that there were big questions that might take a very long time to answer, or she lost interest in the answers and the questions both. She answered her buzzing phone and forgot about Niles.

Students weren't the only ones who were trying to figure out the hows and whats and whys of who to be. Geit and Niles would have very similar discussions when there were no students around to be distracted.

They were in Geit's room again. His feet were on the desk in their usual place. "What would you be doing right now if you weren't a teacher?"

Niles thought about it. Geit must have been feeling more amiable than usual. "I don't know. I'd probably be dead."

"Well, that went downhill fast." Geit's eyes were big. "Why would you be dead?"

"I don't know." Niles had to think some more. "Teaching gave me a purpose. Without a purpose, I'm fairly certain I'd have self-destructed by now."

"That's pretty dark. You should probably see a therapist."

"And then some. Anyway, what would you be doing?"

"I was going to be a detective."

"What? Seriously? Like a P.I.? Like Tom Selleck in *Magnum P.I.*? That's pretty sweet. I can't see you in a Hawaiian shirt though."

Geit smiled. "Not like Magnum, more like Sam Spade. You know, from *The Maltese Falcon*. I love Dashiell Hammett."

Niles laughed aloud. "Really? There are layers to you, you know that? The longer I know you the more I see that there's a lot more to you than you like to let people know."

"Well, I can't tell people everything." He shrugged. "I even took a bunch of courses in criminal justice and got licensed here in Michigan."

"Before you started teaching?"

"No, I was too young back then. You had to be at least twenty-five to get licensed. I got it after I was already teaching."

"You were doing this and that at the same time? That's pretty crazy." Niles was duly impressed. "So why are you doing this now instead of that?"

Geit leaned back in his chair and switched his top foot. It was his favorite conversational pose during their plan period.

"Money and insurance. I got married. Now I have a kid."

"Good point. Nothing kills a man's dreams faster than a wife." Geit laughed at him, then glanced over at his wife's picture that hung on the wall behind him. He didn't have any photos of his son up yet, but he always carried dozens on his phone.

"It was worth it."

Niles tilted his head playfully. "You mean having a pretty young wife is better than sitting in your car for hours at a time watching for guilty behavior from cheating husbands and insurance frauds? No way! I'll believe it when I see it!" He was exaggerating of course. Geit guffawed.

In some other reality, Geit was a private eye. In some fractal offshoot of potential universes, he was living that particular childhood dream. Maybe it was the same one where Niles was a farmer. In that one too, they had become friends.

25. Demarr

Sam was a perfectly average white kid. Like most Americans, he considered himself to be middle class even though he wasn't. His family was poor, working class, and "broken." His father was in prison in another state, his mom worked two part-time jobs. His step-dad was "alcohol-dependent" if not a full-blown alcoholic and would sometimes become violently aggressive with Sam. Just the sort of young man who didn't understand what privilege was - all he "knew" was that he didn't have it. His family would struggle, or at least struggle as much as he knew about struggling. Clothes were hand-me-downs or thrift store finds. He wasn't a great student, but depending on the teacher he could be a very good student. Like many other teens, if he felt a connection to his teacher, he would perform better in class. He liked Niles. Niles treated him like a favorite nephew. He didn't know that Niles tried to treat every student like they were his favorite. He would listen when Sam had something to say and he took him seriously. That's why Sam would tell him some of the things that he couldn't tell his stepdad.

Niles didn't have Sam in class anymore during his senior year, but he would often stop by before and after school or at lunch to sit with Niles and fill him in on events in his life.

It was spring, when a young man's fancy turns to thoughts of love according to Tennyson. Niles knew that was true, but he also knew that it wasn't necessary love of either sex or even people in general. For boys like Sam, their fancy turned to their cars. Sam had just gotten his dream car, or as close to a dream car as he would have access to. It was a 2004 Mustang, a true hot rod in Sam's eyes. Just the week before he had excitedly filled Niles in on a host of technical specs that Niles had little to no appreciation for, but he did his best to mirror Sam's excitement. Sam couldn't wait to get it out on a dry, snow-free road.

Sam walked into the classroom rather hurriedly at lunch, seeming to check behind him as if he were being followed. Niles gave him a quizzical look.

"What's up, Sam? You look a little anxious." Sam laughed nervously and was having trouble making eye contact with Niles.

Niles tilted his head expectantly. "Did something happen? Are you in trouble?" His brow wrinkled and Sam crookedly smiled.

"No. Not really." He huffed into a chair opposite Niles. "Kind of." He rolled his head from side to side. "Well, almost. Almost got in huge trouble." Finally he looked at Niles.

"What happened? Tell me. You know I won't think badly of you..." he paused, "unless you did something really stupid, and then we'll work things out."

Sam tried to smile nervously. He was anxious about telling Niles, but he started talking with lowered eyes, shamefully.

"I almost got arrested."

"What do you mean almost? What were you doing?"

"Speeding. Down Pike Street..."

"Right in front of school?"

He grimaced, "No! I ain't that dumb! Down the road, past the taco restaurant and the post office."

"How did you do that? There's so many stop lights on that road...?"

"It was around eight o'clock last night. There wasn't much traffic. The lights were green..."

Niles nodded. "Go on."

"I was doing eighty-eight in a thirty-five."

Niles was shocked. "What? Are you serious?" Sam nodded quietly, looking back down at his shoes. "How are you not in jail? You just turned eighteen, right?"

Sam affirmed his age, still nervously smirking and looking away. Then the encounter came spilling out.

"Mr. Niles, I was so scared! I knew I was busted, right? The cop just came up to the side of the car and looked at me for a minute. Then he asked me how old I was. I told him. He asked me if I just got the car, so I told him yes. He asked me for my license and registration, so I gave them to him, and he took them back to his car, and all I could think about was how my step-dad was going to beat my ass!"

Niles looked at his face more closely for bruises and then tried to redirect him, "So what happened then? Going that far over the speed limit is a felony. You're not in jail, so did they just give you a ticket?"

"Nothing Mr. Niles, Nothing."

Niles was deeply confused. "You didn't get anything from the cop? He just let you go?"

"He came back to the car with my registration and ID and said, 'You seem like a nice kid. Don't ever do this again. Do you hear me?' and then he let me go."

"He just let you go with a warning?" Niles could hardly believe it.

Sam replied with a shrug. "I guess I'm just lucky." He smiled at Niles.

Niles leaned back in chair and said, "Yeah, lucky you're not black."

Sam was still smiling and nodding until it hit him a second later. He gave Niles a questioning look. "Uh, what do you mean, Mr. Niles?"

"Have you been watching the news at all for the past few years? Have you seen what cops do to black men, black men your age or younger, even when they're doing something that's nowhere near as dangerous as what you just did? Have you thought about what might have happened if you'd been any one of your black friends here at school? Do you think they'd have just gotten off with a nice warning?"

Sam started to stammer a bit. "No, I guess not."

"You're damn right not." Niles was angry, but not with Sam. "Devon or Khalil? Those guys would be in jail today, or worse for doing something like that! I'm glad you didn't get shot or sent to jail, but that's crazy!" Sam was looking thoughtfully past Niles now as he stopped to let it sink in. "That's what we're talking about when we talk about 'White privilege' Sam. Yeah, you all might be equally poor, but you and I don't have to worry about getting shot by a cop! I've been pulled over for speeding before too, twice! Guess what I got!"

Sam paused, but he knew where Niles was going.

"Nothing?"

"That's right. Nothing. I got warnings. All we got were warnings because the cops were white, and we're white. That's privilege, Sam."

As Gunnery Sergeant Hartman once said, the best parts of some people did wind up as a stain on the mattress. Life was never fair, it could trick people into giving up good parts of themselves in anger or bitterness. Sometimes people shed the best parts of themselves along the way through life - a negative response to a negative stimulus. It happened with many boys. Despite the presence of testosterone in the their systems, they could be born with compassion and sympathy for other people including women or people with different colored skin. Sam wavered back and forth into the darkness, and somebody had to be around him often to pull him back into the light. Niles wasn't there all the time. It was impossible. For the times when he couldn't be there, he hoped that something he taught him in class between the predicates, the character arches, and the semi-colons would stick in him and come back to the surface of his thoughts when something or someone in life tried to push him into the darkness.

White, working-class boys like Sam weren't the only ones who needed a good teacher. A good teacher at the right time made a difference in some lives before they got too big.

Somewhere back in one of the pasts that Niles would never know of, there could have been a turning point for a small girl of mixed Chinese and African ancestry growing up in eastern Michigan and another chubby girl in a Northern Michigan commune whose own mixed ethnic background came out in her hair. Maybe the best parts of each girl had still been within her at some point in her personal history, but was lost or driven out. Perhaps there was a small girl who didn't feel like she fit in anywhere, too dark of skin to be Chinese, a face too round and too Han to be African and too much of both sides of her family to be an equal American in the eyes of people who had an impact on her. Somewhere along the timeline, that girl might have been grievously hurt, told that she was less than, deserved less than, perhaps even that she was on the same level as the garbage that someone couldn't taste or smell coming out of his own mouth. Perhaps she was wounded by someone using words as a weapon because they believed she looked too different to be the same as him in the most meaningful and most human way.

The other girl too, that one neglected by her parents who thought others in the commune would pick up the slack, that girl whose skin was as white as the rest of her northern Michigan neighbors with the hair that was so black, so untamable. Her hair was more coarse, more like the manes of the ponies that some members of the commune kept penned up by the compost pile. Perhaps she didn't fit in with the straight-haired popular skinny girls there when she was finally put into public school in the sixth grade. Perhaps they told her she was an animal, the home-schooled, wild-haired misfit from the commune outside of town. Maybe it was one person. Maybe it was a whole class. Maybe, just maybe, it was a teacher.

Niles had his own bad teacher, a man who had bullied and humiliated him in a parochial school where Jesus might have been on the wall and in the church up on the hill, but not in the heart or the mind of a teacher. The difference between Niles and these girls might have been a kind word or a kind moment from another adult in the right place and right time. That was enough to change a life, but not in those wounded and painful moments. Only in reflection and hindsight could an act of kindness come out of the mists of memory and recolor a defining moment. It might be forever too late to change those girls; the women they'd become had no time or patience for thinking back, for reframing those times that had shaped them. They saw their own histories as justifications for the flaming brands that they now wielded, a license to wound or destroy others in the name of retribution. They'd taken their hurts and allowed them to define who they became. That was the danger of allowing the wounds of life to make you align against someone else. A good person could unwittingly allow an enemy to define who they became.

There was no set formula for good and evil, no witch's brew that would guarantee that whatever beast crawled from the cauldron would commit feats of selfishness and evil; likewise, there was no power for good that could set a animal upon the earth with the best of designs and intentions that would be rock solid in its tempered resolve to be without fear or failure. A life never ran on rails. Even if it did, it could go off them. Some people were hurt so badly and got so out of control that they crashed into several others, like cars slipping on black ice on the highway between Chicago and Detroit in January.

Winter was that time. Or more precisely the stretch between Christmas break and Spring break during the school year when the days were short and cold, everything was tedious, and everyone was caught in a metaphorical twilight period.

Michigan in January and February was the literal realization of a metaphorical idea. It was gray, and nothing moved. The days, though short, trudge bent double, like war weary soldiers under heavy packs, knock-kneed, coughing like hags under the gas at Ypres. Teachers and students cursed through the sludge that had burrowed into their lungs in viral packets.

The sparkling lights of the holidays were all unlit, though some still littered skeletal trees and bushes heavy with snow or dangling wetly into the mud, forgotten and ragged until someone was bothered enough to shake off the listless numbness of winter and reel them around cardboard until next Thanksgiving. The high was over, the short break from the grind of preparing for standardized test coming in spring was too short, like the breaks in the clouds that allowed the pale light from a heavy sun to fall upon those wilting flowers of young men and women.

The first day back from break was loud and chaotic, as everyone tried to collectively shake off the snow and ice and get back to work. Students were excited for a day to be around their peers and classmates again. That missed familiarity brought a cold comfort. Teachers were ill, some still tottering with the effort of wringing out lungs and noses wracked with virus and bacteria because two weeks were not be enough for an immune system wracked to recover from both high levels of stress and the daily biomass of bacteria that trekked in and out of their classrooms with every bell.

Whatever lessons there were to teach, whatever lessons there were to learn, there was one that stood above the others: "We must persevere." Everyone wanted to quit. Everyone wanted to roll over and go back to some sort of restorative torpor, but the teacher lead the way through the grinding snow and mud.

The nature of those winter beasts, January and February, had changed much since Niles was the age of the students that he taught. He remembered long, cold winters that never seemed to break. They were hard to bear, but if he could just bear forward and avert his eyes from the freezing wind, they would end in time. Winter in Michigan now was a vindictive and consistently inconsistent hell-beast that could whipsaw from one extreme to the next within days. Climate change had caused it to morph tortuously and constantly. One day would have wind chills of negative ten and fourteen inches of new fallen snow, and the next day the temperature would rocket to fifty-five degrees Fahrenheit, melting the snow quickly and causing overburdened roofs to leak and basements to flood with water that had nowhere else to pool.

Each of those twists and turns and convolutions of the weather cruelly tempted and teased staff and students with visions of early spring and warmth that felt vital and vigorous, but the shifting weather pattern would smash those hopes against chunks of ice within days. Every winter was a dance with someone that you longed for but could not have, and the anger and resentment of constant rejection would ooze or explode out of everyone, even though no one could tell when or why or how they felt so rotten and hateful or why so often everyone turned on each other.

Happiness and joy in winter were rare commodities, but they could exist in community, in kindness, and in the shared sense of perseverance that Niles tried to create and culture in his windowless, whitewashed crypt of a classroom. Others fed on the anger and resentment, cultivating it and growing fat on feeding on it for those winter months. Those were the days when Linn and Demarr could truly shine.

Niles rarely got to see the acts of cruelty toward the students first-hand. How could he possibly? He was in his own room trying to do the right thing for his own students. He heard about things second-hand inevitably and always after the fact.

There was the student who came in at lunch red-faced and crying, trailing a supportive friend. Niles put away his meal and called them both over.

"What's going on, is she okay?" Niles already knew the answer without asking, but he asked anyway. There was a script that he was expected to follow. The student didn't know it, but her mother had called Niles at the start of the trimester to talk to him specifically about her and what was going on in their lives. There was a difficult divorce taking place, and an absent father who had run off with a mistress half his age. Not only was the student suffering crippling panic attacks, but she was already seeing a therapist for self-harming behaviors that she'd begun as she had sensed her parents' marriage breaking apart. The mother had asked Niles to watch her, to be careful and understanding as much as he could with how she was feeling toward the adult men in her life. She also confided in Niles that her daughter was seeing a cardiac specialist for what was either a congenital heart deformity or a stress-related cardiac issue. He knew that even if she hated her father, he'd have to play a "dad" card when he saw her.

The supportive friend was indignant as tears streamed down the girl's face and she drew ragged, sharp breaths.

"I hate Mrs. Demarr so much!"

Niles focused on the girl who was in danger. He looked her straight in her frantic eyes until they caught on his.

"Breathe. Just breathe easy. Let's get this under control. Slow it down. Long deep inhale. C'mon. Do it with me." He exaggerated breathing deeply in through his nose and out through his mouth. She began to mimic him, and her red face lessened in color. "Just breathe for a minute or two, and then you can tell me what happened. Okay? You're here with us, and you're safe." The friend continued to rub her back and Niles kept modeling the easy breathing until she was ready to spill out what had brought her to this state. She pulled a small electronic device out of her jacket pocket, roughly the size of a cellular phone, but less streamlined.

"This is my heart rate monitor. I'm wearing electrodes today that are sending wireless data to this device." She flipped it over so Niles could see it. It clearly was not a phone, blocky and rectangular with a red LED readout.

"Yes?" He was waiting to see where the story went, even though he already had a strong idea.

"It was just sitting on my desk. I wasn't playing with it or anything, it was just sitting there because I didn't want it poking me while I was working. Then suddenly Demarr just started ranting about cell phones, and how we shouldn't have them out during class. She got really mad at some other kids who were texting or something, and then she walked over to me..." At this point in the story, the supportive friend looked like she could spit nails, but the girl went on. "...and she said, 'What's this?' and she was really mad and I didn't do anything, and all I said was, 'It's not a phone.' and then she grabbed it off the table and threw it on the floor. Oh my God, Mr. Niles, I thought she'd broke it, and we don't have insurance right now because of my dad, and I thought we'd have to pay for it and I can't believe she did that she had no right!" And her words were spilling out faster and faster as she went on and Niles stopped her before she went back into panic mode.

"You're okay. You're right. She had no right to do that, even if it was a phone. She was completely in the wrong. Is it damaged?"

The girl slowed down in her breathing again. "I don't think so. It looks like it's still working."

"I know that you've got your phone handy too, it's lunch, and you can stay in here if you want to. I think you should call your mom and ask her to call someone here at school. Either the dean of students or the principal. If you go down to the main office and complain, they'll probably just ignore you. They only take things like this seriously if a parent gets upset." The girl nodded at him. In those moments, it was important to validate her feelings about being wronged in order to calm her down. If he was going to be able to help her, she had to know that Niles was on her side.

She called her mom and talked to her while Niles went back to his lunch. She came back to him and announced that her mom was coming to pick her up. That was the end of it.

Later that week, the girl told him that her mom had called an assistant superintendent to complain, but that nothing came of it. The dean of students moved her to a different class out of concern for the student's well-being. Demarr was never reprimanded.

That was the way things tended to go. Linn and Demarr and others of their ilk got away with bullying the students. Niles wasn't sure what went on behind the scenes in the administration offices, but he suspected that there was bullying going on there as well.

It was easy to justify bullying students if a teacher construed her own story as a victim herself. There were teachers who wanted to be teachers in order to help other people, and there were teachers who wanted to become teachers to gather power and control in their lives. In the law enforcement classes that Niles had taken when he didn't know what to do with himself, the instructors who had been policemen or were currently working in law enforcement were always adamant that they wanted to weed out potential candidates from the program who were in it to enrich their own ego. They didn't want power-tripping cops. They didn't want police officers whose main drive was their own self-interest. There was no one in his teaching programs doing that.

No one monitored how many people wanted to become teachers to address their own deficit in ego or to gain power over others that they lacked in their own lives. There are lives for people who feel frustrated by a lack of agency but teaching wasn't one of those. There are plenty of people who feel that the world owes them some of the power that they feel unjustly deprived of. They shouldn't have been allowed to become teachers.

Teaching on a power trip destroyed the very people that it was supposed to be creating.

26. Thanksgiving

Students often tried to find boundaries because they needed to. Since they saw adults toying and moving them back and forth, they wanted to play at making their own with adults. Niles thought back to the time that Geit had to deal with the young man who thought it funny or interesting to attempt to explain to him how he would rape his wife.

It was all because of a picture. If the picture weren't there, there wouldn't have been an opportunity or a need for the young man to try to find the boundary. Niles learned to always keep his photos of his wife in a safe place despite the fact that "posting pictures of your personal life" was supposed to be one of those prime ways to connect with students. He didn't want to leave an opportunity for a problem to form.

The boy that did it was not a candidate for student of the year. He had trouble keeping his hands off the other students, and he had problems with coping with his feelings towards the members of the opposite sex. Geit had put his seat right next to his desk in front to give the student the feeling he was always being watched. It worked in some measure, but the young man still had a good many confusing feelings and emotions bubbling up that he could no longer harass the female students in class with.

"Hey Geit."

"What?"

"I like your wife. She's pretty. How long you been married?" He motioned with his eyes to the photo behind Geit on his bulletin board.

Geit was grading papers while the students were supposed to be working quietly. He didn't look up, but merely paused for a moment to answer.

"About five years."

"You like puttin' it to her? You know, givin' her 'the D?'"

Geit stopped and looked up. The boy was two feet away, looking over Geit's desk at the photo of her pinned to the wall behind him - unconcerned about the assignment that he was given to work on in class, he had decided that now was a good time to push against his teacher to see how far he could get. Geit tented his fingers in front of him and looked very directly into the young man's eyes.

"That's a very inappropriate question. It's disrespectful and unacceptable. I need you to refocus your attention on the work at hand."

The boy reacted with the sort of defiance that seemed to flow as easily as water. Whether he was to blame, or whether society would point the finger at his parents, or his teachers would point the finger at culture in general, the defiance in the face of otherwise rational decision making stood out as being more than even reckless in this situation based on the look in Geit's eyes. The boy pressed on.

"Where you live? You live in Pianosa Springs?"

"I'm sorry, but you're burning through my patience at an exponential rate. I need you stop. Your questions have no bearing on your ability to do your work. Either shut your mouth and get to work or just shut your mouth."

The kid didn't know when to stop.

"I'm just asking, 'cause you know, I might follow you home sometime, and I don't want to have to drive too far..."

Geit tried to stop him by interrupting him, tried to prevent him from putting himself into a position that he would regret, but the kid kept going.

"...maybe I'd like to be outside your house in the dark, when she gets home. Get my hands on her, give her some of this dick, show her what it's like to be fucked by a real man. I'd get my rape on with that."

Geit reached over the desk, wordlessly grabbed the boy by his shirt, lifted and dragged him into the hall before he could do anything about it. He was quick and quiet, and only a couple of students looked up to see what had happened so suddenly. He slammed the boy against the cinder block wall next to the lockers and pressed his face down into the boy.

"If you ever say anything about my wife again, let alone come near her, I will end your miserable existence. You will disappear. No one will ever find your body and your family will assume that you've run away from home. I will make it as painful as it can possibly be and before I end you, I will hear you beg."

Geit was serious. The man did not joke about such things. Somehow, the boy's brain settled back into his skull; otherwise the situation could have gone so far off the rails that it never would have come back. Geit had a way of dealing with extreme situations that worked for him. Those types of things could never be standardized across classrooms.

Niles was explaining something about the Shakespearean Sonnet cycle when a student raised her hand.

"Mr. Niles, why do we have to do work today when Thanksgiving is tomorrow? None of my friends are doing any work in their classes. My friend in Wein's class said all they did was watch the Charlie Brown Thanksgiving special. I heard that in Linn's class, all they did was sit around and make collages. And in Mrs. Demarr's class, they had a party. Everybody brought in food and Demarr gave them points for bringing in snacks! How come you never let us have a party?"

Niles glanced around the room at his thirty-five young charges. He could see that they were all eager to know why he was asking them to do so much while the rest of their teachers were asking them to do nothing. "Well that's a lot of questions and statements all tied into one." He leaned forward onto his podium and sighed. Every year, every holiday, it was the same thing. Niles would make them work, even make them take a test sometimes, and he felt like he was alone in holding a line. He knew that he wasn't, but the students knew that if they presented him as a lone standout that he would be more likely to give in and capitulate to their desire to do nothing.

"First of all, Thanksgiving is tomorrow not today, and if you want every day off before a vacation or a holiday, then you don't understand the purpose of a holiday. If I'm not going to have you do anything meaningful, then why should any of us be here... Right? We're here, we're putting the time in, so we might as well do something with that time. Secondly, I'm trying to get you prepared to do something meaningful with your life after college. I guess Linn's getting her students ready for being paper mache artists, or maybe for majoring in cutting out pictures and gluing them on paper. That's not what we do in here. I'm pretty sure that you'll be spending the rest of your life thinking and trying to understand the world around you. That's what we're doing here today. That's why we're working when they're not. I know that after this class, you'll probably never read Shakespeare again. I know that you are probably never going to either read or write another poem, but I'm asking you to think and understand words that I put in front of you. You're going to need that every day for the rest of your life. And as far as the whole points for food thing goes, why would I give you a grade for having your parents go grocery shopping? I'm not even sure what that could have to do with anything that we're doing in high school. And how does that even work for them? Does the kid who brings in Doritos get more points than the kid who does the store brand tortilla chips? I don't get that. This is school - not a feel-good social time."

Niles stopped. The students stared at him, waiting to see if he was done.

Finally, one spoke up. "Oh. Well, you don't have to be mad about it. We were just asking."

"I'm not angry. I'm just serious. I take what we do seriously. I guess if you don't feel like being here, you can always stay home. You don't need me to give you a day off, do you?" The students were taken aback by Niles's honesty. None of them knew what to say to a teacher who had just told them that they had some measure of power over their own lives. They hadn't noticed he was attacking anyone and anything that wasted their time in school, even themselves.

Niles could say and do a lot in his classroom, but who would ever notice?

Another end of a semester. Another sneak up to the roof. It wasn't about breaking the rules. It was about what he could see from the roof.

Niles's room was on the windowless interior side of the hallway. If he was fortunate, he could catch a glimpse of the tree moving in the wind outside the window of his neighbor across the hallway, but he was usually too busy to take it in during the few moments available.

During the winter months, it was worse. Michigan's weather may have gotten more unpredictable as the planet warmed, giving him more sixty-degree days in December than he'd ever imagined while growing up, but the sunrise and sunset were always predictable. So was his schedule during the school year. Niles was up and in the building before seven AM each day. Most days, he didn't leave until five PM or later. That meant that for a couple of months, he didn't see the sun.

Those were dark days.

That made the rooftop all the more important. During those dark days, the edges of the world seemed to recede and close in. The walls and hallways got narrower and narrower as the world shrank to only what could be well lit. The world outside was small, cloudy, and thick with shadow. The world inside was doubly claustrophobic and stuffy. Everything was cold and the sun was a distant memory whose return required an immense sacrifice to return to the light. It was no wonder that ancient pagans in the northern latitudes believed in blood rituals to bring spring back.

When Niles climbed those steps to the rooftop and opened the door, light came in. He stepped out onto the roof and could see a wide world.

During the warmer months, it was a sea of green punctuated by houses, but far fewer and far smaller than they seemed from ground level. Up there he could see trees, the tops of trees, in shimmering waves like a wind-swept sea. Being on the fourth floor, he could see the brown strips of manure punctuating the fields behind the houses in the distance like exclamation marks without smelling them. He could see horses in pasture in another direction. He could see how small and meaningless the school itself truly was. He could see a bigger picture. He could see light and dark both, the shadows of the trees and the sun peeking sometimes from behind clouds.

He'd wander around the roof, like he did every time. He looked out over every direction for as far as he could see, trying to fix in his mind a beautiful much more expansive perspective that was so easily forgotten in the darkness that the building cultivated. He did that as long as he could stand it, whether it was too cold or too hot.

The rooftop was more than just an escape, it was an opportunity to remember what it was like to be free; it was a reminder to look at the big picture. Niles needed help to remember these things because working in the classroom was so isolating.

It was as if forces were conspiring to separate and destroy each teacher in turn. Administration saw them as enemies of the students: an impediment to education that couldn't be gotten rid of - a necessary evil. The students too often saw them as enemies because the teachers tried to pull them away from the things that they loved, like games, friends, and social media. The parents saw them as competitors in the struggle to exert control over their children, and in any conflict the parents always sided with their own flesh and blood over a stranger with a mysterious "degree" in an academic discipline that they saw as meaningless in the real world. The most damaging part of the attack on teachers was the way that so many of them could be depended upon to attack each other.

It was especially bad in the English department where both Demarr and Linn took the lead in attacking other teachers they didn't like in a meaningless attempt to have and hold power. They mocked and insulted other teachers in their own classes in front of students. They passively-aggressively attacked other teachers in staff meetings, describing the teacher they wanted to damage in such a way as to leave no doubt as to who they were talking about and threw them under the bus as if the teacher they hated was an enemy to everyone. Niles and Geit were isolated. So were Hippy and Trudeau. Each man tried to find his comfort where he could. There wasn't much to be had, but friendship was a light balm.

One way that schools kept teacher turn-over high was by changing the relevant evaluation measures as often as possible. Paperwork and forms that were required one year couldn't be rolled over into the next. Different forms and different measures were applied each new school year. New titles and measures were introduced annually, each time purported to be more true and more accurate to meeting student needs. Niles and every other teacher who meant well tried to adapt and follow the new measures every year, but the constantly changing standards meant that no one could prepare adequately much less "highly effectively."

Every year the state added to the requirements for the evaluation process, and every year the Pianosa Springs School District tried to be five steps ahead of the state's evaluation requirements. Every change that the state made was amplified by by a factor of three. To the parents who paid slight attention with a split gaze, it all seemed very progressive. To the teachers who were subject to chasing a new moving target each academic year, it was death by a thousand cuts.

Niles had had enough. More and more of the actual work of the evaluation process had been put upon the teachers with each passing year. it was the responsibility of the administrative evaluator to observe and offer suggestions for improvement when he'd started. By his tenth year, the state sentiment had turned so far against teachers that the sum total of the administrators' contributions to the evaluation paperwork was rubber stamping them with negative criticism and signatures.

Niles walked into the principal's office with all of his required documentation in his hand and a heavy sigh. The young new principal welcomed him with a handshake and a smile. Niles towered over him, but he had no interest in intimidating the smaller man. It wasn't in his nature to deal with people in that way. Niles sat down in the chair on the front side of the desk while the principal launched into a practiced drone about evaluations and goals and metrics. The words slid and tumbled past Niles's head like rocks in a landslide. Already he'd heard them too many times and they remained without meaning or value, just as they had the first time when he had actually listened carefully and taken them seriously. Back then he'd been overcautious in listening because he wanted his evaluator to know that he was serious about being excellent. The difference between then and now was that he understood that excellence in teaching was completely unrelated to documentation.

Being a practicing English literature and writing instructor taught him the real meaning of "documentation." Documentation could be created without relation to reality. Documentation existed in the aether until it was pulled down and coalesced into ink and paper without a true need. It was the essence of bureaucracy. "Proof of due diligence" when the reality of practice wasn't good enough. Good teaching could have been measured only weeks, months, or even years after the fact, when the sometimes "too big" ideas had soaked and marinated enough in the sauce of the real world to have germinated, taken root, and then sprung into active, actionable existence in the lives of those students who had "done" instead of "been." There, in the principal's office, effective teaching was all about documentation. Niles knew that documentation was only about documentation. Documents cannot even prove their own existence without further documents.

If a teacher had a group of students who could use the readings and writings of his class to have become better human beings, better citizens in a community, then he could be a "good teacher." But an "effective teacher" was a nebulous, indistinct thing. "Effective" was an amorphous word, a word that was subject to arbitrary interpretation and disagreement. All attempts to prove "effective" on paper would ultimately fail, because "effective" couldn't be objectively quantified any more than first-class, acceptable, excellent, exception-al, favorable, great, marvelous, positive, satisfactory, satisfying, su-perb, valuable, wonderful, ace, boss, bully, capital, choice, crack, nice, prime, rad, spanking, super, superior, worthy, deluxe, first-class, first-rate, gnarly, reputable, select, shipshape, splendid, stu-pendous, tip-top, or up to snuff. Being an good teacher meant that you could connect with your students in a positive way, that they could see you as a mentor, or as an adult with something positive to offer, that they would take the things you taught them and build them into the fabric of who they were as a person and use them to make the society better for everyone, not just themselves. When would the evaluation process be amended to recognize that?

"Mr. Niles, where is your documentation on differentiating your instruction?"

"Right there with my 505 documentation and my lesson plans."

"I can't see anything in this that shows me that you're differ-entiating."

"Are you serious?" Niles seized a folder from the principal's hand that was packed with copies of student work. He pulled a bulging sheaf from it that was clipped together. "Right here. This is the same assignment expressed in different ways for students with different aptitudes. The lesson was from *The Lord of the Flies*. The advanced students worked on examining the philosophy of the dif-ferent leadership styles presented by Jack, Ralph, Piggy, and Simon. One student compared Jack's path to power through violence as a authoritarian dictator to Simon's path of spiritualism and mysticism through mediation in his hide-out in the jungle."

Niles flipped into the bottom of the pile and pulled out a dif-ferent assignment. "This is one is simple information retrieval. This lower-skilled student had to examine and explain cause and effect in the story as the boys' actions made their island dangerous for themselves. I tried to go all the way from basic skills of pulling information from the story to synthesizing meaning." Niles was emphatic.

"Mr. Niles, how many students are in that class?"

"Thirty-seven."

"Is that the only section of that class you taught? I see in your schedule that you have three sections of junior English."

"Yes, last semester I had three sections. There were one hundred and three total students."

The principal looked through Niles's folder, thumbing and pausing briefly as anything caught his eye. "I see maybe at most ten different assignments here. Where are the rest?"

"What do you mean the rest? That's a representative sample..." Niles paused. He was confused by where the principal seemed to be going.

"You have more than a hundred students. How did you differentiate for the rest? Why isn't that in the folder?"

"Are you saying that offering ten different versions of an assignment isn't enough?"

"You're not differentiating instruction. I'll have to mark you down in your evaluation."

Niles frowned and furrowed his brow. He didn't know what to say. The principal resumed filling out the rest of Niles's evaluation and continued questioning.

"And what about technology? You have in here that you're using your computer to make your presentations to the class, but where are the students using technology?"

"There aren't enough computers in the school. I can't get time in the lab more than once every few weeks and the computer carts are always signed out."

"Wein and Linn don't have trouble with getting computer time. I just did their evaluations and they have their students using technology every day."

"You have seventy-five teachers and three computer labs. There are three mobile laptop carts. How do they get technology for their students to use every single day?"

"Have you considered asking the students to use their own cell phones?"

"They're using their cell phones constantly while I ask them not to. Asking them to use their cellphones in class is simply capitulating to their basic drives for constant novelty and stimulation. They're not learning anything from tapping on their pocket screens." Niles suddenly felt exhausted by the thought he'd have to argue something that he knew he would lose even though he was right.

"Have them use them for learning," said the principal, without adding any explanation. "Wikipedia or something."

Niles slouched into his chair and tried not to hate the principal.

It was either the best or the worst thing about modern technology that a simple mistake could make someone look like a fool in front of everyone. Email had been a massive benefit to the bureaucratic nature of education. Now with one simple click of "reply all" anyone's thoughtless response was immediately broadcast to hundreds of people. The results were sometimes hilarious, but there was a darker side too. Even people that weren't on the "to" section were receiving emails in order to monitor conversations and ensure that they were being used only for "school business." Hippy had found that out the hard way.

Niles had started it. He usually started everything that went bad and got people in trouble - not for trying, but just because Niles had reached the point where he no longer put as much care into pleasing people as he was expected to. Even the most patient soul had a breaking point when confronted with constant incompetence.

An email was sent out by Principal Swamp telling the teachers about their new evaluation cycle. It began with an e-mail instructing them to create their own collections to prove that they were having students do assignments in the classroom instead of having a principal come in and watch the students work on a lesson that was delivered in class.

When Niles was a student, a principal would come in to evaluate, collect a few samples, take notes, and do their work themselves. When Niles was a teacher, they would come in with their district provided tablet to sit in the corner where nobody could see what they were typing and spend time catching up on their social media. One of Swamp's vice principals was in charge of monitoring the social media accounts that Swamp had set up for the cheer team and pep rallies. Their responsibilities changed with each new administrator, and Swamp was just the latest to modify the system to suit her own needs.

The teacher's role in the evaluation process grew each year. The teacher was responsible for submission of the lesson plan and the examples of student work, including a written record of both his own questions to prompt discussion as well as the student responses which he had to remember and record after the fact. All of the work of the evaluation was done by the teacher, and like any reasonable individual would, that teacher chafed under such a burden on top of what he did already to teach the students.

Evaluation was tough because it added to the workload of the teacher and moved his focus from the students and placed it on to doing the administrator's job. The teacher now had to create mounds of documentation to prove that he was doing his job. Niles felt that documentation was about hiding the forest behind piles of dried and matted wood pulp. No one was allowed to see the forest for the trees.

It was the same every year. Each year it got worse.

Every last week in August, Niles and the other teachers returned to the classroom they taught in after being in someone else's classroom to put in their time doing what was necessary to remain certified to teach. The two or two and a half months that they were not engaging in daily instruction of others was only a reprieve from that very action and little else.

All school year, the pressure to be highly effective was on. It built all year, amping up in the spring with the standardized tests. Teachers were encouraged to take ownership of student success so as to form a personal investment. The energy needed to love and care for the success of over a hundred teenagers was exhausting, but the standardized testing period that stretched from March to May wore down every teacher involved. By late May, many were running on fumes. The summer break that started in mid-June should have been a restorative period - a time for teachers to take a break from the stress. Instead, it was a shift to a different kind of stress. It was the best time for the teacher to get back to maintaining their certification which depended on investing more time and money into meeting ongoing certification requirements. Teachers got to focus on their biological children for two and a half months, vacation, or take more college courses. Then they went back to school in late August to prepare for another year of instruction. This went on year after year until the teachers were completely used up and quit or simply crumbled. They did exactly what they were expected to do. Everyone could say, "He was a good teacher. He never tried to leave." It was often the only good thing said about them.

Teachers worked in a culture that treated them negatively because of their jobs. The negativity was ongoing - it didn't break for two months in the summer. The only cure was a safe space where all of the negatives got pushed away, where some of what was subtracted was added instead. If there was nothing to restore some of what was lost, then there was no way to recover.

Niles and many of the people he worked with never found restoration.

There were to be no escapes.

Every teacher got four sick days each school year. There were many ways to appreciate using them and as many ways to avoid using them. Niles was sensitive to how the public and the administration perceived teachers using their sick days. Certainly, teachers were entitled to them - perhaps more than most people. That didn't matter to Niles. He went to work every day no matter how sick he was.

Teachers worked all day in an undeniable stew of filth, virus, and bacteria. In Niles's building in Pianosa Springs School District, the cleaning staff employed by the district had been eliminated years ago and was replaced with a contract organization that was the lowest bidder. Since it was the lowest bidder, it employed the lowest number of people for the lowest wages. It was a treadmill-type business: the cleaning staff was constantly being replaced because of the low wages; the few employees that were there were tasked with far too much work to do in the allotted time span. They weren't supervised because a supervisor cost too much money, and they weren't being paid enough to work so quickly as to accomplish the daily tasks. They often quit the job after only a few weeks because of the constant pressure to do more with less for next to nothing.

The ongoing result was that nothing was cleaned well if at all. The carpet in Niles's latest room was never vacuumed, only swept. He watched the cleaning person come by in the evenings when working late, park his or her vacuum outside the door and sweep with a broom and dustpan only the most highly visible scraps of paper and litter on the floor. Hallway floors and walls were sticky. Bathrooms were consistently adhesive with strange colored and obnoxious fluids that clung to every available surface. Filters in the air conditioning system were not changed because the person whose job it was to change them had been deemed too expensive to keep twenty years ago. The building was sick.

Students came to school deathly ill or not, because school was a free babysitter and missing school would inevitably put the good student behind. It would give the economically disadvantaged free breakfast and lunch. It give almost everyone social connections and everyone the railings, doors and desks to paint with germs.

When Geit missed too many days during his son's first year of life, he had his schedule changed so that he lost his "good" classes and was punished with "repeater" courses of students who had failed the course at least once if not twice or more. Of course, such maneuvering on the part of administration was illegal, but when Linn ran the union in the building. there wasn't any help available to Geit. She hated him almost as much as she hated Niles, and she'd sooner sacrifice whatever professionalism she possessed than help him regardless of what the Teachers' Union was for.

Teachers had to come to school, ill or not. That was the message. There would be retribution from Swamp for taking a day off even though the staff was contractually entitled to them.

Niles wasn't for taking sick days anyway. His father went to work in the factory every day that he could remember except one. That was the day that he was cutting wood with a chainsaw behind Niles's house and had it kickback and cut into his thigh. Niles was riding his bike home from school and had stopped at the New Salem General Store with his friends to buy some penny and nickel candy when Grandpa Niles's truck came rolling up in front where they were sitting on their bikes. He immediately recognized his father's sideburns through the windshield in the passenger seat and leapt off the bike to peek in through the open window to see his dad. Grandpa Niles went in the store to purchase some road sodas and Niles looked in the window at this father's lap. Father Niles was unconcerned, but there was a straight cut through his bloodied dungarees and a clean trench of bloody flesh exposed through the quadriceps muscle.

"Had an accident with a chainsaw. It'll be fine. We're just going to have a doctor clean it out. Make sure the wood chips are out and that it doesn't get infected," said father Niles calmly. He even smiled, as if the accident were a joke. Young Niles was impressed. He was shocked and frightened for his father just for a moment, but only for a passing moment. Father Niles knew that as an adult, he was not going to do or say anything to let his child worry about him. That was an unwritten rule of parenting, a thing done for children as an adult. It was part of the job to keep them from feeling scared, and father Niles was good at that. Little Niles often remembered that in the classroom. Even if he felt lost or things were falling apart, or there was a hole in his leg, he kept the students calm.

It was becoming too much.

Niles called in using a personal day and drove to the coastline alone. He didn't tell his wife he was going there. He didn't want to explain to her his decisions made in the interests of preserving his own mental health. She considered his depression and anxiety to be signs of personal or moral weakness. He found no sympathy there.

It was a casual Friday in a warm spring, so he didn't have to wear a tie to create an illusion of scholarship. He was wearing jeans and a t-shirt with the original cover of *Catch 22* on it. His wife never cared enough to ask about work in the morning anyway, usually only waking up enough to say goodbye as he scrambled out the bedroom door.

He drove through back roads that were indirect - a zig here, a zag there, to avoid the busy main roads. He also drove toward one of the smaller and less well-known beaches, one of the "roadside parks" that sprung up in small municipalities on Michigan's west coast during the early twentieth century before the giant highways were paved when a two or three hour drive was required from the state's interior to get to one of those small shaded roadside attractions. He passed by an empty roadside stand that still shouted "Tomatoes, Cucumbers, Squash!" from the previous autumn and pulled left into the beach parking lot. The playground equipment swung empty in the lakeside breeze and his truck was the first in the gravel. This small sandy beach was deserted, as it was early and most of the folk who would visit the beach wouldn't be far enough past their morning routines to appear amidst the flat stones and driftwood. The sun still looked orange coming over the trees from the east and most of the grassy part of the shoreline was shaded. The sand was just starting to warm.

Niles found a tree trunk washed ashore from parts unknown that now served as a makeshift beach-bench for weary shell and stone collectors. He had technically walked past the boundaries of the park onto private property, but he could see no houses on the hill or paths leading out of the trees and so he didn't care. There were no sounds now except for the wind moving through the leaves on the shore echoing a mournful, muted tamborine, and the water shifting its mass forward and backward on the sand and gravel beach. The waves were like a slightly out-of-balance metronome, sometimes coming closer to his feet before turning back like an irregular polyrhythm. The movement of the water was consistent compared to the sound of the winds. As the water and sand heated in the sun, they would become more chaotic, less slave to the overhead currents and more unraveled by variations in the local weather.

Niles felt unraveled himself. Like a child learning to play music needs a meter to grasp on to for guidance, Niles needed this day by the waves to get his head out of his head. There were so many dissonant tones being directed at him in addition to the dark one that he was swimming in. Being a servant of the public good was never an easy task, but it was always worse when it was taken for granted. There were so many needy children who needed parenting, who needed confidants or confidence, who needed something outside of themselves to think about in those troubled tough days when their brains were just breaking out of shells of egocentrism. They needed guidance, but having all of their parents working and fighting to survive didn't give them the guidance they needed. They were crashing about trying to figure it all out for themselves with only their peers for support. Niles remembered those days of his own well. If an adult had taken him by the shoulders and shaken him awake, it would have made things easier in the years since. Some students didn't want help, but young Niles was looking for it and it wasn't there. He could see the same searching he did behind the eyes of some of his own students. Eyes that search have a consistent look.

He was doing his best to be what his students were looking for beyond simple classroom instruction in grammar and literature. It was draining to give so much away and to get nothing back. Young people didn't know better. They took and took, their hungry little egos always searching for more. But adults knew better and they did worse. Adults who worked in education could be the worst because they were surrounded by hundreds of examples of children who didn't know better. And somehow, some of them thought that was an excuse for them to take and give nothing back as well.

Was Geit right though? Did none of it matter anyway? Was it meaningless? Were they and their efforts all to be simply forgotten, brushed away and ignored as time went by? And if it didn't matter anyway, why bother? Why bother to do anything, to smile or frown, to laugh or cry, to mock or to encourage, to love or to hate? If none of it made a difference to the lives of the people who were entrusted to their care, to their en loco parentis, then why did Niles have to drive thirty miles on a Friday morning in late spring to a deserted lakeside beach to sit on a desiccated driftwood tree trunk to try to fix his own internal rhythm?

The answer, of course, was to make it mean something. To use the force of will to bring meaning into existence. Geit wasn't wrong, but he wasn't right. There was a space in the between places of meaning and meaninglessness that had yet to be explored.

The following Tuesday marked another point on the time-line. The inaugural parent-teacher open house was a smashing success and Niles took no pride in making it so. He showed up on time, left on time, and in-between he gave a short presentation to parents that consisted of him showing his syllabus on the projector. For the two extra hours that he was there that day, he presented his material twice to three different people, and only one of them was a student that he was going to see five days a week for the next semester anyway. The student brought his grandfather with him to meet Niles and the rest of his teachers. Even though Niles and the grandfather hit it off over a shared philosophy of education, Niles still wasn't sure that this had been the absolute best use of his evening given that six people out of a potential two hundred had shown up.

As he sat in his empty classroom at the close, Swamp came over the PA and announced that the event had been a "wonderful success" and thanked "everyone involved, but especially the parents" for making it so. Niles rose from his seat and wandered into the empty hallway where there wasn't even the sound of a footstep. He found Bradley leaning against his closed classroom door, his bag in hand and his face incredulous. Niles shrugged and held his empty hands up in the air.

"Are we in same world as this woman?"

"You got me, bro. It's her world and we're just here taking up space. I'm leaving though. I've been here enough hours today."

"Good night, Bradley. Drive safe. It's a crazy world out there."

"You too, Niles." Bradley slipped out into the darkness leaving Niles standing with his hands on his hips in the hallway. Niles's back and head hurt. He felt like another brick in the wall.

27. Economics

Niles dropped into Geit's room while Geit was dozing off during his first period planning period. His feet moved when Niles closed the door behind him. Niles wiped his feet on a non-existent floor mat and dropped into Geit's extra ergonomic chair. He often struggled with his feelings of inadequacy - it was inevitable in a business where he never received positive feedback, and if it was given it was always from the students. No matter how good he was, his feedback from the students was going to run fifty-fifty both ways.

"They're trying to fire me."

"No one is trying to fire you."

"Then why am I getting so many unscheduled walk-ins from administrators? The district ELA coordinator popped in unexpectedly yesterday, and today Swamp was in my room. She's not even my evaluating administrator. They all hate me."

"They're doing pop-ins on everyone. They'd probably like to replace all of us with cheaper less-experienced teachers that they don't have to pay as much. I don't think you're any more of a target than any of the rest of us."

"What difference does that make? Nobody around here likes me. Swamp talks to everyone. She doesn't talk to me. Our department head hates me. Everybody hates me." Niles's face was turning red and tears of anguish were building behind his brown eyes.

Geit tilted his chair back, but his hands were still folded in his lap and his feet were still propped on the desk. Geit wasn't worried about it. He wasn't worried about anything. Niles's eyes started watering. His eyes always watered when he believed that people were out to get him.

"They're just doing their job. Don't take it personally."

"How am I not supposed to take it seriously when they're out to take my job? I take my job seriously!"

"Who are they going to replace you with?"

"I don't know. Aren't English teachers a dime a dozen?"

"Yeah. A lot of bad ones are. You're not bad. Just relax."

Geit knew he was correct, but Niles had proof. Everybody did hate him. It was everywhere. Every time that Niles went online to read articles about education, the comments section was full of posts from average citizens stating that all teachers were terrible, that they all got too much time off, that they all got paid too much, that they were all lazy and worthless! Every politician politicked on a platform of cutting teacher pay and benefits and making it easier to fire and replace them. The students hated him too. He was sure of it. The ones who didn't make it obvious were too polite to show him every day that they hated him like all of the others.

Geit chuckled at Niles's discomfort, but it wasn't funny. It wasn't funny at all, and there were many things that were even less funny than losing his job. Like drowning.

"Hey, have you been out to Lake Michigan lately?" Geit knew Niles liked to drive out to the lakeshore when he was feeling overwhelmed at work to watch the water.

"Yeah, I took my kayak out there last weekend and was going to go for a paddle, but the water was too damn rough. Five to seven foot waves and it looked like a storm was coming in. I was just going to go in anyway, but I had second thoughts when I remembered that a guy got lost out there last week."

"That guy in the kayak who went missing? Whatever happened to him? Did they find him?"

"Yeah, he washed up in Big Shores, about 30 miles away and 3 days later than his kayak."

Geit scowled. "Damn."

"Sometimes I think drowning would be the way to go, you know? Like in a story, where some guy walks into the ocean with his pockets full of rocks. Kind of romantic in a way." Niles was dreaming.

"What? How is drowning romantic? Your lungs fill with water, you choke and sputter and flail in spasms as you die, and then fish eat your eyes and lips, nose and ears. Then some kid walking his dog on the beach finds your putrid corpse and has nightmares about the smell for years." Geit smiled as he pointed out what Niles missed about death, but he wasn't mocking him.

"Yeah, you're right - but nobody ever writes it that way."

"That's because nobody wants to read that kind of stuff. Life is tough enough as it is without having to confront death and what it looks like to die. That's why when my mom dies, I'm going to ask that they paint her up like a whore at the funeral parlor so I can have a good laugh."

"Your mom would make an ugly whore," smiled Niles.

"She sure does."

They laughed together. Niles walked back to his classroom feeling a bit lighter, a bit better for all the wear. Geit had invited him over to his house again to watch people fight on television. Niles had to think about it, but thinking about it made him feel better - as if someone was on his side.

Another day past. Another page turned. It was still a gray day there at the school building. Both inside and outside. Niles and Halverson took a few moments to talk while Halverson was on his way out.

"Hey man, did you know that Tibbs doesn't have his professional certification?"

"Do you mean that he's just been extending his provisional one?"

"Well, what the hell? Why? I mean we all basically have to have enough credits to earn a Master's degree to keep teaching anyway, so why wouldn't he just do that? I mean aside from the fact that we'll never make the money back that we spend on getting the advanced degree."

"He's got a plan."

"A plan?" I have a plan too. Marry someone rich. Of course I'll have talk about it with my wife first. She probably won't care for it much."

"How many years has he been doing this?"

"I think this is his eighth year. Is it your tenth?"

"You know, I lost track."

"Okay, it's my tenth, and you came in after me, so it must be your ninth. And he came the year after you, so it's his eighth."

"That sounds right. So he's extending his provisional and hasn't done any course work?"

"Yup."

"I'll tell you, I hope it's a great plan. He's the best math teacher we have, and I'd hate to lose him because of a stupid mistake." Niles hated to lose anyone who was a good teacher, but especially a good math teacher. When Kyder was across the hallway she had a sign on the wall opposite the door that Niles could see from his spot that said "Ask three before you ask me." It was Kyder's way of avoiding answering questions about how to do math. Students told Niles that even after they had asked three other classmates for advice, that she would still refuse to answer questions, directing them instead back into the textbook. Sometimes if they questioned her enough, she would simply give the answer without explaining how to do the problem.   No one was sad to see her go. However, losing Tibbs would be a problem for which there was no answer in the back of the book.

There was no secret that the Pianosa Springs School District had a problem retaining quality young teachers. The teachers and the community knew it, but the school board and the superintendents did not. To them a teacher was a teacher, and none of them were any better than any others.

Kaseman and his hand-picked underlings knew teachers well. Some teachers won "Superlative in Education" awards and some won "Inspirational Teacher" awards, but that often meant that they manipulated the young impressionable students who chose the teachers the way that Linn's did. Some teachers were manipulative, hateful people who did whatever it took behind the scenes to make themselves look better except honestly try to be good teachers. They were simply replaceable cogs in a machine, none with any more value than any others. The belief was that anyone could "teach" to a test and that teachers who led their students to high standardized test scores on the MEAP, or ACT, or SAT, or AP tests were no more than a baseline competent animal trainers. All teachers who did not do that were simply below average pseudo-intellectuals who were lazing about in their tenure-protected gravy trains.

This attitude was wrong, but it was also uniquely American. No teacher mattered any more than any other and all were equally replaceable. The attitude was a transfer from the industrial era, but since the education system was also a holdover from the same era, why not keep these ideas as they were still applicable? The older teachers who stuck around were simply milking a system meant to protect them from criticism or fault. Even though none of these things were true for every teacher, it didn't matter in Pianosa Springs because the people in charge said that it didn't matter.

Even if good teachers could make a difference in student lives, it wasn't worth the financial investment in an era of lower school funding. Money trumped quality, and if there wasn't enough money to retain quality teachers, they had to be replaced. The school board considered the money more well spent in securing the services of Dr. Kaseman who for several years running was the highest paid school superintendent in the state by a wide margin. In an environment where one person was given the authority to determine his own financial worth, as well as the financial worth of everyone who worked for him, that outcome was inevitable. It was peak modern capitalism, and everyone knew that capitalism was the best possible system because it had come after feudalism and monarchy and looked better than authoritarianism.

Capitalism reduced students to products and transformed teachers into replaceable cogs on a Fordian line, but the legislators who built budgets for the state's schools had set up an inane and unreal pyramid of bureaucratic accountability with standards that no one could meet.

Teachers had to be like toasters if the university was going to be like a factory. They had to be disposable and easily replaced. There couldn't be any repair or upkeep available, no way to keep the good ones from wearing down and out early, becoming ruined or quitting. There had to be constant demand to keep up with the constant supply being generated. They had to be broken, and it was best if they could break each other. That was why Linn and Demarr were so valuable to Swamp. She outsourced the degradation of the profession in the building to them. They were highly effective.

Niles was crumbling, falling apart, and needed something to keep him going, a positive in a business filled with negatives.

Niles finally took Geit up on his offer and made plans to watch a MMA event on pay per view at his house. It was on the same side of town as the school, adjacent to one of the university's many student enclaves, but Geit's neighborhood was still wholly a place for families. Directly across the street from his tidy well-kept house was an elementary school where his son would go when he aged in. Like many suburban neighborhoods planned in an era when no one thought that urban areas would continue to expand, the roads to his home were labyrinthine. Niles met a handful of dead-ends and wrong-turns, odd switch-backs and circular cul-de-sacs that had become roundabouts as the development spread and grew like cancerous cells upon the formerly green landscape. Geit's house was as nondescript as he was descript, blending in with every other drab, colorless, fenced-in property on the block. If the home reflected anyone's character, it wasn't Geit's - except in the way that the exterior hid a deep richness inside.

Niles parked on the street and then hemmed and hawed in his car before knocking at precisely 7:55 PM. He wanted to give them five minutes to exchange pleasantries and settle in before the televised undercard began. Geit himself came to the door dressed like a regular person which made Niles uncomfortable because he was so accustomed to only seeing him as a teacher. Compounding Nile's discomfort was the slight bit of embarrassment that the undeserved attention that the invitation into Geit's inner sanctum made him feel. It was a special reward that he wasn't sure he deserved.

The house was normal on the inside too. It looked exactly as if a young married couple who sometimes shopped at Pier One lived there. The only thing that marked it as Geit's was the basement. After briefly introducing his uninterested wife, Geit invited Niles to his basement.

The basement, though mostly unfinished, was Geit's haven. He had a small office tucked into the corner behind some storage totes. He unlocked the door and showed Niles inside. It resembled nothing so much as as a more compact version of a private detective's office in an old noir film. Geit had finished the room with wood trim and wainscoting, white plaster walls and a refinished oak desk that shone in the light from the overhead bulbs. Along the wall was bookcase filled with classic hardcovers, a first edition Dashiell Hammett *Maltese Falcon* with a bright yellow cover, and several hardcover first editions of H.P. Lovecraft from Arkham House Press, printed in the '50s with slipcovers still intact. Niles's jaw fell open.

"What do you think?" Geit was smiling.

Niles stammered wide-eyed, "I'm impressed." Geit motioned for him to sit on an overstuffed couch opposite the desk that looked like it had come through a time warp from the 50s as well and sat behind his private detective desk in front of a wooden coat rack that held a gray overcoat and fedora. "This room represents quite an investment, right? Those books alone had to be expensive."

"I have protection."

"Like the hand of God?" Niles quipped.

"Nope, one of these." Geit pulled a handcrafted wooden box from a desk drawer and sat it on the desk ledger, opened the lid and carefully lifted out a .38 caliber snub nosed revolver for Niles to inspect in his hands.

Niles looked but didn't touch. "Wow. This is your office."

"Yeah, I grade papers down here. It makes me feel closer to living my dream."

"I feel like you sit here and solve mysteries."

"Speaking of mysteries, who's going to take the main event tonight? 'Shuga' or 'The Iceman'"?

"I think 'The Iceman' is due for a win."

"Let's go up to the living room. It's almost ten after. They should be getting to the first fight shortly."

Geit led the way up from his domain into the house that he shared with his indifferent wife as the two men settled into the living room to watch fighters in swim trunks pummel and grapple with each other. Drinks were shared and Geit's disinteresting wife drifted away upstairs shortly after ten, leaving the two men to drink and trade stories between fights.

The final bout of the night ended abruptly with the former champion dropping to the mat like a corpse kicked out of a speeding car. There was stunned silence in the arena and in Geit's house as the man who had been picked to win took a worryingly long time to regain his violently removed consciousness. Then the replays came, from angle after angle, the slow-motion replay showing the exact fraction of a second that a man's soul was almost severed from its tether.

Throughout the evening Geit's book collection had been a recurring topic in between bouts. Niles was fascinated that Geit had managed to assemble the first editions of such sought-after books on a teacher's salary, so at the end of the fight card Geit invited Niles back down to the office despite the late hour for a closer look.

"And here is a first edition Murakami from Japan. Published in 1978: *Kaze no uta o kike* or *Hear the Wind Sing* in English. Niles took the white book with the art deco style image on it in his hand and relished it. It was Geit who'd introduced him to Murakami two years ago. The author had quickly become Niles's favorite.

"I love Murakami's protagonists. Each one seems like the same character viewed through a different prism each time. It's always a lonely guy looking for meaning and having some level of existential crisis. I can relate." The alcohol had fully taken hold and Niles was letting his feelings rise to the surface from an otherwise uncharted depth. He put the book down on Geit's desk and sighed, slouching back into the vintage sofa. Geit too, was feeling the effect of the late hour combined with watching a man become brain damaged on tv. He rolled back in his desk chair, put his feet up on the desk and started talking like it was two AM on a Sunday morning.

"You know what Niles, you think too much. You're always going. I've noticed it in the hallways and in meetings. The world doesn't move fast enough for you, does it?" Geit wasn't so much asking as telling.

Niles sat back up, tried to regain his composure. "What do you mean? I can hardly keep up with all the stupidity going on."

"No, not that stuff, I mean you actually think. You think more than anyone I've ever met. It's damn near all you do. I can see the wheels turning in you non-stop. Like right now. You're not even here right now. Where are you? Do you even know?"

"No. Part of me is here, but the rest is scattered. I feel like I have three narrators in my head fighting for which story to tell." Niles was short circuiting. He relaxed into the couch again.

"You should find a way here. Find a way to where your body is, these spaces it inhabits and drag your head along with it." Geit was as supportive as his life allowed him to be.

Niles was drained. "There are nights when I fall asleep asking, 'What will save me from myself?' And mornings when I wake up, knowing with absolute certainty that the answer is 'nothing.'" That anyone who could is merely nothing more than a figment of an overwrought imagination. That the people I've looked for don't exist, and never will. That ultimately, I will fall and it will make no difference. It will simply be as if I never was. It seems terrible, but it's true. And I have to make peace with that."

"You do, Jo-jo. You're right. The real question is how do you make your peace once you know what you have to do. The worst thing you could do is wait around for someone to give you an answer to your questions. At least, that's what my therapist tells me."

"You're seeing a therapist too?"

"Isn't everyone?"

"If they're not, they should be. It's the best decision I ever made in my life." Niles sighed with relief. He wasn't alone in needing help.

"Mine smokes a meerschaum and looks like Hemingway."

Niles laughed. "Fitting. Mine looks like a Jewish Tom Cruise and is named after a beer."

"Wouldn't that have been funny if we were seeing the same guy?"

"A cosmic coincidence on a literary order is what that would have been."

"Geit."

"Niles."

"Thanks for inviting me over. I haven't been invited to someone's house since elementary school."

"That's because you're weird, Jo-Jo. I don't mind that though. I appreciate that." Geit reflected. "You're not supposed to be the way you are, you know that?"

"What do you mean?" Niles was perplexed.

"You came from a farm, you drive a pick-up, and you hate country music. You're full of contradictions once you let people get to know you, just like a real human. You treat every kid like you're their dad. You're the most interesting hick I've ever met."

Niles glowed. "Thanks man. Thanks for letting me in."

Geit closed his eyes and rubbed his face. "My wife wants me to go to church with her in the morning."

"Are you serious?" Niles chuckled. "Are you going to do it?"

"I don't think so. I'm afraid the altar might spontaneously burst into flame. Did I ever tell you that I used to be Satanist?"

Niles laughed. Both at the absurdity of Geit as a Satanist and at Satanism itself.

"Yeah, as a teenager. Mostly to piss off my mom." He smiled a toothy grin.

Niles laughed again. More anxiety drained from his face. "I went to church every week with my mom until I was almost eighteen. My version of Satanism was to insist that I needed Sunday morning to sleep the summer that I left for college. But that was only after I'd decided against becoming a priest."

Geit laughed with Niles "You, my friend, are the devil."

Niles walked out of Geit's door into the early morning coolness that night feeling something profound that was unfamiliar to his experience. He felt connected to something besides an aching loneliness. Niles felt friendship.

28. Fire Alarm

Fifth periods on a Thursday in February went by slowly. There was nothing that Niles could plan in his lessons to change that. It was the nature of the beast. He felt that a day given over to Thor the Norse god of thunder, storms, and farming should be more exciting, but not strongly enough to change it. Niles wasn't the only one who felt that way. The students felt it too. For them, Thursday afternoon was the cusp of something greater. Friday night and Saturday were within their field of vision, but the hours between seemed far too long to contemplate.

Niles was making rounds in the room, watching and directing and facilitating and assisting students who were working on textual research in Hamlet, examining how Shakespeare might have used his monologues to both prove and disprove the meaninglessness of life. A student raised her hand and Niles went to her enthusiastically. She always had good questions.

"Mr. Niles, nothing exciting ever happens in my life. I'm bored with it." It wasn't the question he anticipated.

"What do you mean you're bored with it? If you're bored, I can give you more work to do.

"I don't want to do more work. I just want something exciting to happen."

"What's exciting to you? Do you want some kind of fireworks display? Should I break into a song, maybe dance for you?"

Her eyes lit up. "Yes!" Her grin was still large, but she reconsidered. "No, I wouldn't want you to embarrass yourself like that. I've seen you try to dance."

Niles played along. "What? That was you stalking me at the club last weekend! Oh my gosh! How'd you sneak in? You're too little!" She laughed, covering her mouth so as not to disturb the others in the room. She didn't know that Niles hadn't been to a club since college and had rejected every attempt to get him to "dance" for years on the grounds that his rhythm was worse than Navin Johnson's prior to his journey of self discovery.

She straightened up in her chair and got serious again.

"No, but really I'm serious, Mr. Niles. This school is dry. It needs something different to happen once in a while. Do you know what I mean?"

Niles knew what she meant.

"It's too dry here, so you want it to flood?"

She rolled her eyes backward as far as they would go, and then her head followed all in the same motion. She laughed hard, not hiding it this time.

"You're crazy, you know that?" She smiled her million dollar smile at at him.

Niles switched to being serious. "I know what you mean. Here's how I look at it. Usually when something exciting happens, it isn't very good." He looked in her eyes, and knew that she needed an example. "Like for example, aliens show up and start kidnapping people to experiment on. That'd be pretty dang exciting, but probably not very good." He paused there and feigned a pensive look. "Unless they were going to kidnap me, take me to their planet in another galaxy and experiment on me to give me superpowers, then use time travel to return me to this very spot where I could become the world's greatest superhero when I'm not teaching. That would be great. But when people get taken by aliens it doesn't go very well for them, at least from what they show on TV, right?"

Before she had time to answer, their conversation was interrupted by the shrill buzz of the fire alarm. Niles looked at the clock.

There was still almost 30 minutes left in the period. This was an awful time to have a fire drill. Students were always told in the event of a fire drill to just leave everything and exit the building, but Niles had a gut feeling.

"Everybody, let's take our stuff with us, just in case, okay?" Students that were already headed to the door came back and collected their things quickly. Niles thought of the day when he was an intern when there was a gas leak. Some teachers had left their coats and keys in their classrooms and they were not allowed back into the building to retrieve them. Niles was younger and more naive back then, but he still took his coat and his keys.

Construction on the new undersized theater facility in what was once a combination of empty field and teacher parking lot next to the school building had been ongoing. Occasionally, students would sneak over to smoke cigarettes with the construction workers, but the only real impact of the work next door to this point had been the sounds of building taking place in that overlapping time frame with class, interrupting the teachers with windows facing the new construction during their lectures and giving Linn another thing to complain about when she wasn't bullying teachers and students. Miles Smithson was the reigning administrator, and there was no plan in place for what to do in the event of a gas leak.

The workers broke a line and the possibility of a fire or explosion was a major concern. Niles and Cook were at lunch, talking over some aspects of classroom management while also entertaining the six or seven students who invariably came back to her classroom for a calm, safe haven.

The fire alarm went off and Smithson's stuttering voice came over the PA.

"St-st-students and faculty. There is a gas leak next door at the construction site. Please exit the building as quickly as possible on the..." There was a pause. Students were noisily gathering their half consumed lunches to flee, but Niles could still hear Smithson's voice faintly over the PA asking where the kids should go. "Which side is the football field on? Should we have people go out there?" The murmurs in response to the question must have been the secretary taking control of the situation in her normal fashion when Smithson was clueless. "People, evacuate toward the football field side of the school..." He paused again. "... which is on the south side of the school. Please exit the building using only the southside exits and go towards the football field, but not to the football field." He paused again. Then Niles clearly heard him ask the secretary "Where should they go?" since Smithson had completely neglected to remove the phone from his mouth this time. More murmurs, and then he went on. "Follow the access road between the football and baseball fields and meet your teachers in the practice football fields near the cemetery. I repeat, do not exit through the north doors, but instead leave the building and meet your teachers in the practice football field near the cemetery." Niles and M.A. Cook made perfect eye contact and started taking materials.

"You grab the attendance clipboard, and I'll get some extra coats out of my closet." It was still hovering around freezing outside and the gray sky threatened rain. She saw the questioning look on Niles's face and before he could even ask, she answered. "We'll still need to be able to take attendance of who is with us and who's missing. A clipboard will make it easier." There was no possible way to account for all of the students who were in the cafeteria where no one took their attendance. She took the students who were with them. "I'm heading out there now to meet students as they get there. Stay

402

back a bit and make sure that teachers are the last ones out, then find me." Smithson might not have had a plan in place, but Cook did. The extra coats were for the students who didn't bring their own and would be standing in a freezing field for the next hour. She was good like that.

From then on, Niles tried to be like M.A. Cook.

He took his coat and his keys as the fire alarm's shrill sound drowned out the worried voices of his students.

"Remember ladies and gentlemen, we meet at the side of the football field, away from the building that might explode when the fire hits the gas lines." Students were filing out the door when one of the first through stuck his head back in.

"Mr. Niles! There's smoke out here!"

"Well, you know what they say about smoke, right? Let's go! Everybody out!"

It was difficult not to smile. Maybe this was just the right type of excitement for the students on a Thursday. Niles followed the last student out the door and locked it behind him. There was smoke visible down the adjacent hallway and the everyone was ushered out the door by grim-faced teachers. He zipped his coat and made his way out behind them and to the fence by the football field. Sirens were already approaching in the distance. Niles found Halverson who was disheveled and breathing heavily.

"So, an actual fire, eh?" Niles had his hands in his pockets like a bemused bystander.

"In the stairwell next to my classroom. I pulled the alarm." Halverson was still panting, spitting out the story in pieces. "I didn't smell it at first. The kids said it smelled like burning plastic, so I looked out into the hallway and saw smoke coming out of the stairwell. I grabbed the fire extinguisher off the wall and went in there. It was pretty thick, then I saw that the window was on fire. I tried to put it out, but it was too big, so I just ran back and got the kids out of the building!"

Both men turned to look back at the building. Indeed, the fire could be seen through the melting plexiglass window in the stairwell that faced them.

"Good job, Halverson. The life you saved may have been your own."

As both men stared into the flames, Niles asked the question that was burning on both their minds. "How did they set the window on fire?"

"They must have covered it with something flammable..." Halverson, suddenly thoughtful, gazed up at the window with his hands on his hips.

Niles suppressed a laugh. "I have to say, I wouldn't have given most of our kids enough credit to be able to do something like that. I think we just narrowed our list of culprits down to chemistry students."

The crowd of students surrounding the building had to be pushed back by security to make way for the fire engines. Several dozen teens were in the act of taking selfies with the window in the background. Niles imagined that it was already trending on the local Twitter. He went to the fence to take his attendance. Every student was out and most were there. He saw the three that weren't when their car nearly collided with the fire trucks as they made good their escape. Already student vehicles were lining up to hit the street, and one of the vice principals was waving her arms and shouting impotently that no one could leave as the cars pulled out into traffic. In front of where the first fire truck pulled to a stop, a group of girls had organized an impromptu dance troupe and were performing a chore-ographed routine in front of the smoke billowing out while other students recorded the dance with the fire in the background for dramatic effect.

Niles leaned back against a car that wasn't his, crossed his feet and smiled. It was like watching a cheap 1970s disaster movie unfold. Firemen pulled out hoses and headed inside through the doors below the fire. The vice principal who earlier had been shouting at students in cars that they couldn't leave as they drove past her had now been given a megaphone and was hyperventilating while telling the assembled students to "Remain calm" while she was clearly losing her mind. Chaos bloomed and Swamp panted and ranted trying to rein it back in. She marched around between the students and the smoke, shouting and stomping her feet like a cheerleader gone off her meds. To Niles, it all felt normal.

The chaos seemed trivial to Niles. Everything was chaos now.

It was a cold, dark morning like most in Pianosa Springs. Niles was running late. That was not normal. Niles was never late.

That morning he walked into the building with Tad Irvine. Irvine was a prematurely balding psychologist who'd decided to become a teacher in the late eighties when the path to certification was easier. He was grandfathered in and maintained a corner of the history department that was comfortable and solid. He had worked with Psychology professors who believed strongly in experimenting on themselves. They were mostly old, white men who had learned their trade in the free-wheeling sixties before budgets shrank and drugs were locked away behind schedules that made experimentation difficult. Irvine liked drugs. They worked without fail.

Niles shuffled quickly between the rows of cars toward Irvine and caught him on the lane before the sidewalk. "How's it going, Irvine? Happy Monday!" Niles often switched from perfectly serious to perfectly ironic in the same sentence. Irvine was one of the only people who understood both parts at once.

"I am good to go, Jo-Jo. I'm happy to be here. Always happy to be here."

"I'm jealous of you, Irvine. I don't know how you do it. This place is dangerous. It makes me a little bit nuts."

"I'll tell you how I do it, all you have to do is ask."

Niles looked at him confusedly. "Okay, I'll bite. How do you do it?"

"I got skills in pills son, skills in pills." He turned and looked Niles squarely in the eye as he held the door open for him." Niles stepped in and they faced each other. "The first I take against depression. The second is pure energy. The green one for my self-aggression. Then the red one - ecstasy."

Niles tilted his head and looked at Irvine like a confused dog. Irvine translated for him.

"It's all about balance my boy, balance. If you need help, you have to get it. If you get help, you have to use it."

"I guess."

"It's not hurting the kids. They don't know. Did you know?"

"No."

"I'm here every day. I can do my job. That's what counts, isn't it?"

"Yeah. I suppose it is.

They walked up the steps side-by-side to the second floor and parted at the top by the doors.

"Have a day, Irvine." He winked.

"You too, Jo-Jo."

Geit's door was the first one on the left after the steps, and for once when Niles got there, the door was open already.

Niles was late, Geit was early. Ever since his child was born, he was showing up for work barely ten or fifteen minutes before the students instead of a half hour. Having a child was a time-consuming proposition. Geit had his feet up on the desk and seemed to be meditating. Since his footsteps had already broken the silence of the near empty hallway, Niles broke through the open door.

"Geit. How the hell are you doing?"

"Lovely, just lovely."

"You were gone yesterday. Are you okay, the kid okay? The wife okay?'

"Yeah, I just had a bad reaction.

"Do tell."

"I've told you about my therapist, right?"

"Yeah."

"Well, I'm on a lot of prescriptions. There was a bad interaction."

"Isn't your doctor supposed to make sure that kind of thing doesn't happen?

Geit nodded. "Supposed to. I guess nobody's perfect." He shrugged his shoulders.

"How many prescriptions are you on?"

"Eight."

"Holy..." Niles was taken aback. "You are joking, right? You must be joking."

Geit shook his head no. "Nope. Eight."

"Wow. Are you chemical or man?"

"I almost died."

"Why did you come to work today? Shouldn't you be some-where recovering?"

"I don't have any sick days or personal days left. Junior has been sick a lot. My wife used up her sick days a couple months ago, and now mine are all gone too. I have to be here."

Niles felt sick to his stomach. "Is there anything I can do?"

Geit shrugged. "Keep talking with me and check on me be-tween classes?"

"Yeah, at least."

"I was doing my normal thing yesterday, when I started get-ting warm, like really warm. Way too warm. I had to open the win-dows all the way, and my students were complaining about being cold. Then I started shaking, and I just couldn't stop. The tremors started out small and just got bigger and bigger. I felt like I was los-ing all control of my body. Then I started getting tunnel vision. That was when I called down to the office and told them that I had to leave."

"Why didn't you say anything to me yesterday? All I knew was that you had to leave early."

"By the time I realized what was going on, it was all I could do to drive myself to the emergency room."

"You had to drive yourself to the emergency room? You should have asked me. I'm your friend you know."

"You mad at me because I didn't ask you to take me to the hospital? Oh, I'm sorry, I didn't know it was about you."

"C'mon. You know that's not it. It sounds like your doctor is trying to kill you. I feel like as your friend, I should talk to him vio-lently."

Geit ignored Niles's concern and continued. "Serotonin Syn-drome. Apparently the drug cocktail I've been on was generating too much serotonin in my brain and not allowing enough of it to be reabsorbed, so it was pooling."

"What kind of doctor doesn't know enough about the drugs he's prescribing to prevent that kind of interaction?"

"I don't blame him. I'm on uppers for the depression, downers for the anxiety. I got another pill for the mania, one for the migraines that messes up my blood pressure, and another one for the blood pressure. I got pills to help me sleep because the anxiety meds keep me up at night. I got pills to wake me up because some of the other ones make me so tired I can't stand up. Those are just the ones that I remember."

"What the hell, Geit. That's like playing roulette with your health."

"No, more like rolling craps with eight dice."

"Jesus." There was a long pause as Niles tried to evaluate Geit. "What now?"

"Right now I'm off all of them. I had a cup of coffee this morning and I feel like I'm submerged, but I'm off everything for a while to try to prevent this from happening again."

"God damn, man."

"Yeah, I know."

"Now what? What do you do next? You can't go cold turkey on all that, can you?"

"I'd rather go cold turkey then have a repeat of yesterday."

"Just do me a favor and let me know today if you feel anything bad coming on, anything at all, okay?

"Okay."

That was Niles's signal to go. He was running late already and he had things to do to get ready for the students to show up. There was always too much to do.

Geit didn't let Niles know. That was his thing, he was an interior man. He kept things to himself. He was one of few people who were like that in the building. Sure, Niles was another, but most teachers were more like Halverson.

Halverson was blowing up. Over the past week he'd been impressed mightily by the lack of effort and general high level of apathy demonstrated by his students that particular February. The Honor Society was doing next to nothing, waiting for Halverson to do everything for them. His AP classes were in the same mode. February depression and lethargy had set in for the students, but Halverson wasn't having that. He went off.

"This is unacceptable. These test scores, these essays, all of it! These are inexcusable! What is going on?" He paused to add dramatic flair, but the class was immunized by their cell phone inoculations. "Do you not care? Is that it?" He stalked around the front of the room like the mad man that he was.

The class was silent. They just looked at him.

Just then, when the timing was perfect and Halverson was in peak teacher rage mode, the phone rang.

He walked over and picked it up. The voice on the phone shouted a single phrase then slammed down in disconnection. Halverson's fuse hit the dynamite.

He slammed the phone back down on his end in a state of explosive rage.

"This is the kind of bullshit I'm talking about! This kind of slapdick asinine goofshit! You all ought to be ashamed!"

The students' eyes were wide. What was the phone call? What did someone say to cause the otherwise usually cucumber-cool Halverson to blow his top? He stalked, he ranted, he raved.

"God damn it, I'm so sick of the bullshit around here! Do you know what we're trying to do here? Do any of you even care?" A student's hand started to rise up, as if to volunteer an "I care" but Halverson didn't care. His face was red. Whatever that phone call was, it must have been the worst possible thing anyone could have said. Halverson was on fire. He launched into a full twenty minute shame speech, berating first the class effort before moving into a full condemnation of the whole age group. Whether or not he was effective in encouraging them to feel any shame, they were quiet and averting their eyes from his angry gaze.

Meanwhile, in Niles's classroom, his AP students were in an excited buzz. They were reading *Catch 22* and even though no one seemed to love it as much as Niles, even the hardest students found a joke or two that was funny. Now motivated by the text, one of the greatest classroom pranks ever played had just taken place, and there was nothing to do but wait for the fallout. A student stood by the classroom phone, elated and anxious. Who else could they call? They wanted to call every teacher that they liked in the building, pranking them all the same way, but Niles warned that a joke put on repeat loses the element of novelty that often makes it amusing.

What they knew and wanted to share was the answer to the question that no one was asking: "Any fool can make money these days, and most of them do. But what about people with talent and brains? Name for example, one poet who makes money."

The student punched in the code for Halverson's classroom phone. The phone rang. The classroom was silent with expectation. They heard the other side on the line pick up. Everyone held their breath.

He shouted "T.S. Eliot." into the receiver and then swiftly slammed the phone down on the cradle.

29. Trudeau

Niles had copies to make before tomorrow, but Geit's door was open. He hadn't seen him in the last week. As the the only person in the building who could reliably tolerate Niles, he had become indispensable to his ability to keep Niles's own level of crazy at a manageable place. He entered Geit's door from the side, head first like a rookie soldier navigating trenches in the Somme. Geit's feet were on his desk, he was slouched in his chair, fingers tented, resting his head which looked exceptionally wearied by something even darker than his hair.

"Hey, are you rushing out of here?"

Geit's eyebrows popped up, but he didn't speak.

"I just wanted to bother you for a while. Haven't done that in a few days."

Geit gestured for him to enter, looking nothing so much as like a weary king marking his brother, the Duke of Something.

"You doing okay? You look like yourself." Niles's attempt at dark humor was acknowledged by an uptick on the left side of Geit's pale face, an eighth portion of a smile made solid only by a twinkle of his eyes.

"Just thinking."

"Thinking about what? Man's insignificant significance? The way we're employed with buckets to drain a planet-sized body of ignorance? Or something more Nihilistic? Don't tell me that you're thinking about all of the other Erics in history and feeling like you don't measure up?" That last one made the other side of Geit's face curve toward the sky as well. Niles perked up too. Geit got his jokes. The students might not, none of the other staff would, but if he could amuse Geit, then he'd done something that day.

"I was thinking about God. Do you think we go someplace when we die?"

"Dude, are you serious?" Niles laughed, put his hands on his hips incredulously. "You're thinking about God? Eric Geit, the man who practiced Satanism as a teenager just to piss off his mom, is thinking about God?" Geit's hands turned from tents under his nose to a splayed finger question mark. "You know how I feel about it. God is something we made up to feel better about all the things we can't know."

"I figured you'd know, since you were ready to be a priest at one point."

"Yeah, I read all about him. Read a few of those books that supposedly he wrote using other people. Read the whole things, not just the parts they replay in church like the priest's favorite hymns. It's tripe. I've read better and more cohesively themed work from the bottom rung of my creative writing students. The only thing it proves is that if you can get a lot of people to repeat the same thing over and over again that it magically becomes true. I thought you knew that too?"

With that, Geit's face became unreadable to Niles. His hands gestured the universal motions for "I don't know," and hidden deeply in lines that Niles couldn't decipher was a kind of hurt that seemed alien to men. There were lines that Geit hid in and behind that Niles couldn't compute, at least not yet.

"I've started going to church with my wife. I just wanted to know what you thought." Geit's hands fell to the armrest of his chair, expectantly.

"I think Eric Geit sitting in church is something that I would pay a hefty ticket price to see. Catholic church or one of the other thirty-three Protestant ones in town?"

"The ones in the middle. My wife is searching for one that feels right." He paused slightly and then corrected himself. " We're searching for one that feels right." Geit's pale face was mostly blank, not questioning, not judging, just being. Niles folded his arms across each other and tilted his head in consternation. "The Catholic one had the nicest choir."

Niles was confused. Geit was a rock upon which whole fleets of superstition and religious folly both pagan and Christian had crashed and sunk. He was an anti-matter man, a being whose doubts had solidified into beliefs themselves the way that some men had taken the words of their fathers living unexamined lives and turned them into lonsdaleite bedrock. More than any of that, Geit had been the freest man he'd ever met. Now he was getting fitted for chains? Niles's reaction was knee-jerk. Religion coming from Geit was like a tap on the nerve with a hammer.

"I could think of better things to do with your time if you want a suggestion." Niles's playfulness was dismissive of the idea, not of the man asking the question, but what did Geit see? There was no indication on his face. "I think everyone has to decide for himself what is going to work for him in the life that he wants to lead and that anything I could tell you about how I see it would be useless to you. You're more your own man than anyone else I've ever met. Participating in a religion means that you give the reins to someone else, that you ask someone to tell you what to do when the questions become difficult. And the only reward for doing what they say is social acceptance. People around you pat you on the back and say good job, no matter what you feel on the inside. To me, it was a slow poison."

"I wanted to know what you thought." Geit gazed thoughtfully out the window. "I washed my face with the dew and combed my hair with the wind..." He kicked off the desk and put his feet on the floor. He changed the topic of conversation to something else, and Niles would never be able to remember what that was, not in the days, weeks, months or even years of thinking about it. His last conversation with Geit was about church.

Things got dark quickly. Darkness wasn't always a matter of the cloudy days and the seemingly endless winter. Sometimes it was the people -- the dour, serious people, still suffering the lingering effects of any number of borderline tragedies. Wins and losses didn't even out. Geit had a fight break out in his room, a fight between two students who knew that he was too worn out to control or prevent. They belligerently attacked him first, before attacking each other. Geit didn't make it to the phone, but campus safety walking by the door heard the ruckus. Desks were overturned, punches were thrown and landed. Geit wanted them gone for the full ten days prescribed in the school handbook. He did not get what he wanted.

Both students claimed that the fight was incited and inflamed by Geit, that he'd made vague statements that sounded racist. Both boys being black complicated the issue. The district was already under fire for suspending too many minority students, rightfully so. For all the "cultural sensitivity" training foisted on the teachers, the administrative mandate still included no means of restorative justice for students who had broken school rules. There were only two options for responding to violations of the behavioral code: suspension or not suspension. Not suspension meant that there was a meeting with an administrator - in this case White - and then the student was returned to the class. No further administrative paperwork or follow-up was deemed necessary.

In this case, both students had their bloody lips and facial cuts treated and they were returned to Geit's room the next day. Geit was livid. It was a slap in his face, not just as a professional teacher, but as a human being with the right to feel safe on the job. The boys came back and taunted him, flaunting his powerlessness over them. Geit tried to be professional in the face of accusations of racial bias and bit his lip and tried to teach. Without the specter of punishment to deter the boys, there was nothing to curb their disruptive behavior. He couldn't send them out or write them up without advancing Swamp's belief that he was a racist.

Geit's classroom was suffering. His marriage was suffering. His ability to take care of himself was suffering. He was still struggling to cope with the effects of having gone off of his medications. He was a good teacher when he had support, like many of his peers. But the opposition that he faced from the students compounded by the ways in which Swamp deliberately undercut his authority made him feel sicker than he was already.

By lunchtime on Wednesday, Geit had had enough. He called down to Swamp's secretary and told her that he had to leave. He was too sick to continue. He left that day without saying a word to anyone else. He was not at work on Thursday or Friday. Niles, who had not spoken with him in days wondered what was going on, but was too buried in his own work and too exhausted to pursue any answers.

Swamp was livid that Geit had left work during the day, forcing a scramble to find teachers to cover his classes. It didn't matter how sick he was. She determined that as soon as he returned, he needed to be spot evaluated for keeping his job. She was out to trim dead wood, and to her, dead wood was anyone she didn't like. She called Geit herself, warning him over the phone that he should probably look for work elsewhere. When Geit complained, threatening to bring the union into the matter, she put her administrative staff on notice that they were going to do surprise evaluations on the whole building. None of the teachers would know when she or her lackeys would show up, just that they would. The whole building was on edge again. Linn and Demarr blamed Geit and made sure that everyone else on the staff believed it was his fault too.

It was the atypically typical Sunday. A sense of dread engulfed everything like a fog. Every teacher and every student felt it to some degree. The death of freedom and the encroaching shadow of structure, of work, of the potential for discomfort. It was amplified by Swamp's efforts to undermine everyone's comfort with the surprise evaluations on the table. That weekend, Niles was feeling the shadowy dread more acutely. No one could have predicted what the lingering chill would bring them that Spring.

Niles received a phone call just after seven PM from someone who had never called him before. Phone calls from people not prone to calling are rarely good if ever at all. This one was the worst. Geit was dead.

Niles was undone on that cold evening. Nothing could make losing someone close, someone your own age, someone who wasn't ill or visibly suffering, feel normal. Geit was gone. That phone call had unraveled him, exposed breaks that were hidden, uncovered wounds that had never healed well and made new ones on top of them. Geit was gone and would not be coming back.

At first, Niles tried to wake up from what was clearly a terrible phantasm, a nightmare drawn from a pool of his own worst fears of loss. But he couldn't wake up. It was real. He first wandered up and down the stairs in shock. "The Art of Losing" was stuck on repeat in his head: "Lose more, lose faster..." He'd taught the poem so many times in class, always pairing it with a protagonist in a novel or short story losing something meaningful - a friend, a parent, a lover, innocence. Now it rang like a bell in his head. It was true, but what could he do with truth right now? What good does it do to know something like that? The other line from a book that was stuck in his head like a skipping record was the one that told him what to do next: "Put on your shoes." The words of Loyd Peregrina to Codi hung like the moon on a night devoid of stars.

So that's what he did. What else can someone do? He put on his shoes and went outside. He stood in the driveway staring up at the night sky and paced up and down the hill in his yard in the darkness. Moving his feet kept him upright. "Keep moving" he told himself. He needed someone to hold on to.

In the darkness he found Heller's name on his illuminated phone screen and touched it. She would know something. They hadn't talked lately, but she was still a trusted friend. She'd be able to dispel the nightmare, to cast away those dark thoughts and reveal the truth that had to be there. It had to be a rumor grown out of control, some half-formed creature made only to crush joy and make him bleed. She would know the truth that Geit was still there and that it was all the very worst of rumors.

But that wasn't how it was, and she couldn't save him from the truth. The news spread throughout the community. The former principal Fitzgerald, now living and working in Lansing, had called her, but she'd heard first from a half dozen students. News traveled quickly in Pianosa Springs. She knew all the details that the other call couldn't provide Niles. Knowing was as equally awful as not knowing and sharing the knowledge only made the burden of knowing more bearable. Niles's knees buckled and he fell in the driveway, crying, short of breath. Heller sniffled on the other end of the line.

"I'll see you tomorrow morning before the kids come in."

Niles could barely hear her. He ended the call and mustered himself. He rolled back from his knees to sit on the dewy wet grass. He called Cook in her retirement bungalow. She knew. Voices were spreading the news quickly. Such things never move slowly. Grief and the voices that bear it move like swift clouds on the horizon, coming close and wreaking devastation upon shelters thought safe and dry.

He'd left them without warning or ceremony; he would never cast his shadow in the hallways again. The list of names who had now passed through them never to return was long and dark, like looking at the rolls of young men who had left small towns and gone off to the Great War, never to return and shuffle past shop windows with children of their own. Those men left hollow spaces that only the eyes of the wanting could see. Niles felt the same way as allies dwindled in the hallways. Others had gone before Geit, in ways that were more normal and less shrouded in darkness.

There was the wise old Shepherd, a mustachioed Gandalf in the History department, who had been first to retire on Niles's career. Back when the teachers' union was a union of teachers, he'd come sweeping down like the white wizard leading the Riders of Hill and Dale against enemies within and without the Keep. He was young yet, only twenty-two when he first strode giant-like against the dark forces of ignorance and division, and though strong and hale, he knew that his own ship to the Greyhavens was setting sail, so at fifty-two he bid adieu from the dock, a hero who had conquered and made way for lesser ones to follow.

M.A. Cook, Mother Nurture herself, had set out soon after. She'd spent two life-times of energy and mass lighting her room and all parts surrounding like a blooming sun, though more daughter. She was crafted of mother of pearl and shone like the combined radiance of all of the pearls she'd mothered in her years of classrooms and after thirty years she left to rest, leaving her pearls to care and maintain the next generation. Among her pearls she counted

Trudeau, Geit, and Niles, who had all played fiddles to her merry Queen Cole in those very halls. All four had made a merry quorum at every meeting, like a gender-swapped Fred MacMurray ruling a comedic roost of three sons in real time. She'd left them in each others' hands and the students' too, trusting that all things would be good and right as far as she could see.

There was Coach Tower, a history teacher who'd blotted out the sun like a giant at every football game and track meet. He had moved on as well, when life-long injuries from the sports he'd loved as much as he loved the students he had coached made hovering around a classroom too painful to endure. His hips were replaced, but he wasn't. The giants to come were smaller. All of these and more were in the building, lighting the halls when Niles arrived, and all of them were only memories in the minds of those who persisted by the time Geit was lost.

There were some yet in the building who might be giants, maybe even Niles, but the world that was fostering these was not the same that had created those giants now striding off into the sunset. They grew in a world and a time that had esteemed them, built them up, told them that they were pillars of the community, and thus made them all the greater. They came from a community that valued them, helped them become the most that they would be. Niles's world was different: smaller, more crass and less kind, less forgiving, and most strongly - less encouraging and more cold and indifferent. How could these young people grow to be giants when they were constantly attacked on all sides before they had a chance to grow to their full size and strength?

It was no one's fault that the world had changed. That was simply the way things went. Those giants, though kind and benevolent, had assumed that the world had become better because they'd made it better. They'd lost sight that always at the edges of their better world there were forces working to push back against them. Linn and Demarr were the opposites of these titans, but leviathans still. Lurking like icebergs, mostly below the surface. They allowed only their thin false fronts to rise while they were being watched, and below the surface, rot became all. They were shoggoths, formless and shapeless while their betters were on watch, but once those betters went on their natural course, they coalesced, becoming the succubilike wraiths that corroded and hollowed out the building from the inside.

Now Geit was gone far before his time and Niles was at ground zero for the fallout. Every day when he went to work for two weeks, he had to walk past Geit's classroom, with his name still above the door, like the most recent headstone in a series of remarkably awful victims of an drowning. If anyone who'd been on the outside wanted to know about Geit, they came to him. There was no putting any distance between himself and Geit's absence. Everyone had known that the two men were friends.

Geit was a cult figure and a teacher. If there had been action figures of the staff, all of the students would have wanted to collect his. He looked like a handsomer, younger, and darker version of Severus Snape, and his mastery of the dark arts was as cynical as it was thorough. To the students, he was the arbiter of coolness. He knew everything about cool movies and cool music, cool locations and cool history. He did things before they became cool and knew exactly when to stop. Nothing could offend his inherent mastery of everything that was great before anyone else ever caught on to it being good.

Unlike everyone else, Niles knew him well enough to see the fault lines. To the rest of the world, Geit was an icon and an iconoclast all at once, he could have formed and led a perfect cult if he hadn't claimed to hate people so thoroughly. The thing was that his misanthropy was a defensive mechanism. Geit used it to preserve himself. Everything about him that would have been perfect for a filmic anti-hero was real. It was who he was and not some sort of construct meant to win admiration or affection. If Niles had asked him before he left during that last conversation who he was trying to be, he would have only been able to answer with "my best self."

The recently retired Sven Bobsdottir had returned to the building to work as an after-school tutor for the math classes, and he was the first figure from the past to seek Niles out at school. Niles always stayed late grading, sitting in the classroom that was more home than home, and Bobsdottir had stopped by to talk to him before, to catch up and catch on, as it were, to the moods and musics of the school. This week would be no different in that regard, but only in that one way of seeking comfort in loss. Bobsdottir and Geit had always gotten on well, and even though there was little time for Math and English to bond, Geit had talked about him as if he were some kind of father figure to him, a distant but significant replacement for the man that Geit had lost himself to a heart attack the day before his own high school graduation. Bobsdottir mourned Geit as well. That week he roamed the empty halls after the tutored students went home, pausing at the goat above Geit's door, before making his way to Niles's open door to talk to him as old men do about the passing of young men before their time.

For fourteen days, that goat hung over his door before anyone had the courage to remove it, to remove him. It was as though it were a lamb's blood talisman of protection for a blind and angry god who would know no other way to spare the family inside more animal blood on the floor. Through that door was an answer that no one

423

wanted. He was gone but he would stay yet for the eyes of a few that had depended on him.

Niles would see him in places where he wasn't because Niles would still go to the places where he wasn't supposed to go. Everyone else avoided the answer that was Geit as if he were a half corpse washed up on a foreign shore, a victim of a propellor and a wind gust, like a grim "No Trespassing" sign on what was once a favorite swim spot, so that it was not just one life that had gone out like a candle suffocated, but several. On that beach where rapacious eyes could be fed and young couples could find a dune or three to cover passions running unfettered there would be no more life, none until the seasons had gone full circle once again, and winter storms and high tides had changed the landscape so that no one who had been there before would recognize it again. The only guidepost for the eyes would be the water on the horizon, and that would never change, nor would it ever be any less same than the view from any other beach that faced the sea. Those small lives were lost too, moments that would now never be, memories that would never form, and memories that would be forgotten because they invoked something altogether too painful to acknowledge.

And so it was that finally when Niles went in to work on a Monday that all vestiges of Geit were wiped clean. Very little of him remained in the first place, as Geit had been as thorough in cleaning the whiteboard and his room as he had been with everything else. He was gone and nothing would change. Niles tried to make changes happen, but the sluggish weight of apathy combined with the momentum of routine would keep things the same. As Kaseman made it clear so many times, teachers were absolutely replaceable, none better, none worse than any other. It wasn't true for the students. They may as well have been shoved abruptly face first into a canyon while

they were gazing up at the sky. Classes were rearranged to give Demarr and Linn the ones that they had been coveting and the rest were
fed to a long and almost unceasing parade of "long-term substitutes"
whose plans superseded their titles. The students suffered for it all.

They were left to drift, and Swamp was trying to cover herself. Everyone said that it made no difference even though Niles saw
that it did, but it was no good to see what he could not do when his
hands were tied and weighted down by grief. Memories of that weekend kept coming back up as Niles tried to deal with the weight of his
grief, cycling with the pulsating rhythm of a broken bone or a con-
cussion.

For weeks, that one Sunday echoed within Niles. Geit had
left them without warning. His leaving was the most painful leaving
of all.

30. The Cellar

Geit's leaving deeply wounded Trudeau. He wanted to escape as well and had been thinking about it for several months. Trudeau was seated at his workbench in his garage, laboring over his grading and fretting about getting wood shavings in everything. His phone started vibrating and nearly shook right off the edge of the desk. He grabbed it and saw Hippy's name on the caller ID. He took the news and his insides turned to a sack of sawdust. He trembled as he sat the phone down and began to hyperventilate. He was no longer a Christian, but he instinctively asked God that Niles, Hippy, and his other friends would be okay, then he berated himself repentantly because he knew it wouldn't help. If there really were a god, he wouldn't have been torturing Trudeau like he was. He thought about Geit's wife and his son, and he wondered if they too had been lost, or if they were like him, struggling with an empty space.

He then thought of his own wife and daughters. Life was cruel. His wife had reminded him so many times that there were so many other men who could prove more satisfying to her sexually. When he thought of his wife, he always thought of death; when he thought of his wife he always thought of losing her.

Sunday night ended nearly sleeplessly for Trudeau, and Monday came without remorse. On his way into the darkly familiar building, he was accosted by both Linn and Demarr. They surrounded him, two constrictors wrapping the same numbed prey. Their hands on his arms on either side, they led him to Demarr's classroom to sit on a destroyed sofa. He felt weak and ashamed. Where was Niles? Where was Hippy? They should have been with him now. He needed them.

Trudeau opened his mouth to talk, but Demarr held a finger to his lips, silencing him. Then she pressed the side of her head to his shoulder and crooned softly.

"I know you're feeling sad right now, sad and lost. But just because Geit is gone doesn't mean you're alone. It doesn't mean anything at all actually. We're still here, and we're your real friends, right? We'll stay with you, and we won't leave."

Trudeau was confused. He hadn't slept well after receiving the news and he had half rolled, half stepped into work today. He tried to reason through, to walk through his own thoughts, but they were to be buried under seventy-two inches of wet sod, gravel, and sand, and Linn and Demarr were with him right now. Linn's hand was still holding his right arm, but her body was distant as if Trudeau's weakness repelled her even as Demarr snuggled his left. Wire mother on one side and the soft mother on the other, but where were his other friends?

Trudeau was breathing shallowly, and the world seemed to shrink and contract then expand like traversing as series of tunnels in pace with his breath.

"Make yourself comfortable. Lean back and relax with us for just a few minutes. We'll make things okay." It was Demarr again. Her voice had the rhythm of a condescending lullaby, like a stepmother comforting a child that was not hers in front of her partner.

He was utterly powerless and at their whims. His sizable frame, though growing gaunt, still towered physically over both women, but he had never felt so small before.

"Now Trudeau. We're on your side, but we've got to stick together, don't we? We can't have you acting like you don't like us. We need to show everyone that we're still united and strong through this, right? If you let anyone see how much Geit's suicide bothers you, they'll think you're weak. Right now people need us to be strong, don't they? The students need you to be strong. You can't show anyone how you feel right now, no one but us, because we're your friends, and we're going to get through this together."

Trudeau shuddered as he tried to catch his breath. A tear caught in his eye.

"No, you can't do that. Don't cry. Don't let anyone see you cry. Ever. If you feel like crying, come to us. We'll make sure that no one else ever thinks you're weak. You're safe here with us." Demarr crooned in that same sick lullaby.

Trudeau's head rolled and crashed like an abandoned boat tied against a stone sea wall. He couldn't think straight.

Trudeau gathered his own strength and mustered it in combination with the two smirks on either side of him. He stood, slightly swaying, looking like nothing else so much as a grim Ahab in his darkly worn peacoat surrounded by shadows. He balled his fists as he breathed, trying to remember the meditative, calming breathing he had taught himself years ago. He gritted his teeth over the murmuring of Demarr as she continued to tell him how she and Linn would help him through whatever problem he was facing, and that he wouldn't have to worry about ending up like that silly Geit, who had never accepted their friendship or even had the polite sensibility to pretend that he liked them in front of groups of people. But he was gone now, and Trudeau was free of his bad influence to become the best of friends of Linn and Demarr. Trudeau like that idea. He'd never felt comfortable talking about his feelings with anyone except his wife, but that had become more difficult lately because she was so free and comfortable talking about all of her feelings to him, including how she freely lusted for other men who she'd told him were much more inspiring that he was, much more of what she needed, now that she had mostly used him up.

He was brought back to the present from the cold something that his wife whispered in his ear by Demarr again. "We're here for you, Trudeau. If you're feeling weak, just come to us, okay? We are here for you." She emphasized the last sentence, squeezing his arm for a punctuation mark. What time was it? Trudeau wondered. He was in a fog. Suddenly he was brought back to the hallway by the sound of a bell. Linn and Demarr slithered back into the shadows. He knew what the bell signaled and he had to get himself together. A dull roar of teen noise crashed into him like a long, low powerful storm surge. Like Pavlov's dogs, he responded to his operant conditioning and went to his classroom to meet a wave of questioning eyes that had seen rumors on social media and were looking to him for answers and meaning. It was a good thing that he had been caught be Linn and Demarr on his way in that morning, yes indeed. Where were Niles and Hippy and all the rest when he needed them?

Across the building, twenty minutes before the bell, in Trudeau's room waited Heller, Hippy, Halverson, and Niles. Heller's room had the same door key and was adjacent. Niles arrived first, then waited outside her door, unable to think about his lessons and what he'd have to say to the students when they arrived. Then Hippy came up out of the depths of the far wing of the school, looking for Niles and found him there at Heller's door first, where the two men hugged like long-lost brothers and cried with each other. Then Heller arrived, eyes dark from not finding sleep where it was supposed to be a comfort for her. The clock ticked on, closer to the time when the deluge of students would hit them. Halverson joined them and they tried to reason, to plan together how to handle the loss of someone so important, but most pressingly as the clock continued to tick to come to a consensus about how to deal with Geit's death.

Ten minutes to go until students. They waited for Trudeau. Heller went to his door, opened it, and they moved into Trudeau's room to wait for him. They needed him too, all of them needed each other for support under the unimaginable weight that had been given them the night before.

One minute left to the bell. No Trudeau.

The waiting teachers had to abandon his room, turn out his light, and return each to their own spaces to prepare the environment as much as they could for the challenge of addressing death.

Each was crumbling too, and in the environment of the school building there was no opportunity for support. Every teacher was cut off and separated until he or she too would be broken and have to be replaced.

Niles was exhausted. The funeral on a Saturday drifted further and further back into memory as the weeks of school piled on. Niles sat with Heller and Cook. Cook held his hand while Heller held his shoulders. Niles delivered a eulogy on friendship and recited "Manifesto: The Mad Farmer Liberation Front" on Geit's behalf. Trudeau skipped the funeral and avoided Niles from then on. He wasn't the only one. Niles's visible grief marked him with a red letter, and no one wanted to be tainted by being close to him.

For Niles, the loss of his closest friend combined with the evaluation process and the piles of work that continued to grow under the pressure that he felt not to let up on the students was crushing. Spring brought no comfort even though Niles could find sunlight in the evening after leaving school.

He was working late grading papers and thinking about leaving the building for the day when his phone rang. It was Woodley.

"Niles. It's time for your evaluation meeting."

Niles had forgotten about it. He went zombie-like to Woodley's office with his box of materials and "evidence."

"Sorry that this is last minute, Niles. We've all been busy. I have to have the paperwork in by the end of the week." Niles was blank. He looked at Woodley without reaction. Woodley was waiting for any kind of response to tell him how to move forward, but Niles felt nothing. It made Woodley uneasy. "Look Niles, I know you've had a rough year. It hasn't been easy for any of us. I shouldn't be telling you this, but I can't give you an effective evaluation."

Niles was too numb to feel anger. He said nothing. His face registered nothing. Woodley continued speaking as if he were frightened. "I know you're a good teacher. If I had a kid, I'd want him in your classroom, but the best I can give you is 'minimally effective.' Only two people in the building are getting "highly effective. You know who they are." Niles was impassive. He looked through Woodley instead of at him. Woodley continued rambling on. "It's out of my control. I don't need to look at any of this stuff you brought to know how good you --"

"It's fine, Woodley. I don't care. I just don't care." Niles's gaze drifted to the floor.

Woodley had sympathy for Niles. "You know what? I'll talk to Swamp and see if we can do something."

"I appreciate the sentiment, but I don't need anything really except to get this stuff over with and filed away. We need to get our paperwork in. Let's just do that. Okay?"

"Sure. No problem," Woodley stammered.

Niles left his box of evidence on the desk and walked out.

31. Graduation

A comment that "I wish I could graduate with you" to one of his seniors was the tiny speck of dust that had caught ice on a wind current as it drifted from a cloud earthward. It picked up more and more ice as it fell, still light on the wind, but no longer able to drift with the clouds, instead gathering weight and momentum as it drifted downward, losing its lazy pace and gaining mass. She told another senior, who told a class of mixed juniors and seniors, who told a teacher, and before Niles could hack off this leg and twist a tourniquet on the bleeding stump a rumor was off and running.

Niles was walking back from the restroom hurriedly when George, an art teacher with an eye for the abstract, caught him by the sleeve.

"I heard you're getting out..?" The question hung in the air for a bit. Niles was nonplussed. He wanted out, but without Geit to talk to about it, no one could have known - especially not a casual acquaintance in the hallway.

"I just got in, why would I get out?" blurted Niles, and he hurried along on his way, ducking slightly and moving to blend into the swarming mass of sweaty teens. It wasn't time to confront any aspect of leaving. He had students to attend to. Everyone else did as well. George disappeared forever into the swirling mass.

Niles stayed in his classroom the rest of the day. Students didn't ask if they had heard the rumor. For most of them, a teacher was a teacher. Some were cruel, some were not, but they were only a small part of a daily set of rituals. One face meant as little as any other.

It was at the end of the day, after even most of the straggling students had trickled out. Bradley had poked his head in and said "See you tomorrow!" Niles sat behind his desk, feet up again, grading more papers. The hallway was silent after the door at the end of the hallway had closed behind Bradley on his way out. Fifteen quiet minutes passed. The hallway motion sensor flipped the lights off. Suddenly, in the darkness, there was movement outside the door. Through the forest of chair legs on desks, Niles could make out a ghostly face. The face made eye contact with Niles and crept closer, glided from the far side of the hallway to the near, and then into his doorway, then to a table, using the chairs and table as a barrier. It was O'Connell, a first year math teacher from the third floor. Niles didn't know her, but he knew of her. The building was structured to keep people from becoming friends.

She took a deep breath. The motion light in the hallway outside flipped on.

"Mr. Niles, I'm sorry to bother you, but I heard a rumor about you. Is it true?"

"Depends on the nature of the rumor."

"Some of the students were saying that you're leaving at the end of the year."

"I didn't know we had any of the same kids."

"I don't think we do. Most of mine are freshmen, but you know, kids talk."

"It's true. That they talk, I mean," Niles deflected. "A lot of us look every year. I think any teacher has to keep looking for opportunities to grow. If you don't feel like you're in a healthy place, then you owe it to yourself to keep looking."

She was timid. Still hiding behind the chair. The hallway light flicked off again, leaving her in shadow. She looked down at her shoes.

"Yeah, it's not healthy, is it?"

"It's rough here. There's not much support. If teachers are going to be good, they have to support each other. For whatever reason, nobody cares about anyone else here."

She stuck her left hand in her pocket, and clutched a pile of fresh copies tighter to her chest like a breastplate that was a size too big.

"I just bought a car. This is the best paying job I've ever had. There's not a lot out there for teachers."

"No, there isn't." Niles was apologetic.

"I can't quit. I just had my hours cut at my other job. I need this." She spoke timidly.

"Then don't quit this job. Keep trying to find ways to make it better. Carve out some safe space for yourself. Make sure that you have a good support structure behind you. There's nothing here." Niles wanted to say more. He wanted to reassure her, to help her feel safe and supported, but he couldn't. He was one person standing against an entire culture.

"I know." She moved backwards toward the door, still facing him.

"Good luck."

She drifted backward, like smoke on a zephyr, never breaking eye contact, until her pale face was lost in the gloom of the empty hallway. Niles listened, but there were no footfalls in the hallway. The light didn't come back on. She was like a ghost already, even more so than she had been when their paths had never crossed. Niles went back to grading. The dusty hum of the overhead fluorescents remained unbroken.

Niles felt hollowed out. The school year was the toughest yet, even before Geit left. He was more isolated than ever. He wanted the teachers he worked with to act like a caring, professional community.

No one in the building had any investment in each other. Geit left, but nothing else changed.

Some teachers stayed for the students like he did every year, but some of them stayed for other more selfish reasons. He needed support. Geit had been broken by a lack of support on all fronts and Niles was breaking too. How could anyone support anyone else if everyone was breaking down?

Niles looked down at the papers still crowding his desk. He had a lot of work to do before leaving for the summer. The students had made progress in their writing over the year. The time needed to grade each AP response paper had dropped from an average of fifteen minutes each to only six for the full five pages. The Creative Writing class, in the span of less than a trimester had gone from giving less than the very smallest damn to trying their best to impress each other. They wanted the constructive feedback in the workshop. It was a taste of something new and unexpected for them, but it was addictive. Even the English 11 students had shown marked improvement from the start. That class lacked the doers of the AP group and the dreamers of the Creative Writing group, but many of them had grown to begrudgingly respect Niles and wanted to impress him. He didn't condescend or belittle. He treated them like the adults that they thought they were.

Niles went back to grading. Minutes clicked by on the wall clock. The light in the hallway flickered to back to life, resurrected by dragging footsteps in the hallway approaching the light from his desk lamp that sprouted jaggedly into the hallway through the door frame.

The tired shuffle lit by his door and a face peered in. It was McCall, another freshman teacher from the third floor. His face was haggard and pale, masked by his week worth of heavy, thick stubble that Niles couldn't match in a month. He looked sick.

"Hey man. Is it true?" The words felt sharp, but their points were not at Niles. McCall crept closer, weaving through the jungle of tables and chairs toward the point of light in the darkness. He looked so weary and spent, holding his sheaves of classroom copies, that Niles couldn't bear to disseminate.

"It's true that we should all look every year when we've found ourselves in a bad predicament. No one should feel trapped. Nobody else should have to leave like Geit."

McCall sighed heavily and shuffled heavily backward. The mention of Geit caught him off guard, as if he had forgotten an important message. McCall's mouth opened in a slight gasp, but he caught himself. His gaze became more intense.

"I didn't know him. I'm sorry."

"I don't know if anyone did. Thank you though." Niles turned back to his task at hand with wet eyes.

McCall went on, as if to assure himself that everything was fine. "My wife's job is here in town. We have a house here. We just had our son. No one else within thirty miles will pay anything near what this district pays."

Niles didn't look back up. "You have to do what's right for you. This place is a lot to take. There is a lot of negativity."

McCall, unable to speak further in the gloom, left and continued his wounded walk down the hallway.

The building was emptying out of teachers as well. Hearing silence in the halls, Niles walked to Heller's room to see if she had left for the day. As he neared her door, he heard laughter, so he checked his speed. Heller had gotten close with Demarr and Linn since Geit left, and while he didn't speak to her as much as he had when she started, he still felt like she was a little sister to him. He neared the door lightly, not wanting to interrupt anything when he heard Heller's voice ring out clearly: "Well, I for one won't miss him if he's gone. He's an inconvenient person to be friends with. Too much work involved for me."

What came next in the conversation he'd almost interrupted didn't matter. That was the only thing he heard. Niles didn't know who they were talking about, but he didn't want to. He stopped and turned around, hastening on quiet soles back to his own room lest he be accused of spying. Not many people would be sad to see another meaningless new face in an ongoing cascade in the teacher directory next year.

That night was graduation. It felt like an end. Trudeau was MIA. Hippy, Halverson, Tibbs, and Heller were all too busy to go. Geit was gone. All of the wise, old teachers with the most experience who had shown the way forward were gone as well. Niles wondered: if he stayed, would he be irreparably broken too? It was what the system needed, but not what Niles could bear. Despite his sadness, he knew what he was doing. He was staying, and he wished that the rumor would crawl back into whatever hole it slipped out of.

He stepped lightly in with the other teachers in their procession, his shoulders back and his head up, proud to be included in the backdrop of what was the class's achievement. All the teachers looked like mourners in shiny robes - save their smiles. They were cowled in the colors of their Master's degree programs. Only Niles cut the scene with a mournful aspect. The students were jubilant. Their high school purgatory had come to an end, the sins of their fathers were no longer to be visited upon them without the mercy of choice. They were moving on. Niles lacked their joy, their sense of accomplishment. He lacked anyone to share it with.

It was the third of Niles's graduation ceremonies that year. The first two were family; nephews who were walking the stage of the own high school auditoriums to applause and high fives. Each of those first two ceremonies were mostly the same. They were short, an hour or so and focused on the students. In each of them the staff and students entered to music. There was a short speech from the super-intendent, less than four minutes. Then the guest speaker - in each case a former student made good - who spoke for less than seven minutes. Next, the principal introduced herself only to bring the students forward and passed out diplomas as each student came to the stage. The photographer was set up to the side, focused on a mark on the floor below the steps where each student could pose holding their diploma for the camera. They went quickly and smoothly. Students were allowed to be excited.

The Pianosa Springs Public Schools High School graduation was as different as could be. The students walked in to music, but the parallels drifted far off course from there. The ceremony was opened by a fifteen-minute speech from Kaseman in which he spoke at length about his initiatives for school improvement, including some of the ongoing initiatives that started well before he came in that he claimed as his own. He talked about himself and all of his "hard work" at length, before turning the microphone over to Swamp. The students were already shifting uncomfortably in their seats. Families in the audience also moved from side to side and frequently shushed small children, in some cases taking them to exit the auditorium. Swamp began by speaking about herself at length, how she'd perse-vered as the child of one of the wealthier immigrant families in town, playing sports and leading the cheer team, making homecoming queen, but being kept from prom queen by teacher politics. Faces in the auditorium looked confused. She went on for twenty-five min-utes, illuminating the audience about how the success of the students was due to her and her efforts, how she, through her belief in God and the community had lifted graduation rates. How she strong-armed reluctant and lazy teachers into doing the right things for "her kids" and how much she did for the community at her church and "her" school. She talked about the cost to her, how her dedication was causing her to gain weight, how her family was making the sacrifice of eating out daily, supporting the local businesses, but how everything was progressing according to God's plan and she would be the last person to ever question that.

Students were adrift in their seats and the winds had bled from their sails. Grandparents were nodding off or escaping to stretch their legs. Swamp went on and on in her personal liturgy. Finally she finished and brought out a special treat. The school cheer teams filed out of the back and posted themselves in front of the stage. The music rose, a throwback Paula Abdul number from Swamp's youth that she had overseen the choreography for herself. She beamed behind the podium, shaking her hips to the music. Kaseman looked proudly on beside her. The music pumped until finally the jumping and gyrating came to a close but the cheerleaders remained in front of the platform.

The orchestra music rose, and graduating students on their cues began to rise and walk toward the front. They lined up expectantly on the right side of the elevated dais. The cheerleaders posed in the front, the photographer just left of center and aiming where Swamp and Kaseman were waiting with the diploma placeholders. At Swamp's signal, the first graduate advanced and his name was called. The cheerleaders applauded, did jump kicks and leg scissors as the boy walked toward Swamp. When he reached her, she grabbed him and faced him toward the camera, her arm around him as if she'd met him before or at least knew his name (she didn't) and the photo was taken. It was the only photo that was part of the official program, and the one that each family would have the privilege to receive to commemorate the event.

That routine repeated another 320 times, like copies ejected from a machine. The tired student did her or his best to smile. The glad-handing Swamp grabbed them for their official graduation photo and an arena full of staff and family members applauded and howled. Everyone performed on cue as though Swamp's self-centered theatrics were normal for a well-trod course of events. Niles felt like this graduation ceremony should have been quick and painless, focused on the students - just like the others he had been to that year. He felt alone again there in his seat, surrounded by hundreds of people.

Finally, the end came. The students filed out, back past the smattering of teachers on the side. The music dropped. The ceremony was over. Niles rose and applauded as the graduates were released, but then sank back down into his seat, defeated, as the lights came up and parents flooded the floor to collect their offspring from this most recent rite of passage. There was a flurry of energy as half the cheer team skipped past him. He felt crazy, as if the world was inverted.

Niles was standing alone when there was a tap on his shoulder from behind.

"Mr. Niles."

It was a tall dark young man still clad in his gown who had come back on to the floor as people milled toward the exits. Niles had him in class for two semesters that year. He was holding his hand out to Niles to shake.

"Mr. Niles. Thank you. Thank you for not being a jerk."

Niles laughed softly. "You're welcome. I tried."

"You know, when I first saw you in the hallways, I figured you were a real asshole. You always just stood there, saying "hi" and nodding at people, but you had your arms crossed and you looked so serious and mean. I was afraid to take your class. I was afraid you would be like the rest of them. But you weren't. So thank you."

Niles felt hot and wanted to escape into the cool night air, but he smiled for the young man. "Thank you for giving me a chance."

"What did you think of me when you first met me, Mr. Niles? Did I give you a first impression that was wrong?"

"You know, you did. I saw you, and I thought you looked angry. You always looked angry. After I got to know you, I figured out that you weren't mad at me personally, you were simply mad at all the people that I looked like. All the people who looked like me who'd ever judged you, everyone who ever said terrible things to you because of the color of your skin, all of the teachers who'd ever discounted you. That made sense to me. I would have been angry too. Once I realized that, I knew I had to work to gain your trust. I had to earn it because people who look like me tend to be pretty awful to people who look like you. People sometimes have children because it gives them an opportunity to be better people than they were. You are my children. You made me want to be better."

The young man's mother called out to him. He melted into the flowing crowd. Workers were already dismantling the stage and taking chairs away as building security ushered people toward the doors.

Niles was left staring into an empty part of the arena, thinking of Geit, thinking of the faces who were leaving. He heard his name. Someone was calling it from behind him, but he knew who it was so he didn't turn.

She kept repeating it, saying it louder and louder each time in turn, but Niles pretended to be still lost in thought, ignoring her shrill repetition of his syllables. That hateful voice carried with it a tone of condescension as it cut through the joyful murmurs that still reverberated from exiting crowd.

"Mr. Niles, Mr. Niles! Yoo hoo! Mr. Niles." The last repetition of his name was spit from her mouth with an ugly sing-song rhythm, directed at him the way a nun might mock a daydreaming child in Sunday school. He turned to face Swamp again. She waddled toward him in her off-red blazer that was still the size she was last year even though she had expanded noticeably. "Mr. Niles, make sure that you stop by my office tomorrow. Mr. Woodley talked to me. I have something for you before you go for the summer." They made eye contact only for a moment before her attention was swept away again.

Niles didn't say a word. He felt sorry for Swamp. No one would ever appreciate her, even though she wanted that more than anything. She was never real. The only thing appreciable about her was how good she was at being inauthentic. Niles didn't know if there was anything genuine in her at all.

He looked around again. Most of the teachers had melted away, but Trudeau was hovering near an exit talking with Linn and Demarr.

Niles walked alone in the opposite direction.

32. Literary Devices

"Mr. Niles, please come to the principal's office. Mr. Niles to the principal's office please."

Niles sighed heavily.

The secretary greeted him and ushered him into the cramped, overflowing conference room where there were a handful of seats around the table, surrounded on all sides by messily stacked banker's boxes filled with Swamp's detritus.

He stood on one side of the table; on the opposite side were Kaseman, Swamp, and two extra chairs. There was no chair for Niles. He waited, arms at his sides.

"Who is this man?" asked Kaseman. Even though Kaseman's daughter had him as her junior English instructor and he'd spoken with Niles at conferences, he could not remember who he was.

"He thinks he's someone who's actually important, sir," answered the school psychologist, Dr. Conway, who had stuck his head in from the door that had been closed to the hallway on Niles's left. He disappeared again and the door clicked shut.

Halverson appeared in the doorway that Niles had come in through, grabbing a bag of Swamp's expired candy to pass out to students. "Whoops! Sorry."

Niles turned around to see Halverson, but all he caught was his heels as he turned the corner. As Halverson disappeared through the door on the left, Demarr and Linn entered the conference room from the right, wearing ugly Cheshire grins as they advanced to the empty chairs opposite Niles.

They sat heavily and Demarr gestured at Niles while talking to Kaseman. "He thinks he's old 'Broom' Bromden, escaped through the window and roaming Canada bringing the Gospel of Randal to the fragile, underprivileged masses." Niles could smell the cigarettes on her breath from across the room.

"I'm Mr. Niles." Niles replied.

"He's nothing," said Linn to Kaseman, shaking her head.

Niles laughed. He had nothing to lose.

"I'm the apostle Thomas Didymus," said Niles, dripping with doubt.

Kaseman looked confused. "I thought you said there were two of them?"

"See, I told you, he thinks he's an Indian!" said Demarr.

"Geit was my brother," said Niles.

"What?" Kaseman was still confused.

Niles repeated himself. "Geit was my brother."

"The other one took his own life." Swamp looked at him with distaste.

Niles's head was throbbing. He was angry. "Why am I here? None of this makes any sense." Niles moaned audibly and rubbed his bald pate.

"You're not effective, Mr. Niles. We're having a meeting to address that. Your effectiveness has gone downhill since Mr. Geit left us."

"He was my friend. Grief has a way of breaking things."

"He's gone. Get over it." Linn hissed from her chair. Kaseman looked confused. Geit was below his notice. Just like Niles. Most of the time.

"I'm not going to demean his memory by acting like he didn't matter. Eric was a better teacher than anyone else in this room. I won't betray him or the things that mattered to him."

"Who is this Eric? Why are we talking about him?" Asked Kaseman.

"He was Geit. He was beaten down and lost things little by little." Niles was mournful with remembrance. His anger was fading quickly. His voice became soft. "You didn't know him. You didn't know anything about him." He looked around as if searching. "He lost everything, and then we lost him."

Demarr mocked him. "Are you sad? Are you going to cry because he's dead, or because you're upset that no one else is upset?"

Kaseman was apathetic. "Everyone is replaceable. Shortly, he'll be forgotten about. They're always forgotten about." He turned to Niles, "You're nobody. You don't matter. When you go, you'll be forgotten too. Is that why you're upset?"

""He was my friend."

"You'll meet others." Demarr drew the last consonant out painfully.

"That's not true. I never have. I never did. He was my friend."

"That doesn't matter. No one cares. No one will remember." Linn was cold and hard.

"Stop making such a fuss. You're making us look bad. Stop acting like that." Demarr took the condescending tone of a parent talking to a child over a dollar store toy.

Niles furrowed his brow, but he couldn't look at them.

Demarr went on, looking down her nose at Niles. "Be friends with us. Forget about him. We'll be your friends. You don't need anyone else but us. Just tell everyone the truth about us. Tell them all how much you look up to us and respect us."

"Tell them you want to be like us," hissed Linn.

"Send us your lesson plans. Do what we do. Be like us," said Demarr.

"Join us." Linn drew her sibilant "S" at Niles.

Niles looked up at the smirking witches.

"No."

Kaseman interrupted the exchange between the English teachers. "Mrs. Swamp, is it common practice for your teachers to run their lesson plans through their department heads?"

"No, not yet. I think it will be."

"Yes. Make that happen. Particularly if the department head is 'highly effective' like Ms. Linn. I think that's a new 'best practice.'" Then he turned to the grinning women on his other side. "Is this the troublemaker? The one who doesn't get along with the rest of his department and is always stirring the students up to trouble? The one who tries to undermine you?"

Linn nodded.

Swamp assented. "That's him, Dr. Kaseman. Can I fire him?"

"Yes, I think so. But not yet. We have to make sure that he gives us no other choice. You don't want to make us look bad, do you?" They both turned to look at Linn and Demarr.

Linn stood up first. "Thank you, Dr. Kaseman, thank you, Mrs. Swamp. I know that you'll do what's best for the students. Demarr stood up and both stalked out of the room. Demarr sneered at Niles as she closed the door behind her. The smell of smoke and sickness lingered.

"You're all mad," said Niles, "Mad as hatters. I've had enough."

Swamp was taken aback. "Dr. Kaseman, he's not even a Christian. In fact, I heard that he was an atheist! Those people should not be allowed to work with children in the first place!"

Kaseman turned back to Niles. "Is that true, Mr. Niles, that you're working here with children in a public school and you're not even a Christian?"

"Well sir, I am an ordained minister."

Swamp's jaw dropped. "Oh my Lord, so am I!"

Kaseman was grim-faced now. He'd caught Niles in a lie and he was going to crucify him for it. "That cannot be true. I heard from a young Christian math teacher who was a part of your small learning community that you refused to join her prayer circle after several high school students were gunned down by a boy who wasn't receiving the treatment that he was entitled to."

"I am ordained. It cost me eight dollars on the internet. Now, which school shooting was that? I don't remember. There have been so many."

"Are you implying that thoughts and prayers don't make a difference? How dare you try to say something so terrible!" Swamp was nearly apoplectic. "I pray for my teachers everyday, Doctor Kaseman. Even ones like Niles." Swamp pouted. "Can I fire him now? He's not a Christian. He won't pray for the victims of school shootings. Clearly, he's not against shooting up a high school. What if he comes here and tries to shoot me?"

"Is that true Mr. Niles? Are you planning to bring a gun to school and shoot as many people as you can?" Kaseman pulled out his cell phone.

"Not believing in your version of God doesn't mean that I'm going to shoot anyone."

"Well, you've already admitted that you're not a Christian, what else are you lying about? Are you even who you claim to be? Are you even Joseph Niles? A man who would lie about being a Christian would lie about anything, wouldn't he, Mrs. Swamp?"

"People who aren't Christians are a danger to us all!" She was clearly alarmed. Kaseman, a practicing Jew, looked sideways at her.

Niles was adamant. "I haven't done anything wrong."

Swamp countered: "I have your evaluation. It has a list of things you've done wrong. You didn't even differentiate your instruction."

Before Niles could answer, Kaseman broke in. "If you haven't done anything wrong, why are you guilty?"

"Who said I'm guilty of anything?"

"If you weren't guilty of something, you wouldn't be here, now would you?"

"I didn't realize that this was how it worked."

"You better believe that this is how it works. We're going to get rid of you, Mr. Niles. You're a troublemaker. You refuse to cooperate. You're destroying the community here. You won't even agree that Linn and Demarr are the best teachers in the building."

"They're not. Your evaluation system is capricious and arbitrary and you made it up."

Kaseman became stern. "Exactly, and that's why we're going to force you out, Niles. If you don't do as I say, we're going to make your job very unpleasant."

Niles sighed and rubbed his shorn head.

Kaseman did not wait for Niles to respond. "Do you think we have time to waste on you? Do you think our time is worthless? We're going to get you. I have a signed statement right here from your principal that you said you were thinking of shooting up the school."

He held out his hand toward Swamp while staring up at Niles and his drooping shoulders. Swamp was confused for a moment, then hastily scribbled something on a piece of paper and jammed it into his hand. Kaseman folded it securely in half so the writing was hidden and showed it to Niles.

"Mr. Niles, do you even know why we called you to this meeting?

"To make me feel smart?"

"No! To show you how foolish you really are. Tell him, Mrs. Swamp."

"Mr. Niles, I have witnesses who say that you haven't been giving your juniors the mandatory summative assessment that Linn and Demarr designed."

"That's all? That's what this is about?" Niles felt relieved that he hadn't actually made a mistake. "That's true. That 'test' is garbage and any second grader who paid attention in school could get a B minus on it."

"Aha! So you admit it! So the scores that you've been entering in the grade book for your assessments are false, even though those scores are a part of your professional evaluation!"

"No, the scores are real. I made my own test."

"We've got you now, Niles! Mrs. Swamp, put this on record that Mr. Niles admits to: number one, not giving the mandated test; and number two, using falsified information to attempt to get a better evaluation in the arbitrary and capricious system for evaluating teachers that we made up!'

"The scores are real."

"You're using the wrong test."

"No, the district is using the wrong test-- that's why it's terrible and doesn't measure anything at all."

"Write this all down, Mrs. Swamp. This is going in the letter in your personal file, Mr. Niles. You won't be able to escape this! We've got you on record admitting everything."

"I don't have to put up with this kind of treatment."

"Oh yes, you do. If you walk out of here, we'll tell everyone that you don't like us because you're a racist. I can tell just by the way you look at me that you hate Jews. Anti-semitism! And you hate black people too, don't you? I know that's the real reason that you won't admit that Ms. Linn is the best English teacher this district ever had and you probably hate Swamp for the same reason."

"That's not true. Linn is an egomaniacal bitch who bullies her students. I'd hate her if she were the whitest woman that ever lived. And Swamp? She's just miserably myopic and incompetent. Those aren't qualities that I associate with skin color. In fact I can think of a short, white man who embodies those things."

"You're a liar, Mr. Niles, and I can see right through you. If you walk out of here before I say you can, or if you leave this district we'll make sure that everyone knows it's because you're a racist. We say that about every white teacher who leaves this district because they're all the same. Teachers are interchangeable." Kaseman was insistent.

"That's not true. I love my students. They know that. A good teacher is not a replaceable cog in some kind of machine."

"They'll know whatever we tell them after we fire you for insubordination and falsifying documents in your evaluation and replace you with anyone else. That's what we'll do if you don't start to toe the line."

Kaseman stood up from his chair and stepped toward him. He tilted his head back so he could look down his nose at Niles.

"Mrs. Swamp. Take care of Mr. Niles. I have an important meeting with the Baptist Church Association about getting more ministers into the district as security guards. He abruptly turned and strode from the room.

With Kaseman's exit, Swamp's tone softened. She became a one woman good cop/bad cop. Her condescending smile intensified.

"Mr. Niles, have you ever considered becoming a principal, or an assistant principal? Or even just having the power of an assistant principal in this building? You could stay a teacher, but if you make a deal with me, I'll make your job so much easier. I'll back you up, and you can boss and tell teachers what to do. You can be like Linn."

His right eyebrow shot up.

She went on. "Be on the side of right, Niles. Be on my side. With your help, I can really whip this building in shape, but I can't have you going around being disloyal to me. You want to change our English curriculum, don't you? To make it more difficult? I could help you facilitate that. But I can't have you talking to the kids, telling them that I'm not the best principal this building ever had."

"I don't volunteer my opinion to them. They ask. I don't claim to know what the best is, but you're not it."

She ignored his response and went on. "You're just hurt and angry. I know you are. That's why you've been saying bad things about me to the other teachers. Have you tried praying to Jesus Christ our Lord and Savior for relief from your pain? Perhaps if you started coming to my church weekly or joined in my daily prayer meetings here in my conference room when I get here between 8 and 11 AM."

"I won't. I can't lie to the students. I can't lie to my co-workers. All I've done is acknowledged the terrible things around here that everyone already sees."

"Why not? They lie to you. I won't lie to you. I haven't done any bad things."

"You lie all the time. You just don't believe it because in your mind every lie you tell is justified. You believe your God gives you license to do whatever you want as long as you can find some line out of context in your version of the Bible to justify it."

"You're taking things out of context. You're judging me. You don't like me because I'm black, a child of immigrant parents, gypsies who fled the Stalinist purges in the Soviet Union."

"No, I don't like you because you're selfish and cruel, and you think 'making a deal with the devil' is justified because you share similar goals. You should ask why your goals coincide with the devil's before you pursue them." Niles was getting angry again, his rage rising through the fatigue, biting his tongue after each statement.

"Niles, why don't you have faith? Everyone else has faith in me. Ms. Linn has faith in me. Everyone on staff has faith in me except you."

"Everyone pretends because they're afraid to cross you. They know that Kaseman needs you, and they know that he'll let you get away with anything in this building."

"That's not true, Niles. I can't believe you'd think something like that. It's no wonder you tell lies about me." Swamp put her hands on her ample hips and stood over him. "Mr. Niles, I think you should ask me for forgiveness."

Niles smiled down at her. "You know what I think? I think you'd get farther in life if you treated people the way you expect to be treated by them."

This comment confused Swamp. She was already a high school principal and a head pastor at her church. She was a direct line to God for dozens of people and there was nothing that she wanted for that wasn't already hers for the taking.

"I pray for you. I can hardly imagine what it must be like to have so much hatred in your heart."

Niles sighed. "Here's what I've learned while working here: It doesn't matter how much good you try to do, or even how much good you actually do. Unless you're the one in power writing the story, you won't be remembered as a good person, if you're even remembered at all because there is always someone else who will benefit by making you look worse than you actually are."

"Mr. Niles, I think I'm done with you. You can leave now. A fool has no interest in understanding and only wants to air his own opinions."

Niles turned toward the door, still looking at Swamp. "Are you speaking of you or me?"

Niles stormed from the office, shoving the door to the hallway out of his way forcefully. He almost ran face-first into Geit.

Niles snapped back in breathless shock.

"There are a lot of ways to commit suicide, Niles. Some are quicker than others..."

Niles sat up sharply in bed, his heart racing. He clutched at his chest, gasping for air in the dark. The alarm clock read 3AM. He scanned the dark room and struggled to regain his breath. His eyes burned and his nose stung. His wife snored quietly, unbothered, on the opposite side of the bed. Tears rolled down his cheeks.

There was no return to sleep for Niles.

33. Niles

The last day at school dawned like many others. Students had a half day of exams and teachers had a full day of grading and closing up their classrooms. The underclassmen were all gone just a week after the seniors, and Niles had closed his door for lunch when McCall came knocking.

"Demarr says that you made a deal with Swamp."

"I don't know what you're talking about. I didn't make a deal with anyone."

McCall was confused. "But Demarr says that you're good with her and Linn now, that you finally admitted that you were wrong about them, that there was nothing wrong with the junior curriculum and they really are the best teachers in the building."

"I wouldn't lie like that."

"But I just talked to both of them. Trudeau was there too. He said he was glad that you'd finally come around."

Niles felt sad that Trudeau was lost now too, in a different way than Geit. "He is mistaken as well."

"But why not? It's a good deal, isn't it? You get to stay here, you get good evaluations from the administrator, and all you have to do is tell everyone that Swamp is the best principal that we've ever had, and that Linn and Demarr are the best teachers in the building?"

"No offense, McCall, but there was no deal. I haven't talked to any of them. I would never say those things. That would be me saying that the way they are is okay - that it's acceptable to lie and bully. I can't do that. I'm supposed to be a role model for teenagers. I'm supposed to show them how adults should be."

"Niles, these kids need you."

"I know that they do, but if I stayed under those conditions, I wouldn't be any good. That compromise requires me to become someone who doesn't deserve to have people look up to him."

The air conditioning was never turned on during the last week of school. The district was dedicated to saving the money that they might spend to keep buildings cool and comfortable so they could pay it to Kaseman in his annual salary. Both men were sweating. McCall ran his fingers through his greasy hair.

"Why would they tell me those things if they were not true?"

"Linn and Demarr only tell the truth when it benefits them. The rest of the time, they lie. I don't know what's going on with Trudeau."

"Niles, you can't quit."

"Who said I was going to quit?"

"They're saying a lot of bad things about you. They say you falsified your test scores to get a better evaluation. They say you've been doing it for years. They say that you weren't even giving the right test. If you try to quit, they'll fire you."

"McCall, that's a lie. They'll lie and try to use fear to manipulate anything and anyone.

"That's not the only thing I've been hearing about you, Niles.

"What do you mean, that's not the only thing?"

"At our last department meeting, people talked about you because you weren't there."

"I'm not surprised. So what?"

"Wein was saying that she's heard a lot of students complaining that you were saying racist things, and teaching racist books. That you believe that black people are inferior savages..." McCall trailed off.

Niles thought for a moment that he might actually be guilty as old habits kicked in, but then swiftly regained his sense as McCall started up again.

"And Kringe said that she heard that you were coming on to the girls, trying to coerce some of them to stay alone with you in your classroom after school."

"McCall, you know that's not true. You know me well enough to know that any student who stays after school is coming to me for help of their own volition."

McCall's face was frozen, uncommunicative. "Niles, Kringe says that you've tried to come on to her. That she's not comfortable being around you. Linn and Demarr were telling her to report you to Human Resources."

"I can't stand her. I don't even want to be around her, let alone touch her! Niles was shocked, but not as shocked as he should have been.

"If she does, it's her word against yours, Niles." Niles looked at him quizzically for some sort of support. McCall's face was blank. "She said Geit harassed her too, before he passed away."

Niles shot back immediately, "That's a lie. Geit would never have done that to anyone!"

"Maybe you should quit, Niles." McCall was still deadpan, saying things that should have put emotion on his face. He looked like he was in a trance. "They say that only guilty people leave."

"So what should I do? What would you do, McCall? If I leave, they'll poison the well, if I stay, they'll poison the well. I'm damned if I do, and damned if I don't." As Niles spoke, sounds of hard heels slapping the floor in the hallway approached. McCall looked at the open door to the hall and turned back to Niles nervously.

"I have to go. I don't want them to know that I was talking to you." He slipped past Niles trailing sweat as he left through the library by the back door of the classroom.

Niles looked through the door to the hall as the sound of heels approached. He expected Swamp, instead he saw Dallas Austin, peeking nosily through the door from the far side of the hall. Austin saw Niles looking at him, then nervously sped up down the hall, his cowboy boots clicking on the floor as he went around the corner and trailed off.

Niles sank back into his chair, defeated. His heart sank. He didn't hear Halverson come in through the door that McCall had fled through.

"Niles, did you hear that Tibbs quit this morning? He's already gone. Packed up a few things from his classroom, put his grades in and left."

"No kidding? To do what?"

"He got a job with a tech firm in California. He's done teaching."

"I thought teaching degrees were useless outside of education?"

"No, just yours. He's going to be fine." Halverson paused for dramatic effect. "He's not the only one who's leaving. Dr. Conway's going to work for a consulting firm in the state capital lobbying for education. Bradley's quitting to become a principal over in Hastings."

"Is anyone staying?"

"Everyone else that I know of. Roberts and Freyburger have less than ten years to go to retirement. Why would anyone in that position leave? Speaking of leaving, you're not thinking about it, are you?" He cocked his eyebrow at Niles.

"Should I not be?"

"You should talk to Swamp." Halverson leaned in conspiratorially. "You know, if you do things for her, she'll make it easier for you. If you do enough, you might even get a 'highly effective' evaluation." He winked at Niles.

"How do you know?"

"I just volunteered to become the leader of the 'Chain Gang' next year. Things are going to get a lot better for me!"

"What the hell is the 'Chain Gang' and why would you volunteer for anything extra duty around here? You realize it's more work for less pay, don't you?"

"'Chain Gang' is a new program for our young black males, to mentor them. Swamp said they were going to be like the Israelites, freed from bondage in Egypt and led back to the holy land!" Halverson was in a pleasant daze, dreaming about all the good that the program was going to do.

"Are you serious? She wants to take all of our black boys when they come into the school and put them in the 'chain gang'? And you don't see anything ridiculous about that? Are we now a Louisiana prison? That's ridiculous." Niles was red-faced with anger. "Where are the people who should veto this garbage?"

"Niles, calm down. It will work out. You should join me. I can tell Swamp that I need you to help me run the program."

"Halverson. I like you. You're a good teacher, and more than that, you're a good person. You need to get out of here before this place ruins you."

"You're right, I am a good teacher. These kids need good teachers. I'm staying here to work with them."

"We're all here for the kids. Nobody does this job for the money. You have to know your limits though. This job can ruin you. You can't do it until it ruins you."

"Geit left, and he did it in the worst way possible. Geit was sick. And he wasn't a good teacher. Swamp told me how he'd gotten an 'ineffective' evaluation. He was going to be fired. She was going to make sure of it."

"Halverson, we're all ineffective no matter what! Geit was sick, but that was just another boulder on the camel's back. And you know damn well that he was a good teacher. He wasn't well, and he was dealing with problems at home, but he still came in here and did everything he could for them."

"He should have been better--"

"Goddamnit, Halverson, you try being teacher of the year when your life is falling apart at the seams!"

Halverson stepped back. "Calm down, Niles. All I'm saying is he could have tried harder. He could have done more. Like I do." Halverson seemed to be gloating.

"You're not going to stand here and say bad things about Geit. He was a friend to you, and he deserves better than that."

"Whatever, Niles. You know what? Maybe you should quit. I'm starting to see that your attitude isn't right for this. Swamp needs people who are willing to work together, people who are willing to make sacrifices. You're only out for yourself."

"I've been here for the kids, but I know now that if I stay here, then I'm going to have to be someone different, someone willing to sign young black men up for a "chain gang"-- and if I stay here now, then I'm teaching my students to sacrifice themselves to elevate people who do not give a damn about them. If you think that Swamp, or Kaseman, or anyone else with any power in this district cares about you and what you do, you're fooling no one but yourself."

Halverson glowered at Niles disdainfully. "Swamp was right about you. The worst thing about you is that you actually think you matter. You don't matter. Some people do, but you're not one of them. You're a nobody." He stalked out of the room.

Niles sat at his desk, stunned. If Halverson was right, then it didn't matter if he quit or not.

After Halverson walked out angrily, the halls were silent. Grim-faced, Niles finished grading and double-checked the last of his grades on the computer. He turned it off and covered it. He looked around the room. He'd taken his students' senior photos off the wall and packed them in a box to take with him. Only those and few of his own copies of annotated texts went with him each year. He glanced down at the teachers last day check-out sheet, the final thing remaining on his desk.

He looked around his classroom. There were the bulletin boards he'd made, the "word wall" of important literary and grammar terminology he'd created one year when administration had told them all that "word walls" were going to make a dramatic increase in student engagement, and all of the Classics Illustrated comic book covers he'd copied and printed to hang on the walls. Niles locked it all into his memory. He shut down the computer and was preparing to turn out the lights when the clicking of high heeled shoes came from the hallway. It came from two distinctly different directions and with two distinctly different paces. Each was too fast to be Dallas Austin again. Niles went back to his desk, dropped his building keys on the unfilled check-out sheet and waited. Through the doorway, Niles could see as Linn walked by from the left, heels still clicking a metronomic death rattle. Her heels converged with the heels from the other direction and Niles heard her shrill voice joined by Swamp's. They were eight Linn paces past his door to the right, just by the main stairwell.

It was better now than later. He could slip out the back door, through the library, taking the long way and running the risk of walking into more teachers on their way out, or he could walk out through the door past Swamp and Linn, past the door that had been Geit's and down the second set of steps directly to the teacher's lot.

Niles took one final look around his classroom with his students safely in a box under his arm and walked out of the door.

Swamp and Linn's conversation stopped. He could feel both sets of eyes on his back as he strode toward the exit.

"Mr. Niles!" came Swamp's voice, calling down the hall. Niles walked on, not turning back. "Mr. Niles! Come back! I have something for you!"

Niles turned to look back, spurred by irresistible curiosity. Swamp was holding up a red and white coffee cup with the school's emblem on it. He turned back to the exits and said nothing as he continued walking away from Swamp and Linn and everyone else.

He passed the door that Geit had stood by so many times and then walked through the exit just beyond it. As the door closed behind him, he heard the sound of a coffee cup smashing on the floor and Linn's cackle echo into the stairwell.

Niles jumped down the stairs, two steps at a time and took off.

Made in the USA
Middletown, DE
11 March 2022